Wolfskin

A TWO MONARCHIES NOVEL

W.R. GINGELL

For Dad, with love from his "boy"

One

It was bright summer in the Dingle, the triad sweeping in a high, hot arc across the sky with its littlest sun just above the horizon. Sheep bleated in the tottering remains of the old fort, where patches of purple lavender fluctuated on the breeze in warm, scented gusts; and sunshine fell crisply over the plentiful woods, creating welcome pockets of shady green. It was clearly a day to be outdoors.

In spite of this obvious fact, I, sulky and dismal, was stuck indoors to mend a huge rent in my second-best petticoat. I had been hunting among the hills and crags of the ruins for a falcon fledgling to train as my very own, when a sudden crumbling of ancient masonry left me dangling precariously with a bloody shin and the sound of tearing cotton in my dismayed ears. Mother sat me down promptly the next day and warned of dire consequences if I didn't mend the tear—and mend it *well*—and I was feeling distinctly put upon. It would only get ripped again, and then where would my hard work be?

I tried to explain the sense of this to Mother, illustrating my point with the myriad other mended tears decorating my petticoat, but she only said significantly, "It had better not get ripped again, Rose."

The veiled warning was one reason for my put-upon feeling.

The other reason was my younger sister Gwendolen. She sat opposite me with her own sewing, the early summer sunshine spangling a halo over her golden hair that was entirely appropriate. She *liked* sewing. It just goes to show that insanity runs in the most commonplace families, I suppose.

"You've sewn a wrinkle in," she told me helpfully, looking over my work. She was only ten months younger than me, and often acted like she was at least one year older. I suspected that the two months in the year when were were the same age were her favourite two months. "It's going to pucker."

I poked my tongue out at her, but my heart wasn't in it. There's nothing hypocritical about Gwen: she really does love housework, and her advice is *always* sincere. She even sings while she does the washing up. Mostly, I mutter. And break dishes.

It seems like such a waste of time: I don't intend to be married, so why should I be in training? Gwendolen's storybooks say that to have adventures one must be either the seventh son of a seventh son, or at the very least the youngest, most beautiful daughter of a bevy of seven, but I haven't ever had any trouble finding adventure. Mother says it's my unique perspective on life; *I* say that if you want adventure, you have to march right up to it and kick it in the shins. It makes life more interesting.

Life at this juncture stretched out before me, as long and tortuous as the tear in my petticoat. My father, amused and indulgent of a daughter who swore black and blue at the age of seven that she would be a bloodthirsty pirate by the name of Cutlass Rose, had been willing to allow me to follow him out into the fields and woods without demur as soon as my little legs could keep up with him. He taught me to fish and trap and fight and, much to my delight, referred to me as his boy. Father had died several years ago, but I had been left with the conviction that there was not a boy my age that I couldn't out-hunt or out-fight, and a series of black eyes and bleeding noses had not been sufficient to convince me otherwise.

Gwendolen, on the other hand, was perfectly happy to be turned by my sensible mother into a Marriageable Prospect; and now at almost fourteen had already refused two proposals of marriage. Girls married young in the Dingle, some even as young as Gwendolen was now. Mother wouldn't hear of it for us. She was determined that we would be at least sixteen before we became engaged.

"You deserve to know your own mind," she told us, when Gwendolen complained. She hadn't been married until she was past twenty, and it had been a very happy marriage. "You're a child yet. It's not just about being chosen by a boy, you must choose for yourself. For heaven's sake, have a bit of sense, Gwen."

"I choose freedom," I grumbled, throwing down my petticoat and looking longingly out the window.

I prowled toward the square of sunlight, careful not to let Mother see me, and peeked out. She had her back to me, nipping off spotted leaves from a sparse but healthy rose bush. The black spot had gotten into the roses last year, decimating them, and Mother had become paranoid over the smallest blemish in any of the bushes.

"You should sit down," Gwendolen said, tugging briskly at the sleeve she had finished to test the set of it. "Mother said no lingering and no lollygagging."

I huffed out a breath, considering my options. There didn't seem to be any, so I pumped one fist in the air vigorously, shouted, "Freedom!" and scuttled back to my chair before Mother saw me.

A few moments after I had picked up my sewing again, Mother's flushed, inquiring face appeared at the window. "Do I hear the stirrings of rebellion?"

I tucked my chin in, trying to hide the mulish set to it, and her eyes twinkled.

"I've got a good mind to let Akiva have you, after all," she said.

I bit down very hard on an excited yell. Akiva was the village witch, a most interesting and exciting person, and I had slightly *accidentally* overheard a conversation between her and my mother that suggested she was looking for an apprentice. More, that I was her first choice.

"I'm nearly finished," I said. The slap-dash stitches shoring up the torn petticoat were anything but satisfactory; hopefully Mother would forget to check on it once I was done.

No such luck. Mother held out an authoritative hand, the twinkle in her eye more pronounced, and said, "Let me see."

I got up and gave it to her with a sigh, mentally consigning the rest of the day to unpicking and resewing, but Mother's eyes were creased at the corners—a promising sign. I allowed myself to hope. I held my breath as she examined the petticoat in silence, turning the fabric to the bright sunlight.

"Well, Rose," she said at last, with a sigh: "I suppose I will just have to make the best of a bad deal."

Startled, I raised my eyes to hers.

"I spoke to Akiva this morning," she said, turning the petticoat to observe the other side of the darn. There was a small smile lingering at the corners of her mouth.

"Mama, you're *cruel!*" I said indignantly, bouncing up and down in an agony of impatience. "What did she want?"

"Well, in spite of knowing you, she still seems to want you," said Mother. She patted my cheek, leaving a smudge of dirt, and for an instant I fancied I saw the bright sheen of tears in her eyes. "I told her she might have you."

ONE SHORT MONTH LATER, I WAS WALKING DOWN THE road that led out of the village, dragging my small, battered trunk behind me in the dust. Bare-legged and bare-footed in the summer, I kicked up dust as I went, eager to reach the cool, shady sanctuary of the forest. Gwendolen had waved to me from the front doorstep, dancing from one foot to the other in vicarious excitement, but Mother had been grave and quiet with the little furrow between her brows that meant she was Not Giving In To Her Feelings.

The Daring Cutlass Rose setting out on her first Gallant Adventure, I thought, a little defiantly. I was determined to vanquish the tiny ache in my throat that told me Mother was now a luxury rather than the everyday commodity I was used to. The road blurred briefly at the thought, and I blinked fiercely, saying aloud to no one,

"The road is dusty today, but we pirates fear no dirt. The forest will tremble before us!"

Before I knew it, I had left the dusty road for a soft, moist forest track. The air was cool and sweet in the forest, intoxicatingly free, and I began to feel in good earnest that my adventures were beginning. The ache in my throat subsided, leaving in its place a feeling of light-headed expectancy, and before long I was charging through the trees with a stick for a sword, slashing indiscriminately at branches and briers alike and leaving a wide trail of destruction in my wake. My trunk bounded behind me, becoming very quickly the worse for wear with each chunk of grass it tore out, but since I was as happy for my clothes to form a straggling line through the forest as I was for them to remain in the trunk, I continued heedlessly as I was.

I was gleefully engaged in the process of reducing a blackberry bush to small, thorny pieces, on the principle that it was an enemy to the crown and traitor to the country, when a thunderbolt out of the blue struck me hard by the left ear and sent me tumbling into the blackberry's wilting embrace.

I dropped my stick-sword, the better to rub my ringing ear, and turned an aggrieved face to my attacker, conscious that strands of blackberry bramble were clinging threadily to me, and that my petticoat now had a new tear.

Before me stood an old woman I recognised as easily as I did my mother: her face was lined and brown, and she was a little bent, but her eyes were as uncomfortably sharp as ever. It was Akiva. The hand with which she had boxed my ear was now on her hip, but I didn't put it past her to raise it again, so I released the handle of my trunk, which thudded heavily to the ground, and stood to attention as best I could.

"*What*," she demanded, without preamble, "Do you mean by tearing up my forest?"

I would have liked to have pointed out that it was everybody's forest, but the look on her face convinced me that it wouldn't be safe to risk it. I tucked in my chin and mumbled, "Sorry."

She snorted and strode away down the grassy path. "I dare say you are."

The snort left me indignant. It suggested that I was only sorry because I had been found out and punished. It was true, of course, but *she* couldn't know that.

"Pick up your trunk when you walk!" Akiva threw over her shoulder, as I scrambled to keep up.

I did so, panting, and was attempting to cut the corner to catch her up, when she snapped back at me, "Keep on the path, girl!"

She must have eyes in the back of her head, I thought resentfully, backtracking with a scowl. I was too new to Akiva to know how far I could push things, so I followed her bony back scrupulously along every curve of the path until at last I caught her up by an old, shabby garden gate, and discovered with some stupefaction that I was standing in front of a house. I hadn't seen it as we approached, by board or beam.

I reflexively glared at the house, too, wondering why I hadn't seen it, then noticed that Akiva was doing something fiddly to the crooked little gate, muttering crossly beneath her breath. While she muttered, I put down my trunk and gazed about me. I could just see the road to town through the trees, and even the crooked weathercock atop the roof of my old house. I regarded the sight thoughtfully as I trailed into the garden in Akiva's wake, my trunk once more clasped in my arms, and barked my shin on the white picket gate for my trouble.

"I thought your cottage was further in," I squeaked, one hand clapped over the afflicted area and the other desperately grasping my trunk.

Akiva snorted again in a way that would have earned me a box on the ears from Mother, and said, "I dare say you did."

She stumped on up the path, choosing not to notice my frantic one-legged dance, and passed through the front door. It was bright green but peeling with age, and I was surprised when its hinges didn't squeak. Akiva didn't leave it open for me.

Following her with some difficulty, I found myself in a high-ceilinged room with four tantalizing doors, low beamed and as brightly green as the front door. The back door was the most easily recognizable: it was open and almost straight ahead.

I would have stood gazing around me for some time longer, but Akiva poked a hard, skinny finger between my shoulder blades, shoving me toward the door I had assumed to be the broom cupboard, and told me shortly to stow my trunk. I had to duck my head to fit through the door, which led to a small but airy room with just space enough for a bed and a small dresser with three drawers. When I turned around to thank Akiva she had already disappeared, and I could hear her rummaging around in the other room.

In spite of the size of the door the ceiling of my bedroom was as high as the ceiling in the main room. The walls were whitewashed, pleasingly light, and the floorboards glowed a gentle gold in the triad's light. I liked it very much. Most likely after a week or two of occupation it would be dirty, cluttered and over-run with my mess, but just then it was perfect. I crossed to the window and kneeled on the narrow, cushioned seat, leaning my head and shoulders out into the leafy green of the side garden. The forest was very close here, trees over-reaching the fence to brush against the walls and throw soft green shadows that mottled with the gold. It was pleasant and quiet, and I was tempted to stay where I was; but it was my first day after all, so I left the quiet greenness and went in search of Akiva once more. She wasn't in the main room, and I took the opportunity to study it without danger of being told not to gawp or earning a clout from Akiva's firm old hand, which I already had reason to respect. It was whitewashed, as my room was, and very, very clean. There was a fireplace, with a rack of herbs tied high above it and a coal scuttle beside it, old and rusty. A table stood back in the far right of the room with bread and cheese atop it and a washtub beneath it; and by the back door, a green hooded cape hung.

I narrowed my eyes accusingly as I gazed around the room. I began to have the feeling that somehow, and in some way, I had been conned. It didn't look at *all* as if a witch lived here. A workbench stood along the wall that held the front door, with a smallish window for light. I noted the mortar and pestle on the desk without much enthusiasm, but eagerly approached the rows of variously sized glass jars and phials, hoping for such exotic magical specimens as dragon's blood or newt's tail to alleviate the general lack of magic that the room radiated.

Disappointingly, whenever I could read Akiva's crabbed little writing, the labels described only such mundane things as 'St. John's Wort', 'Coriander', and 'Foxglove'. Regretfully leaving them, I stared briefly out into the front garden, giving the innocuous flowers a hard look; and then, failing to sight Akiva, wandered into the back garden.

She was there, by a bed of newly sprouting summer greens. Her back was toward me, her rump in the air in the traditional manner of elderly gardeners, and for the first time I realised that she was barefoot, her toes disappearing in the deep green grass. Her skirts had been kilted up so that most of her scrawny calves could be seen, and I stared at her with my eyes bright and calculating, wondering if I would be allowed to tuck up my skirts just so. I had been mutinous when Mother lowered all my skirts three months earlier, since it had made tree climbing and exploration that much harder in proportion to the extra amount of skirt I now had. Maybe that's why she did it.

Akiva's grey, dry voice cut in on my wonderings. "Stop staring and get to work, child." Her back was still toward me, and I jumped at the sound of her voice. Perhaps she really did have eyes in the back of her head. "I want you to turn the soil in that bed in the corner."

I did as I was told, digging and watering and fertilizing as ordered. Once or twice I spoke with the idea that it was rude to let the silence stretch on, but the first time I spoke Akiva only grunted. The second, when I asked about my empty window box, and what was supposed to be growing in it, she gave a short crack of laughter and said: "Whatever grows, of course. Don't ask foolish questions."

I relapsed into silence and let my thoughts wander where they would. It was a nice garden, as gardens go; surrounded by the same grubby white picket fence that surrounded the front garden. The forest, as it had outside my window, seemed to press in and encroach upon it. Trees leaned over the more delicate herbs, providing shade, and at certain places the picket fence bowed slightly around an especially large trunk.

I plied my trowel viciously, fairly itching to explore the forest, and each time I straightened to stretch out my back I found my gaze wandering unconsciously to the cool green shadows. As the day wore warmly on, these moments became more frequent and my gaze more longing.

By the time the triad had sunk behind the trees in a welter of golden glory, taking with it most of the heat of the afternoon, I was dishevelled, hungry, and excessively dirty. I didn't mind the dirt, but I did regret the hunger. After lunch, Akiva had stood over me, a scrawny, bent slavedriver, and made me dig a new garden bed, continually insisting on it being *bigger* and *deeper*. It seemed that Akiva's garden needed a ridiculous amount of work done in it. I wondered how long it had been left to its own devices, and then, if Akiva had left it especially for her new apprentice. I darkly suspected she had. Nightfall couldn't come quickly enough, in my opinion, and by the time it did I was so hungry that my stomach had long ceased even putting up the pretence of grumbling. As I trailed into the house in Akiva's wake, there was a queer lightness to my head.

The kitchen was bare but for the plain bread and cheese I'd noticed earlier, deflating my hopes of a hearty dinner, and when Akiva began to cut the bread, I watched with glittering eyes. I was too tired and hungry to voice my bitter disappointment, and food was food, after all; but Mother's rich meat stews were a very present, mouth-watering memory. I ate without complaint, feeling self-right-eous, because even if I *was* a hoyden, at least Mother had made sure I was a polite one. Besides, I didn't put it past Akiva to tell me shortly that if I didn't like it I could go to bed without any dinner, *and* to box my ears for good measure.

Akiva was as taciturn during dinner as she had been the rest of the day, but I didn't notice so much because I was dozing over my bread and cheese. I fell asleep after my third slice, and the last thing I remember is the creak and pop of Akiva's bones as she settled down in her battered old armchair.

When I woke it was dark and my neck was stiff. Akiva had left me where I was and there was a flat, sore patch on my forehead

9

etched with the grain of the table. I found that I was too sleepy to feel as outraged as I would have liked to feel so I merely wiped away the damp patch by the side of my mouth and blearily headed for my bedroom door, feeling my way along the walls. In the darkness Akiva's cottage was unfamiliar, the door handles at a confusingly different height than I was used to, but I made it to the safety of my room with no worse injury than another scraped shin.

As I slid between the cold sheets of a likewise unfamiliar bed, it seemed that I could still feel the grainy wood handle of the trowel in my hand and smell the rich, hearty scent of fresh turned earth.

I woke earlier than usual the next morning in a hum of excitement. The first in the triad had slipped over the horizon and was only just beginning to light my whitewashed room from grey to white, but I scrambled out of bed and into my clothes as quickly as I could, lacing my boots with the mischievous idea that I might even be up before Akiva. However, when I tumbled out into the main room, messily plaiting my hair as I went, she was already bending by the fireplace, a kettle over the low burning coals.

She gave me a swift, critical look, and said without preamble: "Shoes off, girl."

I gave her a suspicious look to make sure she wasn't joking, then hastily tugged them off when her one sardonically raised eyebrow informed me that she wasn't, hopping on each foot successively to do so. I banished the satisfied grin that wanted to spread across my face and straightened again. I was subjected to another stare, this time longer.

"You're a bit on the skinny side," she opined. Her eyes pinioned my toes, which had been wriggling with delight at being free, and I hastily scrunched them tight against the floorboards to keep them still.

"Yes," I agreed, inspecting my own familiar, wiry arms and briefly indicating my entire lack of hips. "I haven't got the voluptuous bits yet."

Akiva gave a crack of laughter. "If you're anything like your mother, you won't get that until you're well past your sixteenth birthday."

"Good," I said, in some satisfaction. "Gwen's got hers and she can't step outside the door without three or four boys following her."

"Neither could your mother," retorted Akiva. "And that when she was skinny as a broom handle. But she always acted like a lady."

I thought about this, unashamed. "She washed her face every night, too, I s'pose."

"She did," Akiva said dryly, and I could have sworn her sharp eyes saw the ring of dirt that lay beneath my collar. While delighting to swim like a fish in any passing stream, I was a past master in the art of avoiding baths. My wash last evening hadn't been thorough, and I cheerfully suspected that most of the dirt had lodged itself just out of sight behind my ears. They were certainly itching, but that could have been the effect Akiva's prolonged, sarcastic gaze.

I was relieved when her attention went back to her kettle, and blew out my cheeks in silent respect. Even Mother didn't have a look like that. It was a *scorcher*.

"Collect the eggs and feed the chickens, there's a good child," she said, without looking up. "The henhouse is in the clearing outside the back garden gate. You may have breakfast when you finish."

I uttered the requisite 'Yes'um' and turned to go, but Akiva's bony old fingers grasped me by the wrist, surprisingly strong.

"Stay on the path," she said.

"Path, huh!" I said loudly. The back garden gate hadn't wanted to open any more than the front gate had, and I'd stubbed my toes kicking it open. In my opinion, Akiva cared a great deal too much about her grass. The chook house was outside the main garden, a little ways into the shady forest, and I had been looking forward to exploring a little before I fed the chooks. I looked sourly down the dirt path and said another hearty *'Huh!'* to relieve my feelings, then glumly set out down the path.

The chooks mobbed me at the wire gate, and I hopped on one foot, shooing them with the other to prevent their escape until I could scatter the seed far enough to distract them away from beckoning freedom. As they scrambled for the grain on spindly legs I regarded them with a certain amount of fellow feeling, and gave them a half-measure more of the mix to make up for another day of imprisonment. That done, it was only a matter of displacing a few broody chickens in order to collect the eggs. I peeked behind the chickenfeed bin and a few of the nesting boxes in a hopeful sort of a way, supposing that Akiva must keep her arcane supplies *somewhere*, after all. The house had been disappointingly normal. Herbs were all very well, but there should be at least a dragon about the place.

I dangled my basket disconsolately on the way back, counting on my fingers. Common-or-garden herbs, no dragon, no exotic supplies, tending garden beds—apprenticeship was beginning to look more and more like work, and less and less like adventure.

On the other hand, the savoury smell presently emanating from the kitchen window promised bacon and eggs for breakfast, and anyone who fed me bacon for breakfast couldn't be *all* bad. I thought, graciously, that it might be possible to give Akiva another chance.

"Wipe your feet," said Akiva shortly, as I presented the eggs. I skipped a few steps backwards, did a little more than my usual shuffle on the mat to help good impressions along, and danced forward again.

"The garden gate needs greasing," I announced in a spirit of helpfulness, eyeing the bacon that Akiva was deftly snatching out of the frying pan.

"The goose-grease is in the cupboard."

I scowled. "What, me?"

"After breakfast. Next time you'll remember not to mention a problem if you aren't prepared to fix it."

I certainly would! I thought indignantly. Mistress Pennypurse said I was too pert by half, but she couldn't do anything about it: it was quite another thing to have Akiva think so and be perfectly capable of administering lessons.

The bacon softened my mood somewhat, but when Akiva set me to weeding an overgrown corner of the garden while she donned her hooded cloak with every appearance to suggest that she was going out, I let myself fall into simmer of sulky grievance that was not helped by knowing she was well within her rights to do so.

I was almost too preoccupied in my sense of injury and the fact that none of the weeds would come out to notice that there was something not quite right about that hood, but the idea planted itself in my mind to be explored as soon as Akiva was gone. It certainly looked like a proper hood: there was nothing unusual *there*. The oddity, I thought carefully, pursuing the thought as I tugged heartily and entirely ineffectually at any convenient weed; was in the pattern of green summer leaves. Pattern wasn't the right word, though. It didn't look so much like a pattern as it did leaves sewn together, right down to the rustling late summer leaves make against each other as they prepare to brown for the autumn. I looked speculatively at the trees surrounding the cottage: and sure enough, but for a few evergreens, most of the foliage had gone dark, dark green with spots of brown and gold, promising an early autumn.

I smiled a benign smile around the garden at large. Magic at last! Not even Gwendolen could sew leaves together to make a cloak! I made a note to watch and see if the leaves in the cloak changed with the seasons, and wondered speculatively just what function a magical hood served. Invisibility, most likely. I was considering this interesting possibility when another gaze around the garden brought me to realise that I was no longer alone. There was a young man propped up against the fence, watching me with interest, his arms folded casually on one of the lower boughs of a patchy weeping willow. I returned his look with one of my own, because I hadn't seen him arrive, and I *should* have.

"You have to sing," he said. He was a nice looking boy with tawny-brown eyes under a shaggy mop of golden hair, and a smile that reminded me of Father, so I was polite.

"Pardon?"

"You have to sing to the garden to get the weeds out."

"Why?"

He shrugged. "The garden likes it. It won't let go of the weeds if you don't sing."

"That's blackmail!" I said, impressed.

The boy grinned. "I broke two shovels on my patch before I learned the right songs. Can you sing?"

I shrugged. I certainly used to sing at home, but since my idea of singing was to bellow sea-shanties at the top of my lungs, Mother usually thrust me out of the house as soon as I began.

Momentarily suspicious, I narrowed my eyes and regarded the tawny-haired boy. "Akiva didn't tell me that."

"She didn't tell me, either," he said sympathetically. "Akiva never tells you anything if she thinks you can learn it for yourself. She didn't have a teacher, so she had to learn everything by herself. Now I've got my own wardship I thought I'd come to see her next victim."

"What do you mean, wardship?"

This time it was his turn to gaze at me thoughtfully. "I don't think I should tell you if Akiva hasn't."

I stuck my chin out mulishly. "But you said—"

"I know, but this is different. Look, what's your name?"

"Rose."

"I'm Gwydion. I was Akiva's last apprentice."

I looked him up and down. "Well, you survived."

He grinned again. "You sound just like her," he said, and straightened. I opened my mouth to reply indignantly, but he turned away with a wink, and disappeared.

I was inclined to scowl after him, but it occurred to me that Akiva's old apprentice was using something very like magic, and the thought cheered me up. I plumped myself down on the dew-damp grass, resting my forearms on my crossed legs, and frowningly considered the garden. I couldn't recall that I knew any gardening songs at all. I knew that there were many, because Aunt Myra also sang to her garden; though when Father was alive he had said that this was more because of the quality of the liquid that Aunt Myra drank from strange-smelling jugs in her garden shed than because she fancied it did the garden any good.

But as I sat there considering the garden, the thread of a song seemed to trail through my head, a half remembered catch of tune.

Soil is rich, roots run deep...

Now where had I heard that before? And what were the last two lines? I hummed the tune beneath my breath, singing the first two lines over and over to myself until the last two lines followed naturally.

> *Soil is rich,*
> *Roots run deep;*
> *Weeds loosen,*
> *Moisture seep.*

I sat up straight in exultation. *That* was it! I wriggled my backside to settle myself more comfortably in the turf and sang the song through twice.

I wasn't sure if the song did magic or if the woods and soil were magic and simply liked being sung to, but the weeds came out more easily after that. In fact, they came out rather more easily even than ordinary weeds did. Gradually the earth grew damp and rich under my fingers and the pile of weeds beside me rose to mammoth proportions. Eyeing the huge pile askance, it occurred to me to wonder again just how long it had been since Akiva had weeded this particular garden patch. When I had asked her yesterday evening, she had only given one of her rather rude cracks of laughter and said: "Yesterday."

I *had* wondered if she was having a private joke at me, but it seemed to me that I could remember her weeding the garden beds in this section as I sweated away at digging the new garden bed yesterday. I wondered if singing to the garden would have made my job easier then, too. I had an idea that it might have. I was in half a mind to ask Akiva if it was so: and if it *was*, why she hadn't told me, but I had a feeling that it would just be another of those things that she expected me to work out for myself. I saw her briefly in my mind's eye, looking at me indifferently and demanding to know why I should have it easier than she had.

Two

The weeks passed quickly with Akiva. Not all of my time was spent in the garden: some days Akiva would don her leafy hood and I would know that we were going in search of particular herbs and plants that didn't grow in her garden. Bad weather didn't keep us indoors, much to my gleeful approval; we sallied forth into garden or woods whatever the weather.

Akiva, crabby old crone that she was, mustn't have got over me tearing up the forest with my trunk, because whenever she allowed me to come with her into the forest I was always ordered to stay on the path. The command made my eyes snap and my chin stick out mulishly, but I had learned by now that it was only a shade more useless to argue with Akiva than it was to try and pump her for information. When I complained once too often about having to stay on the path after being sharply told off for attempting to lean out and pluck a blackberry that was two feet from the path, and sulkily asked her *why* I was forever to remain on the path, Akiva only said brusquely, "Because it's safe. Do as you're told."

Since she enforced the command with a none-too-gentle box on the ears, I had felt aggrieved for the rest of the walk.

. . .

A MONTH AFTER I ARRIVED AT AKIVA'S COTTAGE, I WAS allowed to go home for a half-day. I'd been lethargic for some days, at first unaware and then unwilling to admit that I was feeling homesick, and I hadn't expected Akiva to notice. If she *did* notice, though, Akiva didn't comment upon it. She merely remarked after breakfast that it was about time I made myself up some pinafores.

"Off to town with you. Tell Mina Pennypurse there needs to be enough material for two pinafores," she said. "And tell her to put it on my account. You may spend the afternoon with your mother and sister so long as you're back before nightfall."

I said, very primly, "Thank you, Akiva," but I could feel the heat of excitement causing my eyes to sparkle, and Akiva looked at me with a dry amusement in her old eyes that suggested she knew perfectly well what my emotions were.

"Get along with you, child. Stay on the path and be back before nightfall."

It wasn't until I was some way into the village that I became aware of the stares. A flutter of curtain or a pair of eyes peeking over the shutters was quite normal if the fair was passing through, but I wasn't prepared for the same level of scrutiny to be directed at *me*. I scowled at a mother who gave her big-eyed child a none-too-gentle tug to hurry him out of my way, and she scurried away with a frightened look that puzzled me as much as it amused me. What had struck the village? Fortunately, I wasn't one to blush, and I strode up the main street with a fierce smile that made matters worse, much to my satisfaction.

The general store was crowded when I got there, filled with the same stares and quickly averted gazes as the street had been. I bared my teeth at them all in another fierce smile; and then, feeling better, I spent some time looking over the bolts of cotton with mingled disinterest and foreboding. The choice of dress stuffs wasn't to me the excitement that it was to Gwendolen.

I was turning over a bolt of sensible brown cotton that would give me as little trouble as possible to sew, when Mina Pennypurse herself rapped me across the knuckles and told me sharply not to touch.

17

"I need new pinafores!" I said indignantly, scowling up at her gold spectacles. They were mirror-like and hid her eyes, but her sharp nose quivered as if she had smelled something nasty. "I'm a customer the same as everyone else, so there!"

"The likes of you can wait outside!" she retorted, and gave me a clip across the ears for good measure.

I wasn't expecting it, since Miss Pennypurse (although muttering at my general and particular evils) had never raised a hand to me before, and I was too surprised to duck. I retreated in bad order, clutching my ear, and sat down on the front porch to dangle my bare feet with a feeling of injury. At least when Akiva clouted me it was for a reason. I felt gloomily that I had lost this particular round.

"They don't like you not wearing shoes," said a voice to my left. I looked around enquiringly and found myself meeting the blue-eyed gaze of a girl I knew vaguely as Elizabeth Gantry, the sister of one of Gwendolen's bosom friends.

"*And* you came in right when they were talking about Akiva," she added, licking a finger that was coated with sprinkles. She had a small paper bag of the brightly coloured candies that she was dipping her forefinger into at a steady, thoughtful rate. Now she offered it to me, and I helped myself. "Miss Pinchface thought you heard her. She thinks you'll carry tales back to Akiva."

"So I will," I said vengefully, scowling over my shoulder at the shop window. I wouldn't, of course: there's nothing worse than a tell-tale. I would just have to be injured but honourable. I sat straighter in the self-righteous knowledge, and drummed my bare heels against the porch.

"What are you in for?"

"New dress," said Elizabeth laconically. "My custard exploded. Burned little holes in the bodice and stained the skirt."

"My custard did, too," I told her. "Gwendolen's didn't. It went beautifully."

"Hers *would*," said Elizabeth. "Anyway, it was getting too short."

I blinked a few times before it became apparent that she was now speaking of her dress, and not the custard. Elizabeth Gantry's legs had certainly lengthened since the last time I had seen her, and she was now a head taller than me: tall enough to have lengthened her old dresses without any marked difference. I didn't really care what length my skirts were as long as they didn't encumber me, so my fellow feeling was only good for a sympathetic look. Elizabeth, however, took it in good part, and offered me the sprinkles again.

"You're lucky," she said. "Akiva doesn't care what anyone thinks. I suppose you don't even have to learn to cook."

I shrugged. Akiva had certainly made no such attempt. That her forbearance resulted from the certain knowledge that I would ruin whatever dish I tried to cook, was more than likely. I felt a vague sense of accomplishment at the thought.

"Mostly I dig and weed," I said. In my opinion there had been entirely too much digging and weeding. It seemed remarkably excessive for a garden that size. "Sometimes we go out into the forest."

She looked at me with an expression I was unable to decipher. "Mama won't let us go out in the forest because of the Wolf. Have you seen him?"

I regarded her sharply, unwilling to be made a fool of. "That's just a story. I'm not afraid of stories."

"My grandam saw him," she remarked equably. "She was out with her sweetheart. They say he eats the hearts of girls."

After another thoughtful moment informed me that Liz's habit of skipping subjects had once again confused me, I gathered that it was the Wolf, and not Liz's grandam's beau, who supposedly ate hearts. "What, just the heart?"

She nodded solemnly. "Just the heart. They find the bodies waxy white with a huge bloody hole where their heart should be."

"Fussy eater, isn't it?" I knew a little something about wolves, and nothing I knew of them suggested that they were in the habit of eating hearts and leaving the rest of the organs untouched.

"Gives you the shivers late at night. Me and Harry tell each other stories across the lane sometimes; his window is right next to mine."

I grinned. "What does your mama say about that?"

"She doesn't know," said Liz, with a cool look. "She better not find out, either, Rose Grady!"

"I'm no tell-tale," I said carelessly. "Gwen has boys talk to her through the window, too; they go away pretty quick when you pour the washing water on them, though."

Liz gave a surprisingly elfin grin. "And what does Gwen say about that?"

I returned her a conspiratorial wink, but the appearance of her mother sent Liz scrambling to her feet and cut short our conversation.

Mrs Gantry, looking me over in a thoughtful manner not unlike Liz's, nodded once and said, "Good morning, Rose. I think Mistress Pennypurse is ready for you now."

I nodded my thanks, shot another grin in Liz's direction, and set the little bell above the door tinkling again at my entrance.

Fortunately, my business with Mina Pennypurse didn't take long, and I was soon able to feel myself in possession of a proper holiday despite a certain, quivering nose and spitefully short-cut cotton. I also purchased a length of silky blue ribbon for Gwen's approaching birthday with my own money, which precipitated the short-cut cloth. Mina had looked at the ribbon, then at my bare, dirty feet in open disapproval, suggesting to the initiated that she'd expected me to steal the blue silk, and plied her scissors with more than her usual vicious rapidity.

While I didn't mind Mina's frown, it had reminded me just in time that Mother wouldn't stop at a look to express her disapproval of my bare feet, and that I had hung my boots from their laces over my shoulder for just that reason. So I scowled up at Mina, daring her to make a remark as I thumped my boots to the floorboards, and used her counter as a prop while I tugged them on. I even, glumly, untucked the bit of my skirt that had pulled the wealth of material out of my way over the last month, allowing it to sweep irritatingly against my shins. I then gave Mina one last glare for form's sake as I took my parcel, and let it linger as I clumped heavily out of the shop.

My dirty feet felt odd and unnatural in the boots as I strode back down the road, ignoring stares. They took the fun out of the walk, cramping my poor toes and rubbing my feet in places I didn't remember ever hurting before. I would have slowed my pace and favoured the right foot, which hurt the most, but eyes were still watching. Instead, I put out my chin determinedly and forged ahead, scowling more and more fiercely as each step grated at the back of my heels. Horned hedgepigs, I was certain it was scraping away my skin one layer at a time!

I forgot my pains the moment I saw Mother's face in the kitchen window. When she saw me, a rare smile swept across her face and she disappeared from the window in order to throw open the door. I clattered through the front gate and threw myself into her arms, careless of the fact that my parcel had dropped into Gwen's carnations.

"Rosie, my darling! You have no idea how much your old mother has missed the banging of doors about the house!"

"You're not old!" I said, my voice muffled. I had buried my face in the front of her apron to hide the tears that caused my eyes to glimmer in a less than piratical manner.

"*I* didn't miss your tossing and turning," said Gwendolen. I knew she wasn't serious, because she was glowing with pleasure. "I've had lovely *long* nights of sleep ever since you left."

"That will be why you felt it necessary to share my bed for the first two weeks, I suppose?" inquired Mother mildly, shooing us into the house and rescuing my parcel from the carnations. "Rose, I've made up a parcel for you with some vests and underthings for the winter. There's also a new best dress for you. How long are you staying?"

"Just the afternoon," I said regretfully. "I have to be back with Akiva before dark."

"Very well; remember to take them with your parcel. New pinafores?"

I scowled. "Yes. Akiva said I needed two."

"Make sure you make them large enough to let down the hem once or twice," she advised. "I believe you're about to go through a growth spurt."

I said: "Hah," without much hope, wondering how she knew. Both Mother and Gwendolen were dainty and petite, and while I couldn't be said to be either, I was certainly scrawny enough in my own right. I'd given up on the thought that I would grow any taller, shrugging away my disappointment as best I could. Tall pirates are more imposing than tiny, scrawny ones, but we scrawny pirates kick *harder*.

"You're just in time for lunch," Gwendolen said, with slight exultation, dismissing such mundane things as pinafores. I guessed that she had made the leek and garlic stew I'd been smelling with bliss ever since I entered the house. "What's it like, being an apprentice? Is Akiva really a witch? Does—"

"You can tell us the Awful Adventures of Cutlass Rose over lunch," Mother said firmly. "We are not going to stand talking while the stew goes cold."

Happy to oblige when obliging meant consuming as much stew as was humanly possible before Mother noticed and rationed my intake, I settled myself down to the business of eating until Gwendolen's questions bubbled over again. Then, sitting back with a sigh of relief and a newly filled bowl, I was able to turn my attention to answering them at last. Gwen sounded slightly envious, and I wondered, grinning a sharp, brothy grin at my sister that made her eyes narrow, if having Mother's full attention all the time was so easy, even for her.

"I don't think Akiva is really a witch," I told her, answering her second question first. It had been borne in on me, regretfully and at long last, that there were no arcane supplies hidden about Akiva's home or person. Nor was she in the habit of wandering off on full-moon nights to gather herbs that stories said simply *must* be gathered in moonlight to be effective. "She talks to her plants, but she doesn't mutter spells or anything."

"What a disappointment," said Mother promptly, but there was a distinct gleam of amusement to her eyes that said she knew Akiva a little better than I had given her credit for. I *had* been conned.

"Well, I think it is," Gwendolen opined. "Think how useful it would be to be able to charm away warts, or freckles! Or spots, for that matter. One always comes out in a spot just before a party."

I made a rude noise through a mouthful of stew. Trust Gwendolen to think of that first. "You can do all that with plants. And what parties do you go to, anyway?"

Gwendolen lifted her chin haughtily, a more elegant copy of my chin thrust, but there was a dimple in her left cheek. "In case you've forgotten, Madam Pirate, *I* am now old enough to attend the dances on the green. Just because you never cared to go doesn't mean I don't."

I pursed my mouth to make another rude noise but caught Mother's eye and refrained. "Pirates don't dance, bufflehead. Not that sort of dance, anyway: we do hornpipes and things."

"I learned a hornpipe just last week!" Gwendolen struck in, with triumph. "So there! You wouldn't have liked it at all, it's very dainty and light. Robert Tenny danced with me."

"*My* hornpipe would not be dainty and light," I said with conviction.

Mother laughed. "Not if you were dancing it, Rosie darling. I've never seen a clumsier set of feet in my life. I will never understand why anyone who can dance so quickly in a circle while being spanked, cannot dance creditably."

I grinned, recalling several memorable occasions that had displayed that particular prowess. The most that could be said about my constant encounters with discipline was that I always thoroughly deserved any spanking that was meted out.

"I s'pose it's the lack of motivation," I said. It wasn't quite true, but it was the closest thing to the truth. Barefooted, I was as light as Gwendolen: once booted, I tripped over my laces and caught one foot over the other, stomping on my partner's toes with abandon. I thought, grinning a little wider, that even if I *had* chosen to attend the dances, there wouldn't be a boy brave enough to stand up with me.

"Well, there's no need to look so *proud* about it," said Gwendolen.

I wolfed down a third bowl of stew before I left. Gwendolen

was determined to show me the two new dresses Mother had made her: and so, despite my complaints, I was dragged upstairs to watch the show. I refused to be parted from my stew, however, and Gwendolen was forced to twirl for a slurping audience.

On my part, I was forced to admit that the frocks were beautiful. Mother had that touch of flair about her that always chose the right colour and material to set us off to best advantage. With Gwendolen, all gold hair and blue-green eyes, she had gone to some expense to get up a dress of the most ravishing green satin. The neckline was modest, but nothing could hide the fact that Gwendolen had already begun to develop a figure, and the layers and layers of light, foamy petticoat gave the dress an air of weightlessness. It was a creation, even if I wouldn't have said so to Gwen. Gwendolen, dancing effortlessly around the room, was as light and fine as thistledown floating on the summer breeze. It would shortly be too cold to wear it on the dancing green, but Gwen wouldn't care a rush about that: she would brave sleet and hail if it meant looking just right.

Her other dress was muslin and only slightly more practical; cream with rich amber stripes that brought out the golden tints of her hair. The petticoats were a little thicker in a nod to the approaching autumn, but I noticed with a grin that both the frocks were rather longer than any of her others: Gwendolen must have persuaded Mother that she was old enough to have her skirts lowered. More fool her.

Prancing in front of the mirror in the amber-striped creation, Gwendolen said over her shoulder, "Open yours, Rose."

I blinked at her in the mirror, my eyes blank and pebbly. I disliked dressing and undressing just to twirl in front of the mirror.

Fortunately, Mother said, "Rose's dress is not to be worn yet." Gwendolen was pouting and beginning to look stubborn, and that always meant trouble. That stubbornness is our most similar feature. "It's to be kept for a few years. The vests and underthings, on the other hand, are *not*, Rose. I don't want you wandering around barefoot in the winter: those woollen stockings are meant to be worn."

I nodded, and Mother gave me a sharp look that softened after a moment in a smile. "I know you, Rose. When the winter comes you catch every kind of cold because you won't wear your shoes and stockings."

"I'll wear them," I said grudgingly. I didn't know how Akiva was going to feel about it, but it was impossible to say no to Mother. Speculatively, I wondered if I could wear them to bed for warmth, thus obeying both Akiva and Mother, and pleasing myself.

I stayed until the afternoon was just beginning to darken around us. When I tied my two parcels together ready to leave, Gwendolen's lower lip trembled, and she looked distinctly tearful. I set my chin and refused to let myself acknowledge the luminous sheen to her eyes, since Gwendolen cried best for an audience, and I was feeling unusually forlorn.

Mother said, "The house has certainly been peaceful since you've been gone, Rose. Come back again when you can."

I didn't look back until I reached the corner, where I waved to Mother and Gwendolen. I continued to wave obligingly until I was out of sight, then sat down with relief and some guilt to remove my shoes and tuck up my skirt. The fresh air went a long way toward putting me in a more cheerful frame of mind: it smelt of rain, and forest, and freedom. I hung my boots jauntily over my shoulder by their laces again, whistling loudly, and by the time I reached the darkening cool of the forest, I had the odd sense that though I had just left home, I was also going home. The mossy path felt cool and pleasantly damp beneath my feet, and my eyes glittered in the dusk as I saw Akiva's cottage between the trees.

The feeling of coming home was so strong that when I entered the cottage and found it empty, it was a nasty jar. I noticed the silent dusk as I unlatched the gate, and wondered at it, because by this time Akiva should have lit the lamp and set it in the sconce beside the front window where it beamed brightly both inside and out. It wasn't close enough to winter for the nights to be very dark yet, but the light had been a comfortable beacon to navigate the yard by until now.

I dropped my parcels by the door and lit the lamp myself with narrow eyes. My hands felt clumsy as I placed it in the sconce, and if I told myself it was from the cool evening air, well, it wasn't exactly a lie.

A warm circle of light spread around the room and glanced off the empty space where Akiva's hood was usually kept. I looked at the bare wall, frowning, because Akiva hadn't been prone to night ramblings since I had become her apprentice. I stood by the lamp for a long time, scowling into a dark corner of the kitchen and trying not to feel the cut of cold that wasn't really cold. Then I sliced myself some bread and cheese and scowled at the kitchen table instead.

Later, I unpacked my parcel of pinafore cloth and set myself down at the table to cut the pieces, encouraging myself with the thought that there wasn't really anything else to do, anyway. I even remembered to brush away the crumbs first, and the pieces weren't *very* crooked. When my eyes were blurring from concentration and lack of light, I folded the pieces away and sank down on my footstool. Akiva's chair was free, but I didn't sit in it: I darkly suspected that somehow, she would know that I had. When I found myself glancing up at the door every few minutes, I took myself off to bed.

Akiva wasn't home when I woke the next morning. I was awake earlier than usual with a buzzing mind that confused me with its noise until I remembered why; then I tumbled out of my room in nothing but my shift to check the cottage. I padded through the length and breadth of it, and even dared to foray into Akiva's bedroom. She was nowhere to be seen. The lamp had burned out some time ago, but the morning was bright enough to navigate without the extra light, so I left it unlit and cut a tasteless round of bread for my breakfast with glittering eyes.

I ate it as I dressed, scattering crumbs around my bedroom with careless abandon, and let my mind touch briefly on the tasks of the day. It didn't occur to me that in Akiva's absence I might conceivably get away without doing my work: if it had, I would have laughed humourlessly at the thought.

I didn't dawdle with my morning preparations, scattering a few drops of water more as a warning to the dirt than an actual purge, and knotting my hair untidily at the base of my neck. A few minutes later I was scampering for the back gate with the egg basket clutched in my hand.

I was prepared for a long, busy day. I was prepared to find myself slightly out of my depth. I was even prepared to have to fetch my own lunch and dinner.

I was *not* prepared to find that the chook house path had disappeared. I set the egg basket down and hung over the fence to gaze at a perfect and unmarked green expanse of grass between silent trees. Even the henhouse had disappeared. The lack of path bothered me more than returning to an empty house had done, since I expected Akiva to be odd, after all. I didn't expect old, well-worn paths to disappear on me. I glared at the silent trees, daring them to move, and backed away carefully to check on the front garden.

The village path had also disappeared. I scowled, refusing to acknowledge that the little wriggle in my stomach was anything but excitement, and tried in vain to locate the main road that should have been visible through the trees. It, too, had disappeared. I was having my first contact with magic; real, unpredictable magic, and to my surprise, the most noticeable thing about it was that it was distinctly uncomfortable.

I sat down in the grass with a quick pulse ticking behind one ear and ran my fingers through my hair. No way in—no way out. I smiled fiercely at the garden around me. No way in, and no way out: but Akiva would still expect me to do my work. So I did.

The chickens went without food that day. Even if Akiva hadn't sharply warned me each and every day to *stay on the path!* I wasn't rash enough to leave the safety of the back garden to find a henhouse that had vanished from sight overnight, on a path that was no longer there.

I tended the garden beds instead. My month with Akiva had taught me that her choice of which garden beds to work on wasn't random; there was a strict circular order that made sure each bed was seen to three times a week. This morning I was supposed to be tending to the bed of something Akiva told me were aloes. The aloes were a spiky, pulpy kind of plant which either required or generated a kind of warmth around them. They had always fascinated me. The air about the aloe bed was constantly several degrees hotter in temperature than any of the other beds, and the soil was different; drier and sandier.

Only this morning the aloe bed was cooler than usual, almost the same temperature as the other garden beds, and the soil was damp from last night's rain. It wasn't until I was gazing at the rain-darkened soil that it occurred to me that I hadn't ever seen this bed soaked with water, even if it had *poured* rain during the night. I frowned at my own stupidity: of course it must be Akiva who kept the garden beds at their different temperatures. I had been so certain, poking and prying around Akiva's cottage for arcane supplies, that magic was batwings and mumbling and potions. I hadn't seen the real, practical, plain magic going on under my very nose.

If I had known Akiva was singing spells, I thought injuredly, I would certainly have troubled myself to learn the words she sang to her garden. Or was that one of the things she expected me to learn by myself? Horned hedgepigs, how was I to learn anything if she didn't teach me? I had no idea of the words I needed to correct the aloe bed. I did know the tune she used, since Akiva (unlike myself), didn't use myriad different tunes to beguile the garden. She used only one: an old, oddly complicated but oddly familiar series of notes that stuck in my mind like the echo of an old familiar lullaby sung to me when I was too young to remember.

I hummed the melody under my breath to assure myself that I knew it well enough, then planted both my hands palms down in the slightly damp soil of the garden bed as I had often seen Akiva do, and began to sing without much conviction. I had a feeling that anything that was routinely bullied by Akiva would be unlikely to be very much impressed with me.

Still, I must have made *some* impression. The moment I began singing, the ground bucked and heaved violently beneath me. I was tumbled head over heels in the surge, biting my tongue: then, as suddenly as it had rocked, the earth was still again and I was able to pick myself up shakily. The salty taste of blood was in my mouth as

I ruefully checked for damage. Evidently Akiva's spells were not for my use. My pride, along with various other parts of my body, felt distinctly bruised, and I scowled at the aloes, feeling vaguely hard-done-by. If Akiva *did* expect me to learn this particular thing by myself, she would be woefully disappointed. I pulled on my lower lip, considering my failure with regret, and then reluctantly began the task of weeding. With any luck Akiva would be back before the cooling nights did too much damage to the aloes.

I was so much into the habit of singing to the plants by then that I didn't notice exactly when I began singing. It was when I stopped to fertilize the freshly weeded soil that I realised I was singing a song that my father had brought back with him from the hot deserts of Lacuna.

> *Fold the warm night air 'round your shoulders*
> *Hang two heavy drops of rain from your ears*
> *And you and I, my love, my rose,*
> *Will drink in the scents of the arabah.*

It was a crooning lullaby that Father had sung to me when I was small enough still to have my cot in with him and Mother. He had told me once that in Lacuna the nights were so heavy and hot that the air folded around you like a cloak, and that the most delicious scents of cinnamon and cloves floated in the air. Perhaps it was the aloe bed that had made that particular song spring to mind. Be that as it may, as I lightly watered the aloes it seemed to me that warm, scented air rose with each drop of water that hit the earth. I tasted cinnamon and cardamom, and when I poked a wary finger into the soil, it was noticeably warmer. I sat back on my heels, my eyes glittering in fascination, because in some inexplicable way, I must have done the right thing.

I didn't stop for lunch. Instead, I checked once more to see if the paths had appeared again. They hadn't.

"Oh, bother you, then!" I snapped, because there was a touch of cold fear in my stomach. I kicked the shovel but all that did was stub my toe, so instead of sulking I climbed the tall pine that stood against the back of the house, to spy out the extent of the danger. I climbed until the branches became too small to bear my weight and gazed out in every direction, clutching myself close to the trunk.

The view convinced me of the extent of my isolation. Just as the main road should have been in view through the trees, the village rooftops should have been clearly in sight. Yet forest spread as far as the eye could see, rising and falling like the moors. Some of the trees were higher even than the one I'd climbed. I clung closer to the tree trunk and thoughtfully considered the prospect. Maybe Akiva wasn't coming back. Maybe I was stuck in this little patch of civilisation. What then?

I *could* venture out into the forest, I thought, excitement warring with a shrewd idea that magic in Akiva's garden would be a very different thing from magic in the forest. The garden had some patches warmer than others, and weeds might grow unnaturally fast in it, but at least it remained the same size.

I looked around again, turning my back on the disturbingly wooded space that should have been the town, and then, with an unexpectedness that made my heart jump, there *was* a path. The fact that it was to the right of my tree and ran under the shadow of the hedge might explain why I hadn't seen it before, but I was more inclined to think that it hadn't actually been there a moment ago. More importantly, it began from a point in the hedge that I knew didn't contain a gate.

"Sneaky," I said gruffly, startling myself at the sound of my own voice. I slithered down the tree, accompanied by a shower of pine bark, and dashed through the garden to the hedge. And, do you know, there *was* a gate there. It was more of a door than a gate, green and covered with a pattern of lightly etched leaves and vines that seemed to shift and curl in the light breeze. I looked at the panels of the door with hard eyes. If it had been here all along, it was careless of me not to have seen it, since although the swirling pattern of vines made it strangely difficult to see, it was a very big door in a rather nondescript hedge. I gave it a last, narrowed look, and chose to believe that it hadn't been there before.

It took me quite some time to decide on a course of action.

Akiva had said not to leave the path. She had not, however, said anything about travelling on magical paths, and to a mind as well trained at spotting loopholes as mine, this practically amounted to direct permission.

I *did* have enough native caution to postpone my adventures until the morrow, when Akiva might conceivably be back and prevent the necessity of my going. It was with glittering eyes and a half hope, half fear that Akiva wouldn't return the next day, that I presently returned to my work.

Akiva still hadn't returned when I woke the next morning. The conviction that I felt upon waking that she *would* be there, however, was so strong that it wasn't until I had searched all the rooms and both the front and back gardens that I could persuade myself I'd been wrong.

Horned hedgepigs! I thought, grumbling under my breath. That meant my work and Akiva's to do again. The thought didn't appeal to me; and since I could, I thought righteously, reasonably be considered as mounting a rescue attempt, I packed myself a lunch basket and broached the hedge gate with a rapidly ticking pulse.

I shut the gate carefully behind, and sallied forth, I thought in sudden glee, to make my fortune. The basket that I had bought with me only added to the light-hearted feeling, and all in all I forgot about magic and danger—and almost, but not quite, about Akiva.

The path began ordinarily enough. As I had seen from my perch in the pine tree, it ran for a little ways under the shadow of the hedge, but it very soon dove into the very heart of the forest, where I found myself warily walking before very long. This path was narrower than the others, and in order to make sure that I stayed on the path as Akiva had constantly adjured me to do, I had to place one bare foot almost directly in front of the other as if I were dancing a slow strathspey through the forest. It was oddly exhausting work.

I hadn't gone far before the forest began to grow darker and cooler around me. I cast a glance around cautiously; but forests *did* get darker the further in one went, after all. I hauled my basket up with a mulish thrust of my chin. I was settling it back on my hip when, from the corner of my eyes, I caught a brief, silent flash of grey between the trees to my right. I sucked in a breath through my teeth, my fingers tightening around the basket handle, and readjusted my ideas. The darkening forest was the least of my problems: whatever it was, that grey streak of menace was *big*. I automatically checked the tucked hem of my skirt and took in another deep breath with the idea that before very long swift and prolonged running might be required.

Nothing happened for quite some time. I saw the same streak of grey several times over the next hour: always too quick to see clearly, always keeping pace easily, and always perfectly silent. I thought I could make out a distinctly lupine outline to the thing, but it was travelling too swiftly to be certain, and the only thing I could be sure of was a blaze of brindled white on its chest.

I set my teeth and continued to walk, refusing to allow myself to be frightened. The idea that it was a wolf grew steadily on me, and to my mind, unbidden, sprang memories of Liz Gantry's Wolf stories. It made a kind of cold hollowness in my stomach, which angered me enough to be brave.

I stopped once or twice and pretended to pick flowers by the side of the path, covertly darting quick glances into the woods, and managed in this way to catch a glimpse of a huge brindled muzzle.

A breath hissed through my teeth, and I blinked twice, very fast and wide. It *was* a wolf, and a very large one at that. Oddly enough, now that I knew for certain, I wasn't frightened; I could hear my heart beating loudly in my ears, but my head was clear, and my blood sang exhilaratingly. It didn't occur to me for a moment that it was an ordinary wolf, but I had the instinctive feeling that as long as I stayed on the path, nothing from the forest could touch me. When the path widened slightly, I continued to walk precisely down the middle of it despite the extra room.

I had hoped to find some trace of Akiva by now, but to my dismay there was no sign of her, or that she had ever travelled this path. In fact, there was no sign that the path was proceeding in any particular direction or for any particular reason, either. The only thing I was certain of was that the grey wolf following me was getting closer, and I began to stop more frequently at flowerbeds in the hopes of catching a covert glimpse of it.

I was carelessly rooting up daisies when a gravelly voice said in my ear, "Clumsy wench."

I sat down rather suddenly in the middle of the path, startled in spite of myself, and found that the wolf was now lounging slightly to my right, huge and grey. It seemed to be grinning, which annoyed me.

"I'm not really that stupid, you know," it said.

I caught my breath and scowled at it. Talking wolf or no, I disliked being made a fool of. "I don't know what you mean."

The grin widened. "Of course you don't. I suppose you merely have a passion for wayside weeds."

Belatedly, I remembered that I hadn't collected any flowers for a posy, and went pink-cheeked with annoyance.

"I was looking for a *particular* flower," I said, tilting a challenge with my chin. Since this didn't even raise me to eye level with the wolf, it was less effective than I'd hoped.

"Yes, a weed," suggested the wolf agreeably, as if he understood perfectly. I glared at him again.

"Why are you following me?" I demanded, scrambling to my feet and seizing my basket. I felt that I had been on the defensive long enough, and he didn't *seem* to be upon the point of tearing out my heart.

Again he seemed to grin, but his voice was innocent. "I don't know what you mean."

I gave him a hard look and walked on at my best pace. Despite this he continued to slink along at my side without effort, and I regretted bitterly not having a longer stride.

"I know where to find what you're looking for," he said at last, breaking the silence.

I looked sideways at him and was unnerved to find that my eyes were not very greatly higher than his when I was upright. It hadn't struck me before how very big he was. "What do you mean?"

"You're looking for a flower. I know where to find a flower."

"A *particular* flower," I repeated, annoyed to be taken up in my lie.

There was a suspicion of a growl from the wolf. "This *is* a particular flower. There are things in the forest that have special properties, things that you know nothing about. Akiva uses this one quite often."

I stopped abruptly. "You know Akiva!"

"Of course."

"Do you know where she is?"

"No. But I know how to find her."

I eyed him with distrust. "How?"

"With the flower, of course. I told you: it has special properties."

"What flower?" The wolf was being annoyingly roundabout. Also, he was smug. "And *what* properties? I think you're just making things up to look important."

"It's for finding things," the wolf said, offended. His outraged stillness made me realise with a shock that he had been gradually edging further into the woods. I was only just in time to stop myself from unconsciously taking a step off the path to follow. "And people. Akiva dries and powders it, but it's stronger fresh."

I tilted my chin and looked at him narrowly so that he knew I didn't really believe him. "Where is it, then?"

"Further in," he said, sitting on his haunches a little further away.

"I can't leave the path," I said. I didn't trust him at all. "I'll just use Akiva's powder. So there."

"Not strong enough." The wolf flattened his ears, suggesting impatience. "Just what do you have against the woods anyway?"

"Akiva said I wasn't to leave the path."

"Still with the path! Aren't we Akiva's precious poppet!"

My eyes snapped. "There are *things* in the forest."

"Oh, if you're *frightened*—"

"I am not frightened!"

"Then stop dawdling and come along."

I took one step off the path, more in involuntary agreement than in decision to go, but in that one step there was a rushing of air accompanied by a feeling of sharp motion that threw me to the ground violently, lurching me into another world. The cool forest air around me darkened and grew silent as if the forest were watching, intent. The very air was heavier here.

"Horned hedgepigs!" I said, in a scratchy voice. I climbed clumsily to my feet with the horrible knowledge that I needed to be back on the path *now*, and that it had disappeared. There was a queer little pulsing behind my eyes that I knew was my heartbeat, and I wondered coldly why it was so hard to draw in a breath all of a sudden.

"*Now*," said the wolf silkily, and at that moment it really did seem likely that he would tear my heart out; "*Now...*"

I turned and ran.

I must have dropped my basket somewhere back on the path. I didn't think of that then. I remember being thankful for my bare feet and kilted skirts, but beyond that was only the single, intent thought of flight. I felt the hot breath of the wolf at my back long before my own breathing had time to grow ragged, and I only had time to yell out the fragment of a song in wild appeal to the forest before his teeth snarled at one ankle and I tumbled head over heels. What madness or instinct led me to sing out those particular words I couldn't tell, but when the world stopped rolling about me, I found myself cocooned in willow saplings. They knit together so tightly above my head and all around me that only slivers of light could squeeze through.

In the gasping darkness I took an instinctive inventory of myself: torn skirt, bloody knee, painful breath. Sharp pain in my ribs—ouch—that was a protruding tree root. So *that* was what I had winded myself on. My mouth was full of mingled blood and grass, and a hot streak on my lower lip niggled at me, telling me that I'd split it.

I spat, and said again, this time in a groan, "Horned hedgepigs!"

The wolf growled, low and savage, from just beyond the saplings. My cocoon seemed suddenly very fragile and useless.

"Where did you learn that spell?" His voice was close, but he sounded grey and old—beaten.

My voice came out raggedly as the words fought with breath for precedence. "It wasn't a spell." My knee had begun to hurt the way injuries do when once you know about them, and my head was aching. "It's a nursery rhyme."

"*Willow basket, willow basket, weave the strands to make a casket; bend not break, casket's safe*," the wolf's voice said bitterly. "Of all the *infantile*—you infuriating little *witch!*"

"You've got a cheek, after trying to *eat* me!" I snapped, spitting out more blood and grass. I was badly shaken and that made me cross. "Anyway, I would have got away if I hadn't fallen; I don't *have* to do spells. I am not a witch."

"Rubbish. If you hadn't come up with that, you'd have been nothing but a few bones and a hank of butter-coloured pigtail by now."

I scowled at him through one of the larger cracks in the willow prison. "I don't wear pigtails, and I'm not fat enough to eat! I'd be stringy and bony."

The wolf gave a derisive half-snarl, half-laugh. "You're not good for anything else; at your age you're useless except as food."

I kicked the willow saplings from which the wolf's voice projected and was rewarded with a short, startled yelp and a flurry of movement. "I'm not anyone's food!"

"You're nothing but fodder! I need a *woman* to break the spell, and you are quite obviously not a woman."

"I never said I was," I told him coldly. "It's your own stupid fault if you thought so. When Akiva gets back—"

"How do you think I was able to get to you so easily? Akiva is off in the southern woods. I put the path out in the opposite direction."

I went very still, considering my options. There didn't seem to be many. "*You* put the path out?"

"Of course." His voice sounded bitter. "I might as well have spared myself the pains for all it got me. From the vibrations coming out of the garden I expected at the least a full-grown woman."

"I don't know what you're talking about," I said. "If you're under a spell it serves you right, and I wouldn't break it if I could."

"Very dramatic," he retorted, on a growl. "But since you can't, it really doesn't make any difference, does it? And I said *vibrations* because the whole forest has been humming with you for the last month."

I propped my elbows on my knees and sank my chin into the palms of my hands, frowningly considering this. "No," I said at last, with certainty. "I don't put out *vibrations*. And I don't do magic, the forest does."

"Oh, really? That would of course explain why you happen to be sitting inside a casket made of willow saplings."

"That was the forest, too," I told him. Stupid wolf. He didn't listen. "I think it likes me. It helps me sometimes."

"Ignorant as well as half-grown," said the detestable voice irritably. "In any case, you're going to have to do."

"I won't," I said flatly. "I won't do anything."

"If you want to stay where you are, very well. I'll be here waiting when you come out."

I pondered this for some time, chin in hands again. There didn't seem much chance that Akiva would come for me, and I knew I couldn't count on another miracle like the willow casket. At last I said cautiously: "What do I need to do?"

"Ah!" the wolf's voice was spiced with mockery and, oddly, hope. "I can't tell you. You have to learn it yourself."

"That's not fair."

"Don't sulk at me, *I* didn't arrange it."

I made a face at the saplings that divided us, annoyed to be dismissed as useless and then summarily told what to do. Stupid wolf. "Is it something I have to find or something I have to do?"

"The curse is in three parts," the wolf said. "The first part needs you to find something, the second part needs you to do something, and the third part needs you to give something."

"It sounds stupid," I muttered crossly. "Why is it so complicated?"

"You need only do one part," the wolf replied agreeably, but there was an undertone to his voice that made me wary. "That will be sufficient for now."

Sitting there in my safe little casket of willows, I knew he wasn't telling me everything. I could almost feel the ruthlessness of his desperation, and the same instinct that had told me he was about to eat me, told me that the wolf was not far from madness in his rage and despair. It was just as clear to me that I had no other way out, and the savage madness I heard in his voice made me certain that he was capable of waiting with no other end in view but to tear me to pieces in revenge if I wouldn't help.

So I stood rather shakily in the middle of my casket, stooped, with my fingers interlaced in the nursery rhyme way, and took a deep breath. I disengaged my fingers one by one, each in order according to the rhyme; and as I did so, to my wonder, each sapling untwisted and became a separate young willow tree, allowing me to stand upright. Despite the danger, I grinned in fierce exultation: I *had* done this.

"Impressive," growled the wolf, but his voice was a threat. Through the newly separated willow trees I could see that his eyes had gone wild and almost black. I knew coldly that I had only so much time before his control snapped and I became what he had called me: fodder. I stepped through the trees toward him, and his eyes followed me each step, hungrily. When I reached out one hand to place it on top of his huge grey head, the wolf ran his nose along my arm once, sniffing deeply and swiftly with his teeth just showing. His growl was low and hungry.

I tried to ignore it, but I think my hand trembled, sending a harsh ripple of laughter through the wolf's snarl. It made a scratchy cold something skitter across my back. I put up my chin, very slowly and deliberately, and thought that time and air had got very heavy suddenly. The forest was intruding on my sight: I could see curls of alternating pitch black and gold swirling around the wolf.

I gazed at him, fascinated, for moments that turned into minutes, until at last I understood. The swathes of pitch black were the madness; the gold a touch of the man this wolf had once been. It had been so long ago that the gold was faded and tarnished, and the blackness of wild animal had almost taken over. He must have been driven mad by rage and despair, over centuries perhaps, and by now there was so little left of what he had been that the hope I'd caused to flare was eating away at him just as the desperation had.

I knew this kind of swirling madness. When I was eight, I found an old, mad soldier who didn't know where he was and couldn't tell me his name. I took him home to Mother, who shaved his beard and cut his hair, making him look much younger; but his eyes had stayed the same—old and desperately mad. He hadn't known who he was, and it had eaten away at him like a maggoty-grub until there was nothing else to him.

Distantly, I became aware that the wolf had begun to growl again in a soft, savage undertone. My hands dropped to my sides, numb and cold, as his growl crescendoed into a snarl; but I knew what to do.

The soldier had wanted a name more than anything else. I was certain that the wolf needed his name just as badly. He needed to be reminded that he was human.

"I know what you need," I told him, finding my chin a little less mulish in the face of his growl. My eyes felt wide and fixed. "I just need to find it."

He snarled, teeth long and bare beneath drawn-up lips. "*Hurry...little...girl.*"

I took one step back, then another. The wolf closed the gap with one swift stride, and I sucked in a quiet, hopeless breath, because his eyes had gone completely black.

I didn't know his name, I thought, ideas flowing fast and cold behind my frozen eyes—but I knew the forest. It did so love to be sung to, and I was certain it could be tricked. I grinned then; a fierce, humourless grin that made my cheeks hurt, and found the right song. It was a schoolyard song, a choosing rhyme to pick teams.

"*Arthur, Martha, Michael, John,*" I sang, quick and low.

I wasn't quite quick enough, for with a suddenness that caught my breath in the back of my throat, the wolf leapt.

I shrieked, "*I name you Bastian!*" completing the rhyme—or was it a spell?—then two huge paws punched me in the chest and my head hit the grass.

Three

I found myself crushed and barely able to breath, spluttering on a mouthful of hair that was long and dirty and very human. I gave a small, angry yell that was too breathless to sound like anything so much as a yelp, and struggled vigorously beneath a heavy body. To my annoyance, I wasn't able to wriggle away. Someone's bare, dirty chest was squashing the breath out of me, and two powerful human hands were pinning me to the grass by either shoulder.

I scowled up at Bastian, for of course it was him squashing me. His eyes, deep hazel and confused, stared sickly down at me; then they sharpened and fixed on my face in fierce wonder.

"I am human again! Little witch, am I dreaming?"

My mouth opened uselessly, dragging painfully at my lungs, but the very breath had been forced from my lungs.

Bufflehead! I raged silently.

Bastian's eyes flashed with the same dark desperation I had seen in his wolf-eyes, and one of his hands closed around my neck, further cutting off my air supply.

"Am I dreaming?" His voice had become harsh and dangerous. "Am I dreaming? *Speak!*"

I groaned, shoving with both hands, and to my relief he pulled himself off me, allowing me to draw in a much-needed gulp of air.

"Horned...hedgepigs! Of course you're not dreaming...stupid wolf! Couldn't speak with...pounds of wolf *squashing* the breath...out of me."

He swiftly crouched, surprising a defensive scowl from me, and gazed at me with a kind of painful hunger in his face. "I'm human again?"

"Yes." I said it quietly, slowly—as if he were a small child.

The next moment I was caught up and spun around, crushed breathless once more to Bastian's chest, while he shouted in amazement and joy. "Little witch, little witch, you're a wonder!"

Both my cheeks were kissed soundly despite both my squirming and yell of outrage, and I was ruthlessly spun in another wild, euphoric circle.

At last, I worked an arm free and boxed his ear. "Put me down!"

He did so, laughing; and I promptly collapsed on the grass, my head still spinning.

Bastian lowered himself to the grass beside me more in the manner of a wolf than a man and regarded me sideways. "I was wrong about you. Infuriating little witch, yes; but not so young. How old are you?"

I looked at him in disfavour. "I'm nearly fifteen. I am *not* a witch."

"You look like you're ten," he said. He looked me up and down critically. "Possibly it's the dirt. What's a horned hedgepig, by the way?"

I scowled at him, because he wasn't so clean himself. "If it comes to dirt—"

"It does. You've got it all over you."

"So do you," I pointed out, not to be put off.

"You have a smudge on your nose," he added, flicking it carelessly as he spoke.

I scrambled to my feet, eyes snapping, but Bastian lounged where he was, wolf-like and grinning. "Where are you going?"

"I'm going home," I said coldly. There was always a smudge on my nose, but I didn't think it was polite of Bastian to bring it up when I had just helped him break his spell.

"Don't sulk, little witch, it's not becoming. Besides, how will you find the path?"

I shot him a distinctly nasty look. "I'll manage. You and your flower!"

Bastian grinned even more broadly. "I knew you wouldn't get off the path unless I told you I could help find Akiva. No, don't scowl at me; I'll show you how to get back."

"Fine," I grumbled. "But no twirling! And leave my nose alone."

Bastian did leave my nose alone, but after he led me to a huge oak that had been felled in some long-ago storm, there was another mad twirl as he threw me up on it.

I gave a muffled snarl of annoyance that made him grin and said: "Bufflehead! What are you doing?"

"I thought you wanted to get back to the path, little witch?"

"The path was much further back than this," I said haughtily. It was easy to be haughty when I was taller than him.

"Don't I know it," he said feelingly. "You led me a merry dance to get here. Near or far is not the point; the point is the path."

"That doesn't make sense."

"Only if you don't have any sense with which to make it," he retorted unkindly. "Don't think about it, and don't look for it; just jump backwards. The path will find you."

I sucked in my cheeks and regarded him in stony silence for a long moment. "I helped you break your spell, wolf. You could at least say *thank you* instead of insulting my wits."

He shrugged. "You haven't broken the curse, little witch; only a part of it. I reserve my thanks for a completed task."

"How do you mean?" Interested in spite of myself, I sat down on the oak log. This allowed me to be even haughtier since I could now dangle my feet in Bastian's face.

"I told you the curse was in three parts; one to find, one to do, and one to give. You've done the finding, and I'm man again for two hours of my choosing each day, but there are still two parts to go."

"Well, I did the first part," I pointed out, lightly drumming my heels into the dry bark.

"That was the easy bit," mocked Bastian. "I told you, I reserve my thanks for the completed task."

I glared down at him. "You aren't the least bit grateful, are you?"

To my surprise, instead of answering, Bastian bent his head and gravely kissed first one and then the other of my bare, grass-stained feet.

"I am more than grateful," he said gently. "Thank you, little witch. Now, jump."

So I jumped. I meant to argue, but the kisses put me so much off balance that I obeyed unthinkingly, scrambling to my feet and leaping backwards from the log. I found myself back on the path with a jarring bump, and just barely escaped biting my tongue. There was a frantic whirl of skirt and torn petticoat as I very nearly rolled off the other side, and when the world stopped turning, I sat up carefully, feeling more shaken than I liked to admit.

The lunch basket proved to be within reach when I looked around to gain my bearings, and although the sandwiches in it were a little squashed and grass-stained, they were still mouth-wateringly edible. I stayed where I was and ate them in the middle of the path, so worn and tired from my adventures that it seemed the only sensible thing to do. When I was done, I shook the crumbs out beside the path, watching with owl-like attention as they disappeared before they ever hit the grass.

Then I said, "Ouch," in a thoughtful voice, remembering my various injuries, and climbed painfully to my feet. It was time to go home.

Night had fallen when I emerged from the forest. The great, bright, full moon shed a glowing twilight on the forest that had deceived me into thinking that the afternoon was still lingering, and it was a shock to find that it was already night. Apparently time ran more quickly in the different kind of forest I had found myself in. My footsteps dragged as I made my way wearily to the side gate and into the back garden: I was more tired than I ever remembered being before, and so far behind my work in the garden that I knew I wouldn't ever catch up, even if I worked all night.

I was so gloomily caught up in my thoughts that I was partway through the garden before I realised that Akiva's two daily garden beds were tended. I gazed at the garden for a long, stupid moment, then threw my basket aside and dashed for the house.

Akiva was sitting in her chair as if she had never left when I crashed through the door.

"Shut the door, child," she told me placidly as I stood staring. "Good gracious! What a mess to bring into my nice clean house!"

I grinned ruefully at her, causing a jagged slice of pain across my split lip. I was almost overwhelmingly glad to see her again. If I had been Gwendolen I would have rushed across the room and hugged her.

I was glad enough to see her that I didn't even protest when she jabbed one bony finger in my back by way of encouragement to enter the bathroom, in which a tepid bath had already been drawn. I might have enjoyed it. I don't know. I think I was nearly asleep by then.

I slept until nearly noon the next day. The first thing that I saw when I woke was a golden beam of early afternoon sunlight, swimming with dust motes at the very end of my bed. I sat upright in horror, tumbling my pillow to the floor. Horned hedgepigs, why hadn't Akiva woken me?

There was a mad, fumbling hurry, as in my haste I took twice as long as usual to button myself up, then I scurried out to the main room, plaiting my hair as I went. I was prepared to encounter sarcasm, irritation, or even weary resignation. Instead, I found breakfast ready for me on the table.

Akiva, eyeing me with what I thought was grim approval, only said: "Sit down and eat your breakfast."

I opened and closed my mouth twice before I finally found my voice. "I thought you'd be angry."

She said, "Ridiculous!" but I saw the shadow of a smile at the corners of her mouth. Akiva was only being gruff. "Deep forest is not to be toyed with, and it's important to rest well after your first taste."

I was blissfully helping myself to bacon and eggs, but at that point I slid a sharp look at her. "Did you leave me alone on purpose so I'd have to go into the forest?"

Akiva gave a dry cackle of laughter. "You're not nearly as important as you think you are: I left because there was a need. I was in deep forest myself."

I stopped mid-mouthful of bacon, assimilating the term. *Deep forest.* So that's where I'd gone when I stepped from the path after Bastian. "How did you know *I* was?"

"Child, if you imagine I wish to see your breakfast in that disgusting state, you're fair and far off. I knew you were in the forest because every tree and energy thread in the forest was humming about you when I got back. I suppose you helped the Wolf?"

I closed my mouth and contented myself with nodding, eyes wary.

"Hmm. That could bring more trouble than you're prepared for. Never mind, it can't be helped now; and something certainly had to be done."

"Why trouble?"

"The person who laid the curse on him won't be happy," Akiva said. "Eat up, child; work goes on."

And so it did. The next day, I found myself carting the weekly washing down to the creek behind Akiva's henhouse. I was burning with excitement. Washing was, after all, washing; but Akiva had tacitly repealed her orders for me to stay on the path, and the entire forest was now at my disposal. There was also a part of me that expected, and was excited at, the prospect of seeing Bastian again. I hadn't met anyone quite like him before.

This time, prepared for the disorienting shift between path and forest, I didn't fall over. The wash basket jerked and the chook house disappeared, but the stream was directly ahead and just a few steps away, sparkling golden and cool in the warm sunshine that broke through the trees. Autumn hadn't yet overtaken the afternoons, even if the mornings and evenings were cooler.

Gleefully, I skipped from stone to stone until I was within leaping distance of a huge, sun-warmed rock that had caught my eye; and in a matter of moments, I and my basket had made it safely there. I found it as promising as it had looked from the bank; flat and baking hot, perfect for drying clothes and for sitting on to dangle my feet in the water.

By the time I was wending my way home with the basket of semidry clothing, I was pleasantly sunned and splashed. The last of the moisture in my skirt dried while I pegged the clothes by the chook house, but I still hadn't seen Bastian. I was disappointed but not really surprised; he was quite likely to be looking for someone who could break the rest of the curse. The fright and weariness of the previous day's adventures had faded overnight, leaving behind a sense of adventure and accomplishment. Akiva's rare approval had been sweet, and it had convinced me as all Bastian's protestations had not been able to, that I had in fact done magic. I wanted to do more.

When I got back to the house, Akiva wasn't in the garden. Surprised, I put my head around the back door, and was further surprised to see her sorting through the herbs on her work bench. I didn't remember Akiva staying in the house during the day before.

She said: "Don't hang off the door, child. If you're coming in, come in."

I indicated the collection of phials that Akiva had separated from the rest. "What are those?"

Akiva, choosing to take me literally, rattled off a string of names: some that I knew, more that I didn't. "Sit down if you want to learn."

I did so, curling the fingers of one hand into a tight fist in my pocket. I didn't dare show the full extent of my joy in case Akiva changed her mind, but I was fizzing with suppressed excitement. As it was, she reprimanded me almost immediately for fidgeting and slapped the hand that I was turning bottles with.

"If you think I want a flurry of continual movement next to me, you're very much mistaken," she snapped. "Do you know what this is?"

I inspected the glass jar with a wrinkled nose. "Yuck. Honey-blossom."

"What do you know about it?"

"It stinks," I said, sitting back to get away from the cloying honey-scent of it. "Gwen uses it for love potions."

There was a saturnine gleam to Akiva's eyes. "Does she? Yes, they used it for that when I was a girl, too. Piffle."

"Oh. Why?"

"Because it's natural sugar and nothing more. You might as well make a love potion from sweetcane."

"*And* it would taste better," I agreed. Akiva's lips gave the tiniest twitch upwards, and she held up another jar, this one thinner and tube-shaped.

I gazed into swirling green that seemed to make faces at me, and found myself shocked. "That's lillypilly oil!"

Now where had she been hiding *that*? I had poked my nose into every phial and jar on this workbench: I would have noticed something as contraband as lillypilly oil.

"Familiar with it, are you?" said Akiva, with a short crack of laughter.

Since lillypilly oil was used only by the very rich or very desperate, I ignored this remark as the mockery it was, and said, eyeing the vial in fascination, "Someone I know had some. It's for dreams and forgetting."

There was another dry cackle from Akiva, but she said: "That's close enough. Three drops of lillypilly in a palmful of honeyblossom, then stirred warm into a cup of fresh water—what does it make?"

"Something you keep drinking because you forget how much it stinks," I said, grinning. The remark earned me a clip over the ear, but it was worth it, because just for a moment, Akiva had grinned too.

"A longer lasting sleeping draught, you stupid child. Honeyblossom makes the lillypilly cling a little longer, and the water dilutes it so that the sleep feels natural. *Fresh* water, mind, and free running. Still water collects too much residue to use."

"All right," I said, since she seemed to expect me to say something. "Still water is bad, honeyblossom clings, and lillypilly is only for a few drops at a time."

"Close enough," Akiva said again, and went on.

Akiva was a good teacher. Unlike Gwendolen, who was always annoyingly helpful and earnestly determined to make sure I understood absolutely everything, she was quick and to the point, explaining only if I asked a question, and sometimes not even then. Her dry voice, with its short, terse sentences, was easy to listen to and easier still to remember.

We spent the afternoon making two potions. Teas, Akiva insisted on calling them, much to my disgust. Apart from the lillypilly oil, my gloomy suspicion that the herbs and roots she used were medicinal only and without any magical qualities, was confirmed.

"Which is quite enough to be making mistakes with," Akiva added dourly, raising one brow at my crestfallen face. She wouldn't tell me the use for which the teas were made, and I sank my chin crossly in the palm of one hand, glaring at the bottles as if they could be induced to tell me themselves.

"Tea making is touchy work," she said, corking the second finished bottle. "One wrong step and you'll have a villager curling up on your floorboards, dead."

I brightened momentarily, eyes glittering. I hadn't thought about the possibility of poison.

"And if you want to know what they do, work it out for yourself, ignorant child," added Akiva, raising the other brow at me. I tried not to look so obviously bloodthirsty.

"You know what the ingredients are, the rest should be simple."

"Cough syrup," I said, making a face at the first. I gazed at the second for some time, deliberating. "And...a rheumatics tea?"

"Rheumatics, eh? It's bone strengthener, child. That sailor from the village has a young wife who's with child again, and I promised that I'd give her a tea next time. The first young boy is forever breaking his collarbone or his arm."

"How do you know she's with child?" I demanded. There hadn't been visitors to the cottage for *weeks*.

Akiva gave me one of her looks. "It's not any magic of mine, child: the young sailor was on shore leave three months ago. She should have found out by now."

I blinked a little at Akiva's casual way of mentioning such things. Babies were usually a matter for blushes and coy subterfuge.

"What about the cough mixture?"

"I had a vision," she said, and I looked up at her suspiciously, unsure if I was being laughed at or not.

"Really?"

"Maybe, maybe not. You seem to have an unhealthy desire for everything to be accomplished through magic, child."

She sighed, and hobbled away to the door, beckoning me to follow. "Shift yourself. I can see I'm not going to get any peace until you do some real magic."

She led me out through the front garden but turned off the path immediately after the white gate. I found myself once more in that vast, pathless forest that Akiva had called *deep* forest.

"Now," she said abruptly, coming to a sudden stop. "Close your eyes."

I did as I was told, and stood there with my eyes scrunched shut, feeling the grass soft and damp beneath my feet and the unexpected warmth of a beam of sunlight on my face. The forest stirred around me with all the usual rustles and chirrups, and beside me I could hear Akiva moving in the abrupt, jerky way that older people move. Nothing remotely magical happened.

I shifted impatiently from one foot to the other, and had my ears promptly boxed for my pains.

"I can't hear anything!" I complained, feeling misused. I didn't open my eyes because I didn't put it past Akiva to hit me again if I did. "Did I say anything about hearing? I don't want you to listen, I want you to *feel*."

"Oh," I said, in surprise; because as soon as she said it, I knew what it was that I was supposed to be sensing. Beneath my feet, not in the grass nor yet in the soil; not real, yet not unreal, were faint but definite threads, gleaming with magic or perhaps magic themselves, crisscrossing and stretching far. Mentally, I followed the one that ran by my big toe, and caught a clear, vivid sense of smooth lush hills, and a stretch of green. *The dancing green!* I realised, even as my brain protested at this impossible form of sight. My eyes snapped open, glittering with excitement, and the dancing green abruptly vanished.

"If you want to see both at once you'll need to practise," Akiva told me, catching my look of indignant confusion. "The energy lines are a tool for you, but they're no good if you can't see them with your eyes open. No more questions until you come to me and tell me that you can."

I agreed, my excitement mounting; because at last I was within reach of magic, *real* magic! Akiva left me there, and I closed my eyes again, confident that it would not be long before I mastered the art of it.

One short afternoon was enough to teach me that this was very far from being the case.

I returned to the cottage shortly after the triad sank, discouraged and inclined to give up. It seemed that the only way I could see the forest lines was with my eyes closed: the minute I opened them, the glowing lines vanished.

Akiva laughed rudely at my woebegone face. "You've had a few lucky spells go right and you're suddenly convinced you're the next great enchantress. You have a slight gift but it's nothing out of the ordinary; you need to practice like any other young apprentice."

I flushed hot and dark. There was enough truth in the accusation to make it sting. I had very much wanted to believe that I had a special gift.

"Exactly, child," said Akiva. "Wash up for dinner."

AFTER SOME TIME, I RATHER FORGOT ABOUT TRYING TO see the energy lines. It was just too hard.

Akiva had given me every afternoon off to 'get to know the forest' as she said, and I felt myself as free as a bird. There was so much to distract me in the forest: wonderfully climbable trees; old, dry riverbeds crying out to be explored; and the opportunity of seeing Mother and Gwendolen every freeday when I came to the village to buy meat.

In fact, I would probably have continued quite happily in my state of lazy ignorance, content merely to wander through deep forest, if it hadn't been for what happened on the day of Gwen's fourteenth birthday.

It was a month or so since I had met Bastian, and I was wandering in deep forest. I was aggrieved because Akiva had called me a feckless, shiftless child, and had told me irritably not to come back home until I had learned something; and I was annoyed because I had seen nothing more of Bastian though it was now more than a month since I had helped him. Akiva had given me permission to go to Gwendolen's birthday party, but from her grim tone this morning I had an idea that this permission was in danger of being revoked. I wasn't particularly keen on the party, but I would be very much annoyed if I missed out on the abundant spread of party edibles.

I stomped crossly through the forest, scowling at the blackbirds and alternately opening and closing my eyes in a vain attempt to see the lines with my eyes open. Sometimes I thought I had done it, when with my eyes half open I could see a vague, vein-like net spread over the forest; but by the time my eyes were fully open, the nebulous structure had vanished. My time was fast running out: one of the triad had slipped over the horizon, the other two quickly approaching it; and when they, too, sank, I would be too late to go to the party.

A little after the early evening sunlight began to coat the leaves of the forest in warm gold, I began to be aware of a vibration to the forest, elusively real yet not real, that set my bones warmly buzzing in my skin and my teeth in my head. It wasn't unpleasant, but it was a strong sensation, and I looked around me, frowning; expecting from the strength of it that the vibration must come from something visible. But around me there were only trees and grass, and it gradually occurred to me that the sensation had started in my toes and made its way upward.

"Hah!" I said in surprise, closing my eyes. In the darkness I saw the line, glittering gold and pulsing, that ran directly under the soles of my feet. I cast a curious look around at the other energy lines, but they were all the same quiet green of the forest, and none of them were vibrating. My interest piqued, I followed this thread to a tiny clearing with a fast-flowing stream that wound its way through the trees. I gazed at it speculatively for some moments, wondering what it was about this particular stream that had caused the energy thread to vibrate so strongly. There was a white disturbance frothing at the edge of the stream, air bubbles joyfully breaking the surface of the water, and after some moments of frowning contemplation it occurred to me that someone was swimming.

Lucky! I thought, enviously. As I watched, the water parted with a surge near the opposite bank, and someone stood upright, waist deep in the stream. It was Bastian. He was in his human form, rather cleaner than I had last seen him, and quite naked if his bare chest and torso were anything to judge by.

He seemed to see me at the same moment as I saw him, because he waved, tossing glittering gold droplets of water into the air. "Little witch, come through!"

He surged toward the nearer bank, and I realised in some shock that, naked or no, he was about to climb out. My eyes snapped open, and Bastian and the stream vanished. The energy line beneath my feet throbbed, and I heard him muttering something derogatory; then the thread gave one, massive hum, and Bastian was there in front of me with a huff of forest-scented air. I was relieved to see that although he was still dripping, he was also clothed from the waist down.

"Why did you run away?" he demanded, shaking water from his hair. It made him look like wolf-Bastian.

"I didn't *mean* to," I said. "I still can't see the lines without my eyes closed."

He shrugged. "Not everyone can. Perhaps you won't be able to."

"But Akiva told me not to come back unless I had learned something!"

"Learning what you can't do is still learning," Bastian pointed out.

I didn't find this helpful, and gave him a scorching look to inform him of the fact. "I *can* do it," I said grittily. "I just need time."

Bastian threw himself down on the grass and stretched out. "Time we have. Go ahead."

"I'm tired now," I said, in the mood to be contrary. "Tell me who put the curse on you instead."

"Who is not as interesting as how," he countered, looking lazily up at me. I think he was trying to change the subject. Then he seemed to relent, and added, "I fell in love with an enchantress."

"She put a spell on you because you fell in love with her?" The question came out unexpectedly like an accusation, and to my surprise, a tinge of red came to Bastian's cheeks.

Immediately I pounced. "Liar!"

"Human bodies!" Bastian said in exasperation. "I must be out of practice. Very well, little witch; I *did* court an enchantress."

"And?" Again there was a touch of red in Bastian's cheeks.

"And two other women," he admitted.

"You were courting two other women at the same time?"

"That's the shortened version for young ears," Bastian said shortly. "Take it from me, little witch; never court three women in the same town."

"I'm not going to court anyone," I told him. "I'm going to be a pirate, and pirates don't marry."

"Is that so? Obviously I should have come to you for advice, but it seemed a little late for celibate piracy by the time Cassandra was pointing her finger at me."

I frowned and sat down, crossing my legs, and returned to the point of contention. "Why were you courting three women at once?"

"My dear child, three women is the minimum requirement for happiness: one never finds the qualities one requires in any less than three, much less in one woman."

"It serves you right," I said. I disliked the smooth undertone of arrogance in his voice.

Bastian was startled. "I beg your pardon?"

"It serves you right. If someone did that to Gwendolen I'd curse him, too. If I could."

"Woman's spite," Bastian retorted in annoyance.

"It's not: it's teaching you a lesson," I told him. "If a lady did the same to you—"

"I'd shrug and move on," interrupted Bastian.

"You wouldn't; you'd try your best to make her fall in love with you really and truly," I argued, realising as I said it that it was true. It was *exactly* what Bastian would do. I took advantage of his unusual silence to continue. "If a girl treats a man false he can go away and travel, and forget. Women have to sit at home and remember through every chore and moment that when he said *this* it was a lie, and when he said *that* it was in order to get something. There's no getting away from yourself and all the people who know you've been made a fool of."

Bastian cupped his hands behind his head and eyed me balefully. "And what do you know about it? Who broke your youthful heart?"

"No one, and I *do* know. When Father died Mother was never the same again, and it was better for her, because she knew he'd always been faithful. When you sit there longing for someone and then remembering that they're not worth longing for, it's worse."

He gave a derisive snarl. "Saccharine. Poppycock. No woman is worth that amount of soul-searching."

"You're embittered and old," I said excusingly, watching with interest the coughing fit that came over him. "Gwendolen says that often happens to men in middle age."

"Middle age!" gasped Bastian, sitting up to catch his breath.

"When you get middle-aged and embittered you need someone to care for, Gwendolen says. Mother had me and Gwen to look after. It seemed to take her mind off things."

"I'm not surprised," Bastian retorted sourly, recovering himself. "You would have been a horrible little handful. In fact, I imagine you were much the same as you are now—little witch, I'll have you know that I'm barely twenty-three if you count the time I've been human! I've a good mind not to help you with your magic!"

"I don't need your help," I said defiantly, and climbed to my feet.

"Oh, really?" One of Bastian's eyebrows went up. It was obvious that he was taking it as a challenge. "And who scared you into performing your first acts of magic, I would like to know?"

I eyed him in fascinated wonder. "You're trying to make an attempt to eat me into a virtue!"

Only the memory of what Bastian had been when I first saw him—black, almost mad, and more animal than human—stopped me from telling him crossly that I was glad Cassandra had bespelled him.

"In a hurry, little witch?"

I allowed the change in subject. "It's Gwendolen's birthday party tonight, and I know Akiva won't let me go if I haven't learnt to see the energy lines with my eyes open by the time I get back." With a burst of rueful self-knowledge, I added, "I should have been done weeks ago, but I was too lazy. And there was a stream bed that cut right back into the forest, beneath all that wild ivy, and then there wasn't any more time."

"Why are you so set on this party?" enquired Bastian, eyeing me narrowly. "You don't care for 'em."

"Apple pie," I said promptly, ignoring his cool assumption that he knew what I cared for. "And cream pastries and stuffed duck. Oh, Bastian, *please* will you help me?"

Bastian looked up at me lazily. "Are you sure you want to learn?"

"Of course I want to learn!"

"I meant, are you sure you want to learn from *me*?" Bastian said, grinning wolfishly. He leapt to his feet in a single movement, startling me. "Very well, you've been warned."

"Warned of what?" I demanded, and then squeaked in surprise when Bastian casually swept me off my feet.

"Put me down! Where are you taking me?"

"Where is not as much fun as how," Bastian said.

"Put me down!" I said again, in my fiercest tones. "I am *not* a sack of potatoes!"

Bastian's grin widened. "I'm counting on it, little witch. You have no idea. Close your eyes."

"Stop telling me what to do! And *put me down!*"

"Suit yourself," Bastian said, with his most charming smile. He shifted his weight as if he were about to take a step, and the forest blurred around us in impossibly fast motion. I clung round his neck for dear life as the forest flew by, then Bastian's foot jolted down again, completing the step, and the forest stopped its mad, dizzying rush.

I loosened my death grip on Bastian, who grinned more broadly still and said, "I told you to close your eyes, little witch."

I glared up at him, snatching my arms away from his neck, and opened my mouth to demand again, in no uncertain terms, that he put me down. Much to my discomfiture, he did so before I could spit out the words. But instead of dropping to solid ground, I was tossed, willy-nilly, into a slow-moving stream that had appeared at the end of the thread. I had only time to give a short yelp before icy cold water closed in a rush over my head; and when I emerged, gasping, it was to the sound of Bastian's laughter.

"Just you wait!" I promised him wrathfully, surging up from the stream with violent shivers and dark thoughts of revenge. "I'll get you for this!"

"But first," Bastian said, his eyes laughing wickedly, "first, you have to catch me, little witch!"

He waited, tantalizingly, until I had sloshed laboriously up the bank toward him, then took a negligent step backwards and disappeared from view.

"Cheat!" I cried indignantly, stomping forward heavily in my wet skirts. When I closed my eyes, I could see the thread that Bastian must have gone down, still quivering, and I stepped down on it gingerly with my eyes shut. It didn't carry me swiftly and seamlessly as it had carried Bastian and I: it was an exhausting effort to lift each foot, and a kind of entropy dragged heavily on my legs for each step forward. It felt as though I was walking through thick mire.

I continued with a dogged tenacity, determined to show Bastian that I could do it just as well as he could, but with my eyes closed to see the glitter of the forest threads, I didn't notice I had come to the end of Bastian's trail until I tumbled off it into soft, sweet-smelling grass. I opened my eyes to the familiar sound of Bastian's mocking laugh and picked myself up with all the dignity that a smudged face, dangling petticoat and dripping skirt would allow.

"What took you so long?" enquired Bastian's most sarcastic tones. He was lounging on the grass and playing idly with a stray, flexible twig of greenery that was oddly out of place now that I had time to gaze about and notice that I was somewhere in the middle of a huge, grassy field without a tree for miles around. In contrast to the greenery, wide swathes of purple wild-flowers made scything sweeps of brilliant colour through the lush grass. As the wind swept languidly over the field, the patches of colour swayed and sent up a heady perfume. It didn't *look* like forest, but it somehow was; soaked in the last warmth of the triad and sheltered from the slice of the stronger autumn winds.

"The forest's gone squiggly," I said in surprise, gazing my fill at the view and basking in the out-of-season warmth of the sunshine. I had an idea that Bastian and I might have travelled further than it seemed: the triad didn't seem to be so far sunk over the horizon here.

Bastian cocked an eyebrow and sat up. "Trying to change the subject, little witch? You are not here to admire the view; this is practice. Catch me if you can." He rolled sinuously to his feet, and in the same movement disappeared down a thread. I swiped a few, damp, straggling hairs out of my face crossly, and closed my eyes to find the new thread, regretful that I must leave the strange warmth.

This time it was a little easier to drag myself along the thread after Bastian, but I was panting by the time I stumbled off at the end of the trail. I managed to catch myself before I fell over, with a wild flickering of my eyelids that showed a mad mix of forest-line glitter and swelling, grassy field.

"Too slow, little witch," said Bastian chidingly, sauntering around from behind me. He was just out of reach, twirling the twig between his fingers; then a step back, and he was gone. I sensed him behind me, a quick, smooth slide of movement, and the twig of greenery switched mockingly across my rump. I whirled, molten anger churning in my belly: I may not be Gwendolen's equal in flirting, but I knew that a slap on the backside went far beyond what was allowable.

Bastian twirled the stick again, one eyebrow raised at my wrathful face, and I dashed at him with renewed vigour. He let me get close before he slipped away, but I blinked my eyes shut and darted right after him, more quickly again this time, and I emerged swiftly enough behind him to considerably startle him.

Bastian narrowed his eyes. "I can see I'm going to have to change tactics," he remarked, dodging my unheeding rush with a swift, casual turn and a swish of the twig.

I rubbed my stinging rump and glared at him. "Just you wait until I catch you!"

"I'm waiting, little witch, I'm waiting! I've been waiting this past half hour and more!"

He slipped down a thread before I had a chance to do more than take one step forward. I'd just blinked my eyes closed when a familiar *swish* behind me and another stinging pain across my misused backside told me too late that Bastian had only travelled a few feet. I spun swiftly, snatching at Bastian, but only caught a pinch of bare skin before he disappeared again. My eyelids fluttered uncertainly open and shut as conflicting instincts urged me at the same time to give chase, and not to stir. At last, I closed my eyes in despair and stepped blindly after Bastian. As before, he had removed only a few feet from where he last stood, and my stinging behind received another blow before I could turn to meet Bastian's onslaught.

"You'll have to do better than that, my little witch," he said chidingly.

He slipped away on a thread, blinking in and out of sight, close and then distant by turns; never in the one place for more than a second, and exiting the forest lines to tiptoe sneakily behind me and pull my hair if I closed my eyes for more than a second to find which line he had taken. When I changed tactics and kept my eyes open, Bastian used the forest lines with abandon to appear and disappear, plying his switch of greenery with careless mockery until I was wild with rage. With the heat of my anger came a subtler, deeper sense of the forest, and in a moment of cold rationality, I realised that my emotions were spurring the forest on to help me. Of course! My first real spell had happened when I was frightened to death.

Now, I thought exultantly, my anger fierce and joyous, *now* I was getting somewhere. I let the rage simmer, reflexively rubbing my sore backside and brooding on my wrongs, and gradually, a glitter of gold net spread itself out at my feet. In the midst of this delicate operation, Bastian nipped in behind me and tweaked my hair, inducing a fresh snap of irritation that made the net of forest lines leap and grow in intensity. I darted around, snatching at Bastian again, and caught the tips of his fingers as he turned, chuckling, down another thread. In a blaze of triumph, I saw the thread flare with my eyes open; and then, with a chuckle of my own, I seized it and turned it back on itself. An instant later Bastian stepped lightly from it, and when I punched him in the nose my fist connected with an entirely satisfying solidness.

Bastian made a startled sound, his eyebrows flying up. He stumbled backwards over a swell in the ground and sprawled on his back in the grass. I pounced on him with a gurgle of glee, bouncing my weight down on his exposed stomach with an exuberance that caused him to expel his breath in a surprised groan, and crowed shamelessly.

"You're dripping on me, little witch," he panted, recovering his breath with an effort. Water ran down his nose, mixing with the blood, and I inspected my handiwork with appreciative wonder.

"I hit you, Bastian!"

A gleam of amusement lit Bastian's eyes. "Oddly enough, I did notice. Just what did you do to that thread?"

"I turned it round!" I declared triumphantly. "I could *see* it! I can see them all!" Horned hedgepigs, but it was stunning! The grass showed through faintly beneath the glitter as if the lines were real and the grass merely illusion, but when I blinked carefully, the bright gold became less prevalent; more at one with the greenery. I turned my gaze back to Bastian with all my forest sight, looking past the mingled blood and water he was wiping away, and caught my breath in wonder. "Bastian! You're beautiful!"

The threads leading to him were too numerous to separate: they swirled in huge skeins around him, forming a glowing ball of glittering gold around him. Tones of rich amber and dark gold made shadows in the skeins, and I had to blink several times over before I was able to see Bastian through the gold.

I studied him, and he looked back with a smile playing about his lips at my fascination. Then the threads enveloping him burst with an explosion of brilliance that even the lines in the field had not equalled, the air around me rippling with the power of it. When my vision returned to normal Bastian was in his wolf-shape, and the forest threads were a faint suggestion in the corners of my eyes.

"You shook the forest lines," I said accusingly.

"Interesting." Bastian sat on his haunches, but his muscles were bunched, as though ready for sudden action. "That gives me some little hope, after all. Now, little witch—now that you are content, I'll race you home."

We each picked a different thread, and skimmed effortlessly through the forest, laughing like children. Everything was so new, so beautiful. We leapfrogged at the intersection of the threads, Bastian soaring high above my head in one of his great leaps, or my flying feet just barely clearing his huge, shaggy back. Miles flew by in seconds, and I was disappointed to find myself tumbling back onto the path just before the garden gate. Bastian sat on his haunches by the side of the path, sides heaving and tongue lolling, and I rested my hands on my knees, panting.

"I'm too old for this," Bastian groaned, but there was a laugh in his voice and I rather thought he was having a joke to himself. "Go in, little witch. Enjoy your party."

I waved carelessly, too light in my elation to care about the mocking note in his voice, and scrambled back into the garden. Akiva was waiting at the front door, arms folded, when I opened the gate.

"It's about time," she said.

"I can see them, I can see them, Akiva!"

She eyed me somewhat grimly. "So I see. I repeat: it was about time."

I ducked my head partly to display proper contrition, and partly to hide the grin I couldn't prevent from spreading across my face.

Akiva eyed both the grin and my token of contrition with the same, amused eye. "Be off with you; go to your party. I'll come for you a little before midnight."

I bolted before she could change her mind, snatching up my boots from beneath my bed and darting back out the gate without stopping even to change my clothes. The evening was now darkening to real dusk, but the forest lines called me off the path very quickly, promising adventure and magic, and I followed heedlessly. Gwendolen and her party could wait a little longer.

Four

The buzz and noise of Gwendolen's party annoyed me. We were out on the dancing green, canopied by strings of lights that had been gaily hung between the trees, but after the quiet hum of the forest the mixed laughter and chatter was bothersome, even loose in the night air.

Besides, I was wearing my boots again, and the additional discomfort had soured my temper. I was beginning to dread the onset of winter as the autumn drew on, because unless Akiva had a spell to keep feet warm, I would be wearing shoes continually for the next three months. Even I didn't try to brave winter barefoot.

I stifled my annoyance by application of a large plate of mixed good things, and observed the general throng. Gwendolen was dancing with one boy while sparkling demurely at another over her partner's shoulder, which didn't at all surprise me: Gwendolen has always been a flirt. Almost every other boy watched her as she danced. While she was thus occupied, I escaped to the matron's trestle bench, where Mother was sitting by herself and smiling indulgently at the festivities, a fluffy blue shawl spread loosely over her shoulders.

"Gwen's looking beautiful," I said, seating myself beside her. I was fully aware of the amount of time it must have taken to set Gwendolen's hair.

Mother turned her smile on me. "Hallo, Rose! You look beautiful, too."

I crossed my ankles and regarded the black tips of my boots. "No."

"Well, perhaps I should have said *presentable*, then. What are you hiding in your pockets this time? Not a frog again, I hope?"

I grinned, recalling more interesting times, and showed Mother the silken ribbons I had bought for Gwen's birthday.

She touched them with an expert finger. "Expensive, Rose. I hope you're not spending all your money on fripperies for Gwendolen."

I shook my head and tucked the ribbons back into my pocket.

"Akiva isn't much of a talker, is she?" Mother said, and I wasn't sure whether or not it was a change of subject.

"It's peaceful," I said, and she laughed. I found myself telling her about Bastian and his curse, making an effort to speak, and discovered as I did so that there was only so much I could say about the curse, and no more. It had attached itself to me as much as to Bastian; and, like Bastian, there were things it wouldn't let me say. I found myself crosser still: I didn't care to have an interloper in my head, censoring what I could and couldn't say.

To my surprise, Mother seemed more concerned about Bastian than about the magic I was practicing.

"Be careful, Rose," she said. "Some people are so set on what they want that it leaves no room for what is right. Mind that you do as Akiva tells you to do."

I leaned my head against her shoulder and nodded, allowing her to put an arm around me. It was companionable and...*different*. I didn't feel like the child who had left home half a year ago, muddy and tangled and wild. For an odd, unbalanced moment, I felt old and distant and sober. I shied away from the feeling instinctively, and from the sense of loss and isolation it gave me. When Mother kissed my head in farewell at the end of Gwendolen's party, I hugged her tightly, afraid that I was losing her. But her arms were tight and comforting; and when she left me at the outskirts of the forest with Akiva, she said, "Mind you wear your socks to bed tonight," and I knew that nothing had really changed. At least nothing important.

I fell asleep in front of the fire when I got back, my head leaning against the arm of Akiva's armchair and my tea mug sitting on the floor before me. Akiva had settled down, most unusually, with a rather proficient bit of knitting. She purled away fiercely with no sign of going to bed, nor of shooing me off to mine, though it was past midnight. I was too sleepily content at being back home to want to take myself off to bed.

Consequently, I woke quite some time later to a darkened room. Soft firelight was dancing with dark shadow, and Akiva wasn't in her chair. My sleepy ears caught the sound of her voice through the front door just as I felt the slight, cold draught of night air on my cheeks. I murmured protestingly.

It seemed to me that she was in the front garden, talking to someone outside the gate, but the back of the chair prevented me from seeing who it was. I settled back down to the business of sleep. The voice murmuring from outside was nigglingly familiar, however, and curiosity eventually chased away sleep. I listened vaguely until Akiva's voice cut in on the other voice, sharply negative despite hushed tones.

"Absolutely not! I won't have it. If you try anything of the sort, I will do a lot worse than Cassandra ever did, wolf."

Bastian, I thought sleepily, mistily uncertain as to whether I was awake or dreaming, since it didn't make sense for Bastian to be talking to Akiva over the fence in the middle of the night.

There was the sound of Bastian's voice murmuring again, and then Akiva said firmly, "On no account. Seventeen at the very least."

This time Bastian's snarl was loud enough for me to hear. "By that time one of the village idiots will have stolen a march on me! I found her first!"

"May I remind you that Rose is nobody's property?" inquired Akiva acerbically. "She is still a child, and I won't have you poking your long hairy nose in before she has learned to defend herself!"

There was an indignant but softer growling, and Akiva said

absolutely, "No. If I sense you within a hundred furlongs of Rose in that period, you will have more than a curse to regret. Her seventeenth birthday, and not before. Count yourself lucky that I've given you barely more than two years, and be off with you."

I think there was more, but I fell asleep very shortly after—if I had ever really been awake. When I woke the next morning, I was in my own bed, with curious glimmerings of a dream that contained Akiva, Bastian, and red-gold flames.

The fading memories of the dream vanished over breakfast. Akiva was in a mood, and the bacon had burned to crisp, blackened chips—perhaps as a result of her mood, perhaps causing it. I didn't know which, but I was glad to escape into the garden for the morning's work, leaving Akiva to stomp around the kitchen washing dishes; and afterwards around her workroom to prepare more potions.

I was horribly heavy and sore from my magical exertions of the day before. The only thing that really seemed to make the day worthwhile was the fact that now that I could see the forest lines properly, I could also see the garden as it really was. Each of the garden beds had its own specific threads, some crisscrossed with millions of tiny, fibrous filaments that told me the earth in them was bespelled very heavily. Akiva's aloe bed was one of those that sparkled the brightest. I observed the lines in great satisfaction, because now I understood how Akiva remembered them all: each bed knew its own specific needs and all I had to do was pay attention.

My morning's work was done in less than half the time it would have taken just a week—or even a day—ago. I poked my head back into the house a little after mid-morning to find out what Akiva wanted me to do next, very greatly pleased with myself.

Since there was no washing to be done that day, I was able to make my escape to the forest earlier than usual. It was with a sense of relief that I stepped off the path to find the herbs Akiva needed, and with a sense of real pleasure that I felt a familiar tremble to the forest threads that meant Bastian was nearby. I followed it almost without thinking, and after a moment of swift travel I cannoned into his huge, hairy body. Bastian gave a startled yip as I crashed into him, and then we tumbled head over heels in a tangle of paws and arms and legs and tail, before coming to rest under a blackberry bush.

Bastian wheezed for breath, and I giggled. I had come off rather the better of the two of us: my head was cushioned on his furry side, my face just inches from the threatening blackberry brambles. Bastian was tangled in the thorny vines, and it would take a little trouble to extricate him.

We stayed as we were for a little while, me still giggling madly and quite comfortable with my wolf-pillow, until Bastian began to laugh as well. His flanks heaved underneath my head with his laugh, an odd feeling that made me laugh all the more.

At last I sobered and lay there looking up at the patches of leaves and blue sky through the brambles, smelling the Bastian-smell of rich earth and grass, and enjoying the peace. Bastian's flank contracted, and I felt the snuffle of his nose in my hair, nudging my resting head.

"What's amiss, little witch?"

I sucked in a deep breath and huffed it back out again. "Akiva is in a mood."

Bastian stretched out again. "Akiva is always in a mood," he said lazily. "It's merely that some of them are worse than others."

I heaved a second sigh in agreement and relapsed into silence, prompting another contraction of Bastian's stomach muscles as he swivelled his huge head around to look at me. "You're a child of surprisingly few words," he remarked. "It makes me nervous."

I turned my own head to observe him sideways. "Why?"

He gave a lazy shrug. "I'm not used to it. In my experience a woman is quietest when she's plotting something, second only to when she's sulking. What are you thinking about, little witch?"

"Rosemary and rue," I told him. The herbs were the only two ingredients that Akiva *did* have out of a list of nearly twenty that she insisted had to be gathered this afternoon. She had told me to make myself useful in the forest by collecting them; and I supposed, puffing my cheeks out, that my task was no closer to completion while I lay under a blackberry bush with my head cushioned on my Bastian-pillow.

But I was comfortable and disinclined to move, so instead of climbing to my feet and going about my business as I ought to have done, I continued to lie where I was, gazing dreamily up at the alternating views of sky and tree that could be seen through the brambles.

We continued in companionable silence until it occurred to me to ask, "Bastian, what is the first thing you would do if you could break the spell?" I knew what I would do: I would hug my mother, revelling in the dexterity of human limbs; and then I would eat a full, cooked meal with herbs and spices. I had a feeling that even in the guise of a wolf, raw meat would not be so palatable for a human to eat.

Bastian's sides shook slightly, informing me that he was laughing softly. "Never mind what I'd do first, little witch. What I'd do next would be to find Cassandra and make sure I made her life as much of a misery as she's made mine."

"How long have you been a wolf?" I asked, tilting my head to see his face. His voice had gone quite hard after the amusement. His curse was old, I knew that: exactly how old was another matter.

Bastian only looked at me with his golden-hazel eyes expressionless, and said, "Too long."

"Come with me to the village when you change," I said gruffly. "See the people and the fuss and the stalls."

"Too dangerous," he said, though his voice was dark with regret. "If I'm caught out of the forest when I change to wolf, the change will be permanent. It's built into the curse."

"That was cruel," I said fiercely. I could understand and even approve of the curse on principle, but there was a point at which punishment became torture, and Bastian's curse had long since ceased to be punishment. The enchantress was more vicious than I had expected. If Bastian had no contact with humans during the entire length of his enchantment as wolf, then it was no wonder that by the time I met him he was more beast than man.

"I thought you were convinced it served me right?" enquired

Bastian. His wolfish face was somehow smiling: I think my fierceness amused him.

"Yes, but that's *cheating*."

"She wanted to make sure it was unbreakable."

I wondered in sudden coldness where Cassandra was now. Akiva had suggested that she wouldn't be terribly happy with me for beginning to break the curse, and if Bastian was anything to judge by her wrath wasn't to be encountered lightly. As I huddled back into Bastian's warmth, a fine sense of self-preservation suggested that it might be wise to ask Akiva a few, pointed questions when I returned home.

We spent almost the whole afternoon beneath the blackberry bush, sometimes talking, sometimes silent. It felt oddly like a goodbye. The time passed so quickly that I was startled when Bastian's furry flank rippled and changed into a smoother, harder, human stomach beneath my head. I found myself lying with my head on human Bastian's stomach and sat up regretfully.

Bastian opened one eye and demanded, "Where are you going?" He seemed to notice the change for the first time and said: "Ah. That's interesting."

"I have to find herbs for Akiva," I explained. I detached the few blackberry briars that had caught in my braid and stood up, slowly and stiffly. Bastian stretched and yawned wolfishly, and then also stood. He was wearing the same clothes he had been wearing yesterday: at least, as far as they went. His chest was bare, as usual, and he was wearing the same grass-stained and dirty fawn-coloured trousers as he had been yesterday, down to the deeply red-and-orange woven belt that was tied around his trousers at the hip. The trousers seemed to blend with the colour of his skin, and it came to my mind that he had also been wearing the same clothes when I had broken the first part of the spell, and that his chest had been just as bare.

I gazed at him curiously and came to the tentative conclusion that it was just something that Bastian would do, a kind of show off.

Testing the idea, I said bluntly, "Why don't you ever wear a shirt?"

There was a band of dark red high on Bastian's cheeks beneath the stubble. "Because that's how I was dressed when Cassandra found me," he said, running one hand through his hair. "Enough of my sordid past, little witch; what are we searching for?"

I recited the list hopefully, and Bastian's expression grew rueful.

"You should have told me earlier, while I still had my wolf nose. This short human one doesn't seem to work as well."

"I didn't think of that," I said. "I got distracted."

"So did I," said Bastian. "That is, if you call being knocked to the ground by a little girl who has had one too many good meals, being distracted. If that's what you would call being distracted, I was very distracted."

I stuck my tongue out at him, hands on hips, but he only laughed at me and headed further into the forest, so I abandoned my offended attitude and dashed after him. We stayed on the same thread this time, the forest rushing past around us as we strolled along it. I wanted to move more swiftly and cover more ground, but Bastian said that the slower we moved the easier it would be to see, and I reluctantly yielded to his superior knowledge.

I was scouting ahead for signs of the last of my quarry when I saw the danger. It was shooting along the threads at an incredible speed; black, sticky, foul-feeling tendrils of black that seemed either to be consuming the threads as they came, or to be wrapping so tightly around them as to make no distinction between the two. I saw them and stumbled with a sudden flash of *knowing* that they were searching for Bastian. Bastian's firm hand under my elbow steadied me, but the tarry tendrils had found us by that time, reaching hungrily for him. Seizing him around the waist, I hauled us both off the path.

I heard Bastian howl, "Not while I'm taking a step!" and then we were both thrown violently to the ground, jarring teeth and bones. I found myself on my back, shaken and headachy, and tasted blood. Bastian's face appeared somewhat hazily above me, first concerned and then furious as I sat up dizzily.

"You had better have a good reason for tossing us off the path, little witch," he growled.

I groaned and cautiously explored the interior of my mouth, searching for the source of the blood.

"It's your own fault," Bastian said roughly, but he took my face between his hands and tilted it for inspection. "You've split your lip and serve you right. What were you thinking?"

"Didn't you see the blackness?" It hurt to speak, and I tasted fresh blood. Bastian was right: the cut in my lip had opened again. "It tried to wrap around you."

Bastian's face went quite pale. Something came and went rapidly in his expression: panic, or determination—or perhaps both. I didn't know his face well enough to be sure.

"Rose, go home as quickly as you can; find Akiva and stay with her."

I scrambled to my feet. "What about you?"

"I won't argue with you, Rose. Go." There was a finality to Bastian's tone that I obeyed instinctively. He disappeared on another thread before I had a chance to say goodbye, so I found my own thread, this one home-bound, and travelled down it a good deal more swiftly than last time.

When I stepped from the thread to the path leading to Akiva's front gate, there was a woman between me and it. She was so beautiful. I'm not sure why I expected her to be otherwise. Her hair was black and glossy, and hung loose to her waist in a sleek, rippling sheet that mingled with royal purple satins and silks that were as sleek as her hair. Her eyes, framed by impossibly long, dusky eyelashes, were of an equally impossible shade of violet. I saw them and my herbs scattered themselves on the path, dropping heedlessly from my nerveless fingers. Those twin violets gleamed with the same darkness I had seen in Bastian's eyes the first time I met him.

Horned hedgepigs! I thought, swallowing. It could only be Cassandra.

She looked me up and down with those brilliant, purple eyes while I regretted fervently that I hadn't been a moment quicker, and then said, "You're not pretty." Her voice was bell-like in consideration; and, like every other part of her, breathtakingly beautiful.

"I know," I said. Even if I had been as beautiful as Gwendolen, I couldn't have hoped to compare with Cassandra. I eyed her unblinkingly, wondering why it mattered to her.

"You're not pretty," she repeated—a statement, not a question. A crease appeared between the perfectly arched brows. "I didn't expect that. He must be desperate."

"I don't know what you mean," I said, scowling. I was coldly frightened, and that made me angry. Black, tarry magic was stirring around her, creating nasty pockets of corruption in the air that made me feel ill: it was vastly more powerful than anything I had ever seen.

She looked at me contemptuously through the haze. "Beauty is all that matters to him, stupid child. You can only lose."

"Bastian isn't here," said Akiva's voice suddenly and startlingly. I tore my eyes away from Cassandra's and saw her, knobbly and infinitely welcome, leaning on a stick behind the enchantress. For a horrible moment it had felt like I was drowning in the brilliant lavender of Cassandra's eyes.

Akiva hobbled past her and put a hand on my shoulder. I felt a sense of her power, welling up deep inside her, warm and comforting.

I think I was still looking up at her with wide eyes when she said quietly, "Go into the cottage, Rose."

As I closed the gate with cold fingers, I heard Akiva reiterate, "The wolf isn't here."

"I can smell him all over her!" hissed Cassandra.

There was a silence suggesting that Akiva was shrugging; then her old, firm voice said, "I sent him away: he knows what I think about him. Today was goodbye."

Their voices faded with distance, but as I loitered on the garden path, I saw the warm glow of a formidable power rising to meet and match Cassandra's. I recognised it as Akiva's, hale and hearty, and stronger than I could ever have imagined. After that I hurried to get into the safety of the cottage, feeling the hairs prickle on the back of my neck, because I knew that it was no longer safe for me to be out in the open. Once inside, I plumped myself down in Akiva's chair, absently staring into the fire and contemplating the extraordinary power I had just witnessed. For the first time in the excitement of my new magical prowess, I felt thoroughly humbled and weak. My own power, puny in comparison to that shown so effortlessly by both Cassandra and Akiva, was pitiful past thinking about. I was suddenly very thankful for Akiva's protection. In the coldness of the moment, I knew there was no chance that I could ever hope to fight against Cassandra and win.

I sat in Akiva's chair, cold and unmoving; and then, as the minutes lengthened into an hour, I fetched out my pinafores and worked on them with glazed eyes. It felt as though there was a soundless, savage storm raging outside.

A little later I rose and prepared myself supper. Along with the usual bread-and-cheese I hung the kettle over the fire, ready to brew one of Akiva's strong, restorative teas. She would probably need it when she came in.

It was some time later that I heard the sound of her foot on the threshold. I had taken up my sewing again after supper, and as the door opened I threw it down, regardless of the loose needle, and dashed to hug her. She looked weary but well, and suffered me to hug her for a moment before disengaging herself.

"Gently, child, on my old bones," she said. "Here."

It took me a moment to realise that she was holding out my stray needle. I looked at her inquiringly.

"It's difficult to stop sometimes," she explained; and it occurred to me, belatedly, that her magic was still swirling around her in a state of excitement. The needle had been a reflex action. I felt enviously that it must be wonderful to have such power.

"What happened?" I asked, conscientiously affixing the needle to my half-finished pinafore and hanging the kettle a little lower. "Did you kill her?"

Akiva's eyes came sharply to bear on me. "Of course not! My wardship doesn't permit me to kill anyone except in self-defence."

"Well, I thought she was going to kill you," I argued. "That's self-defence. What's a wardship?"

"The villagers call it being the Witch of the Forest," Akiva explained, accepting a mug of strong, milk-less tea from me and allowing herself the weakness of sitting down. "My magic is bound up in the forest and I have power in it. I am the caretaker of this portion of the forest, and I may not kill without sufficient reason."

I sucked in my cheeks. "What would happen if you did?" I was very certain that Cassandra was not going to be as understanding about killing without reason.

"I don't know for sure," Akiva said shortly. "Most likely the spell would rebound, and I would be stripped of my power. Wardship power allows bending of the rules, but not outright breaking of them. Even the bending comes at a cost."

I cupped my hands around my own mug of tea and regarded Akiva thoughtfully. "Does that mean you're more powerful than Cassandra, being a warden?"

"Cassandra is also a warden. I'm stronger in my own wardship, in her wardship she has the balance of power." Akiva roused herself a little and sat upright. "Which means that you, child, will keep strictly to the boundaries of my wardship and go no further."

"I didn't know there were boundaries," I said, a little aggrieved. I hadn't even known that there were different—what had Akiva called them? Wardships? I had thought that the forest was simply forest, as far as it extended. It seemed that there were many things I didn't know. And now that I thought of it, that was the word Gwydion had used, too.

I opened my mouth to ask another question, but Akiva sank back into her chair with a groan and said, "Tomorrow, child; tomorrow."

Five

My legs were aching so badly that I was gloomily certain they would fall off before long. It was Tomorrow, and I trudged along behind Akiva with the sour thought that if I *did* die of exhaustion, at least I wouldn't have to do the gardening tomorrow.

We had started out at first light without stopping to do more than the most rudimentary gardening, much to my secret glee, but by midday my glee had sunk under the twin discomforts of sore legs and an empty belly. Stopping for lunch had repaired my empty stomach but only increased the dull ache in my calves. Horned hedgepigs, why did I have to ask the wrong questions! For the past hour we had been walking along one of the boundaries, which turned out to be an extremely uncomfortable experience. Whatever the boundary was, my forest sight stopped abruptly where it began, leaving me helplessly blind and considerably indignant about it. I hadn't worked so hard to see the lines—well, *fairly* hard, anyway— only to find it vanishing at the edge of Akiva's forest.

When I complained to Akiva, she snorted and said, "Of course you can't see over the boundary, child. The forest isn't one: all forests meet and merge in deep forest. This border belongs to Gwydion, and his forest happens to be in Civet. Look at the trees over there."

I did—at first uncomprehendingly, and then with light dawning. "They're pines and that. Cold weather trees."

"Exactly."

"But that doesn't explain why I can't see the lines," I grumbled, returning to the point of contention. "Doesn't Gwydion's forest have lines?"

"Of course it does!" Akiva stopped short, I think in exasperation, and I saw something pass across her face. "Deep forest is very... possessive. It chooses a warden and sticks with them to the exclusion of everyone else. Only Gwydion can see the lines clearly in his own wardship."

I grimaced, very far from satisfied. "How can you bear it?"

Again, an expression I didn't understand came and went on Akiva's face. "I have my ways and means," she said cryptically, and much to my indignation she refused to say any more. She did tell me that Cassandra's wardship also bordered on hers in some remote part of it. Maybe she said it to distract me. I tucked away this interesting tidbit for later consideration and asked Akiva exactly where Cassandra's forest really was.

Not wholly to my surprise, she only grunted and said, "Very far from here. Near or far doesn't matter to the forest."

It made me grin to think how closely she had come to saying what Bastian had, and despite my sore legs I began to feel more cheerful.

As we passed around the boundaries, we found increasingly more of the sticky black tendrils that had attacked Bastian, and Akiva began to look rather grim.

"Traps," she explained shortly to me. "They're attuned to Bastian on alternating threads. She has no business setting traps on my wardship."

"Is that breaking or bending the rules?" I asked, angry on Akiva's behalf.

"Neither. It's bad manners," she told me, dismantling one of the traps. "It's as if I went into your mother's kitchen and cooked my breakfast, then left the dishes for her and went on my way."

We found three more traps after that, and it struck me that

Akiva had suggested this outing not just to teach me of the boundaries, but because she had suspected something of the kind. It was a long and wearisome business: even travelling at speed along the deep forest threads the distance was massive, and it was some time after dusk when Akiva and I wearily returned home. I hadn't sensed Bastian anywhere in our journeying, which worried me, but Akiva was dismissive.

"The wolf knows how to take care of himself. Now that Cassandra has her eye on him, he'll have to be more careful. I doubt very much that he'll risk his hide by coming too near you again."

I frowned to myself at the inflexible certainty of her voice. "You told Cassandra you sent him away."

"Cassandra was getting too close for comfort," Akiva said, shooting a sharp look at me. "I may very well be stronger than her on my own wardship, but I can't protect every inch of it at the same time. If I'm right, she'll come unstuck without any help from me. The longer Bastian avoids her, the better for him. Possibly the better for you, too, child."

Later, drying my hair before the fire and toasting bread and cheese, I asked, "What do you mean, about Cassandra coming unstuck?"

"Sooner or later all her bending of the rules will catch up with her. Now stop talking, there's a good child; finish your pinafore and then off to bed with you."

I did as I was told, licking my fingers carefully to avoid greasy patches on the material, but my eyes were dropping shut every other minute and my stitches were looser and more uneven than usual. I would have to unpick all of my work the next morning. Somehow I didn't mind. Akiva looked over my shoulder and gave the snort that was her laugh, but I was too sleepy to mind that either.

When I woke the next morning, it was with a fully formed question in my mind. Akiva had taken me on as an apprentice: was I to be the next warden of the forest? Gwydion had been her apprentice, and he had his own wardship. It was food for thought, and I thought about it at great length, sitting up in bed with a fierce, thoughtful frown. I thought about it so long, in fact, that I was late to breakfast and sent out to work hungry.

Unhappily for me, there was extra work today: weeds and plants alike had grown out of hand in the last two, distracted days, and had become mischievous and defiant. For each weed I pulled, another two immediately grew in its place, filling the bare patches of earth more quickly than I could weed them. My lingering thoughts of the wardship swiftly gave way to a creeping anger as the tomatoes, joining the rebellion with the rest of the garden, refused to be trained aright. Their new tendrils, growing at an observable rate, unwound themselves from the stakes I was training them on and spread out gleefully across the garden bed, fighting with the green beans.

Akiva cackled with laughter but refused to help, and before long I was close to losing my temper or bursting into tears. It was my temper that went first; when the green beans, which I had been disentangling from the tomatoes, tried to strangle me. I gave a growl of frustration and drove my hands into the rich, warm soil, punching with somehow *more* than my muscles and shocking every energy line in the back garden with bright magic. The green bean creepers froze, and then crawled meekly back to their trellis, followed closely by the tomatoes. Every other bed in the garden had similarly frozen: not a rasp of wind on leaf, or leaf on leaf sounded throughout the garden, though a light breeze was softly caressing my ears.

Akiva gave another cackle of laughter, leaning on her hoe. "That told 'em! Less power next time, child."

I watched the tomatoes crawl back to their stakes somewhat ashamedly, but I couldn't help feeling a thrill at the effect. By way of reparation, I sang to the plants as I weeded and watered, and before long they relaxed their unnatural stillness and began to undulate whisperingly to the breeze once more. I was surprised at the feeling of contentment that the sound gave me.

I expected to see Bastian that afternoon. Akiva said she had sent him away, but I interpreted that to mean that she had sent him away while there was danger from Cassandra, and I was disappointed to find no sign of him along the forest threads. Still, there was washing to be done and the forest to explore, and if I didn't have Bastian's company, at least I was as happy with my own. After I attended to the washing I darted gleefully into deep forest, going wherever it pleased my fancy to take me, and found myself some time later running side by side with one of the boundaries. I had been skimming along delightfully quickly on one of the energy lines when I became aware of it, and when I did become aware of it I stopped to look.

I gazed long and curiously into the next wardship, feeling amusingly as though I were leaning over the back fence. There was no discernible separation to the naked eye: it looked just like Akiva's wardship did, except that this forest, instead of being decked in late autumn colours, was just coming into the lushness of fresh new leaf. Enamoured with the idea of testing the dual occupation of the forest, I cast about me for a real, normal path through the forest. I found one and, remembering Bastian's injunction that near or far did not matter, closed my eyes and took a step forward. There was a moment of dizzy travelling and then I was on a path, real and cleared.

To my left was deep forest, if I stepped for a moment off the path. To my right the trees were thinning as they faded into a field. There was certainly no sign of the next wardship. Instead, it was the edge of the forest: *my* forest. As I gazed, grinning in delight, I became slowly aware of an odd, unfamiliar sound ringing through the air; steady and rhythmic. It took a moment for me to recognise the sound of axe on wood.

Curious, I trotted down the path, following the sharp thuds and wondering with not a little indignation who it was that was cutting down trees in the forest. I cast about for the energy lines to tell me which tree was being abused in such a way, but either the threads were unreliable when I was on something so solid as a path, or the tree being cut down was not quite in the forest. I was forced to rely on more conventional means to discover the spot; and, following the path to its natural conclusion at the edge of the forest, I very soon did discover it.

It was only a boy, after all. He was very little taller than myself, but the swing of his axe had all the power of a man and I guessed that he was a year or two older than myself. He was chopping at a strangler fig that had grown into the neighbouring field, sending out huge roots and solid, slow creepers. I frowned at his stupidity: every life-line that flowed into the tree was writhing in furious energy, and the creepers that would normally be abysmally slow, moving only a few centimetres each month, were beginning to move rather more briskly. The strangler fig, close enough to the forest to have more life in it than an unforested tree, had begun to snake out creepers toward the woodcutter, who was blind in his regular, rhythmic swinging.

I huffed an unimpressed sigh and started forward to warn him, but by that time the strangler fig's creepers had crept around his waist and yanked him away from its trunk. The boy gave a startled yell, dropping his axe. It fell at the base of the tree, sinking deep into mossy earth while its owner dangled several feet above it. He scrabbled with his fingers at the unyielding creepers and threw a rather wild look around him for help, but the axe was easily out of his reach.

He saw me at the same time and called out urgently: "Stand back, miss! The tree's possessed!"

"Stop wriggling, bufflehead!" I told him impatiently. "The creepers will only get tighter." I approached until I was near enough to grasp the life-lines that extended to the tree from the forest, and experimentally bunched them tight in one hand. Much to my fascination, this stopped the flow of energy and life that was running through the tree limbs and pooled it somewhere unsafe and unsteady. I felt the imbalance and hastily fed it all into the ground at my feet instead, scorching my fingers. Grass and flowers sprouted beneath me in sweet smelling bunches, tickling the soles of my feet, while the creepers, deprived of their energy, dropped the boy carelessly into the moss below. He rolled, scrambling to his feet and out of reach of the longer creepers, and I released my strangle-hold on the energy lines.

He didn't seem to have sustained any injuries, so I advised him shortly that he shouldn't try and cut that particular tree down, and headed back for the forest.

There were hasty footsteps behind me, then an eager hand grasped my arm and hauled me around with boyish strength.

"How did you do that?" he demanded, his face still flushed from his adventure. Closer to, it was obvious that he was older than I had first thought; seventeen or eighteen, perhaps. My automatic assessment of him as a boy had been unconsciously based on a comparison with Bastian who, (I assumed) from the decades he had spent as a wolf, sometimes had the manner of an older man than even his admitted age.

I scowled down at the hand on my arm, then up at the young man, and he let me go sheepishly.

"I'm sorry," he said. His hand hovered as if he wanted to touch me again and reassure himself that I was real. "How did you do that?"

I frowned, backing away minutely from both the boy's hand and the warm, eager presence he projected. Yet for every tiny step I took backwards, he followed, still pushing at me in a subtle, enthusiastic way that sent a sharp stab of alarm through my stomach. When I recognised the alarm, I scowled more fiercely than before, daring him to come another step forward.

He grinned, accepting the dare, and I hastily tweaked one of the forest threads. Something rustled conveniently, and his eyes flicked toward the sound just long enough for me to dive off the path and into deep forest like a turtle into water. I heard his confusion along the energy lines as I ran, and I began to have an inkling of why Akiva was considered to be such a mysterious figure by the villagers. It pleased me that I was in a fair way to being considered in the same light.

The thread continued to hum softly with the young man's calling as I moved away, but I ignored it because I could feel something different buzzing along a thread further in.

I darted from thread to thread, enjoying the speed and lightness of travel, until I was close enough to feel the thread itself. It was vibrating with distress and pain but when I tried to sight along it, my vision came to an abrupt and almost painful halt. It was another border. I let go of the thread, scowling and rubbing my sore head; and stood irresolute. Akiva had said not to go beyond the boundaries. But that was because of Cassandra, I was sure: and this *couldn't* be Cassandra's wardship. I distinctly remembered Cassandra wearing thin satins and gauzes, and this snowy landscape ahead of me was no place for satin and gauze.

I stooped to the ground with my palm flat against the grass to better feel the thread, and a bolt of agony shot through it, crying out of pain and rage. The sudden conviction that it was Bastian took hold of my mind, and I didn't hesitate. I caught up a stubby, weathered little stick from the ground for a cudgel, and crossed the border.

I found myself in a section of forest that was distinctly unfamiliar, layered with the pristine snow. I gazed around in wonder, shifting from foot to foot in the biting cold. I was uncomfortably blind without being able to see the forest lines, and when I turned around to look back the way I had come I could no longer see the border. Behind me were only black and white shades of tree trunk and snow. I felt a chill that had nothing to do with the snow, and curled my fingers more tightly around my little cudgel. A harsh, bird-like scream tore through the frigid evening air. I heard my own startled exhale through the pounding of my heart, and it occurred to me to wonder if I actually *wanted* to find the creature that could make such a noise, injured or otherwise. It was certainly not Bastian. My feet, however, were already taking me in the direction of the noise. I passed through a narrow hall of hardy evergreens, feeling the distant, cold-numbed prick of pine needles through the snow, and came upon an uneven clearing that was heaped with snow at its far end. Here I halted, unsure of which direction the scream had come from. As I dithered, the mass of snow trembled and moved. A huge, bird-like head with a dangerously curved beak and a snow-crested ruff rose through the white powder, scattering white crystals like sand. A liquid gold eye focused fiercely on me and I knew that I was looking at a gryphon: or, more accurately, being looked at *by* it.

My first instinct was to run away as fast as I could, but my treacherous feet again refused to obey me. I stood where I was until it was borne in on my frozen mind that there was a scarlet stain spreading across the ridge of snow that covered its wing.

Help me, said a huge, golden voice. Its voice thrummed in my bones, as if the magic of the creature was so much beyond my own that my body couldn't comprehend it. I heard the ragged huff of my breath again.

I shivered and said hoarsely: "I've only got a little bit of magic."

The eye looked at me unblinkingly. *I don't need magic, human child: I have all the magic I need. You must set my wing so that I can heal myself.*

I looked up at it with desperate boldness. "How do I know you won't eat me?"

The gryphon's beak snapped with something like grim amusement. *You don't. You must take comfort in the thought of doing a good deed.*

"That won't help if I'm dead," I said. I was made more comfortable, perhaps stupidly, because the gryphon reminded me of Akiva. Besides, if the blood mingling with snow had not been enough to prove that the gryphon really was injured, its eyes, sometimes bright and fierce and sometimes clouded with pain, convinced me. I moved toward it slowly, stumbling on numb feet; then I saw its wing, draggled and twisted at a horrible angle, and forgot my fear in hastening to help.

Immediately, the gryphon's ruff shot up threateningly. It hissed, snapping its beak at me, then stilled at my sudden stop.

Apologies, it said, politely rather than sincerely, and lowered its ruff. *Perhaps you could move a little more cautiously.*

I swallowed with a suddenly dry throat and said, "Yes. Sorry."

I scowled at the broken wing for some time. If it had been in Akiva's wardship, I could have seen the life-lines running through the gryphon, and acted accordingly. Here, blind to all intents and purposes, I gazed at the wing for some minutes before I realised that the wing was not only broken but twisted all the way around from the second joint so that it flopped painfully upside down. It was going to cause the gryphon considerable agony to set, particularly since I was too small to be able to do anything but heave the broken section up and let it drop to the other side.

"This will hurt very much," I told the gryphon. "I'm not big enough to lower your wing to the ground."

Do it now, it commanded, and the one eye I could see was burning fiercely. I thought that it was trying to brace itself.

I knelt beside the poor, damaged wing and shuffled my fingers delicately underneath the bone. I found myself with a face full of spiky feathers and clinging down. It took all of my strength, pushing against the feathers with my face and shoulders as well as heaving with my arms, to twist the wing back around. There was nothing I could do except let it fall, but I was horrified at the heaviness with which it flopped into the snow.

The gryphon shrieked, shredding my eardrums, and its beak slashed through the frigid air impossibly quickly, sending me flying. I landed with a breathtaking thump in a pile of snow, my stomach and ribcage aching from the blow. Across the clearing the gryphon had reared, its ruff upright and quivering, its beak wide open to hiss. It had closed its beak at the last moment: I had been bludgeoned by the smooth, rounded part of the beak instead of the sharpened end. Apparently, I could consider myself lucky.

I didn't feel lucky.

That hurt! The voice shrieked through my body, and I yelled in agony, uselessly covering my ears.

When the hurt died away, I heaved myself up, staggering. "Horned hedgepigs! I *told* you it would hurt, you great, stupid *bird*!"

The head turned and I was stared at by the other eye. Recognition came to it, and the gryphon said, sincerely this time, *My apologies, human child. I forgot myself. Please approach.*

"I won't!" I retorted. With every breath I took, pain shot through my ribs. I had a horrible feeling that I had broken at least two of them.

Please. I did not intend to hurt you.

I remained where I was, sucking in shallow breaths with one

hand pinching at the pain in my ribs. "I can see your wing healing. What do you need me for?"

It will heal, but I need energy, the gryphon said. If its golden eye had not been so fierce, I would have thought it was pleading. *I can help you, too. Your warm-blooded little human body is almost too cold to recover. I can heal you at the same time.*

I hadn't noticed the frigidity for some time because I'd become so cold that everything was numb. Even the shivers had stopped. My mind was decidedly hazy, and as I took the first step back towards the gryphon, the snowy landscape began to spin around me.

"Bother you," I grumbled, but I knew it was right. Each unwilling step toward the gryphon was headily swaying, until at last I was within reach of one of its front claws. It had hauled itself up to sit on its haunches, one wing neatly folded and the other still hanging uselessly at its side. It reached out and gripped me easily around the waist. I whimpered as my ribs were crushed again, but the pain was short-lived, fading as an alien apathy settled over me. I don't know how long I flopped there like a ragdoll, unsure whether I was dead or alive and somehow unable to care much either way, while every second drained more of my faculties.

Minutes or centuries later, I wasn't sure which, there was a deep, powerful rumbling that shook the earth and my bones, and the world turned upside down. I was woken abruptly, dropped carelessly into a pile of snow, and murmured a faint protest at finding myself catapulted into a world of pain again. It felt as though every part of my body was on fire: in fact, the only advantage of the whole situation seemed to be that I was no longer cold.

I pushed myself up on burning hands that seemed, nonsensically, to melt the snow beneath them in a great hissing of steam. The floating sensation was gone but confusion still fogged my mind, so that when I looked around to find out what had become of the gryphon, my fancy saw the figure of a woman standing in the scattered pile of snow that had lately covered the gryphon.

Cassandra, my mind suggested automatically, but this woman's salt-and-pepper hair was nothing like Cassandra's glossy jet mane, and her figure was straight-backed and stern rather than willowy. Of the gryphon there was no sign. I took this as a good omen. It seemed to me that the strange woman must have rescued me, and I opened my mouth to thank her; but by then she was no longer there, if she ever really *had* been.

I managed to climb to my feet with the help of an obliging tree trunk, whimpering at the pain in my ribs. The sensation of burning didn't abate as I took the first few faltering steps forward, and I blindly reached out my hands to gather snow from the foliage around me. One of my hands felt unnaturally thick and clumsy, and it took me some time to discover that this was because I was again gripping my little cudgel in one hand. It was just long enough to be used as a walking stick and I used it as such, forcing one step at a time. From the passing trees, I pressed blissfully cold handfuls of snow to my hot, tight face. My hands were fevered, and with each step I heard the hissing of melting snow under my bare feet. Warm, moist clouds of steam seethed around my legs.

I clutched at my cudgel, stumbling on until I seemed to smell the scorching of crunchy autumn leaves, and until there was no more snow to relieve the burning of my poor, fevered face. It should have meant something to me, but the only thought that occupied my mind at that moment was the dreadful heat of my skin and the lack of any kind of relief. I found myself inevitably falling, and the dry autumn grass rushed up with dizzying speed to hit me in the face.

Intermission

I dreamed for the longest time. At first my dreams were of fire and pain, while my body burned in an eternity of agony. Later I heard voices, angry voices: one snarling that if it had been there this would never have happened; another answering sharply that it was quite capable of looking after one child on its own.

The other voice didn't seem to agree, because it snarled again, and said: "Not this one!"

I seemed to hear Mother's voice, and Gwendolen's, and tried to open my eyes in vain. I thought, or dreamed, that my eyelids had turned to stone.

After the fire and voices came the peace. When the fire was gone, I sat up; a wasted, whispy little body that wasn't quite solid, and critically observed my limbs. Horned hedgepigs! I could see right through myself.

Well, I thought hopefully, at least I wasn't dead: perhaps I was dreaming still. I was inside Akiva's cottage, and I could see her searching through her cupboard full of herbs. She seemed cross: in fact, crosser than I had ever seen her. I had the guilty feeling that whatever it was, it was my fault.

I wafted up behind her with the mischievous idea of frightening her, but when I yelled her name the sound died an inch from my lips, and my breath didn't even stir her hair. It occurred to me, belatedly, that I had been in my bedroom and had floated right through the wall without thinking about it.

I said, "Horned hedgepigs!" in my new, queer voice, feeling dubiously that saying something a little stronger would have been more satisfying but unable to think of anything sufficiently bad. Akiva turned with a handful of rosemary leaves and walked right through me. That made me feel so odd that for a little while I merely floated where I was. Perhaps I was wrong about being dead.

I tried to move things that day. If it **was** a day. I did see the morning come and go, and later on Akiva went to bed while the house grew dark, but despite the darkness I found I could see just as well as ever. I waited for a little while to see if I would get sleepy, but I didn't; so I went on trying to move things instead.

Nothing I tried worked. I tried pushing, pulling—I even tried rushing at things with my transparent body, but all that did was send me rushing through the other side of whatever I tried to manipulate. Before long I was so wild with frustration that I would have thrown something, if only I could. Behind the frustration was a cold fear that I had somehow become stuck in a limbo from which I would never escape.

I spent the rest of the night scrunched up against a wall with my knees at my chest, floating a little above Akiva's floorboards. It gave me a tenuously safe feeling that dissipated every time I forgot I couldn't actually lean against the wall, and accidentally passed through it.

Akiva got up earlier than usual the next morning with a grim look about her mouth. I watched her stump about the kitchen with an odd feeling of homesickness and floated along curiously behind her when she unexpectedly left the house. As she passed into the forest from the garden she glanced briefly to the side of the path, and I saw, with a growing sense of indignation, that my body—my **real** body—was laid out in the grass of the forest. It was marbled and hard and absolutely motionless.

Horned Hedgepigs, what was I? A potted plant? Why wasn't I laid out in my own bed? I hung over my prone body as Akiva strode *on, studying my own features with slightly ghoulish enjoyment. It seemed to me that my face was too fat and my limbs too gangly. I pulled a face at it, but left in a hurry when I realised that I could very easily lose Akiva if I didn't pay attention. I caught up with her just at the outskirts of the forest. She didn't hesitate, striding on through the dappled morning light into full sunshine, but when I tried to follow I couldn't. The forest, implacable and inexplicable, held me inside. I tried pushing, but there was nothing to push against. I tried running at it with my eerily light body, and found myself wafting backwards instead as Akiva's bony back disappeared down the road. I tried rhymes and tricks and screams, but the forest wouldn't be persuaded, and Akiva was gone.*

At last I sat down at the edge and glared at the spotted sunlight that gleamed off the dew, fiercer and fiercer so that I wouldn't cry. I thought determinedly of loop-holes.

By and by I began to notice that there was a little more leeway where the forest extended spars of trees into the green grass of the road-side. I edged myself along one of these until I felt as though I were a bean just too big to fit into a peashooter. The thread for the spar continued on in a patch of mossy green right to the road, but it was too narrow to squeeze myself down and I had to own myself defeated. I retreated into the forest and sat down again, exhausted and breathless.

*Akiva came back later with Mother and Gwendolen. Mother had a straight, deep line between her brows and Gwen was sobbing tragically into a crumpled little hanky. I watched her exasperatedly because I wasn't **dead**, after all. I was sorry to have worried Mother, though, who was looking tired and perhaps a little bit exasperated herself.*

They argued over my body for quite some time. Mother seemed to be of the mind that I should be inside the cottage, but Akiva was still more emphatic that I remain in the forest. I could see their lips moving, but the sound was intermittent; and although I tried to lip-read I was left with very little idea of the conversation. As I watched, frowning in savage concentration, I heard fragments of her conversation that seemed to hiccough along like so: "...Margot...

patience...tried to...in the house but...forest wasn't having it...no, the wolf is..."

This interested me greatly, because of course Bastian must be the wolf, but Mother made her sharp hushing gesture. Gwendolen, who had perked her ears at the mention of Bastian and was watching them both with bright eyes, retired once more into her handkerchief.

I tried moving my fingers and toes for Mother to show her I was there, but my real body wasn't connected to my unreal one in any way I could understand, and I was still looking rather glumly at my motionless limbs when Mother and Gwendolen went back home. I don't think Mother wanted to go, but Akiva had gone firm and magical, and insisted upon her leaving in a way that, even without complete sound, was unmistakable. I was grateful to her for that: Mother didn't weep into handkerchiefs or wring her apron, but she did look after Gwendolen and me up to and beyond the endurance of her own health.

I didn't try to follow them when they left. There didn't seem to be much point. But by the time the triad had gone down I was so pale and cold with boredom that I trailed away wispily to the edges of the forest, willing to try and fail at anything rather than hover around the cottage any longer. Akiva, horrible old woman that she was, had merely gone on with her work without so much as a single apron-wring of distress at my condition. But she was forceful and cross as she stomped around the garden, and I began to wonder if that wasn't the same as apron-wringing in Akiva's case.

I left her striding between garden beds and hovered by the edges of the forest again, trying to squeeze myself down the ever-narrowing channels that stretched, green and inviting, right to the road. I'm not sure what I thought it would accomplish, since I would have been baulked by the road in any case; but it annoyed me to be stopped, and so I pushed and pushed until I was exhausted. I was so intent on my task that I didn't notice the growing darkness or the great glowing moon above me, and by the time the triad was rising in a red-gold arc of glory it still hadn't occurred to me that I wasn't sleepy. I merely glared at the searing brightness of it all and went back to trying to stuff myself into a thread that was by far too small for me. It *reminded me unpleasantly of the time Gwendolen had insisted on trussing me up in a corset; squeezing, squeezing until it felt as though my stomach was about to burst through my backbone.*

*"It's no good!" I said at last, in a gruff, thready voice that was only just loud enough to be a voice. "I'm too **fat**."*

*It's horrible to be a ghost. You can scream and yell in your patchy little voice, and pretend to stomp your feet, but you can't throw things and your feet only sink into the ground anyway. I felt as though I could **burst** with frustration, but there was nothing I could do about it. In the end I floated crossly about a foot in the air with my arms folded—floating being a deedy little trick that I had found fascinating at first, but ultimately useless—and thought hard. Body too fat. Body that floated. Too many things that I couldn't properly touch. Too many things that were frustratingly incorporeal.*

But not the threads. I instinctively fanned my insubstantial fingers through the air, touching cobwebby threads that were somehow more real than they had been when I was properly solid, and pinched one of them meditatively. It constricted slightly, giving off the scent and image of quiet green shadow, and when I released it, blinking thoughtfully at a new idea, it sprang back into its old place and size immediately.

"Horned hedgepigs," said my voice thoughtfully, startling me. "It's just a picture, after all. Bufflebrain!"

*I looked narrowly at my whispy ghost hands, and instead of desperately trying to use them as though they were flesh and blood, I told them to fade. And do you know, they **did** fade. I wondered when I had become so frightened I was dead that I had wilfully deceived myself into thinking this smoke-and-shadow body was real.*

*When I was nothing but a consciousness bobbing against the barrier at the end of the forest, prickly and excited and scared all at once, I narrowed that consciousness out still further, and just **slipped** along the feather edge between forest and road. There was no pretending to have a voice down there, where the threads were raw streams of power and it was all I could do to stop myself being swept away in the great, fierce being of it all. I let myself be carried a little way further down, feeling as though I had gotten to the very roots and* *foundations of the forest. I thought dizzily that if I had Bastian here, now, I could unravel his curse with one flick of my nonexistent finger.*

I only just stopped myself from being dashed into nothingness at the end of the forest, where huge green life met brown, dead gravel and drove its roots firmly to a stop. It was a surprisingly violent ending given the usual peace and rest of the forest, and I lingered there for quite some time, catching my entirely metaphysical breath. Here was raging green life, potent and deep. There was brown, dusty death, the cessation of all life. The idea of it sent a shard of pain to the place that used to be my heart, until I realised that it wasn't entirely death: beneath the unyielding hardness of the village road was more life. It wasn't seething and strong like the forest; it was quiet and solid and sleepy. It was alive, though. I wondered if I could liven it up—send the forest energy out there to make it green again. But when I tried the same quiet sleepiness rose up against me in dogged rebellion until at last I understood that it was meant to be that way.

I returned to the topside forest, trying not to feel absurdly hurt that the outside had refused my help. Mother, after a particularly frustrating family meal with Father's relations, had once said, "Help that you don't want is no help at all." I hadn't understood it then, but I did now.

*I made my whispy little body appear again once I was back in the forest proper. I didn't exactly need it, but it was a comfort to me. The triad, its foremost sun sinking low and its last, small and hopefully lingering well above the horizon, sent shafts of dusty orange-red through my limbs, and made me wonder for the first time just how much time had passed. I floated my way carelessly back to Akiva's cottage, more aware than before of the forest around me with its hidden quirks of life and its boundless length. If I was to be much longer out of my body, I thought, tossing a glance at my real body as I passed it, I might like to explore its length, just to see where it ended. Just to see if it **did** end.*

Akiva was just coming in from the garden when I breezed through the walls. It didn't occur to me until I was watching her try to wash the dirt from her leathered old hands that the grass in the front garden was overdue its scything by a few days at least. I was inti-

*mately familiar with the differing lengths of the grass, since it was my job to scythe it as soon as it became too long, and not a fortnight had passed that didn't see me pleading with an unmoved Akiva that the grass could wait 'just **one** day longer!' I'd scythed some days before I met the gryphon—pesky creature! Horned hedgepigs, if I came across it again, it would be sorry!—but unless I had been insensible for the better part of a week, I had lost three days trying to squeeze myself into a thread at the edge of the forest.*

*"I didn't even **notice**," I said aloud, partly for the practice and partly because it was impossible to be as annoyed as I felt in silence. "Where did they go?"*

Akiva, unhearing, dried her hands briskly on her apron and fetched the cheese in its chequered wrap from the coolbox. This prompted me to think wistfully about bread-and-cheese without having the hunger to justify it. If I didn't become hungry or tired, how was I to keep track of the days? And it was suddenly so very important to keep track of them: just one tiny reminder that I wasn't as alien as I felt. I tried scratching marks, prisoner-like, on Akiva's tidy old walls, but my insubstantial fingernails didn't flake a single spot of plaster; and while I could float myself, it proved impossible to manipulate anything else into moving.

*It wasn't until several days later, which I counted as carefully as though I were measuring out ingredients for one of Akiva's teas, that I realised that although I couldn't manipulate anything about the cottage, I **could** manipulate the forest itself. I was in one of my determined fits that made me want to travel to the farthest edges of the forest and see what there was to be seen: impatient with my unresponsive body for just lying there, irritated with Akiva for just letting it lie there, and worried that Mother was spending too much time with it. I'd travelled well out of Akiva's wardship and into the next one, only realising the difference with the changing of the seasons, since at this level the forest didn't seem to have boundaries or wardships. It was simply The Forest.*

I came across golden-haired Gwydion as I travelled. That was nothing unusual: I'd frequently seen one or another of the wardens in my peregrinations about the forest. It made it easier to tell which part of the forest I was in.

Gwydion was kneeling by a deadened tree with one hand resting lightly on the bark, and I thought he looked puzzled. I wafted up behind him curiously, following a browning trail of forest thread that made me frown, and skirted the trunk while Gwydion remained on one knee before it. It wasn't ordinary dead: it was drained husk dead. The piece of forest around it was a little out of synch with the rest of the forest, its lines almost severed from the smooth continuity of the forest, making me blink away a sense of double vision.

"What have you done to it?" I said crossly to Gwydion. He didn't hear me, and I couldn't really convince myself that he'd done this to any part of his wardship, either by mistake or deliberately. Had Cassandra? I circled the trunk once more, distaste wrinkling my insubstantial nose by habit, and then sat down and crossed my legs—also by habit, since I was hovering a foot in the air and sitting or not sitting didn't really matter.

I ran my fingers along the longest, brownest thread, studying the tiny flecks of gold and green that were still present in it, until I came to the jagged join where it met with the rest of the forest. It looked, I thought, gazing down at it with eyes that were tight and hot despite being not quite real, as if someone had grabbed a handful of forest and tried to tear it out.

Wouldn't I just kick them when I found out who they were!

I felt a vague tickle in the forest lines and looked around swiftly. Gwydion, his mouth tight, was feeding power into the lines—power that reached the bottleneck and could go no further. It pooled and grew dangerously.

"Stop it, you bufflehead!" I yelled, ineffectively swatting his shoulder. "It's going to—horned hedgepigs, there it goes!"

Gwydion, shoving harder than was wise, burst the dam of power and was laid flat on his back by his own magic.

"You've got to **fix** it first!" I told him impatiently, wishing I could kick him. The solution was as plain as the nose on his face.

Gwydion sat up ruefully, shaking his head, and gazed at the dead tree trunk with his lips quirking. He seemed to be at a loss, so I heaved *an insubstantial sigh and began to fix it for him. I unravelled the thread to its base fibres, delighting in the sensation of touching* **something***, and then joined them again, rapidly rolling the thread between my palms as if it were rope. Father had shown me how to make rope once, and though I'd never been much good at it, rolling the forest thread was much easier. Magic, I decided, must be sticky.*

I did the same for all the others until the piece of forest no longer looked like it was out of focus, then busily fed all of Gwydion's pooled magic back down the threads. The tree trunk creaked and grew rapidly, spreading new limbs and new greenery, and the surrounding grass leapt into better focus. I could almost feel the forest let out a breath of relief.

"Oi!" said Gwydion in surprise. His voice was patchy, but easier to hear than Akiva's voice. Perhaps I was getting better at deep forest. "What—who—Rose, is that you?"

"Bufflehead!" I said fiercely, my eyes hot and tight again. I couldn't touch him or talk to him, but at least I'd fixed the forest. That was that.

I went home after that. Exploring the forest had lost its appeal for the moment, and I had had an interesting thought. I'd been looking for a way to keep track of the days for some time: as far as I could tell, I had been bodiless for nearly two weeks now, and the days were beginning to merge. Pushing Gwydion's magic into the lifeless tree trunk had been an epiphany. As I watched it grow and live, it had occurred to me that if I couldn't mark out the days with scratches on a wall or a tree trunk, I could do so with flowers. Nothing simpler. Just grow a flower for every day that passed.

So I sat in Akiva's front garden and tried to make a flower grow. It was harder than I anticipated, pushing that thing up through the soil, and when it came out it looked nothing like a flower. I was trying for a sunflower: they're big and brash and happy, not delicate and perfumed like the others. But when it sulked from the soil, it was a blackened, shrivelled head bobbing unconvincingly on a dark green stalk that looked more like soggy rope than a flower stem. I glared at it by reflex, but my heart wasn't in it. I'd got something wrong.

There was a crack of laughter, and when I looked up, Akiva was gazing at my pitiful attempt at a flower with an ironic eye. "There's something you've forgotten," she said dryly, and went back inside.

*By the time there were about thirty of the things, they were beginning to look more flower-like. They were still black and weedy, but the blob at the top had begun to unfurl what **could** be petals if you looked at them sideways. I didn't know what Akiva meant by forgetting something, but I'd begun to enjoy the daily ritual of growing a flower anyway, despite her derisive snorts. It's not that there was nothing to do in the forest: I was constantly surprised and even on occasion disgruntled by the amount of small botherations that existed at this level of forest. But that small, everyday chore gave some distinction to the days that they otherwise lacked, and helped me to feel a little more human. Wafting around in my tired little mist of a body, I had begun to feel as though I was more a part of the forest than an individual being. It wasn't a bad feeling, exactly. It just didn't feel like **me**.*

Sometimes I pushed on through the forest, exploring threads and dabbling with forest magic, interfering with the wardens as they went about their business. Sometimes I sat for days on end trying to remember what it felt like to smile or frown: trying to form my dream-facsimile face into the right shapes. I visited my body less and less as the days wore on. It never changed, anyway, and it was becoming unfamiliar to me in a way that made me uneasy. By the time I had grown more than a hundred flowers I stopped looking at it altogether, hurrying past it without a second glance whenever I came to grow a flower.

I snuck over to Cassandra's wardship, of course. In this deeper kind of forest, her house looked huge and white and blurred. That meant that it was made of some kind of stone. I wouldn't be able to get into the house: there were no forest lines in or out of it. I was familiar with stone, because Gwydion's house was also made of it, but his was small and cottagey and less blurry. Sometimes, hovering around it, I had the fancy that the stone was almost living, and that Gwydion had the same kind of affinity for stone that most wardens had with the forest. I spent a lot of time around Gwydion's stone cottage: it was quiet and peaceful, and Gwydion had a habit of talking to himself that meant I could pretend he was talking to me. Maybe he was.

Cassandra's wardship, on the other hand, left me feeling sick and cold inside, the fair façade of its surface only a thin veneer through which I could see the troubled roots of the forest, twisted out of shape in dark, silent coils. I tried to reach through the veneer to smooth them out, but even this deep in the forest Cassandra had such a strong hold on her part of it that I couldn't breach her defences.

I did try more than once. Horned hedgepigs, it hurt to see the forest like that! I thought that if I could just niggle at it long enough, I might touch something, change something; in the same way that I'd finally squeezed myself into the thread by the edge of the forest. If stubbornness could accomplish the thing, I thought determinedly, I would do it. I'd forgotten how to put out my chin but I remembered the tug of it on my soul, and I felt it then.

I forget how many days I spent in Cassandra's wardship trying to puzzle out the trick to her defences. I think there were some days that I forgot to return to the cottage and grow a flower, but I must have remembered most of them, because the sunflowers had grown in population by another hundred or so by the time I allowed myself to feel that I most likely wouldn't succeed.

I had a splendidly ineffective rage in Akiva's front garden on that particular afternoon; furious that I couldn't change things in the forest, more so that I couldn't get the sunflowers to be yellow, and beyond myself that I couldn't throw something to ease my frustration.

Horned hedgepigs, was I to be a ghost for the rest of my life?

I screamed that afternoon. I screamed and yelled and kicked my whispy legs. My ghost-voice seemed less real to my frightened ears than it had in the beginning, but I'd forgotten how to cry and in the end all I could do was float above the sunflowers, feeling somehow too stretched and thin. It wasn't until I'd settled into a sort of quiet despair that I noticed mechanically that the ground beneath me had blossomed with tiny wildflowers and reedgrass. Unwilling to shake off my gloomy sulks but interested in spite of myself, I poked a see-through finger into the soil, tickling the roots with their dead seed husks and tangling myriad tiny, thready forest lines. The seeds must have been lying dormant until that tiny bit of magic, exuded in frustration, pierced them and made them spring into life, seed dying and cracking to sprout with new life.

Horned hedgepigs, I was a bufflehead! No wonder my flowers didn't look like flowers! They **weren't**. Flowers grew from seeds, they weren't something that could be produced at a whim. Irritating as it had been, Akiva's snort was justified.

I gave a low chuckle of laughter despite myself, shaking my head at my own stupidity, and reached out to all the tiny, nebulous threads that were just beneath the soil, searching. When I found one, perfect, dying seed, I snapped it back through the thread towards myself, buzzing with new purpose and new hope. It occurred to me as the seed appeared, almond-shaped and real, that I might not be able to do this sort of thing when I was back in my body. For the first time it seemed a pity that I might have to go back one day.

This time when I pushed the forest magic into the ground, the flower that burst through seed and soil alike was vibrantly yellow and strong, spraying dirt in its desire to reach the sun. To my right, Akiva's head poked suddenly through the window, her eyes keen and gleaming. I heard the laugh again, but this time it wasn't dry; it was amused and approving.

"About time!" she said, and pulled her head back in. I made a rude face at the cottage, remembering **that** particular expression by instinct. She might at least have said 'well done'. Only then, I supposed, she wouldn't have been Akiva. I had a sudden fit of the giggles, silent and not-quite-real, because an apprentice was supposed to learn things, after all: only I don't think that's what Mother had in mind when she apprenticed me. Learning forest magic as I ghosted through the forest, setting gryphons' wings, breaking wolfish curses and encountering the ire of an enchantress: I'd certainly found adventure this time. And if it wasn't all exciting, and sometimes more hard work and frustration than discovery and magic; well, that was all part of the adventure, after all.

By the time there were roughly three hundred sunflowers crowding Akiva's front garden, I had come to the conclusion that it wasn't *possible to reach the end of the forest. There were **edges**, of course. So, so many edges and lands, and summer and winter and half-light: places where only the tail end of the triad could be seen, and light was dim, and all the stars were in the wrong places. It was exciting and fascinating and **wrong**; that the triad should give so little light day after day. I left those far-off parts of the forest largely unexplored, feeling off balance and a little scared, and went on to other parts.*

I came across Bastian quite often: he ranged far and wide in his hunts, by turns wolf and human. I think he preferred to be wolf when it came to dinner. I thought feelingly that I might feel the same if I were trapped in the forest with nothing to eat but berries and roots. Even raw meat would be a relief after that.

He didn't seem to be stopped by the boundaries of the wardships; and, much like myself, roamed the forest freely. He didn't wander Akiva's wardship at all, keeping to the limits that she had imposed upon him. I felt both elated and naughty whenever I was in his company, breaking Akiva's orders without the danger of being caught. He didn't talk to himself or to me, unlike Gwydion, but it was always interesting to hover alongside him and see what he would do.

He killed quickly and ruthlessly. He ate rabbits, fauns, odd little fluffy blobs that were fat and very bloody, and buried the remains almost automatically. I wondered if that was his human side, or if his wolf side was burying bones for later like the village dogs did. When he was human he climbed often, ran joyfully through the forest seemingly for the single purpose of feeling the wind in his hair, and swam very often indeed. His wolf counterpart didn't seem to care for the water. Sometimes, rarely, he would be still for the whole time he was human, sprawled beneath a tree with the dappled sunlight on his face, his mouth frozen in a half-smile that was at the same time mocking and grim. That was when I noticed the faint lines by his eyes that made him look old and tired. I didn't like for him to be sad, so one day I grew him some flowers, which he seemed to like. He didn't name me as Gwydion had, but he did chuckle suddenly, the lines turning to laugh lines by his eyes; and after that I grew him flowers whenever I came across him.

I'd stopped counting flowers by the time I felt a curious tug at my soul. I was hovering by Gwydion's house when it happened, watching him set the leg of a rather battered looking chook and paying close attention to his murmured instructions. There was a tug that made me say "Ow!" in surprise, and then I was being gently pulled backwards through the forest, little by little.

"Hey!" I said indignantly, feeling like trout on a line. The gentle pulling became a heady rush, leaving Gwydion far behind, and I found myself flying through the forest backwards, a delighted chuckle catching in the back of my throat. Then I was no longer flying, but falling: falling with the air whipping past me and my stomach left far behind...

Six

There was no time to be afraid, for a moment after I recognised the sensation to be that of falling, I landed with a shock and a thump in lush, green grass. My heart gave one frantic thump, as if it had begun to beat for the first time. Blood surged through my body, pulsing in my ears and fizzing in my fingers and toes.

I opened my eyes to see green leafy branches swaying above me, and sucked in a huge, ragged gulp of warm forest air as my lungs kicked into sudden action. I sat up, coughing, while the rest of the forest sprang into view around me, emerald green and sweet smelling.

Horned hedgepigs, when had it become summer? And when had the air started feeling so heavy in my lungs, like treacle and honey? I could *taste* it.

"*Rose!* Rose, you're awake!"

The girl bounding toward me was Gwendolen, but not quite Gwendolen as I knew her. I would have thought I was still dreaming but for the tickling of grass seeds on my bare feet. Besides, the arms that Gwen threw around me were real and strong, and my own arms were no longer see-through.

I wriggled impatiently under the hug, and when Gwendolen let me go, grumbling, I was able to look more closely into her strange yet familiar face. Presently, that face was pouting prettily.

"You *might* let me hug you for once!" she complained, her voice real and solid. It struck me that her face was narrower. "After all, you've been sick for nearly a whole *year*."

I felt myself go cold, remembering all those sunflowers. Horned hedgepigs! They *were* all real days. "Gwen? What do you mean? What happened?"

Gwendolen's face fell and her small pink mouth made an *O* in dismay. "Uh-oh. I wasn't supposed to say."

I disentangled myself from her arms and stood up. "I'm going to see Akiva."

Gwendolen scrambled to her feet behind me in scattered dismay. "Rose, you're not meant to get up yet!"

I ignored her fussing, striding on toward the cottage and past a multitude of sunflowers. Fortunately, my legs seemed to remember what to do. I thought I covered ground more quickly than I remembered, and I filed away for later consideration the thought that I must have grown while I was asleep. There were more important things that needed thought right now. I hadn't quite believed the days in ghost-forest were real days, seeped in the unreality of sleepless nights and not-quite-real body as I was. But the forest around me was in the mid stages of summer, and I remembered the dry cold of autumn wind as I went to help the gryphon.

Gwendolen, inured to having no real effect upon me, gave up her vain flutterings and instead dashed ahead of me, shouting for Mother and Akiva. The cottage door swung open, and Mother started down the steps toward her, looking collected but a little anxious. When she saw me, her face lit up with relief, and I found myself yet again swept into a tight hug.

Akiva, making her way a little stiffly down the two front steps, remarked caustically, "And about time, too."

She was actually grinning, which gave her the cheerfully sinister look of one of the Fates, and I could tell she was both glad and relieved in equal measure. Whatever she might say, she had been worried about me. I grinned back at her, because it was enough to know that.

They hustled me inside without further ado, and in very short order I found myself wrapped in a blanket, sitting in Akiva's chair with a cup of strong tea. Everything was so real, so *solid*, and the room seemed unusually crowded to my eyes. It took me some time, wrapping my hands absently around the hot tea mug, to understand that this was because I was used to seeing only Akiva and myself in it. With Mother and Gwendolen in it as well, the room became suddenly small and overcrowded.

"You shouldn't have gotten up straight away," scolded Gwendolen, trying to push a biscuit into my already full hands.

"I'm fine," I told her. And I *was*. I felt healthy and strong and wide awake. "Stop fussing at me, Gwen!"

I shoved the blanket away impatiently but didn't attempt to get up, since the look on Mother's face told me that she would only push me down into the chair again. Besides, the tea was *good*.

I looked up at Akiva as the most likely person to know, and asked: "What happened?"

Akiva's smile became somewhat grim. "You, my child, have been sick with dragon-fever."

Remembering the odd passage of time, and Gwendolen's first words to me upon waking, I asked shortly, "How long?"

"Ten months," she said. "We've come into summer again."

"How did you find me?" I asked, frowning. I remembered the gryphon and the horrible, burning heat, but only vague snatches of stumbling through snow until I reached Akiva's wardship again.

"When you didn't come back that night, I went searching for you. You were out on one of the westward paths: in a fair way to setting the forest alight, I might add. It was clear enough what was wrong."

"It was a gryphon, not a dragon," I muttered. "And what about all my chores?"

"Gryphons and dragons are distantly related," Akiva said, matter-of-factly. "The fever's been known to mutate. Of course, most people have the sense to keep away from gryphons. And despite what you may think, child, I am not yet decrepit! I managed the chores just as I always did before you came; if a little more peacefully."

I grinned in relief, because even if Gwen had grown older and Mother had gained a few more lines to her face, at least Akiva was still the same.

"You were like stone," Gwendolen told me. She was crouched at my feet and evidently felt that she had been left out of the conversation quite long enough. "You went hard and grey, and it took all of us to carry you inside."

I looked at Mother for confirmation, sceptical of Gwen's exaggeration, but to my surprise, she was nodding.

"Every time we heaved you into your bed you managed to get back into the forest somehow, though how you did it I'll never know. In the end we left you there because you weren't breathing or eating, and the rain didn't seem to touch you. Akiva said that you didn't need care, just time."

I threw a grateful look at Akiva, remembering that it was her I had to thank that Mother hadn't worn herself to the bone in looking after me. "How did you know I was going to wake today?"

Akiva shrugged, tending to her pot of tea.

It was left to Gwendolen to answer. "We didn't. Akiva only said that it would be this week, so we took it in turns to watch over you." Her face was flushed with triumph as she added buoyantly: "But you came awake in *my* shift."

They left me alone very soon after that. Mother bundled me to bed despite my protests that I wasn't tired and that I had spent enough time sleeping, and left me there with the curtains drawn open to admit warm sunlight. I was thus at leisure to study the ceiling, which was dancing with prisms of light; and my plait, which had grown a full three inches longer while I was sick. I did eventually fall asleep, comforted by the usual sounds of Akiva fussing about in her dried herbs, and the now less-familiar but still welcome sound of Gwendolen and Mother talking. I slept long and dreamlessly.

. . .

MOTHER TOOK ME HOME FOR A MONTH SHORTLY AFTER my recovery, much to my annoyance. I wanted to go on with my work as usual, gloomily conscious of having missed nearly a full year of my apprenticeship, and of all the things I would have to catch up on. After the incident with the gryphon, it had become blightingly obvious that I could no longer afford my ignorance.

Mother, protective and intractable, insisted. Even Akiva, when pressed, said dryly that she thought I had packed enough experience into one year, thank you. I took this to mean that she was sorry she had taken me on as apprentice and nodded shortly. I fiercely resented not being good enough.

Akiva, with a sharp look, said, "You're not a bad apprentice, as apprentices go, and I'd be sorry to start again with anyone else, but your body can only take so much at a time. You need rest. Go home, rest, enjoy yourself. You'll be working hard enough to make you happy when you get back."

It was nice to rest and do nothing in particular, I suppose. My fifteenth birthday had passed a couple of months after I was lost to the world, but Mother didn't attempt to hold a party for me and conveniently wouldn't hear Gwendolen's increasingly broad hints that one should be held.

"Plan your own parties, Gwen," I said at last. Fifteen didn't feel any different to fourteen, and I found I didn't care very much. Besides, my sixteenth birthday was not even half a year away now. "Stop fussing at me."

"It's not fussing to want your sister to have the treat of a birthday party," retorted Gwendolen, nettled. "You're fifteen, and *I'm* nearly fifteen; we're getting old."

"I'm surprised the wrinkles haven't started yet," I said caustically. "I don't want a party. It's not a treat for me."

"Oh, well," huffed Gwendolen, but not really crossly. She knew me too well not to see the truth in my protest. "At *least* let me dress you and do your hair!"

I groaned at that, but more for the form of it than because I really minded. Being dressed like a doll was annoying and tedious, but having Gwendolyn 'do' my hair would be a treat. It wasn't just that she seemed to be able to do wonders with even my fine, messy hair: it was relaxing having my hair braided and combed and twisted. Gwendolen had once thrown the brush and comb at me for falling asleep while she was fixing my hair.

"I'll make you look beautiful," she promised, and I made a rude snort of laughter that sounded eerily like Akiva's.

"Even you couldn't do that," I told her. I had been correct in thinking that I'd grown while I was ill. I'd grown so much that now I was an inch taller than Mother; and my arms and legs, which had been scrawny, now looked distinctly coltish. My face, once cheerfully round under my heavy head of butterscotch hair, had gone surprisingly thin and narrow, causing my grey eyes to look too big.

Gwendolen said, "What rubbish!" with perfect amiability. She was used to my protests by now and was satisfied merely to get her own way in the matter for once.

Some time later, my scalp tingling and well brushed, I was bundled into one of Gwendolen's least favourite party frocks; a grey-blue confection that had never quite suited her as to colour, or her fancy as to ruffles and ribbons. The hem was six inches short of my ankles, almost the same length as my kilted skirts rose to, and it was distinctly tight under the arms. I didn't dare move my arms any higher than my waist for fear that the sleeves would part company from the bodice.

"I feel like a stuffed chook," I grumbled, making small, jerky movements with my elbows. "All tight skin and silly little arms."

Gwendolen managed to scowl and laugh all at once. "Stop it, Rose! You look beautiful."

"So you say." My voice was glum. Even Gwendolen's partiality could not change the fact that, with a girdle band by far too high, and sleeves by far too short, I looked like the nightmare of a clothes dolly. Even the loose, elegant coiffure that Gwendolen had achieved in my hair couldn't draw attention away from it.

"You are; you just can't see it," complained Gwendolen. "Dear, *silly* Rose; I knew the dress wouldn't fit you: it's the colour I wanted you to see."

I flapped my arms rather helplessly, which made Gwendolen

cover her mouth to stifle the giggles, and looked in the mirror again, pursing my lips. "I don't know what you mean."

"Of course you don't," Gwendolen said soothingly. Horned hedgepigs! She was talking to me as if I were an idiot. "Look again. See what the colour does for your eyes. I *knew* I should have told Mother to make this dress up for you instead of me."

I studied my eyes doubtfully. They were still too big now that my face was narrower, but something about the light (or perhaps it really *was* the dress) made them look somehow luminous and blue-grey instead of just the usual grey.

"Huh," I said, tilting my head. "Odd."

"*Odd!*" almost shrieked Gwendolen. "*Oh!* After all the trouble I took, all you can say is 'odd'!"

"You said you wanted to do it," I said defensively. It seemed highly unfair to be trussed up like a blue-grey turkey and then blamed for the trouble of being served so.

"It isn't the trouble," Gwendolen said tartly, sounding very like Mother. "It's you: being so stubborn and stupid and blind, and— Rose! What are you doing?"

I looked up absently. I had just that moment discovered the faint lines of forest magic running through Gwen's old dress in the plant-based threads; and, amusing myself by tugging on them, I had made the left sleeve an inch longer. Some of the things I had learned in the dream-forest must have stuck.

I met Gwendolen's startled eyes and then suddenly we were giggling like children as I stretched out the sleeves to ridiculous lengths and back again. Mother came up to see what the fuss was about, but by that time we were sensible again and I was looking most respectable in grey-blue satin that fitted as perfectly as any expensively tailored dress. Mother eyed the dress appraisingly and said: "Very impressive, Rose. I see your apprenticeship is coming into its own already."

"I didn't think it would be any use whatever, apart from charming freckles and such," Gwendolen said, with the gracious air of one making a concession. "But I quite see how it could be useful after all. I—why are you laughing?"

She was prettily offended; but Mother and I, who had each unfortunately met the other's gaze at the wrong moment, couldn't bring ourselves to explain that adjusting dresses and charming freckles were hardly the most important things that one could accomplish with magic. She would have listened perfectly politely, and then said in mild disagreement: "Yes, but I still think that dress altering and charming freckles is more important than growing odd plants and messing about with curses in the forest."

In fact, she had already said something quite similar earlier, and her only interest in the wolf curse I had partially broken, was to ask me whether or not Bastian was handsome.

I had eyed her, perplexed, and said: "I don't know; he's quite *old* really. Twenty-three, he said."

Gwendolen looked disappointed, but left it at that. I had a feeling that she was disappointed in the whole thing now that it had lost the romantic element of a handsome young prince rescued from a terrible curse by my hand. I thought that this was unfair, since old or not, the curse really had been a horrible one for Bastian. It was no less horrible because he wasn't young, or swooningly good-looking, or a prince.

ALL IN ALL, I RATHER FORGOT ABOUT AKIVA AND Bastian in the next few weeks. There were walks into town with Gwen, where I was dragged about from satins to silks to cottons, and from thence to the newest, most fashionable dancing slippers. Then there were afternoons with Mother, sitting companionably opposite each other over a tub of washing water, elbow deep in suds, cheerfully occupied with the washing. There was always some little thing to be done, or something Gwendolen simply *had* to show or tell me, and it wasn't until the middle of the second week that I came to feel with certainty that something was wrong.

I had been conscious of a niggling discomfort in the back of my mind, something akin to discontent or annoyance that I had assumed to be because I was almost constantly wearing boots. It was only when Gwendolen said exasperatedly to me one morning that week, "Oh, Rose! Stop scowling at everything! You've frightened two of my beaux away with your frowning!" that I realised there was something really and undeniably wrong.

I said absently to Gwen, "Good", because as far as I could see, Gwendolen was by far too caught up with those beaux of hers. The next morning my boots were not beside my bed, and when I asked Mother about them, feeling rather relieved than otherwise, she only said, "Akiva was just the same whenever she came back from the forest for a week or two. Never mind the boots."

I walked outside in my blissfully bare feet, feeling the faint but certain hum of living threads along the ground and realised how much I had come not only to enjoy, but to *need* the thrumming of life and light that the threads gave me. It wasn't so much that I hated my shoes. I had *always* hated them. I simply couldn't do without the constant humming of threads any longer.

The feeling of discomfort left with the disappearance of my shoes, and Gwendolen's admirers, no longer discommoded by my scowl, came back again. Life regained its constant swing, and the only reminder of my life with Akiva in the forest was the fact that I woke each day promptly at first light as usual, instead of rising with the second sun. Apparently, the habit was not easily to be broken despite my ghostly time in the forest. I used the extra hour in the mornings to potter about in Mother's garden, singing silly little nonsense ditties to the plants that seemed to suit the garden very well, judging by the plump, healthy look to the vegetables. Before long the threads running through the garden, though by no means as vivid or powerful as the ones in the forest, glowed and thrummed at my approach into something approaching the liveliness of the forest.

There were no major alarms or disturbances to spoil my weeks at home, and the third month of summer sped by in a warm, golden haze, pleasantly restful. I took to my old pastime of climbing the cliffs, easier done now that I could go barefoot with impunity. Gwendolen even condescended to accompany me on the occasions when all her beaux were in default due to a prize fight in the next village. She was inclined to sulk at these infrequent defections and her company was not so congenial as it would otherwise have been.

Still, a silent, sulky Gwendolen was better than a bright, talkative one when it came to climbing. While she was brooding over her wrongs she climbed automatically, as light and nimble as she danced, across gaps and up rock faces I could never have persuaded her to attempt if her attention were not wandering. By the time we reached a broad, sunny cliff top, Gwendolen would have worn out her fit of the sulks and be as sunny as the day itself, making the walk back home a much pleasanter one.

Mother, pleased to remark that I seemed to be more sensible lately, despite my triumph against the tyranny of shoes, again undertook to give me the cooking lessons that Gwendolen had mastered some years ago. To her dismay, I commenced, with the best intentions in the world, to burn everything that was really flammable, and a few things that weren't. In the end she had to give up, and the only two things that I learned to cook with any proficiency were apple pie and rice pudding; neither of which could really be called sensible. I've since become convinced that I was successful in those two instances only because I enjoyed eating both so much.

In fact, I had just got back into the lazy swing of life at home when I realised with some shock that the new year was fast approaching. I was due back at Akiva's little cottage in less than one week. It wasn't an unpleasant shock, but it startled me, and I packed my things that very night with an odd sense of urgency. I wasn't sure whether the feeling was one of eagerness to get back or of foreboding that something was about to happen, but in either case it seemed only sensible to be ready.

With my everyday dresses and skirts and blouses, I also packed a light blue-grey jumper that Mother had knitted from finest sparkling wool, and the little matching cap that went with it. I packed them with some care: they were the first pretty things I had owned that I had taken any pleasure in. Perhaps my mirrored reflection in grey-blue silk had done more than Gwen thought. Whatever the reason, I packed them where they wouldn't tumble to the ground if my trunk came undone, and took myself out to the kitchen for supper.

I woke from a deep, dreamless sleep the next morning to the insistent sound of my name being spoken. I sat up in confusion, blinking, because the voice was Akiva's.

I was scrubbing one hand over my eyes when her voice said matter-of-factly in my ear, "Hurry up, there's a good child. I need you."

I scrambled out of bed with a cold thrill that had nothing to do with the slight chill of the early morning air, and forced myself into the only dress that I hadn't packed, turning in clumsy circles to chase the sleeves.

Gwendolen, still in bed and frowning in her sleep at the noise I made, murmured, "Wassamatter Rose?"

"I have to go," I said aloud, giving up any attempts at stealth. Gwendolen frowned again and stirred restlessly.

"But what about the dance?" she mumbled, no more than half awake. I scrambled back over the bed to hug her, grinning; because it was so like Gwen to think of an upcoming dance before she was even properly awake.

"Can't go. Akiva needs me and I have to leave now."

Mother appeared in the doorway, roused by the noise, and silently took in my packed trunk. "Already, Rose?"

I nodded, bouncing off the bed on Gwendolen's side. "Akiva needs me," I said again. "She just called."

One of Mother's brows rose, but she didn't comment. "Can you stop for breakfast?"

"No," I said regretfully, thinking wistfully of Mother's huge weekend breakfasts. "She told me to hurry."

"Very well," Mother nodded. "Tie your pinafore tapes, Rose; or you'll fall over them."

I tied one set and Gwendolen tied the other from her huddle of sheets and blanket; then I hugged them both fiercely.

"I'm sorry about the dance," I said to Gwendolen, because she still looked disappointed. "Love you, Mama."

"Love you, Rosie," she said, and hugged me one last time.

As I stepped gingerly across cold paving stones and looked back, I could see Gwendolen; a pale, blanket-wrapped blur at the upstairs window that raised a sleepy arm and waved at me. Mother stood beside her, adding her own farewell, and as I travelled back up the road to the forest, I felt light and free, enjoying the cool summer morning and feeling in its dryness the promise of a hot, sunny day. Gwendolen would be happy: her dance would be fine and warm.

There was a tint of gold to the horizon, but in the forest it was still dark. The half-light from the unrisen triad didn't penetrate beyond the first rank of trees, and the slight chill became more noticeable once I passed that boundary, particularly since I chose to forsake the path and travel by the forest lines. Once off the path, deep forest was always colder and darker. Today I travelled swiftly, without dawdling. I arrived in a more than typically ungraceful manner just outside Akiva's cottage with a very good idea of why Akiva had always insisted on my being back inside before it got dark. There were many not-so-nice things that I'd briefly glimpsed along the forest threads as I passed.

Akiva's face, crabbed in a frown, appeared briefly in the window as I trod the path through the front garden. The door was snatched open before I got to it.

"Quickly, Rose," she said. "Throw your trunk down and listen closely."

I set my trunk down on the floor, but before my fingers even left the handles, it was whisked away by Akiva's magic, which had been buzzing busily around her since I entered the house. I distantly felt the trunk settle beside the bed in my little bedroom, and looked at Akiva with bright, glittering eyes.

"Pay attention, child!" Akiva snapped, with no patience this morning for my delight of magic. For the first time I saw lines of worry in her face. "One of the wardens has gone missing and I'm needed at the council. It will take two days at the very least: in the meantime, do *not* invite anyone into the cottage or even the garden, unless they've come for a tea or a lotion. If one of the other wardens was responsible for her disappearance as Mara seems to think, you should be safe enough while we're all at the council; but I'd rather not take the risk."

A vague ray of hope made me ask, "Was it Cassandra?"

"No," Akiva said shortly, and I could see that she had been thinking the same thing: if a warden had to disappear, it was a pity it couldn't be Cassandra.

"Maybe it was something nonhuman." I thought of the gryphon, wondering what other, more dangerous, animals populated the forest—not to mention *deep* forest. "She could be dead."

Akiva shook her head, the lines etched deeper. "If she was dead, I would know. Ward magic flows back into the forest when a warden dies; it would have been visible to us all. No, she's met with foul play, and around the forest that usually means another warden."

"Was she a friend of yours?" I asked, catching the note of sorrow in her voice.

Akiva nodded briefly, but said, "Enough questions, child. Listen to me: you need to check the boundaries every day, the way I showed you."

"But I don't know if I remember properly!" I objected, taken aback. "Besides, I thought you only did that once a week."

Akiva fixed a steely eye on me, silencing my objections. "You'll have to remember, Rose. Every day, and wear the hood just in case you stray over a boundary."

"Why will that help?" I asked desperately, feeling as though I couldn't breathe. There was too much information flying at me all at once, and I had a horrible feeling that I would do something dreadfully wrong by accident.

"The hood is something of my wardship," Akiva said rapidly. There was a rustle in the air as she flung the hood around my shoulders. It was oddly light. I had long ago proved my theory that it was a leaf-hood by an exercise of judicious sneaking: now I looked closer at it and saw the forest lines running deep and strong through the leaves. Horned hedgepigs! So *that* was how Akiva saw the lines when she was away from her own wardship: she carried her own little wardship with her. She saw my comprehension and nodded approvingly.

"The leaves are from my wardship. When a warden goes from her wardship to another she needs something from her own: it helps her to get back and it allows her to draw on a certain amount of her power. Even if you absolutely trust the other warden to send you back safely it's still wise to have your own power to draw on."

I said, "Oh," stupidly, because I had just realised why it had been so difficult to get back into Akiva's wardship after the gryphon, and how I had gotten back after all. My stout little cudgel had done it: a small piece of Akiva's wardship, pulling me home.

I opened my mouth, bursting with questions, but Akiva cut them short. "Not now, child: I have no time. The boundaries every day, and never without the hood. Everything else as usual."

She left me there with the cloak of light summer leaves around my shoulders, and light as it was, I felt as though a heavy weight had settled on me. When the sound of her footsteps had faded down the path, I turned around in the cold, empty house like a dog making itself comfortable. I wasn't quite sure what to do with myself. Akiva hadn't taken time to light a fire, so I lit one myself, in spite of the fact that the rising triad would soon make the place uncomfortably hot. I had the desire for a good, strong cup of tea.

I made a leisurely breakfast, but it was still early when I finished. The soft light of the fire showed unusual disorder about the base of Akiva's workbench, scraps of foliage and dried herbs. I set myself to sweeping the mess up. As I swept scraps of herbs from the worktop onto the floor with the palm of my hand I noticed the little phial that sat, stoppered and labelled, in the very middle. There was a scrap of paper pinned beneath it, on which Akiva had written in her small, crabbed hand: 'Kelsey Hale; no charge.'

Kelsey, I thought, narrowing my eyes. I knew Kelsey: she was a heavy woman with lank grey hair and a sour smell about her, and there always seemed to be something wrong with her. I uncorked the small phial, cautiously sniffing, and was both pleased and hugely amused to discover that I knew what it was. It was a simple tea laced with mint, and although it was pleasantly sweet smelling it had exactly no medicinal value. Kelsey, always complaining of this or that malady, and suffering from none, would be neither helped nor hurt by the mixture. I replaced the stopper with a laugh in the silence of the house and was startled at the sound of it. For a moment it had sounded just like Akiva's dry, amused chuckle. I wondered if I would come to be like her after living long enough alone—supposing, of course, that I ever did become warden after her. Maybe I didn't need to go to sea, after all, to live a single life.

I put the fire out when I had had enough tea and retreated to my room to unpack the rest of my trunk. The triad was beginning to creep through the trees, bringing light and banishing the slight chill in the air, and by the time I was out in the garden, the golden light was a warm glow, heating the top of my head. I kept the leaf-hood around my shoulders as I worked, instinctively unwilling to take it off: it made me no hotter and didn't weigh on my shoulders. It wasn't very much longer before I had forgotten about it completely.

I didn't stop for lunch. It was such a beautiful day, and the work was a pleasure rather than a chore after so long away. My prolonged break from Akiva's garden had done me some good—or perhaps I simply had a mind to work—and it was still comfortably light when I finished both my and Akiva's work.

It was an unexpected relief: the triad might have set by the time I finished walking the boundaries, but it would not be by long. I still remembered some of the grimmer things I had seen in the darkened forest.

When I at last set out to go around the boundaries, the littlest sun was high in the middle of the sky. I had a brief moment of panic part way to the northern boundary when I thought that I had forgotten Akiva's leaf-hood, but my swift about turn to go back home flicked the edges of it into my peripheral. It was still weight-lessly tied around my shoulders. And as I neared the boundary I came into satisfying proof of the hood's usefulness: my sight of forest lines no longer ended at the boundaries. I could still see them beyond the borders, fainter than the ones in Akiva's wardship, but true and clear. I grinned, fierce and happy, and decided that perhaps I wouldn't make a mess of things after all.

That first night was full of unseen noises in the deepening gloom, and the sudden, sinister snapping of twigs. Once, a huge, blacker-than-night shadow swept through the forest overhead on silent, strong wings, while I crouched to the grass, still as a rabbit in the gaze of an eagle. It was gone in less than a second, but it was many more minutes before I stood up, blowing out my cheeks in mingled respect and relief, and moved on.

At the western border, as dark was beginning to fall in earnest, I heard distant, savage wailing. I didn't linger there, skimming past threads and giving them only the slightest testing touch as I passed, but the wailing seemed to hang eerily on the air as I hurried, made up of myriad, high-pitched voices that followed me hauntingly. At the meeting of the western and southern borders, I passed a thread that gave off a hint of the black, tarry magic I recognised as Cassandra's.

I backtracked to the thread, where I stood for some time staring uselessly at the trap. I didn't have the smallest idea of how to get rid of it. I didn't seem to recall Akiva actually doing much to the earlier traps. She had made a complicated gesture that looked like she was twisting a spindle back the wrong way, and said: "None of that nonsense, please." And that had been pretty much that.

I looked narrowly at the thick, rope-like strands of Cassandra's magic for a brief moment and came to the conclusion that this was exactly what she *had* done. She'd seen it as thread, and treated it as such.

I knew a little something of that. I curled my fingers into the threads of it and *twisted*. To my satisfaction the rope-like magic did the same for me as it had for Akiva, and before long I had the delight of watching the newly disorganized scarves of Cassandra's magic being absorbed into the forest. I made sure every skerrick was gone before I travelled along again, leaving a plumper, richer section of forest behind me.

The disembodied wailing continued to haunt me as I travelled, though it grew fainter, but nothing else impeded my swift journey around the rest of the boundary. I arrived home at last an hour or so after nightfall, exhausted and glad to be within the safety of four walls once again. It was with some relief that I laid out the fire and prepared my evening meal, and at last sank down in Akiva's chair to prove to myself the maxim that a watched pot never boils. But boil it did, and I sat quite some time in contentment with my cup of strong tea and brown bread-and-cheese.

I remembered Akiva's hood when I took myself off to bed, but the knots she'd tied in the tapes refused to loosen beneath my fingers. Perhaps my fingers were numb. Perhaps Akiva had tied them too tightly. I found that I didn't much care. I undressed beneath it, right down to my cotton shift, and crawled into bed, hood and all.

Seven

⌒〜⌒

I dreamed of Akiva. She must have been with the warden council, because there were ten women and three men seated about a round table with her, fidgeting with their various cuffs and handkerchiefs and aprons. I was thoughtfully surprised at the men: despite meeting Gwydion, I'd gotten the impression that warden was a distinctly feminine calling. He was there, too, looking solemn enough to be merely playing at being an adult. I grinned, conscious of a sense of fellow feeling, and wished I could nudge him companionably.

Cassandra was there too, her eyes darting back and forth from warden to warden. Unlike the other wardens, who were dressed more sensibly in plain cotton and aprons, she wore a scandalously gauzy gown that left very little to the imagination. I saw Gwydion wink at her, ruining his solemn air, and although she didn't return any acknowledgement, at least she didn't freeze him with a look. That surprised me.

I scanned the faces more quickly than thoroughly, but only those three were familiar. There was something about the tall, severe lady with salt and pepper hair that seemed to jump in my memory, and I studied her narrowly, my thoughts speeding away behind my eyes.

As I watched she banged a gavel on the cedar tabletop.

"Order, please."

I winced as the gavel connected with that beautiful tabletop, and half the wardens around the table mirrored my pained expression. The businesslike woman said impatiently: "Stop pulling faces every time I bring the meeting to order, Gwydion."

A voice muttered rebelliously, "We weren't *in* disorder, blast you!"

Unabashed, Gwydion said, "It's a hard thing to watch you ruin a beautifully crafted bit of wood. You do know it's still running with magic, don't you, Mara?"

"I do not now, and never will, coddle my wardship and its every twig and stick," Mara said shortly. "Stick to the business at hand: we're convened today to begin an enquiry into what happened to Kendra. Who saw her last?"

One of the male wardens, flushing, said, "I think I did. She was helping me to put up a warding around some meat-eating trees that migrated to my wardship."

"There's no need to be coy," Mara said impatiently. "We all know you two spend your spare time with each other. When did she leave your wardship, and where was she going?"

The blush on the warden's face deepened. "We really were putting up wards," he said. "She brought a few twigs with her to do the magic but nothing else. She trusted me."

"Perhaps, but wandering about with no more of her wardship than a few twigs when she has to pass through two wardships to get to yours is hardly wise. I take it she burned out the twigs doing your wards."

The male warden looked wretched, and I felt sorry for him. He said, "Yes. She burned them up and said that it didn't matter, because she had to pass through Akiva's wardship anyway, and that Akiva had something of hers there."

Mara's eyes turned to Akiva thoughtfully. "Did she meet with you, Akiva?"

Akiva shook her head, lips compressed, and the male warden

sank his head into his hands with an anguished groan. "I should never have let her go! It's my fault, all my fault."

"David, control yourself!" Mara said sharply. The warden stopped moaning but didn't take his head from his hands. I stared at him, fascinated and horrified to see that he was actually *crying*. My right arm twitched, surprising me with an unfamiliar urge to throw my arms around him and squeeze fiercely.

"There were no traces of Kendra in my wardship," said Mara crisply, ignoring David. Horned hedgepigs, but she was cold! "So I must assume she disappeared between David and Akiva's wardship. Are there any objections?"

"Objections?" Gwydion was clearly startled. His gaze swept around the table and then pinioned Mara. "Is it a statement or an accusation? Are you suggesting that Akiva had something to do with this?"

"Of course not," Mara said patiently. "However, warden law states that in a case of disappearance in a rich wardship, that both the person last seen with the victim and the person to whom the victim was going be remanded in custody. I realise you all think you're above suspicion, but consider how unlikely it is that this could have been done by anyone *but* a warden! Until the matter is cleared up, we have a very rich wardship now free to be reclaimed. Complain if you wish, but those are the facts of the matter."

"Who'll take Kendra's wardship?" Gwydion's voice was sharp and only just escaped cracking. "You, Mara? Of course, as our illustrious head, it would be your right."

Akiva's eyes turned on him, and her dry voice, unexpectedly amused, said, "Oh, we can point fingers as long as we like, Gwydion. But I speak for Mara here: let her control the wardship at least for the present. We've never had reason to doubt her motives."

"How will you like confinement?" Gwydion's voice no longer had the sharpness to it; instead, it was amused. He must be quite fond of her, I thought.

Akiva smiled. "I have a new apprentice, as you are very well aware. It will be a rest for me from her exuberance, and a chance for her to prove she can keep the wardship a few days without major disaster. So far, I am not overly hopeful."

Gwydion threw back his head and laughed. "What has she done this time?"

Cassandra's violet eyes darted toward Gwydion and Akiva, darkening with anger. "Why are we speaking about a stupid little chit of a girl? I came here to talk about Kendra, and now I am bored. I will not stay."

Mara held up one hand. "We still have more to discuss, Cassandra. Gwydion, try to stay on topic for more than two minutes..."

I rose to consciousness gradually, the voices fading as I rose. Remembering my dream-laced dragon-fever, I didn't doubt that I'd dreamed truly, and I woke scowling in sleepy resentment.

My waking was accompanied by a feeling of nausea. I found the room distorted around me and blinked my sleepy eyes, but when I squinted around again the room was still blurred.

Horned hedgepigs, what was going on? The window was somehow too long and smaller at one side, and the panes wobbled as if they weren't quite solid. I gazed around me suspiciously. While I looked at one section of wall it seemed to sit still as the rest of the room seethed in my periphery, yet when I looked slowly and deliberately around the room again, it was still.

I wandered through the house in my slip and cape, touching walls and window frames that felt solid to the touch but moved alarmingly in the corners of my eyes. I sat down at last in Akiva's chair, dizzy and ill, and pulled the cape tighter around my shoulders. There was no doubt that something was very wrong with the house, but I couldn't tell where the fault lay. There was no emanation of magic from any point in the house that I could find, and although my inexperience made it difficult to say for sure, I came to the conclusion that the problem lay outside the house.

I didn't eat much in the way of breakfast that morning: I was afraid that it wouldn't stay down. The shifting walls reminded me unpleasantly of being at sea, and I'd never been much of a sailor: it was the one flaw in my piratical plans. Still, I managed to gulp down a piece of dry toast before I made my unsteady way out into the garden, where everything was mercifully steady and solid. In fact, the garden looked so very normal that I thought for a moment it had escaped the general force of twisting magic that was wreaking havoc in the house.

Normal, that is, until I saw the salamander that was stretched out luxuriously on a hot rock in the aloe bed. The aloes were radiating with a gentle glow of warmth that became scorchingly hot once I reached my hand between them, and the salamander churred contentedly up at me, flicking a white-hot tongue lazily at my fingers. I snatched my hand back with a yelp and put my burnt fingers in my mouth, feeling aggrieved, but the salamander only purred at me again. It sounded smug.

I left it to sun itself in peace and moved around the garden to check on the other plants. The climate controlled garden beds were each more than half in the land of their origin and fuzzy round the edges, but the rest of the garden was only a little more active than usual. I thought, puffing out my cheeks in relief, that at least I knew how to fix *that*. As Akiva had said, it required nothing more than a steady hand and not too much power. I made my way purposefully around the garden again, setting things briskly to rights: beans to their poles, tomatoes to their stakes, and cucumbers to their frames, wary not to come too close to the salamander again.

When I finished my rounds of the more everyday plants, I found that the salamander had left its garden patch completely, and that it was not the only animal to do so. Two young, unsteady, deer-like creatures were prancing down the middle stretch of the back garden, all gangling legs and knobbly knees. Their hide was mossy green and feathery rather than hairy, and two little horns rose atop each delicate head, radiating a pale, pearly green that reminded me of young saplings. I stared at them for a long, perplexed moment. I didn't know which garden bed they had come from, much less how to get them back into their original habitat.

I pushed past the deer-things, discovering to my cost that they had a goat-like appetite for foliage and the cotton of my shift alike, and stopped in dismay when I came upon the patches of garden that they had already passed. They had mown a great swathe of destruction through the garden as they played, leaving broken twigs and torn up plants strewn in a trail behind them. I followed it backwards in the calm of despair and at last found the section of garden that began the carnage. So *that* was where they'd come from!

I tried to herd the deer into it as they leapt and bleated, springing to impossible heights whenever I thought I had them cornered, or skipping nimbly through a gap that I'd thought much too small for escape. There was simply no containing their exuberance. They kicked up their heels at the salamander, who seemed to laugh at me, and as I chased them madly round the garden, exotic birdcalls and growls multiplied in the morning air. Patches of the garden snowed on me as I dashed through them, while others blasted with hot, dry desert air. Plots of humidity left droplets of moisture on my skin as I dodged through them, and at one stage, a huge, brightly-coloured bird flew past my head, squawking in a manner most truly piratical.

My shift grew steadily dirtier and more ragged, but I didn't dare take the time to dress fully because the garden gave the impression that it would wait for nothing in its bombastic growth.

Giving up on herding the two green deer, I tried instead to concentrate on containment, but the animals didn't want to stay in the back garden. The garden fence had begun sneakily to meld with the forest. Already one section was more akin to long, oddly pale grass than the original white picket fence, and the entire back section had turned into a row of milky ash saplings. As I watched, a fist-sized marmoset leapt for them with an excited chattering, and promptly disappeared.

I flopped down on my back with a yell of despair. Unfortunately, I was just a little too close to the salamander, which seemed to be following me, and promptly burned off a chunk of my hair. There was a moment of heat and fire and mad beating at my hair before I flopped back into the grass with a groan, ignoring the nasty smell of burnt hair. There was no fixing this: Akiva would come home to a madhouse. Even the cottage itself was beginning to show signs of disappearing into the forest. I contemplated the sky above me in dumb resignation, surrounded by a cacophony of tropical and subtropical animal sounds, and felt hot breeze tickle my neck. I sat up, wide awake and elated all at once.

Of course! Bastian! If anyone but Akiva knew how to bring things to rights, it was Bastian. The last I had seen of him, he was swimming in a deceptively placid-looking stream three wardships away; but with Akiva's wardship in such a state of excitement and powerful disorder, it shouldn't be too difficult to send a call that would pass through several wardships. And I had Akiva's hood, now.

I leaned forward, propping myself on my palms, and felt a tracing burn along my wrist as the salamander's tail brushed my arm. I barely felt it. I punched into the system of forest lines that bunched in a tangling mass beneath me, sending out the call for Bastian. The garden bucked and seethed under me, and in the confusion I felt the power of Akiva's hood stretch and sharpen as though it were waking from a deep sleep. The forest was masterless, furling its tendrils out wildly, and I understood in a flash of grim inspiration that the wardship was mine for the taking.

The hood belonged to the warden of the forest, and the lines around me were reaching mindlessly for a warden to tend them. The realization left me breathless and suddenly frightened. Akiva hadn't left me the hood to keep me safe. She had left it because she was prepared for the possibility that she wouldn't be able to return as soon as she hoped.

I abandoned my call and gathered the threads to myself, straightening and then sending them back out again, bringing order from confusion. It was almost like dismantling one of Cassandra's traps, or fixing a knotted piece of forest. I didn't notice that I'd closed my eyes until I saw a figure in glowing gold magic standing before me, highlighted against the velvet darkness of my closed lids. I opened confusingly heavy eyelids to see its outer form. A dirty face, growing with corn-gold stubble, grew fuzzily into focus before me, its hazel eyes narrowed with concern.

"Bastian!" I slurred. I seemed to be floating a foot above the ground, but I was too weary for the fact to make as much of an impression on me as it should have. Horned hedgepigs, but I was tired!

Bastian's brows had a crease between them. "Gently now, little witch."

I tried to tell him not to be silly, but my mouth wouldn't make real words. The world swayed once, and I swayed with it. I felt Bastian's hands seize me about the waist just as I lost concentration and fell, then there was only deep darkness.

There was something tickling my nose. I squinched my eyes and wrinkled my nose as Bastian's voice said, "It's going to have to come off, you know."

I opened my eyes to find that my head was resting in the crook of Bastian's arm, and that he was tickling my nose with the tail of my plait. As I glared up at him, he gave my nose one final tickle, and let go of my plait.

"What will have to come off?" I asked, wriggling to sit up. Bastian seized my plait again and yanked me back down.

"Stop wriggling," he commanded.

I subsided back into the crook of his arm, from whence I could conveniently glare at him.

"It's no good scowling at me after you've sent a shockwave through half the forest after me. I thought that Cassandra had got to you."

I gazed up at him unblinkingly and said, "I had a problem, but I fixed it."

"That's one thing," Bastian told me grimly, and held my left arm to the light where the salamander burn was an angry red. "But this is another. Who did this to you?"

"The salamander," I told him pertly, misliking his tone. "That's why there's a hole in my hair."

The grimness went away from Bastian's face, and he laughed. "You look like a scarecrow, little witch. The whole lot will have to come off."

I felt the damage with tentative fingers and cheerfully acquiesced.

"Now," I said buoyantly, "I can finally start being a pirate." It made me laugh, because now at fifteen and some months, my childish dreams of piracy on the high seas were fading to amusing memories, impractical and nonsensical. I had begged Mother for years to cut my hair to a more piratically practical length, but now that it would finally have to be cut, I had outgrown the dreams.

"I should have thought of this years ago," I told Bastian.

"I've been meaning to ask you about that. Why piracy?"

"It's how I'm going to keep Gwendolen in pearls and satin," I explained, allowing myself the nonsense of pretending. "That was before she decided she wanted to get married as well as have fine dresses and jewels."

"What a shame," Bastian mocked, turning my head away and gently untangling my plait. His long fingers tugged softly at knots, and singed portions of hair wafted to the grass. "You'll have to get married, too."

I shook my head vigorously, sending burnt strands of hair flying, and Bastian seized my head with one hand. "Oh, no. I'm not going to marry. Pirates don't."

"Very true," he agreed. His fingers held my head firmly while he unravelled the last of the plait, and the remaining whole strands fell about my waist. "Very sensible of you. Now, little witch: scissors."

We used Akiva's sewing scissors; and great, long hanks of butter-coloured hair fell to the grass to join the burnt strands as Bastian snipped. His fingers threaded through my hair, carefully and surprisingly proficiently; and before long my hair swished in an excitingly short way just below my ears. Bastian stepped back to critically survey his handiwork, and nodded.

"That will do, I think. You scrub up quite nicely when your hair isn't in great big tangles and you've gone to the trouble of washing your face. It's a pity we had to cut it, though."

"I *like* it this way," I said. I felt daring and oddly free. I shook my head until I was dizzy and my hair floated around my face like thistledown.

"Ah, well, it will grow back," Bastian murmured, more to himself than me. "Stop tossing your hair, little witch; you make me dizzy. You look like a proper urchin."

I tossed my head once more to show him that I could do as I chose. "Well, so I am."

"So I see." Bastian's voice was dry. He gathered the strands of my hair from the grass, ignoring my head toss. "Now, little witch— what does Akiva mean by leaving you alone?"

"I'm not alone," I said absently, turning away from him to gaze around the garden. Now that I was not half fainting or otherwise distracted, I realised that I was feeling rather queer.

Bastian threw an impatient look at the two green deer that were cowering behind a tree and said, "That's hardly the point. Where's Akiva?"

"Hush," I told him, tentatively exploring the change I could feel not only in the garden but in myself. I shook off the hand that Bastian laid on my arm and walked away, stretching out both hands as if I could physically feel the difference.

Behind me, Bastian said, as if stunned, "Did you just *hush me*?"

"You're distracting me," I complained. "Stop talking."

"I hardly know whether to be offended or to congratulate you," said Bastian, his voice particularly growly.

"Don't do either," I murmured. "Just be quiet." There was a lightness and clearness to the forest air that was both distracting and invigorating me.

Horned hedgepigs! I had *done* it. I was warden of the forest. Order had been re-established all around me, bringing with it an odd sensation of weight about my shoulders. I could sense the lines that ran through the forest without trying, as if they were a constant thought in the back of my mind. The garden was back to normal even if it *was* riddled with exotic animals, and the back fence was white picket once more. I felt a rare sense of accomplishment that caused a smile of grim triumph to curve my lips.

Then fingers closed firmly on my wrist, and I was swung around to face Bastian, who seemed to be struggling between amusement and impatience. "Little witch, although I appreciate the fact that you're the first woman ever to hush me, I want a straight answer. Where is Akiva, and why did she leave you alone? You could have run into any amount of trouble."

"I'm not a woman," I pointed out, but since this didn't seem to placate him at all, I added, "Akiva had to go because a warden disappeared. And I'm perfectly capable of being left alone by myself, thank you."

"Of course! Which is why a call for help threw me off my feet half an hour ago and left me thinking you were dead or dying!"

"Anyway," I said, ignoring what seemed to me to be unjustifiable anger, "you can't tell off Akiva for leaving me by myself when I only met you because she did."

Bastian looked down at me a little grimly. "That, Rose my lovely, is the point. There are more dangerous things in the forest than I."

I gave a crack of laughter, again surprising myself at how much I sounded like Akiva. "You're not dangerous at all!"

"Once again, I don't know whether to be offended or to congratulate you," remarked Bastian, but his eyes were amused. "I don't think I've ever been so insulted."

I looked up at him with narrowed eyes. "I don't understand."

"I know," Bastian said, grinning. "That's what makes it so insulting."

"You're having a joke at me," I accused, hands on hips.

"The joke is entirely on me, believe me, little witch. Now, suppose you tell me just what you were doing when I arrived post-haste to rescue you."

"The garden tried to merge with the forest," I explained. "The other wardens seem to think Akiva had something to do with her friend disappearing and I think they've put her somewhere inside where she can't reach the energy lines. I called for you because everything was collapsing, and I didn't know what to do."

"You were doing well enough when I got here," Bastian pointed out. "Well, if we discount the floating and fainting."

"I think that was because it was bigger than I expected," I said thoughtfully, creasing my brow. "I only understood it properly when I punched into the forest lines to call you. I was going to send out another call to tell you not to bother coming but you got here too quickly."

"Quickly?" The ghost of a smile played about Bastian's mouth. "No, I didn't get here quickly. The forest was standing still—or at least, so it seemed to me. Akiva does not look after you nearly well enough."

"I don't need looking after," I said again, impatiently.

Bastian gave a short laugh and said grimly, "That's the biggest piece of nonsense I've ever heard. You're as helpless as a babe in arms."

"I broke part of *your* curse!"

Bastian's grin was pointed. "And for your pains you were very nearly eaten."

"But I *didn't* get eaten!" I said triumphantly. "So there!"

"The point remains valid," Bastian said indifferently. He had crossed his arms and was leaning his hips against the picket fence. "You need looking after. Or perhaps locking away where you can't get up to mischief—" he broke off suddenly, and tipped his head to one side, wolf-like, before sharpening his gaze toward the front of the cottage. "Someone's coming."

I looked around the side of the cottage without much interest. "It's probably Kelsey Hale. Akiva had some medicine for her."

"It doesn't look like a Kelsey Hale," Bastian said, and there was something of a growl in his voice.

I craned my neck to see and exclaimed in surprise: "It's that boy again!"

Bastian's eyes narrowed. "What boy?"

"The stupid one who was trying to cut down a tree too near to deep forest," I told him, starting toward the front gate, my interest piqued. "I'd better go see what he wants."

Bastian hauled me back by the collar of Akiva's hood. "Not so fast, little witch."

"I have to see what he wants," I argued, wriggling vainly.

Bastian's fingers didn't loosen. "Not like that, you don't."

"Like what?" I demanded, still struggling.

Bastian looked pointedly down at my dirty shift and raised his brows. "Go put some clothes on, little witch."

I stopped wriggling and glared up at him instead. While my

shift was certainly grubby and tattered from my exertions this morning, it was of sturdy, decent cotton, and it was a very far stretch to imply that it was indecent. Even my bare arms were covered by the hood.

"You're a fine one to talk!" I told him indignantly, bare chested as he was. "Besides, I've been standing here with you half the morning dressed like this."

"That's different," said Bastian, but he looked goaded.

"It's not at all! Let me go!"

"You, Rose, are going to go and get properly dressed."

Before I knew what was happening, Bastian had seized me by each shoulder. I was pushed toward the cottage door at a forced march.

"Horned hedgepigs! Let me go or you'll be sorry!" I yelled, but Bastian only laughed, and advised, "You may as well stop wriggling. I'm not going to let go."

I was being pushed through the back door when bright threads of gold began to trace through Bastian. Linked to the wardship now, I saw them with startling clarity although Bastian was behind me. His hands dropped from my shoulders, and braced against them as I was, I fell backwards into him.

We tumbled back into the garden, and I heard Bastian howl, "Not now!" as a blinding surge of glittering gold energy shocked through the garden. When my sight cleared Bastian was back in his wolf shape, with traces of gold still glinting in his pelt. He looked annoyed, and I couldn't help chuckling my glee.

"Rose," he said warningly. "Into the house, now."

I laughed again, this time a gurgle of mirth deep in my throat, and took to my heels, because he couldn't stop me now.

As I ran, giggling, Bastian called threateningly after me, "Rose! Come back here, you pestilent child!"

I ignored him. The boy at the gate had just shouted for admittance: he must have discovered that he couldn't pass the Keep Out spell on the gate. It would only open from the inside, or to either Akiva or myself.

Bastian shot past me in a blur of grey and disappeared over the fence while I made my way to the gate, rather out of breath. I assumed that he was going away in a sulk. I was wrong. A moment after I reached the gate, while my fingers were still on the latch, he leapt, growling, onto the path behind the woodcutter boy.

The boy said, "Quick, get back into the house!"

"Don't be silly!" I told him crossly, pushing past him to face Bastian. I shook off the hand that tried to pull me back and addressed Bastian. "What do you think you're doing?"

Bastian gave a toothy grin. "Step aside, little witch. I won't hurt him, I just want to frighten him."

I glared at him. "You're such a nuisance today!"

A tentative hand pulled at my hood, and the young man said, "Are you talking to the wolf?"

"Of course!" I said, turning to him in some surprise. "Can't you hear him?"

Bastian, with a look of malicious enjoyment, said, "Didn't I tell you? You're the only one who can understand me without magic."

The woodcutter lad shook his head in wonder. "I hear your voice. The wolf growls, but he doesn't speak."

"Ignorant whelp!"

The boy eyed Bastian nervously. "Does he want to eat me?"

"No. He's cross because he thinks it's indecent for me to talk to you in my shift. He's trying to scare you away."

The boy grinned. "Well, so long as I know he won't eat me, I won't be afraid to come back. It's a very nice shift, anyway."

"There, I told you," I said to the still-growling Bastian.

"I came for Kelsey's medicine," the boy explained. He offered me his hand. "I'm Gilbert."

I offered my own hand in return. "Rose." I rather expected to have my hand shaken, but instead Gilbert bowed and kissed my fingers, smiling up at me while Bastian snarled.

"I've been looking for you ever since you disappeared into the forest. If I'd known, I would have come for Kelsey's medicine before this. I thought you were the fairy queen, the way you vanished into the forest that day."

"I'm Gwendolen's sister," I said, ushering him into the front garden.

Bastian would have followed close behind, but I shut the gate on his nose, feeling as though he deserved to be annoyed.

"She's the tiny one with gold curls," Gilbert nodded. "My brother wants to marry her."

"Everyone does," I agreed cheerfully. Gilbert held the front door open for me, and grinned.

"Not everyone," he said.

Eight

〰️

Gilbert stood by Akiva's workbench, fiddling with the little vials as I searched for Kelsey's medicine. It had been in the middle of the bench last night, but somewhere in the confusion of the morning it had disappeared. Search as I might, I couldn't seem to find it. It wasn't until I moved a pile of rosemary leaves that I discovered what had happened to it.

I said thoughtfully, "Hah."

The phial was imbedded in the wood as if it were a small, glass branch, wood and glass meeting seamlessly together without the tiniest crack of space. The vial was not simply stuck in the bench, it had become *part* of the bench. The glass base poked out from the underside of the table, giving much the same effect as a wood knot, and when Gilbert attempted to jolt it loose by thumping his fist down on the top of the tiny bottle, all the attempt achieved was the bruising of his hand.

"That's no good," I said, when he was red in the face from popping under the table and back up again in his endeavour to see if he had moved it at all. "I'll have to try something else."

"Do a spell," Gilbert said, with interested anticipation.

"I don't do spells."

He protested, "But what about the tree?"

"That wasn't a spell, it was just forest magic. Be quiet. I'm concentrating."

Gilbert obediently shut his mouth but continued to watch in interest as I ran my fingertips over the grainy bench, searching uncertainly for threads of forest magic. I wasn't sure if there would be any, for the bench was old and faded, and it was many years since the timber had been hewn from the forest. The lines were still there in the grain, but glowing only very faintly: if I hadn't had Akiva's cape I probably wouldn't have been able see them at all. I tried pulling at them, but they were too old and tired and sluggish, and the only effect was a prolonged, groaning creak from the bench.

"I don't think it's working," Gilbert said helpfully, raising his chin from his hands. His mute but interested gaze was unexpectedly annoying, used as I was to Bastian's uninterested waiting, and I tried to ignore him. I was beginning to remember my first, uneasy reaction to Gilbert, and regretted that I had brought him into the cottage in the first place.

Trying a new tack, I gave up my attempts at pulling and instead put my hands on the wood, palms down, feeding power from the forest into it to quicken the strands of magic. I closed my eyes out of habit though I could see the glittering lines of magic perfectly well without doing so, and watched as the green life threaded gently through the benchtop. I heard Gilbert draw in a sharp breath but paid no attention, my focus on the glittering whorl that was coiled about the phial. The lines loosened, rejecting the foreign matter, and as I reached out my hand to take the tiny bottle, a shiver passed through the bench; a whisper of rippling magic. I let go of the threads with a sigh of contentment and opened my eyes.

At first I thought that the tiny window above Akiva's desk had come open and a branch had pushed its way through, so much twig and foliage was waving before me. But it was the work-bench itself, growing and sending out new shoots with bright green, furled leaves. Where the glass vial had been was now a branch, growing toward the ceiling and unfurling its leaves to the room.

One of Gilbert's hands curled around mine, fingers rough and warm. He said, "Look!" and pointed.

I did look, and puffed out my cheeks in resignation at what I saw. The bench had become part of the wooden floorboards, growing into them with a seamless grain, and from the place that I stood to a radius of two yards, the boards were as alive and eager as the desk.

Gilbert, looking at me with a disconcertingly wondering gaze, drew in a deep breath, and said, "You *are* the fairy queen."

I grimaced ruefully, disengaging my fingers from his. "When Akiva sees this, she's more likely to tell me I'm a feckless, shiftless child. You should go now."

Gilbert took the phial from my outstretched hand and said: "What do I owe you?"

"No charge," I said in surprise. I had expected him to know.

Gilbert only grinned at me in a way that made me think he *had* known after all, and said, "I'll think of something."

He allowed me to shepherd him to the gate where Bastian was waiting, and this time I wasn't surprised when he kissed my hand instead of shaking it. But he held my fingers still, and said suddenly, "We're having a party this night next week. Will you come?"

Unnerved to find that I couldn't tug my fingers free, I said hastily, "I don't know. Yes, if I can, I suppose."

Gilbert released my hand, grinning, and said, "There will be caramel apples and ice cream, you know."

I laughed then, my sudden nervousness swept away, and ignored Bastian's low, warning growl. "Oh, in *that* case! You should have said."

He grinned and I was able to herd him out of the gate, leaving time enough for Bastian to slink into the yard at a dash. Evidently he was not giving me a chance to shut him out again.

Gilbert lingered by the fence, his eyes mischievous, and said, "I've thought of a payment for the medicine, Rose. I'll give you a kiss for it."

Bastian snarled but stayed in the yard. I snorted cheerfully and somewhat rudely. I was perfectly well aware that I was not pretty enough to be romantically interesting to any boy, and that Gilbert was not to be taken seriously. Gwendolen's older suitors tended to chuck me under the chin and call me pretty lady, and I was reasonably sure that Gilbert was another of those. He had an odd habit of reaching for my hand, I thought doubtfully, but that wasn't anything to worry about: he might have younger sisters.

"I'll ask Akiva if I can come to the party," I said. I left him by the gate and returned to the house with Bastian close at my heels.

As the door closed behind us, Bastian said ominously, "You, little witch, are a shameless flirt."

"Piffle!" I said, standing on tiptoes to peep out the window above Akiva's leafy work bench. Gilbert was still standing by the gate, but as I watched, he turned away and headed back down the path. He was smiling.

"You're not listening!" Bastian accused.

"Piffle!" I said again, leaving the window. "I was just making sure that he was gone."

"You took long enough to get the medicine," he added sourly, making himself a bed and curling up on the fireplace rug.

I pointed wordlessly at Akiva's workbench, which was now beginning to flower, and one of Bastian's ears perked.

"Ah!" he remarked. "I didn't notice that."

"No, you were too busy being rude."

"You shouldn't let strange men offer to kiss you," Bastian rejoined. His voice was brooding, and I knew that he hadn't yet forgiven me for disobeying him.

"He isn't a man, he's a boy," I pointed out, ignoring his ill humour. "I suppose you expect me to gag him? He was only being nice to me because I'm Gwendolen's sister: everyone is in love with her."

Bastian, as Gilbert had done before him, said, "Not everyone."

"That's what Gilbert said, but it's wrong, all the same."

"Oh, he did, did he?" Bastian muttered, but his voice had lost its annoyed edge and was now simply amused. I wanted to know what was funny, but it looked as if he were having a private joke with himself, and I knew better than to ask. Instead, I sat down with a sigh in front of the living workbench. Judging by the blossoms, the wood must have originally come from a peach tree.

I watched a peach bloom and grow, fuzzy and ripe and red-gold, and said glumly, "Akiva will never leave me alone in the house again."

Bastian left the fireplace rug to sit next to me, studying the workbench with curious eyes. After a moment he said, "You poured forest energy into the bench to liven it, little witch. Surely it's only a matter of drawing it out again."

I blew out my cheeks, then scowled. "I don't think I can."

The truth was, I didn't think I could bring myself to do it. Not now that it was living and growing: it would be too much like committing murder.

"Then you really are in the suds," Bastian said laconically. He trotted closer to the bench, sniffed cautiously, and recoiled. "*Whoof*, that's strong!"

"That's because it's forest magic," I explained gloomily. I could almost *see* the cynical gleam that would appear in Akiva's eye when she got back. But there was nothing more I could do, so I gave the workbench a kick and left Bastian in the main room so that I could at least dress myself.

Bastian called after me, "Where are you off to, little witch?"

"Deep forest!" I yelled back, muffled and tangled in my last clean dress. It didn't seem to want to be worn. I tweaked the cotton threads in the material, and the sleeves, which had been resisting my attempts to force my arms through them, hurriedly straightened. "I have to walk the boundary."

"I wouldn't if I were you," Bastian said indifferently, through the door.

I opened the door, rather flushed and untidy, to demand: "Why?"

"You look as though you've been dragged through a bramble bush backwards," Bastian remarked, surveying me critically.

"I *have* to walk the boundaries," I argued, twitching my skirt straight and smoothing my newly short hair perfunctorily with my fingers.

Bastian shrugged. "Do as you please, of course; but there is a full moon tonight and the fairies have been rather active the last few days. It's a bad night to be abroad in deep forest."

I tried to look as though I had known perfectly well that of *course* fairies were real and living in deep forest, and asked, "Well, what else can I do? It needs to be done."

"You could leave it for one night," Bastian suggested, leaning against the doorframe.

"I can't," I said; and I knew it was true as I said it.

Taking the wardship temporarily had made a few things clearer to me. I was now reasonably sure that walking the bounds was not simply to check on the wardship, but that it served the double purpose of safe-checking *and* warding. In touching each thread as I progressed clockwise around the wardship, I was setting up very powerful wards of protection. If anything intending harm did get past them, I was certain I would know about it.

Bastian didn't move away: if anything, he shifted until he seemed to fill the doorway. I gave up trying to tie my pinafore tapes and instead put my hands on my hips in order to glare more effectively.

"If you won't let me through the door, I'll only climb out the window," I told him.

There was the suspicion of a growl in Bastian's voice. "It's not safe out there tonight."

I laughed, because of *course* it wasn't safe in deep forest. It never was. "I've got Akiva's hood, and I should be back before dark. Besides, the forest likes me."

"The forest doesn't like anyone: it simply grows and lives."

I didn't argue because I knew I was right. "I'll climb out the window if you don't move," I repeated.

"Smugness is unbecoming in a young woman, little witch," Bastian said sourly, moving aside. "You are impossible to look after."

I put my nose in the air but ruined the effect by tripping on Bastian's tail as I pushed past him. "I don't need looking after."

"We've discussed this before," retorted Bastian, following me outside. "And it's arrant nonsense. The minute I turn my back you're talking to gryphons and contracting dragon fever, not to mention allowing young country bumpkins to flirt with you."

"I don't flirt!" I said indignantly, annoyed to find that there was only one fault laid to my charge that I could refute. "Besides, it wouldn't be your business if I did! You're not my father, *or* my brother."

"Don't be snide, little witch. In my human form I'm not nearly old enough to be your father."

"Well, you're old, anyway," I argued, closing the gate behind us.

Bastian, looking particularly annoyed, retorted, "I'm not in my dotage!"

"Oh, well," I said comfortingly, since he really did seem outraged. "I still like you the best out of anyone, even if you *are* bossy." I laced my fingers through the fur at his scruff and tickled his ear.

"Just as well," Bastian said coldly, but he didn't shake my hand off. "Onward, little witch. Let's be done with this."

The moment we stepped into deep forest I could feel the difference. It was colder there than in the regular forest and suddenly as dark as if night had fallen. I could hear the same wild, animal keening that I had heard the night before, louder and more urgent; and a rank smell I didn't recognise hung on the air, blanketing us in fetid sweetness. I shivered, and my hand tightened in Bastian's fur.

"What's that smell?" I asked, wetting my lips. The chant around us had quickened to a pulsing, frantic beat, and it left me feeling decidedly nasty around my stomach.

Bastian said matter-of-factly, "It's blood. Touch each thread quickly and leave. And stay close to me: it's a bad night to be out."

I did as I was told, and the new sense I found in the threads told me that the rules were different tonight. The fairies, whoever and whatever they were, in all their savagery were as much a part of the forest as the trees were. Tonight, I was the stranger.

So I trod carefully around deep forest with my eyes very wide and bright, one hand always grasping Bastian's fur and the other outstretched to guide my way between the trees; for though the moon was full it was blood-red, and the light it gave was queer and dull. Once I saw grotesque shapes slipping through the branches before me, saffron-yellow and cobalt blue, and caught my breath sharply. I knew that somewhere deep in the forest there was a sacrifice, a blood sacrifice just like in the old stories.

"It's a seventh year," said Bastian's voice, a soft growl at my side confirming my guess. "It's always blood the seventh year."

"Human?" My voice was gruff, but steady. I felt a remote kind of satisfaction that it didn't betray my sick horror.

"Sometimes. Not tonight. Not while Akiva guards the wardship. She has always taken care to bar the forest to humans when it comes to full moon in a seventh year."

Before he had finished speaking there was a drawn out scream that tore through the forest, and the lines around me gave one massive throb. I saw, quite clearly, the moment a rabbit was slaughtered, the tortured arch of its body and its sudden stillness. They had cut out its heart slowly, while it lived. I squeezed my eyes shut but it did no good. The scream went on and on while the forest gibbered and shrieked with mad blood lust around me. I picked up my skirts and ran, hardly aware of each thread as I touched it.

I completed the wards somehow, and came home at last, shivering, to enter Akiva's garden gate in early, bright moonlight. I blinked in the sudden brightness, bewildered, and swayed on the balls of my feet; but Bastian was there under my hand, firm and certain. I don't remember opening either the gate or the front door, but somehow we were back in the house. The salamander was in the fireplace, glowing red, and I let go of Bastian only to set the wood in order around it. I felt as though I would never be warm again.

The wood combusted without my tinderbox while the salamander churred its pleasure, and I curled myself up on the rug, putting off lighting the lamps until I could feel the warmth in my fingers again. Bastian came and curled around me silently while I gazed into the fire with glazed eyes. It seemed to me that I could still see the rabbit in its dying contortions. After a moment I buried my head in the soft, springy fur of Bastian's chest.

I don't remember falling asleep. I remember the gentle whispering of the branches on the workbench, and then I was dreaming that I was in deep forest while the trees whispered around me. The sky was red as blood, and there was a small animal lying on the ground, still and silent. A moment of tense quiet fell as I knelt to touch it, all stiff and cold in the grass, then a great disembodied screaming began. When I woke, whimpering, Bastian was human and his arms were wrapped around me, his voice whispering comfort and nonsense in my ear. I gave a smothered sob of relief and turned in his arms so that I could cling with one arm around his neck while I buried my face in his chest again. It was less hairy and comforting than wolf-Bastian's chest, but it was warm, and I could feel his heart beating.

I fell asleep again with his voice murmuring in my ear. This time, my dreams were clear.

The salamander was sitting amidst the glowing embers when I woke the next morning. I was uncomfortably warm: the fire had heated the room considerably overnight, and I was still curled up with Bastian, who seemed to radiate heat from his fur. His snout snuffled somewhere in my hair as I shifted, tickling my neck, and I hunched my shoulders, giggling.

Bastian groaned and said, "Stop fidgeting, little witch," without opening his eyes. I extricated myself from the one, heavy paw that was flopping over my stomach, and tugged sleepily at the tapes of Akiva's hood. They untied easily, and the hood slipped from my shoulders. It made a little pile beside me, but it was only after I heard someone shuffling in the kitchen that I realised what this meant. I sprang to my feet with a yell, and Bastian rolled over with a startled yelp of his own.

"Akiva!"

"Who else?" said Akiva irritably.

"Mara let you go?"

Her brows rose. "You're well informed. Child, is that any way to treat my hood?" As she shook it out, she cast a sharp glance at Bastian. "I see you've made yourself quite at home, wolf."

"Last night was a seventh year at full moon," Bastian said, between his teeth. "If you don't know better than to let a child wander deep forest on *that* particular anniversary, *I* do."

Akiva eyed him narrowly, then nodded. "I'm in your debt, wolf. I was unavoidably absent, and I'm grateful you happened to be near. But my injunction still stands, as of dusk tonight. I'll thank you to be off my wardship by then."

To my surprise, Bastian took this in perfectly good grace. I did not.

"Why does Bastian have to leave?" I demanded. It wasn't *fair*.

"You, my child," said Akiva briefly and crushingly, "will be told *what* you need to know, *when* you need to know it. Sit down. Eat. I suppose the wolf had better have something, too."

As she'd done that first morning after I used magic, Akiva had cooked bacon and eggs and sausages. I beamed and took my place at the table with aplomb, but Bastian said, "I've used my allotted time already. The food wouldn't agree with my wolf stomach."

"I think something can be arranged," Akiva said, and twitched a great big *something* in the room. The next moment, Bastian was standing and in his human form, looking exceedingly surprised and not a little bewildered. Akiva drew a deep breath, let it out in an unladylike huff, and said, "There you go. Consider it a thank you. Just be warned: it won't last as long as it usually does."

When we were done with breakfast, Akiva sat back with a satisfied sigh and said briskly, "Very well, child; let us see the extent of the damage. You can do the dishes, wolf."

I couldn't help glancing apprehensively over at the peach-tree workbench, and Akiva followed my gaze sardonically.

"That's as good a place to start as any. What on earth possessed you to quicken dead wood?"

I reddened and explained about the vial, but Akiva began to snort with laughter halfway through my explanation, and I stopped short, unsure whether to be offended or sheepish.

"You foolish child!" she said, cackling to herself. "I expected at the very least that the house would have vanished into deep forest, and that I would have to pull it out again, not to mention all the garden beds that are only half there. As far as I can see, the worst casualties are the bench and your hair. I was expecting to be let go a little sooner, I must admit."

I curled the toes of one foot thoughtfully against the floorboards and frowned. "But what about the salamander and the little green deer? Your workbench is flowering and growing *peaches*."

"Yes, the bench could have been better thought out. You must have pushed a lot of life into that old thing to make it flower like that. As I've told you before, child: everything in moderation. You don't have to bellow to be heard."

My face was hot, then cold. "You mean you're not going to send me away?"

"I'd only have to train somebody new," Akiva told me, giving her own peculiarly dry chuckle. "And goodness only knows what mistakes they'd make: I'm too old and set in my ways to start out again. Better the devil you know, as they say. Now, let's see about getting rid of some of the more exotic animals in the garden."

We spent the rest of the morning chasing queer creatures around the garden while Akiva set magic-laced traps to send them back to their original habitats. Only the salamander and the two green deer refused absolutely to be sent back. Leaping high and nimbly, the deer refused to allow themselves to be caught. Even when Bastian reverted to wolf before them, they were unafraid, and capered around him until I was breathless with laughing.

Bastian was stiff with outrage. He growled at one of the deer, but it only sailed over his head with a gleeful leap, and he sat back with a snarl. "I give up. The creatures are incorrigible!"

He stared balefully at me as I wheezed with laughter, but Akiva said briskly, "No matter. They give an uncommon milk I'll be glad to have."

Neither would the salamander be displaced: it would not leave the fireplace, and when Akiva attempted to pick it up, it began exuding a truly scorching heat. Now that I was no longer warden, I couldn't see exactly what happened, but Akiva seemed to be trying to counter the heat with her own magic, her hands steady around the salamander's glowing skin. The salamander clicked in annoyance, turning almost translucently white, and Akiva dropped it with a grunt of surprise.

"Cheeky!" she scolded, examining her heat-pinked hand. The

salamander curled up again smugly. It knew very well that she was more amused than annoyed. She sat back on her heels and said matter-of-factly, "That's that, then. It could have been worse, I suppose. You do seem to attract the more dangerous of the magical entities."

But she seemed rather approving than otherwise, and I wasn't crushed. Besides, I liked the salamander: and later that day, when we were drinking our tea in front of the fireplace, Akiva stretched out her feet to the warm glow of the salamander with every sign of enjoyment.

Bastian had gone by then, leaving me feeling oddly lonely. I think it was that slightly forlorn feeling that made me do what I hadn't really intended to do—ask about going to Gilbert's party.

Akiva looked momentarily surprised, and then said, "Ah. Kelsey's nephew. Well, why not? You can take a basket from me to Gillian—Gilbert's mother," she added, at my inquiring look. "You may stay on as long as you like: after last night nothing in the forest should frighten you too much. I do apologize for that, child; I was locked in stone, away from anything live. I couldn't so much as send Gwydion to help."

"Bastian helped me," I said, swirling lukewarm tea in my sturdy little mug. I wanted very badly to know why Akiva had sent Bastian away. Instead, I said curiously, "Why did they let you go so soon?"

Mara had seemed as though she were prepared to incarcerate Akiva until the culprit was caught, or Akiva actually proved to be the culprit.

"Gwydion found traces of Kendra in two other wardships as well as mine, and Mara can't imprison Gwydion and Tancred as well as David and me. That's too much forest for Mara to care for alone."

"Not to mention crazy Cassandra darting about," I added, suddenly even more thankful that Akiva was back. I had been too busy these last two days for idle speculation, but now I found myself wondering: if Akiva had been gone much longer, just how long would it have taken for Cassandra to pay me another visit?

Nine

A kiva began to teach me magic the next day. She called it *learning a thing or two*, but we both knew it for what it was, regardless.

First it was learning to raise witchlight, then how to keep the balance in Akiva's multi-layered garden; and finally, how to keep the cottage in its place in the forest. It was in this way that I learned just how far into deep forest we were if the paths were gone, and how frightened I should have been when the paths disappeared that first time.

When I asked Akiva about the sudden change in routine, she said: "Something's brewing and I may not be able to be here as often as I would like."

To my great joy, she added: "Besides, it's about time I made up my mind if you're to be my successor or not, and I rather think you will be."

But by the time Gilbert's party was drawing near and I could still only raise the dimmest and most elementary of witchlight, I was feeling sulky and decidedly sorry for myself. In a fit of petulance, I exploded my latest, pitiful attempt into sparks, and demanded to know *why* she had chosen me as her successor.

"Oh, you'll never be an enchantress," Akiva said coolly,

twitching something in my magic into the correct position. "You'll just have to resign yourself to being ordinary, my child: you've a small talent and no more. Fortunately, great magical talent is *not* a necessity for wardens."

"But you and Cassandra are so strong."

"It helps, but it is not absolutely necessary. Which," she added frankly, "Is a very good thing for you."

I nodded glumly, not really surprised. I knew that I would never achieve more than mediocrity when it came to practical magic. I had seen in both Akiva and Cassandra a depth and talent that I couldn't ever hope to equal.

"Then why did you choose me?"

"Tell me, child: how many deep forest creatures have you encountered?"

"If you count the salamander and the deer things, three," I told her, frowning. "Why is that important?"

"Three encounters in two years," Akiva said, and she was smiling wryly. "Child, do you know how long it was before I saw my first deep forest creature?"

I shook my head soundlessly.

"Five years. I took me five years to catch a glimpse—and *only* a glimpse, mind you—of a mythic. You've seen three in two years, and you're not a warden yet. They seem to seek you out, goodness knows why! I know of only one other person who had that many encounters previous to being a warden."

"Cassandra," I guessed. Only Cassandra could be beautiful, talented, *and* loved by the forest. Horned hedgepigs, but sometimes I wanted to kick her in the shins!

"That's right," Akiva agreed briskly. "I may pick my apprentices, but it's the forest that choses wardens. Wash up and dress for your party, child. Never mind the witchlight; you can try again tomorrow."

It hadn't occurred to me before that day that I hadn't got anything to wear to a party. I stood in my shift, looking down at my meagre (and mostly grubby) collection of clothing in mixed satisfaction and helplessness. The part of me that was still largely pirate was unashamedly proud that I owned no Gwendolen-frocks. The helpless, oddly longing part of me that was no longer pirate but not quite yet lady, felt curiously dissatisfied. I almost opened the package that Mother had given me when Gwendolen had had new party clothes and insisted on me having some too, but something stopped my hand on the strings. When I set off for the party that evening I had on one of my everyday dresses, set off only by the little blue jumper Mother had made me.

Akiva nodded approvingly and gave me a basket at the door. "Enjoy yourself. You're to be up as usual tomorrow morning."

I nodded wordlessly, struck suddenly and inexplicably with butterflies in my stomach. All at once, I wasn't so sure that I wanted to go to the party. If Akiva hadn't bundled me out into the forest without giving me a chance to renege, I might have slunk back to my room and sulked with my witchlight all evening.

It was a cool summer's night outside, clear and untroubled by gnats, and it wasn't long before I began to enjoy my walk despite the butterflies in my stomach.

I went home first to see Mother and Gwendolen. I knew that if there was a party anywhere in the village, Gwendolen was sure to be going, and I wasn't entirely certain I knew how to find Gilbert's house.

I'd only just laid my foot on the steps when Gwendolen opened the door in a flurry of silk and fell into my arms. "Rose! Oh, Rose, I'm so glad to see you! What are you doing here and whatever have you *done* to your hair!"

I grinned naughtily, because her tone was accusatory. "I don't believe you're glad to see me at all," I said.

"But what happened? Your beautiful hair! It's all gone! Just you *wait* until Mother sees you!"

"You're only cross because you want to go to your party," I said, refusing to bewail the freedom of my shorter hair.

"How did you know about—Rose! You're going too, aren't you?"

The open astonishment in her voice brought a touch of colour into my face. I shoved her through the door as I retorted: "Of course! You aren't the only one who was invited, you know!"

"But—but—" Gwendolen stammered. "But you can't go dressed like *that*! Oh, Rose!"

"Don't *'Oh Rose!'* me," I said, grinning to find that my transgressions had been swept away in the all-consuming importance of my dress. "Of course I can go dressed like this. Horned hedgepigs, you're fine enough for the two of us."

"Mother!" Gwendolen protested, appealing to higher authority. "Mother, tell her that she can't go to a party dressed like that!"

Mother emerged from the kitchen to close the front door and kiss my cheek. She stood back to observe my hair and said: "Not as bad as could have been expected, and it will grow back. I'm glad you're here, Rose. Gwen is going without me tonight, and I'll be glad to know you're with her."

Gwendolen gave an exaggerated, world-weary sigh, admitting defeat, and said, "At *least* let me do your hair, Rose."

I let her do my hair if only to distract her attention from my bare feet, and we set out for the party together. Gwendolen's hair was put up high and loose, very grownup. Mine was festooned in a wildly improbable wreath of little blue flowers that sat lopsidedly on my shorn locks and matched my blue cardigan.

We went arm in arm, cotton rustling against silk as Gwendolen tripped along at my side, skipping lightly with every other step. Even the loose curls around her neck bounced with exuberance. I guessed that she was expecting an exhilarating night, especially in the intoxicating freedom from Mother's guiding and sobering hand.

"You will meet Archen and Robert and George and William," she chanted, twirling a step to make her draperies fly out prettily. "And you will dance and laugh and flirt with all the boys!"

"I won't," I warned, scowling, and added darkly, "You're more excited about me being here than *I* am."

Gwendolen put her nose in the air, turning pink.

"I'm not one of your dolls, Gwen."

She huffed. "Well, but you never come along to parties! I want you to enjoy yourself."

"So I will," I said, only half believing it; and added as a hasty afterthought, "But *not* every dance!"

Gwendolen opened her mouth to protest, but by then we had swept into sight of Gilbert's house, where a group of eager young men were waiting. They must have been waiting for Gwendolen to arrive, because when they saw us, we were promptly mobbed. I tried to detach myself from the group, but Gwendolen wouldn't let go of my hand, and clung to me like a small blonde limpet as we were swept through the gates, determined that I would enjoy the party despite myself. I couldn't help being amused despite the discomfort: Gwendolen was in her element here. She bossed and flirted and pouted, ordering this one to get her a drink, and that one to take her shawl, and adjuring still another to dance with me.

Greatly to my relief, Gilbert appeared shortly afterwards. He successfully parted me from Gwendolen, who gave me a coy, sideways smile as I left. I scowled back.

"There had better be a *lot* of caramel apples," I told him irritably. "That's the only thing that would make being mobbed by Gwendolen's beaux worthwhile. She was ordering them all to dance with me!"

Gilbert grinned and said: "Dance with me the whole night, that'll confound 'em! I'll look after you, Rose."

"Not every dance," I said again, determined to sit down in peace for at least *some* part of the evening. "Maybe one. Or two. That will give your feet time to recover from being trod on."

"We might as well get some pie and find somewhere to hide, then," Gilbert suggested cheerfully, and we retreated to a low-hanging branch with loaded plates and no regard to our clothes.

We ate in companionable silence, breaking it only to laugh at any particularly ugly dresses that danced within our orbit, and by the time the first dance was finished I was sitting back with a contented sigh, my belly full.

"Shouldn't you be out there dancing?" I enquired. My experience of parties had taught me that the sons of the house, like the daughters, were almost religiously expected to be constantly on the dancing green.

"If you'll dance with me, I will," Gilbert said promptly, setting his empty plate down on a wobbly trestle that was conveniently near.

I looked up at him curiously. "Don't you want to dance with Gwen?"

"If I wanted to dance with Gwen, I would have asked her," Gilbert said, pulling me to my feet. "I want to dance with you."

"Very well," I said graciously, grandly laying my hand in the crook of his arm. "But don't blame me if you lose your toes."

It had been a long time since I had danced, and my threat was no empty one. There was a master to call the dances, but I lost my way merrily through all of them regardless. Gilbert didn't seem to care about having his toes stood on thoroughly through every other figure in the dance, so we were well matched.

"I'll remember to wear my working boots next time!" he yelled at me over the loud merriment of the music. Gwendolen, passing in the dance, looked much affronted.

When I repeated my apologies after the dance he said dismissively, "You're light, like a butterfly. When the cow steps on my toes, it's another matter."

I laughed aloud at that, and Gwendolen, who was passing by on her way to join the new set forming, immediately demanded to know what I found so amusing in Gilbert's conversation.

"My dancing is being compared to the cow's," I told her, laughing all the more at Gilbert's protests.

Gwendolen looked both disapproving and disappointed, as if she had expected to find Gilbert flirting with me. I raised my brows at her with mischief in my heart, and she scowled and turned on her heel. A moment later I saw her vigorously bossing one of the group of young men surrounding her. The others were evidently laughing at him, but though he looked wretched he also had a mulish jaw very like my own. I wasn't really surprised when, at Gilbert's brief absence to refill the punch bowl, the same boy approached me and asked me nervously to dance.

His name was Harry, and he was one of Gwendolen's regular boys—Liz Gantry's window-friend, too, if I wasn't mistaken. He was too young to be settling down any time soon with Gwendolen or anyone else, so I said to him: "You don't have to do everything she says, you know."

He pushed up his glasses and looked at me properly for the first time, startled. "Sorry, Rose. Only do dance with me, please. She said she'd only dance the next with me if I danced this one with you."

"Oh, all right," I agreed, distantly amused to realise that although every boy present probably knew my name, not a one of them actually *knew* me. I was Gwen's sister; part of the furniture. "But I'm a dreadful dancer and I'll probably trample your toes."

"Oh, just go clockwise no matter what, and you'll be fine," he assured me. "You're trying to go the men's way, I saw you before."

I grinned, because he was right: I *had* been trying to lead. I was so used to dancing the boy's part with Gwen for practise that I could never remember to go the right way.

Fortunately, the next dance only consisted of a few simple polka steps and hops accomplished in a waltz hold, which made it difficult for me to go wrong. Once I got used to the constriction of having an arm about my waist, and being forced to remember to put my own hand on my partner's shoulder, the rest of the steps weren't so difficult. I surprised myself by enjoying it all. Harry, like Gilbert, was informal and boyish, and didn't spend the entire dance turning his head to see where Gwendolen was, much to my approval. Gwen could certainly do worse. He treated me like an agreeable sister, discussing fishing and hunting with a gleeful abandon that I guessed he wasn't permitted to show with Gwendolen. He was an energetic dancer, spinning me for twice the amount of turns the dance demanded and routinely losing his glasses with each hop. I couldn't picture Gwendolen, all polite curtsies and delicate whirls, appreciating his style of dance.

When the dance ended, we parted agreeably. I retreated with Gilbert to the edges of the forest before Gwendolen could send any more boys to dance with me, out of sight but not out of sound of the party. We walked between hedge and forest, being careful to keep just far enough away from deep forest to avoid falling in. I kept Gilbert to my left and the forest to my right, and we shared a half-pie that Gilbert had snatched from the buffet in passing.

"Mother always told us not to go into the forest," Gilbert said through a mouthful. "There were stories about a monstrous wolf who ate the hearts of any young girls who were stupid enough to come in after dark. I thought that if he was after young girls he wouldn't want me and so I used to come in anyway, to find strawberries."

"Liz Gantry said something like that," I said, my interest piqued. Evidently Liz was not the only child to have been terrorized with the story. Bastian really must have been wolf for a long time, to have stories told about him to frighten young children. "Why hearts?"

"I suppose because that's what it always is," Gilbert said. "There was supposed to be a spell on the wolf. My mother said it was nonsense, but she still wouldn't let Betsy and Nan and Grace into the woods after dark."

"Suppose there really is a monster in the forest," I countered, testing how much the curse would let me say before it prevented me from speaking. It was a favourite past-time of mine ever since I had found that if I were sneaky enough, I could tiptoe around the matter. "Maybe under enchantment?"

"We could free it from the spell!" Gilbert was grinning, the light of adventure in his eyes. "What should our monster be, Rose?"

I tossed the question back to him. "What do you think?"

"Oh no, this is your monster! You tell me."

"A wolf," I said, watching the dancers between the foliage and hoping that my voice was just casual enough.

"Just like the legend," Gilbert said approvingly. "Good. Now, what spell is it under?"

I opened my mouth to speak, but nothing came out. The words were there, but no matter how hard I tried, I couldn't make myself say them. I scowled into the forest. Bother! I mustn't have been tiptoeing carefully enough.

At last, I said: "I don't know. It's your turn to tell me."

"He's a prince under a spell," Gilbert said frivolously. "He fell in love with a princess and the evil stepmother put a curse on him because she doesn't want her stepdaughter to marry and take over the kingdom."

It was close enough to the truth to make me think there would be some point in asking Gilbert what he thought would disenchant such a person. When I opened my mouth to ask him it was too late. Other couples were making their way out to the forest's edge, and we soon formed a noisy, cheerful group.

I left not long after, sneaking away while Gilbert was engaged in resupplying the table with food and punch. Gwendolen was horrified, but since the Gantry girls undertook to walk her home and she wasn't forced to leave with me, she soon came around. Cecelia Gantry was a silly little goose as blonde as Gwendolen, but Liz was sensible and not likely to let Gwendolen stay out too long. I wondered, briefly, if Elizabeth remembered sharing a packet of sprinkles with me while we kicked our heels outside Mistress Pennypurse's shopfront those two years ago.

Getting my own back for all the times that Gwendolen had adjured me to make my bed and do the washing, and willing to make Liz laugh, I said to my sister: "Now, Gwen; you're to mind Liz and do just what she says."

I slipped away while Gwen was still opening and closing her mouth in outrage, and Liz laughing, and made good my escape to the forest.

It was peaceful under the trees. Dew had wet the grass and soon my feet were drenched in it, pleasantly cool and clean after the exercise of dancing. I didn't hurry back, wandering among the trees dreamily; though I kept to the path, still cautious of what was to be found in deep forest after dark. The fairies had frightened me more than I liked to admit, even to myself.

But the night was quiet and peaceful around me: friendly, even, and I found myself skipping along the path, light and free, singing under my breath. There was a kind of exuberance in the air, a tickling of excitement in my stomach that made my toes lighter. It felt as though the forest were preparing for something.

Before long I was dancing, spinning perilously close to the edges of the path and unusually nimble. There was a definite pull from the forest now, a heady, gleeful tug that might have set alarm bells ringing in my head if it hadn't been so absolutely clean and joyful. Shadows and lights glittered and danced in the forest beside me, resolving into human-like shapes and then sinking back into the dark green twilight of the forest.

The strange excitement grew in me, along with the sense of invitation emanating from the forest, and in one uncharacteristically graceful leap, I left the path for the forest. Strong hands reached out to welcome me and I was tossed headlong into a wild, laughing dance, where my hands were seized, and I was pulled effortlessly into the moving circle.

The faces of the dancers were beautiful but hard to see, shifting and becoming part of this tree or that hedge, never entirely human yet not disturbingly inhuman. They laughed and danced with quick, wild unfamiliar steps, circling continuously around a couple dressed—or was that their skin?—in vibrant, spring green. At first, tossed about in the circle, I wondered why: then I gave a short crack of laughter at my own stupidity. It was a wedding, with the bride and groom whirling in the very centre.

We circled and laughed, and in the centre of the circle, the bride and groom whirled together as the music became indefinably faster. The ladies, myself included, swayed first to the right, then the left. We were swooped up into the air by our waists and swung in a breathless, graceful arc; only to be let go lightly the next moment in a continuous movement and pirouetted onto the next partner.

I was passed from partner to partner, dancing with tall, beautiful men who tossed me into the air without effort and laughed down into my flushed, exhilarated face. I felt like the youngest sister in a family of older brothers, there to be cosseted and teased, but by no means taken seriously.

One of them, younger than the others, even said: "Here we go, little sister!" and whirled me wildly through the dancers in a mad promenade with barely enough time to swing me into the air before it was time for me to go on to the next partner.

Once, I saw Cassandra in the dance almost opposite me, and for a nasty, cold moment, the world seemed to stand still. But she only nodded at me; a slow, considering incline of the head, and it struck me that she was greeting me as an equal. It occurred to me that the wedding dance was shifting through all the wardships, and that in this dance there *were* no wardships, only forest. My eyes glittered, because that meant I was in a different kind of deep forest altogether. It should have frightened me, but I was too euphoric to allow the feeling to grow.

I forgot about Cassandra after that, caught up in the dance and the wonder. I knew she wouldn't harm me here, where we were both guests; and I knew instinctively that if she tried, these people were entirely capable of stopping her.

The dance grew faster and more complicated, and all my energies were devoted to keeping up with it as it came to the last few rotations. Within the rings of dancers, the bride and groom spun in a tight circle, flicking their bare feet in and out more quickly than my eyes could follow. We did likewise with our partners, feet flashing so high and fast that more than one lady fleetingly displayed a shapely pair of knees. I knew in this gleeful moment that once I left deep forest, I wouldn't be able to dance like this again. It was as much a part of the forest as the trees were.

As we slipped into the final revolution the circle of dancers around me shouted: a high, joyful whoop. The groom lifted his bride into the air in an exuberant, graceful sweep, his hands around her slender waist, and her skirts swirled in a pine-scented whiff of air. There was another shout and then the bride was whirled back down and folded into the arms of her groom, his arm tight about her waist and her arm about his neck. It was graceful and beautiful, and wholly intimate. I looked away, losing myself in the general milling and murmur of voices as everyone else did the same, and the dance broke apart into confusion.

It was hard to remember exactly what happened after that. Perhaps I was falling asleep, or perhaps it was just the way things worked in that kind of deep forest, and one wasn't meant to remember. The last coherent thought that I remembered, before finding myself alone on the path before Akiva's cottage, was a wistful desire to dance again. To my confusion, it was broad daylight on the path. I blinked and rubbed my eyes, bewildered, because *surely* I had only been in deep forest for half an hour! It should by rights still be night. But the triad stretching across the sky proclaimed the day to be some way past mid-morning, prompting the foreboding thought that I might have lost more than just a few hours of night in the dance.

Horned hedgepigs! I thought indignantly. Not again!

"I believe I'm too old for this dance you lead me," sighed Akiva's voice. She was standing just inside the garden gate.

I sucked my cheeks in and said, "Sorry, Akiva."

She raised her brows. "So I imagine. It must have been quite a gathering, to have held you there three days."

"Three days!" I numbly combed my little wreath of blue flowers from my hair and found that they had unaccountably become faded and shrivelled.

Akiva directed her gaze at them with grim meaning. "You've been properly pixie-led, my child."

"There was a wedding," I began, but lapsed into silence at her raised eyebrows. I seemed, I thought mournfully, to fall into scrapes with alarming regularity. There didn't really seem to be any way of defending myself sensibly, and so I sensibly kept quiet.

"Hm," Akiva said, watching me. "Since you can't seem to help your natural stupidity, perhaps it would be just as well to broaden your education."

As reproofs from Akiva went it was a mild one, and I was grateful to escape a boxed ear as I followed her back into the cottage. Despite the three days Akiva told me I had been gone, I felt bright and refreshed. I seemed to remember being given a small cup of something clear and sparkling; something that tasted like water and yet somehow more than water. I wondered quietly about it to myself but didn't mention it to Akiva, since I had a good idea that disclosing such a fact to her would lead to my ears being boxed for the stupidity of drinking anything in such a place and such company.

When I mentioned cautiously that Cassandra had also been at

the dance, Akiva only retorted, "No doubt. Cassandra is not bothered by such trivialities as being pixie-led for days or weeks on end."

I frowned, because my own guess been rather different. "They were *pixies*?"

"Of course not, ignorant child! They were dryads of the deepest forest, and you were fortunate to have lost mere days. Come with me."

She opened a door beside my bedroom door and disappeared through it, much to my astonishment. I gave it a hard look: there had never been a door beside my bedroom door. Interesting.

When I followed Akiva, I found myself in a small library. The walls were lined with books and even the dusty old window was surrounded by shelves stacked perilously with books.

Akiva said shortly, "That section is dryads, and *that* section is Forest. Now for pity's sake learn something!" and left me there.

When she returned with a tray of lunch I was curled up in the fitful light from the window, immersed in a book about dryads. I looked up warily and Akiva set the tray down with a sigh.

"Oh, don't look so woebegone, child. I'm sorry I snapped your head off."

"I'm sorry, too," I said, surprised. I wasn't used to Akiva apologising to me. "It was silly of me. Only it was so much fun, Akiva!"

She sat herself down on a pile of books with a groan and said, "The truth is I was never taught, myself. And I'm blessed if I could keep up with you enough to tell you the things *not* to do before you do 'em! Maybe I started too old."

"What about Gwydion?" I asked. I had never quite dared to ask about him before, but then, neither had Akiva ever seemed so approachable. "Didn't he do anything wrong?"

She laughed. "Oh, I suppose he did. I had him when he was a child of four, and he was a real devil on legs. I don't recall that he was in the habit of meeting with gryphons and dryads, however."

"I'll try harder not to be stupid," I said, with a sinking heart. Akiva's gentleness was more terrifying to me than her frequent, crabbed moods. "Please don't send me away."

Akiva looked startled, and then cackled with laughter. "I doubt the forest would let you go, child, even if I *wanted* to send you away. Which I don't, so let's hear no more fears about being sent home. Unless, of course, you are tired of living with such a grumpy old tartar."

I hastened to assure her I was by no means eager to leave, glowing with relief and a small, warm joy. It was a nice feeling to know that the forest had accepted me, and no less pleasant to know that Akiva had, too.

"That's enough of that!" Akiva told me, with a gruffness that I realised, in some surprise, hid her own pleasure.

So I wasn't taken in, and meekly followed her as she briskly walked around the library shelves, choosing volumes for me to read with decisive quickness and passing them back to me. My armful of books grew quickly, and following behind Akiva, I was at leisure to skim the spines of the books.

In my wandering, I came across a book entitled: *'The Art Of Curse: Theory and Practise'*, which I hooked from the shelf and quickly hid in my pile. It had occurred to me that Bastian was bound to turn up again at some point, and although Akiva had told him in no uncertain terms that this was not to be before my seventeenth birthday, I felt that I would like to be prepared. I didn't know why she'd done such a thing—any more, I thought crossly, than I knew why my birthday had been singled out as the end of the embargo.

When asked, Akiva had said roundly that she didn't propose to consult me as to every decision that she made, and to mind my own business. I felt aggrieved, since I considered that it *was* my business, but I hadn't asked again. Bastian was a touchy subject with Akiva, though she seemed to like him well enough when he was with us.

It struck me that her manner was that of a protective mother, and I recalled Bastian warning me that he was dangerous. Since I didn't see exactly how Bastian was dangerous, I tucked the little red book close in the front of my pinafore and instead turned my mind to things I *could* understand.

Ten

It was a busy year for us after the first few, inactive months. A month into autumn another warden disappeared, spreading a nasty taste of fear through the forest. It occurred to me for the first time that Kendra's disappearance hadn't been an isolated incident, and that if other wardens could disappear, then Akiva could, too.

The disturbances alone weren't what made the year busy, however. Some way into winter, Akiva began receiving midnight guests: mysterious figures that were crabbed and oddly shaped beneath their winter furs. Sometimes I was allowed out of my room to fetch and carry or be stared and prodded at, but other nights Akiva shut and locked my door—at times with a word of explanation, more often without. It seemed as if the days were too short to hold all the necessary tasks, and it was often late into the night by the time I was tucked in bed, reading the little red book I had discovered in the library.

Since I could by now raise a reasonably proficient witchlight, this was not the eye-straining task it would once have been, and the only thing that really troubled me was the lack of sleep. I didn't dare to read the book at any other time: I had learnt by now that it was not a very nice little book, and I very much doubted that Akiva would be happy to find me reading it. The author seemed to enjoy his subject with a macabre blood lust that reminded me of Cassandra, and there were many pages that I skipped over with a grimace of disgust and a hope never to meet the author in the dark of deep forest. It appalled me to learn that a simple curse was one of the easiest forms of magic to perform, easier even than my pitiful little witchlight.

The curses in the book ranged from the simplest spoken curses to more elaborate, webbed constructs that required several speaking parts, each at its own time. The methods for breaking each curse were different, and it was borne in on me that I might not be able to help Bastian until I knew which kind of curse had been pronounced on him. The thing that worried me the most was the fact that curses were not meant to be broken. The author of the book expended much time and much relish explaining this, and it occurred to me for the first time that I had been uncommonly fortunate to have broken the first part of Bastian's curse at all.

All in all, I found myself sickened with the little red book, and one night halfway through winter I threw it down on my bed with a grimace of distaste.

Akiva had been relentless that day, sending me into the forest for fresh supplies of hardy winter herbs that I'd picked only the day before, and with my other duties unabated I was too tired to have the patience to sift through the bad in the book just to find the good.

Yet for all my weariness I didn't seem to be able to sleep; so instead, I crawled out of bed and went to the window, wrapping myself in a warm shawl as I went. Ever since the dragon fever I hadn't needed shoes even in the dead of winter, but the cold still seemed to seep into my back and neck. My witchlight hung above me, glinting a reflection in the window, below which I could see my face, pale and more serious than usual. Through the bedroom door I heard the faint clink of Akiva's tea mug being set down on the little table beside her chair, so I quit the window seat and padded out into the fire-warmed room, glad to know I wasn't alone in my insomnia.

When I wandered into the warm circle of orange light there was a cup of tea waiting for me.

Akiva smirked at me and said, "Can't sleep either, eh? You can help me shuck these toktok pods."

I settled down beside her chair and reached a hand into the bowl for one of the brown, hairy pods. Only Akiva would think of turning a few sleepless hours into work, but I was too pleasantly warm to really object. The toktok pods were tough and wiry, and the task of shucking them involved cracking them open slightly, flicking the kernel out with one finger, and then snatching the finger away to avoid being nipped when the pod sprang shut again.

Sometimes it was hard to tell if a pod had been harvested yet. It was a task that required some concentration to avoid bruised fingers, and with my mind fuddled by the warmth of the fire and the hotness of tea in my belly, I began to find myself more often with nipped fingers than toktok kernels.

I wasn't aware that I'd fallen asleep until I woke up, curled around the half-shucked bowl of toktok pods. A murmur of voices rose and fell in the background, and I opened my eyes sleepily, aware that though one of the voices was Akiva's, the other voices were unknown and strange.

Bright colours danced blurrily in the kitchen beside Akiva's grey form, and I blinked again to clear the clouds of sleep from my eyes. Voices spoke, quick and foreign, and my vision cleared enough to see what the midnight visitors looked like. They were small, quick and colourful; little brown men with long, fat, oddly stiff rolls of hair protruding from bright, baggy caps that were sprinkled with snow. Two of them had threaded beads and pebbles into their round, matted tresses, and tied the bunch in a huge, stiff knot beneath their caps, but the third wore his loose and threaded with feathers.

They all smelled rather peculiar, just like Bastian had at first: evidently they hadn't bathed in some time. They were crowded around the kitchen table as Akiva cut a small portion of something that looked like cheese. Their small brown faces were sharp and acquisitive, and one even went so far as to lick his full brown lips longingly.

The one with feathers in his hair had his fingers curled around the edge of the tabletop, his nose twitching and sniffing just above table level, and his fingers flexed in a way that suggested, had it been anyone but Akiva, he would have snatched up the hunk of cheese and made off with it.

I watched them through my lashes, and a small smile curled my lips. My recent reading told me that they were gnomes, little folk who spent their days in perpetual summer forest, barefoot and chasing leaves. I had longed to meet them since I first learned of their existence, but I didn't dare move for fear that Akiva would send me away if she knew I'd woken. I watched through my lashes until business was concluded and the visitors gone, then allowed Akiva to shake me properly awake and shoo me off to bed.

A peremptory rap on my door woke me early the next morning. I tumbled out of bed, bright-eyed and bubbling with leftover excitement, and opened the door to a grim-faced Akiva.

"David's missing," she said shortly, and flung her hood around my shoulders. I looked up at her familiar, worn face hungrily, suddenly afraid that one day she might not come home either. David was the fourth warden to inexplicably disappear, and the third this year.

"You should have your hood," I said, my chin mulish.

Akiva slapped my hands away from the strings when I tried to untie them, and my chin was no match for her. "Don't be silly, Rose. I have more than one way of slipping through wardships."

Though her voice was harsh, she patted my head briefly, and it occurred to me that Akiva—*Akiva!*—was worried. She took herself off, her front apron pocket bulging slightly with bits and pieces of miscellany from around the house, and I watch her go with a chin tilted higher when I realised that my eyes were suspiciously wet.

The paths remained for only a few moments after Akiva left. Then they silently melted into the snow, and the cold forest closed in on me, bringing an air of deep silence to the cottage. I went about my chores in that silence, followed by the two green deer, who had gone very wide-eyed and were inclined to follow me even into the house, scattering icicles from their thick winter coats. The snow hadn't bothered them at all, but they seemed to be able to taste the unease in the air.

They would crowd close at my heels, treading on each other's delicate hoofs, and then leap away in fright whenever their hides touched. It irritated me but I bore with it: it would have been cruel to shout at them when they were so frightened. Even the salamander stayed close, curled about my neck with its natural heat toned down to a more tolerable warmth. The closeness made me realise how much I missed Bastian: the instinctive feeling of certainty when he stood by my side, and the warmth of his furry body when I leaned into his flank.

I ran around the boundaries as fast as I could that night, feeling the wind cold at my back and the vastness of the forest in its pathlessness. Now that I was used to deep forest the lack of paths didn't confuse me, but their absence was a constant nagging loss in the back of my mind. They were like old, familiar signposts that had become so much a part of the scenery that they were not noticed until they fell down and left a hole in the familiarity of the road.

When I returned at last to the safety of home, Akiva was at her workbench, looking very busy and irritable. Her workbench was overflowing with mixed leafy and dry ingredients, some of which were familiar, but most of which were not, spilling out between the peach branches. She was frowning and crushing something in her biggest mortar, jabbing short and sharp with the pestle, but when she saw me, her face brightened.

"There you are! Quick, child: find a feather—blue if possible— and get me a small pebble."

A tingle of excitement sparkled in my stomach. "Did you find David?"

"Yes. But I need an ingredient, and I need bargaining chips for some little friends of mine."

"Is it the gnomes?"

Akiva looked exasperated. "I might have known! Feather, rock, and *then* explanations!"

I ran off in great glee. A weight seemed to have lifted from my shoulders knowing that David was safe, and I had wanted badly to meet the gnomes for myself.

There was a deeply blue-black feather on my windowsill that I had been saving to make a pen of. I snatched it up without a pang and darted out into the garden to find a pebble. The salamander followed me out, mischievously charring the doorframe as it went, and since I knew that it was very capable of walking through the house without burning chunks out of the floor, I concluded that this was the salamander's way of protesting my neglect of it over the last month or two.

Perhaps I shouldn't have encouraged it to hang about my neck this morning. I had been so busy learning, and Akiva teaching, that we had had little time to spare for petting or talking to it. It had become more and more sullen as the days passed.

Akiva glared at it and the singing smell stopped, but when we were out of her sight the door mat burst into tiny, exuberant flames. Its humour much improved, it sidled off sideways into the blackberry bushes. I let it go and gazed about me with my hands on my hips.

To my left the salamander gave off a faint, pearly glow that made the bush around it luminesce. I could see faintly around me, but I didn't have to see to know that there were hundreds of pebbles in the garden. Speckled and plain pebbles, black-brown and white pebbles. None that I could picture in the eager grasp of that colourful little man, while he cooed over it in pleasure. It had to be something special for a gnome.

I opened up my sight to the full glowing glory of the forest lines. The salamander's bush was a node of pulsing energy and there was a misty patch of green where the two deer were sleeping. The rest of the garden looked just as it had always looked: lively, with its patches of colour and variety, but without anything to interest a gnome. I searched again, this time following each thread until it met with another. Then I saw it, almost hidden within the glowing pearl that was the salamander: a smaller, more moonlike luminescence. It was the very thing I was looking for: smooth, oval, and milky white, glowing with moonshine.

"Aha!" I said aloud, and gleefully burrowed into the blackberry patch in search of the salamander. Some minutes later; hot, dusty and rather badly scratched, I realised that Akiva's garden beds, like everything else in the forest, were bigger inside than out. I scowled into the depths of the berry patch, and gathered the forest lines in both hands, pulling the section of blackberry determinedly toward myself.

Dark branches rushed toward me, and I flinched but went on pulling. In a moment the salamander winked into sight, looking startled and slightly offended. For an instant we stared at each other, then the salamander uncurled and took itself off further into the bushes, leaving the pebble to me.

In the waning of the salamander's white heat the luminescence of the pebble faded, and it became a simple white stone. I held it for some time, unsure, but when I closed my eyes, I could still see the moonlight in it amidst the glitter of forest lines. I tucked it into my apron pocket where it made a small, oddly heavy bulge, and backed out of the bushes.

"Show me," Akiva demanded, as soon as I stepped into the house. I held out the feather and rock for her inspection, and she nodded briefly with what seemed to be relief. "Very good. Now listen carefully, child. There's an old, banded tree stump in deep forest not far from the creek: you'll know it when you see it. Take the feather and the pebble, and find it."

I nodded, biting my lips to stop the questions that were bubbling on the tip of my tongue. I had a feeling that if I spoke out of turn again, Akiva would box my ears.

"Put the calling cards on the top of the stump and turn once, clockwise," she said. "Touch one thread for each pole of the compass, and call out the name of the gnome you want at each one. Call for Hari, or Marj if Hari doesn't come. Repeat that back to me."

I did so, at high speed and in one breath, prancing on the balls of my feet. Akiva gave me a Look.

"I need a distilment of fine-graded blueroot: do *not* under any circumstances allow the gnome to take the pebble or feather until you've seen that it's true blueroot. They are very polite and very sly, and if they can take the payment without giving the items, they will do so. True blueroot will be unmistakable: there's no blue like it. Don't bring me back anything else."

The tree stump wasn't where it ought to have been. I knew the spot well enough: it was a wide, grassy glade just past the rock where I washed the clothes, clear and sunny in the daylight but now cool and mysterious by moonlight. The glade was still there, white and pure in winter, but the stump was not.

I glared at the empty space that should have been filled with tree stump. Akiva needed the blueroot *now*, and I didn't appreciate the forest playing its little tricks off on me.

I drew in the power of the wardship, figuratively stepping on Akiva's toes a little, and pulled the stump to myself just as I had done to the bushes in the garden. It came reluctantly, and I had the feeling that the forest had wanted to play. I ignored its injured consciousness and drew the stump back to the glade firmly, the forest sulky but willing enough to help once it understood that I wouldn't put up with the nonsense tonight. I put the things out on the stump just as Akiva had told me to do, sweeping the snow away first, and called Hari to me.

Dizzy from the spinning, I didn't at first notice the small brown hand with its creeping fingers. When I did, I slapped one hand over the feather and stone, nipping his questing fingers along with them.

"Ah, pretty leddy, pretty leddy; you is too quick fo' me!" said a little lopsided voice, disarmingly.

It was my favourite gnome from the night before, the one with feathers threaded through his dreadlocks. Insensibly, my fingers lost their tight grip on the feather and stone, and I realised in mingled fascination and indignation that I could be very easily beguiled into giving Hari the items out of hand.

I put out my chin and stared at him, searching for the enchantment that he had spun, cobweb-like, around himself. It took only a moment to find it: it was bound up in his voice.

"Cleva, cleva leddy," he crooned, and even knowing about the enchantment, I still felt the pull of his voice.

"You stop that!" I told him, but he only grinned up at me and held up a gold coin between thumb and forefinger.

"For the beautiful leddy I have gold."

"No gold," I said firmly, feeling the added bargaining edge to his colourful voice. "I want blueroot, and *only* blueroot."

"Ah, blueroot. Verra, verra valu-able," Hari said, his voice weaving up and down, and his eyes crafty. "Not for these few, liddle tings."

I shrugged, and held the moonstone up to the moonlight as he had done with the coin, between thumb and forefinger. A shaft of moonlight beamed palely down, and the stone was transformed into the glowing pearly orb that I had first seen, its glow reflecting smoothly on Hari's face and the small white teeth that showed through parted lips. In the shadow it cast, the feather seemed to be a pinion; dark, midnight blue and strong.

Hari's fingers twitched involuntarily. He swallowed, and pulled a vial from inside his shapeless, striped shirt, his eyes still on the moonstone.

I examined the deep blue liquid through clear glass, my hand still firmly curled around the items. I scowled at him. "That isn't blueroot."

He grinned, unoffended. "How did the pretty leddy know?"

"I want real blueroot," I said, pulling my hand out of reach of his clinging fingers. I had been fairly certain that Hari's first offer would be a false one, and I wanted to make sure that this time he would give me the real thing for fear of my pretended knowledge.

Hari tossed another vial to me, this one crystal instead of glass, and I found that I was holding true blueroot, with no uncertainty about it. Akiva was right, there wasn't any blue like it. Not sea, nor sky: not even sapphire.

I passed my two items to Hari, who said cheerfully: "We do business again, yes," and disappeared with his treasure clutched to his chest. I ran home to Akiva, breathless with triumph and excitement, and presented my bottle. She didn't thank me, but her nod was approving and that was satisfaction enough.

We walked out by the main path. When I asked Akiva about it, she said softly, "The less we travel in deep forest for the time being, the better. The attacker has shown an alarming knowledge of deep forest, and I can only assume he or she is watching us all. I believe David will remain safer if people think he's dead. When we're in the forest speak softly or not at all about our business."

I nodded soberly and kept my mouth closed for the rest of the journey. Somehow I wasn't really surprised when Akiva turned in at my mother's gate and opened the door without preamble. Mother was the sensible choice if Akiva wanted to be discreet.

Mother was washing indoors, a thing I had never seen her do before, but when I saw the bloodied water and the watered-down stains on her apron, I understood it.

"No change," Mother said, and I thought Akiva looked relieved rather than otherwise. "Gwen's watching him."

"I'll bring Rose's things around later," Akiva said. Mother nodded, and I realised a little indignantly that I was expected to remain with David. "Come, Rose; I need your help."

David was in Father's study, laid on the bed from our guest room and wedged snugly between the big old writing desk and grandma's sewing cabinet. Father's room was a good choice: the guest room faced the road, whereas Father's study backed onto the open hills, with windows that were shielded by three large evergreens. It would be difficult for anyone to catch sight of David there.

Close to, I could see that David wasn't as young as my dream had led me to believe. In sleep or coma his face was relaxed and untroubled, but there were creases about his eyes and a deepness to the line of his cheeks that suggested he was perhaps only a few years younger than Mother.

The serenity of his face puzzled me: somehow I'd expected terror or pain to be etched into his features. The attack, while bloody, must have been very sudden and short. I wondered if he'd seen it coming, and the first doubts as to the attacker being

168

Cassandra filtered slowly into my subconscious. I felt uneasily that Cassandra would have played with her victims before finishing them, and it left me with the frightening knowledge that the choice was now between the remaining six wardens, all of whom had appeared perfectly sane and reasonable. Somehow I'd been more comfortable thinking that of *course* it must be Cassandra.

"Poor boy," Mother said compassionately. She stood in the doorway drying her hands on her apron and adding to the blood-stains on it.

"Margot, take his head if you please," said Akiva. "Rose, his hands. Hold them fast."

Mother sat on the bed at David's head, smoothing back the long strands of hair that were beginning to curl, her hands competent and gentle. I took a firm hold on his wrists and leaned my weight a little forward, ready to apply pressure if need be.

Akiva uncorked her small vial of potion and said, "Steady now," as she tilted the bottle over David's mouth.

Black liquid flowed smoothly out, a little more quickly than honey but by no means as quickly as hot tea, and David spasmed as it hit his tongue. Mother's hands, which had been gently stroking his brow, fastened with vice-like strength around his head, and I had to lean all my weight on David's wrists to prevent his thrashing from knocking the bottle out of Akiva's hands. He struggled, but we held him tight until every last drop of the black liquid was swallowed and Akiva nodded at us to step back.

David's eyes had opened during the struggle, and now he stared at the ceiling with huge black irises that were horrible in their sight-lessness, insensible to the world.

Akiva straightened with a groan and restored the empty bottle to her satchel.

"That's all I can do for now. Rose, you'll remain here until he wakes: I have some forest business that can't be delayed. You will need to draw wards every night while he sleeps."

Mother's eyes flew to me, startled, but I only nodded.

Akiva said, "Well, Margot; what could I do when she was stumbling over every mythic in the forest? Not to mention Cassandra. She's safer knowing these things."

Mother looked rather grim. "Very well, but I wish to know more of Cassandra. And of Bastian. Rose is still young and heedless, and the young man doesn't sound like the kind of person I would wish her to know."

"We will talk downstairs," said Akiva, nodding.

The stairs were wood, and through the faint lines running in them, I heard snatches of conversation.

Akiva said, "I've scared him off for the time being, but I can't protect Rose from him forever. He has some claim on her."

"Because she helped him? I think not."

"He has one chance," Akiva said softly; and despite the sternness with which she treated him, she sounded as if she felt sorry for Bastian. "And he has waited a very long time: Cassandra's vendetta has spanned some decades."

Their voices faded away as they moved into the stone-paved kitchen, and I wrinkled my nose in annoyance. Bastian, I had always been certain, was hiding several things from me: it was annoying to find that both Mother and Akiva were doing so also.

David didn't recover consciousness that week. He lay silent and barely breathing, his eyes still black-irised and staring uselessly at the ceiling until Mother closed them. I walked a boundary around the house and gardens each night, feeling an odd sort of power drawing in around the house, and was charmed to realise that here at least, I would always be warden. It was like my own, small version of the forest.

Akiva returned in due course with my trunk, and I found that she had packed a great many books in with my clothes, all of which I was adjured to read. I went through them eagerly that night, picking out the interesting ones and putting aside the more ordinary ones for later. Gwendolen tripped in blithely as I was sorting through them by David's bedside, looking unusually studious with a fat little book in her own hand. She looked over my books and wrinkled her nose fastidiously.

"Oh, how *boring*, Rose! What a dull life you must have with Akiva!"

I gave her a scornful look and snatched at her own volume. "What's this, Gwen? Going in for a course of serious study?"

Gwendolen tried to snatch it back, flushing, but I held it out of reach.

"Rose! Give it back!"

"Shush!" I adjured her, looking pointedly at David. Gwendolen shushed, but looked pleadingly at me, so I took pity on her and tossed it back.

"Does Mother know you're reading *The Black Knight*?"

Gwen put her nose in the air. "There is nothing remotely improper in it," she informed me coldly. "It is only a romance."

And in spite of my teasing, she read it aloud to David during the day. Fortunately, David's haggard good looks had appealed to her sense of the romantic, and she was happy to take her turn watching him when Mother and I didn't have the time to spare.

Akiva came by every few days, hobbling in to poke David's shoulder and then grunt in annoyance when he didn't wake. She twice forced more of the blueroot potion down his throat and returned at last, at the beginning of the new week, with two huge black crow feathers.

"This has gone on quite long enough," she told the unresponsive David. "Your stubbornness will be your undoing, young man."

She set the feathers alight with a click of her fingers and held the grossly smoking things beneath David's nose. He coughed and weakly protested with meaningless mumbles, but his irises shrank almost immediately until the grey of his eyes could be seen once more.

"That's better," Akiva said approvingly. "Wake up, man!"

David groaned and coughed again, wrackingly. "Go away, you evil old woman. Stop haunting my sleep."

Gwendolen and I snickered into our hands, and even Mother fought a smile as Akiva glared at David.

"Show some gratitude, David McAvee! Sit up and tell me what happened to you."

The grey eyes studied her warily. "I don't know who you are. Have you kidnapped me?"

Akiva's eyebrows snapped together, and she sat back on her heels. "Hm, I didn't expect this. Do you remember who you are?"

"I was looking for someone," David said jerkily. "I don't —remember."

I watched in horrified fascination as a tear slid down his cheek, following the deep line in his cheek.

Mother said sharply, "That's enough. Out, all of you!"

Even Akiva did as she was told, and we left Mother alone with David. Gwendolen looked distinctly tearful on David's behalf, but Akiva's back was stiff with annoyance as she marched down the stairs ahead of us. I left Gwendolen hovering uselessly in the kitchen and followed Akiva out into the garden, where she was glaring with ferocity into the bright winter morning.

"Do you think he was looking for Kendra?" I asked her warily, quite prepared to be told to go away.

But Akiva only sighed. "I very much suspect so: I found him outside the forest entirely. He may have confronted someone."

"And so the kidnapper had to kill him," I finished darkly, forgetting for a moment that this wasn't an adventure story.

"Whoever it was didn't try to kill him: the forest would have intervened even that far out."

"*If* it was a warden," I added helpfully.

She looked at me sharply then nodded. "*If* it was a warden. There was a curse crawling all over David when I found him, a nasty slippery thing that was very well put together. If it's not a warden, it's a very strong, logical magic user."

"What was the curse supposed to do?"

"I don't know." Akiva looked as if she were annoyed with herself. "I had to dismantle it before I could find out what it was meant to do. However, whoever cursed David doesn't know that we have him safe, and I would like to keep it that way until we know a little more; or at least until his memory comes back."

"I've drawn wards every night," I said quietly, feeling sobered.

"Good, good," Akiva murmured distractedly. She was not

looking at me: she was looking to her left, where the forest stretched out, bleak and barren with the winter. "Continue to do so. Run along now."

I did as I was told and went back into the house. By late morning Akiva had vanished into the forest and I found myself still at home with Mother and Gwendolen, almost as if nothing had ever changed.

WE TOLD PEOPLE THAT DAVID WAS FATHER'S BROTHER, addled from the northern wars. Everyone was kind and understanding, and he was drawn into our circle easily. Thankfully there were no dancing parties at that time of year, and I could spend most nights sitting before the fire with Mother and David while Gwen sewed frocks for the coming spring and dreamed of conquests with a bewitching smile on her cherry lips.

David continued all winter without recovering his memory. I played chess with him of an evening, and sometimes with Gilbert, who turned up with startling regularity along with Gwendolen's hangers-on. I found myself glad of his company, and when David was disinclined to talk to anyone but Mother, Gilbert and I would quite often walk along the borders of the forest.

I missed the sound and the feel of the forest, but more especially of *deep* forest. As we walked, I could always feel the pull of it, yearning and somehow frightened. There was an uneasiness to the air that made me more worried for Akiva and the remaining wardens than ever before.

Mostly we talked of Gilbert's farm, the harvest and his plans for the spring planting. Gilbert was eager and knowledgeable on the subject, and I could tell that he loved the farm very much. I didn't know why exactly he chose me to confide in, but I found the subject interesting enough to ask questions, and Gilbert seemed to enjoy answering them.

Sometimes we talked playfully about the supposed monster in the forest and how we would free him from his enchantment. This subject I found more interesting but of no practical value, since

Gilbert had no better idea than I of how to break Bastian's curse. I kept niggling at the idea, however, and it became something of a joke between the two of us, something to laugh at when we didn't feel like talking seriously.

When spring came with youthful spurts of green in even the most deadened tree branches, Akiva came to fetch me once more. David was doing well by then, though he was still without his memory, and another warden had disappeared. The thought in both of our minds was that Akiva could also disappear at any moment, and it seemed to me that she had come to fetch me because she wanted to have the wardship taken care of if she weren't there to look after it.

"Has the council found out anything yet?" I asked, as we walked through a sweet-smelling patch of pines on our way home.

"The council is rather thin on the ground at the moment," said Akiva, rather grimly. "Gwydion and Mara are still searching, but the other wardens are keeping to their wardships as much as possible. The forest is suffering."

I nodded silently, because I had felt as much. "Did you find anything?"

"Perhaps." Akiva was short. "I have no doubt that it's one of the wardens. What I don't know is who, why, or how."

"That's a lot we don't know," I said dissatisfiedly.

I had been so busy looking after David and trying to find out how to break Bastian's curse that I hadn't had a spare thought for finding the rogue warden. I think that in some subconscious way, I had assumed that Akiva would make it all right: that no one could stay hidden from her shrewd grey eyes for long. It hadn't occurred to me that there might be something that was too big for even Akiva to fix.

But today I felt the truth of it keenly, just as I had felt keenly Akiva's danger for the first time those few months ago. The forest didn't seem so welcoming as it once had.

Eleven

∽

I was shuttled back and forth between home and the forest through the final months of my sixteenth year. Each night I walked home to set the wards around the house, protecting David from notice; then I walked back again. I came to enjoy the quiet of my nightly walks despite the new, uneasy stillness I felt in the forest.

While the days remained warmer and longer, I stayed for dinner; Gilbert was almost as often with us, playing chess with David and sharing a supper plate with me. We squabbled over treats and quarrelled amicably about the Wolf of the Forest.

Gwendolen was rarely without one or two dinner guests, either. Sometimes it was the Gantry girls, whose company I really enjoyed, but more often it was one or two of her beaux, whose company I could have done without. Gwendolen seemed to like them all impartially, but from conversations with Mother and Liz Gantry, I discovered that Gwendolen had also attracted the notice of a certain, older man who had lost his young wife just over a year ago.

Liz as well as Mother seemed to think his chances were good, and both of them seemed to be relieved at the idea: Mother because she liked the man, and Liz, I had begun to suspect, because she was a little bit sweet on her friend Harry. I had a feeling that she would be glad to see him free from Gwendolen's coils.

Gwendolen didn't mention the man at all and looked away when his name was mentioned. This, I discovered to my surprise, seemed to mean that she liked him very much. When I asked her about him, eyeing her narrowly, she would only tell me that his name was Thomas and that he was a blacksmith, and wasn't very forthcoming with any other information. Surprisingly enough, she also didn't mention anything about her imminently approaching sixteenth birthday, when she would no longer have to wait before mother would allow her to be engaged. Since this was another of her favourite subjects, it was likewise mystifying.

When I had a spare moment, I took myself off to the place where Akiva had found David. The field where she had found him was just outside the forest and still in disorder, even after a few months' respite. Leaves had been dashed from the surrounding trees, and the bareness of the boughs made it easy to see where branches were missing.

Others, cracked almost to breaking point, hung forlornly from their trunks, and smaller branches lay here and there on the grass below, as if a storm had passed through. I took it in with silent rage and asked myself what sort of curse could have caused this much damage. There were still streaks of blood in the grass where David had lain, though they should have washed away when the snow melted, and the deep gouges in the earth looked more ruddy than earthy.

The blood was mingled with an oily residue of curse, and I rubbed two fingers over a patch resentfully, disgusted at the way it soiled the forest air around it. I wiped my hand gingerly on my apron and threw another thoughtful look around the clearing. I remembered the gashes on David's arms, and it occurred to me to wonder for the first time if the attacker might have been an animal. The gouges on the ground were large and widely spread, as if the animal had been very, very big. More importantly, they were *familiar*.

Horned hedgepigs, where had I seen those before? Another circle of ruined trees sprang to my mind, these ones snow-encrusted; and the sound of a gryphon screaming in pain seemed to echo in my ears again. They were gryphon claw marks! I was sure of it.

If someone really *had* set a gryphon to attack David, they had probably set it to attack me as well. I puffed out my cheeks in quick surprise. I'd been lucky that time. I was pretty sure that it was Mara who saved me from the gryphon: I had recognised her black-and-white hair when I saw her on the warden council.

No one had been there for David when he was cursed and attacked. My jaw became mulish but this time I didn't try to stop it. Somebody was going to *pay* for David.

I crouched by the greasy scarf of curse again and pinched it between my forefinger and thumb, grimacing. Patchy but clear, it trailed back into the forest. I followed it, unspinning it as I went. It gave me great pleasure to take the twisted nastiness and repurpose it to shore up the fraying edges of the forest, which had been starting to show for quite some time now.

I followed the trail over Kendra's boundary, stopping briefly to snatch a leafy sprig and tuck it into my buttonhole before I stepped over the invisible line. The forest around me went in an instant from new spring green to early, russet autumn. I could still see a trace of the curse corrupting the gold of the forest lines, but the trace vanished after I crossed into Kendra's old wardship. I couldn't tell if it was gone because I didn't have Akiva's hood, or if it really had disappeared.

I scowled, hands on hips, but the forest wasn't to be intimidated into giving up anything else. In the end I had to be content with dissipating the remaining threads that I could still see.

I was scattering those few threads to the breeze when I felt a twinge in the forest lines that meant someone else had entered Kendra's wardship. It was a gentle twinge, but it was enough to startle me: I couldn't help remembering that two wardens had disappeared from this wardship. My inability to see the forest lines here made me feel uncomfortably blind, and I hurried for the border with a chill crawling uncomfortably down my neck.

I had almost reached it when I saw Mara striding through the trees toward me. Relief flooded through me at the sight of her sensible, no-nonsense face, and I waved, forgetting that though I knew her face, we had never actually met.

She stopped, frowning, but wasn't slow to work it out. "Ah. Rose?"

I nodded, wondering if I should curtsey.

"You shouldn't be about at a time like this," she said. "Stay in Akiva's wardship where she can keep you safe."

I nodded again and made my way back home without protest, but as I left deep forest for the path, I wondered very much who was going to keep Akiva safe.

As the spring wore on and Akiva didn't vanish, I was able to push my fears to the back of my mind. She began to teach me the proper modes of communication with mythics (by which I learned that I had not been *nearly* respectful enough to the gryphon I had met) and the forest began to feel safe again: or at least as safe as it had always felt.

Akiva sometimes took me into other wardships: journeys to assist the birth of an oddly-coloured, less-than-human creature, or to find new plants; and once to help bind up a wound that Gwydion had gotten from a wild boar. His wardship was in late summer, only months ahead of Akiva's, and the forest had begun to go wrong for him just like it had for the rest of the wardens. As we travelled through the warden-less pieces of deep forest, we saw the decay and general *malaise* that the forest had fallen into.

"It looks like its fading away," I said in sorrow, when we returned from patching up Gwydion. "Can't it do without a warden?"

"No," said Akiva. "It's the balance. Never a forest without a human warden; that's the way it works. That's how the forest remains Forest even though each of us are in different places and sometimes different countries. If there were no wardens, there would be no deep forest."

I shivered. I couldn't think of existing without deep forest now that I knew of it: there was such a depth of quietness to it, and at the same time such a heady excitement. I didn't know how Mother and Gwendolen could exist in their flat, simple little lives with only parties and villages to brighten their days. I felt as though I had been blind and deaf before I went into deep forest.

"Can't Mara look after it?"

"She is," said Akiva shortly. "By and large. As are we all: the council as a whole is meant to care for empty wardships until a successor is chosen. But Mara has her own wardship to attend to, and it's not so easy to meld wardships. It means more power, but a lot more work."

"How much more power?" I asked curiously.

"Each successive wardship exponentially increases the power a warden can draw on," said Akiva. "I've never known a warden to take on more than three at a time. Six is unheard of. The warden who took it on would be the most powerful warden the forest has seen."

I sucked in a breath and said: "That's a pretty good motive."

"Perhaps, but no one could tell who the wardships would be appointed to. It would make the risk of killing hardly worthwhile."

"Who *are* the wardships going to be appointed to?"

"It'll be decided tomorrow when the council meets. The vote seems to be pretty evenly divided between appointing them all to Mara or distributing them amongst all the wardens. Mara is the elder, so it's really her decision without need of a vote but she insists that a council vote shall decide the matter. Cassandra's the dark horse: she could say yea or nay, whichever drops into her pretty little head at the time."

"Which will you vote for?"

"With more power, Mara should be able to prevent another attack," Akiva said, shrugging. "I don't like any of us having that much power over the others, but if anyone has to do it, I would choose Mara. She hasn't leapt at the chance, and she could have if she wanted to. I like that."

"So you'll vote in favour of Mara?"

"Most likely. We'll see when the case comes up tomorrow."

"Can I come?"

"No. I want you to be with David. I don't think anyone knows that he's alive, but I'd rather not take the chance while all of us are otherwise occupied."

"There's no getting out of it, then," I said gloomily. Akiva raised her brows at me, and I explained, "The first dance of the spring is tonight."

Akiva's lips curved in the first real smile I had seen on her since the summer. "I am very much afraid that you will simply have to suffer, child."

I went to the dance that night feeling rather aggrieved. I felt that I had been shut out of all that was adventurous and interesting, and left to do the mundane chores. I sulked in the shadow of the refreshment table until Gwendolen came and adjured me not to be so grumpy, and David forcibly bore me off to dance. I kept an eye out for Gwendolen's widower, but when I asked her about him, she said airily, "Oh, he's not here tonight; he doesn't always come."

I couldn't help but grin. I liked the man already.

When David wasn't dancing with me, he was dancing with Mother. It had been years since I'd seen her dance: in fact, the last time I had seen her dance was with Father. I was surprised to find that she danced light and fast, almost like one of the deep forest dryads. With her face flushed and her blue eyes bright, she looked like one of the young people. I saw more than one knowing look exchanged between the matrons attending the refreshment table. David, his memory still not intact, looked happier than I had ever seen him. I wondered what would happen when he regained it—his attacker, Kendra, and all—and I wondered if I should mention Kendra to Mother.

After David I danced with Gilbert and also Harry, who was now quite willing to dance with me when Gwendolen was otherwise occupied. Wanting to do Liz Gantry a favour, I'd suggested her as a likely partner, and I had the smug satisfaction of seeing them dancing animatedly together some time later. Harry had at first been doubtful, remarking that it was a bit too much like dancing with his sisters, but if Elizabeth wasn't quite so brilliantly lovely as Gwen, she had her own mischievous charm, and she was looking very pretty tonight. Once he got over the habit of thinking of Liz as his sister, Harry might come to see things in a different light. It certainly wouldn't do Gwendolen any harm to lose a few of her admirers to other girls.

I found myself part of a noisy group of four at supper time, much to my surprise. Liz and Harry had joined Gilbert and me, and we made a cheerful ring around a flat-topped tree stump, which we had turned into our own refreshment table. To my amusement, Harry didn't look as if he were pining to be a part of the crowd around Gwendolen. He joined with enthusiasm in the conversation that had somehow turned to a light-hearted discussion of what Gilbert in sepulchral tones called *The Werewolf of the Forest*, and volunteered the information that his second cousin twice removed had supposedly seen the creature.

"And did your cousin have her heart eaten?" enquired Gilbert, cheerfully bloodthirsty.

"Unfortunately not," Harry said, likewise ghoulish. "She's ninety if she's a day and she must have been fifty then. *I* think her mangy little heart was so shrivelled and wrinkled that he took one look at it and ran."

I grinned, because I had gathered that Bastian did tend to like pretty women better. "Gilbert says that he's a prince put under a spell by someone's jealous stepmother."

"I think he was a villager who wanted to marry a duchess," Liz said. "But her family was a wizarding family, so instead of just horse-whipping him they cursed him."

"How would they break the curse, if a witch did it?" I asked, always eager to hear anything that might help.

"In the stories it's always a kiss," said Elizabeth. "They'd probably think it was poetic justice: a romantic boy steals a few kisses, so they curse him until a kiss frees him."

"It's a good thing most families hereabouts aren't witch families, then," Gilbert said, grinning. "Or there'd be more than a few boys turned into whatever animal or plant came first to mind."

I considered the idea. It certainly sounded very like Cassandra. The irony of it would have appealed to her: a kiss to free the man who had broken her heart.

"What if there was more than one part to the curse?" I asked, neatly snatching the last cream puff from the plate before Gilbert could.

"He would have to grovel on his hands and knees in abject apology for a month," Gilbert retorted, and threw the scrunched napkin from the cream puffs at me. "Not unlike young ladies who steal the last cream puff, I'll have you know."

I gave him a creamy grin and licked my fingers.

Liz said, in slow interest, "You know, I've never heard of a woman being cursed before. Isn't that odd? It's always the prince, or the woodcutter."

"That's because villages are over-run by women," Harry said immediately, and dodged an olive that Liz threw at him. "We're all under the thumb, and we know it."

"Only men get cursed because only women are clever enough to break the curses," she retorted, but she was laughing. "It's the natural balance."

I thought about it later, on my way home. I had absentmindedly set the wards for David and said goodbye to Mother and Gwendolen at the house, but Liz's voice stuck in my head, saying, *It's the natural balance.*

It cheered me, because I knew then that whatever Cassandra had intended, and whatever the evil little man who wrote my curse book intended, curses *were* meant to be broken. Just as man was for woman, and woman for man, or medicine for illness, there was always a remedy for a curse. They balanced each other so that nature always remained in harmony. I thought I understood, dimly, the fairies and their bloody sacrifices.

I arrived home quite late, but Akiva hadn't returned. I sighed a little as I pushed open the door to an empty house. The salamander was a glow in the fireplace that faintly lit the room, and despite the moonless dark, I didn't bother to light a lamp. The peach-desk had begun flowering again and the leaves whispered to themselves in the darkness, active in their spring newness. It was a comforting sound in the semidarkness.

I took myself off to bed early, overtired enough to be brightly wide awake, and spent the next few hours sitting bolt upright on my mattress, staring at the lightened square of my window. I don't remember what I thought about, but when I woke the next morning, it was with the pleasant feeling that my seventeenth birthday wasn't far away now. I scrambled out of bed, displacing the salamander, who hissed at me, and dressed myself. The silence from the outer rooms had already told me that Akiva wasn't back yet. It was going to be a busy day.

When at length Akiva did return, it was with the information that Cassandra's deciding voice had swung the vote in favour of Mara. She'd told me herself that Cassandra could decide either way, but I could tell the result puzzled and worried her.

"Cassandra helps no one unless it helps herself as well," she said grimly, when I asked her why it should bother her. "And at the moment I can't see any reason for her to help Mara. I'm flying blind and I don't like it."

I didn't like it, either. Cassandra was in this up to her white, slender neck. Why was she giving power to someone else? A small germ of an idea came into my head: an idea that said Cassandra needed watching.

How, I wondered speculatively, did a person go about following an enchantress? Whatever else it involved, I was pretty sure that a big part of it would be keeping Akiva from finding out.

Fortunately for my plans, Akiva was kept so busy for the next few months that she barely noticed if I was there or gone. The wardships didn't take kindly to being amalgamated into one wardship, separate as they were physically, and so long as I did my chores and continued to travel back and forth to put up wards around David, Akiva allowed me to come and go as I pleased. She wouldn't allow me come with her when she travelled out in deep forest, and before long I stopped asking.

I wasn't naïve enough to imagine that Cassandra wouldn't know immediately the moment I stepped onto her wardship. I spent the first month in investigation: wandering Akiva's wardship and analysing the vibrations that the forest put out every time a human stepped into the forest. Before long I was familiar with the particular hum the lines put out, but though I could recognise it I couldn't yet stop it from happening. Unless I transformed myself into a tree or an animal it didn't seem possible to walk into Cassandra's wardship without her knowing. For a week or more, it seemed as though I might have to give up on my idea, until it occurred to me that if I couldn't prevent the disturbance from my presence, I could at least *alter* it.

Bastian had told me once that I set the forest buzzing when I went into deep forest, and I regretfully found out that he wasn't exaggerating. No one else who strayed into deep forest set off half the row that I did when I stepped from the paths. Akiva always made the forest lines sing almost audibly, but the repercussions didn't last nearly as long as they did with me. I wasn't sure if this was because the forest liked me or because I was still too unlearned to be able to manage better.

I first taught myself to soothe the lines as I walked, and practised for weeks until they barely murmured when I slipped into deep forest. When I'd succeeded pretty well at the exercise, I turned my attention to altering the *type* of vibrations I set off in deep forest, and practised that at length, too.

By the time I knew that I was ready, late one night on my way home from drawing the wards over David, the knowledge was bolstered by the equally pleasant knowledge that tomorrow was my birthday.

Twelve

"It's my birthday," I said aloud, to no one in particular. I felt as though it needed to be said aloud, because once again, I didn't feel any different than usual. Seventeen, I thought in dissatisfaction, *ought* to feel different.

"I suppose you want the day off," remarked Akiva, surprising me. It surprised me not only because it was the first remark she had addressed to me in a week, but also because it was the first time in nearly as long that she had acknowledged my presence. Still, a day off was not to be sniffed at, and it would give me the opportunity to try out my new skills at sneaking into Cassandra's wardship.

So I said, "Yes please!" happily; and Akiva gave her dry crack of laughter.

"Off you go, then. Mind you come back for the usual start tomorrow."

She went back to her work and appeared to forget about me again, so I left while I could do so unnoticed.

My pounding heart lent speed to my feet, and I fairly flew through deep forest. I knew that if Cassandra caught me things could get very nasty, very quickly. There was a sparkling feeling in my stomach that wasn't quite pleasant; but with the forest suffering and wardens disappearing, it didn't seem right to give in to cowardice.

This conviction lasted until I was standing at the very cusp of Cassandra's wardship and gazing into the expanse of forest that belonged to her. Then I had to blow out my cheeks and scowl before I could persuade myself not to turn around and simply go home as Akiva thought I had.

"Contemplating suicide, little witch?" asked a well-known voice, mockingly.

I turned my head to see Bastian leaning casually into a pine trunk some feet away, arms crossed. His hair had been cut and his chin shaved, and he looked rather...different.

"It's my birthday," I said, to give myself time to think over what exactly was different about him.

"So I was led to believe," agreed Bastian, strolling closer.

He was smiling in a way that I didn't quite like, and it struck me suddenly that what was different about him was that he was like the old wolf-Bastian I had met at the start. The one that had wanted to eat me. I looked at him more carefully with my forest sight and sure enough, there were tiny tendrils of black mixed in with the gold around him.

I narrowed my eyes at him, but he only grinned more widely.

"What are you doing, little witch?"

"Wardens have been disappearing," I told him succinctly, fighting the urge to keep a wary eye on him.

"And yet, I find I don't care," said Bastian lazily, playing with a strand of my hair. It had regrown well down my back and could now be plaited again, but my plaits have never stayed tidy for more than five minutes. "Cassandra?"

"No, she's still here," I said regretfully. "I think she's got something to do with it."

Bastian stiffened. "So you *were* contemplating suicide."

"I'm just going to have a look around her house," I told him lightly, but Bastian's eyes had narrowed. His hand closed vice-like, around my wrist, and there was no trace of the blackness swirling in his aura. He was for a moment the old, bossy Bastian I knew.

"You are going nowhere but back to Akiva, my love."

I grinned up at him and said, "Catch me if you can!" Then I did the little Lacunan wrist slip that Father had taught me years ago, and took off running.

I heard explosive cursing behind me, and sounds of pursuit, but human Bastian was not as quick as wolf Bastian, and I had a head start. He was still some feet behind when I took a flying leap into Cassandra's wardship.

In my hurry, I only barely remembered to mask my entry, with a quick stab of pure terror a moment before my feet hit the ground. I'd chosen to disguise my signature as that of a rabbit, since I mimicked that particular signature best; and when the faint forest lines I could see showed only the presence of a rabbit, I was able to let out the breath I had been holding. I waved gaily to Bastian, who was prowling furiously on the edges of Cassandra's wardship and flitted off through the trees in search of Cassandra's house.

The forest around me rustled like dry paper as I walked deeper into Cassandra's wardship. My forest sight clashed confusingly with my normal sight, and I was left with the impression of deadened trees and dying grass. Thanks to my months of practise, a small bracelet of blue flowers from Akiva's wardship now allowed me to faintly see the lines; but in Cassandra's wardship, this was more confusing than helpful.

I briefly let the forest lines fade and blinked with normal sight at the panorama around me, but the trees looked green and lush, and the grass was plump and fat as it should be. It was only when I allowed my forest sight to come back that I saw the true state of Cassandra's wardship: dying and old. A kind of deadening drain was preying on the forest's energy, but I couldn't tell where it came from. I kept walking, following the thread that led to Cassandra's house.

Before long I was crouched in the bushes outside the house, methodically touching each thread that led to it to make sure Cassandra wasn't anywhere near. Her house was large and ornate, with delicate mouldings around the door and windows, carved in one piece from massive blocks of marble. I gazed at it in awe, wondering how she had gotten the blocks this far into the forest where the trees were so thick. Trust Cassandra to have something so ostentatious in the middle of a forest where no one else could see it.

It looked like the kind of house that would require an army of servants to maintain, but I didn't think Cassandra was the type of person to appreciate mere mortals nipping about her home where they could possibly interfere with her doings. Despite that, I was wary as I pushed open the massive front door, half expecting an old, villainous butler to appear and offer to take my coat in measured tones.

No such apparition presented itself, and I was left alone to wander the hall. It was a grand hall, large and lofty, with its loftiness all the more pronounced by a floor-to-ceiling mirror at the opposite end. A regiment of doors opened off the hall on either side of me, closing in and forcing me to march toward my reflection. More uncannily still, Cassandra had arranged statues between each door: lifelike statues with horribly human expressions of sorrow and terror on their marble faces. The effect heightened my sense of being marched to my doom between regiments of soldiers.

I gazed at those statues for a long, curious moment, trying to pin down the feeling of captivity they gave me. It came to me at last that it was because they had no feet. Their legs each ended in a solid marble block. It was as if their being statues hadn't been enough for Cassandra: she'd had to take away from them even the idea of independence and freedom.

I remembered the darkness in Cassandra's violet eyes. Suppose, I thought, with a sudden cold chill; suppose that the statues were more than just statues; suppose that *this* was Cassandra's army of servants? She had turned Bastian into a wolf, and it was no great leap from there to turning people into living marble statues.

I looked at the statues again, more intently this time, and it seemed to me that I could see a slow kind of life to their faces. A shiver rippled through me, right to my bones. I stopped looking at them after that, unable to meet the hopeful question I thought I saw in their eyes.

I would have begun by opening the door nearest to me, but one of the statues at the very end of the hall began to move, grating down a shallow groove that seemed to have been made for the purpose.

My heart gave one shocking thump loud in my ears and I almost ran, but the idea of going back to Bastian only to admit defeat was not to be thought of. I huffed out a breath that was just a bit too quick and waited to see what would happen. Following the shallow trough in the hall, the statue grated across to the door opposite and stiffly opened it. I started down the hall toward it before my resolve failed, running lightly down the groove in the centre of the hall. My reflection, pale and reflexively scowling, hurried toward me, our feet pattering on marble in perfect synchrony.

At last I stopped, panting, by the statue. It was a little girl, her face upturned to mine with an expression of hope that frightened me with its expectation. The faces of the statues around me were morphing into varied expressions of hope and fear, as slow as molasses. With a sick heart, I wondered what this little girl could possibly have done to be doomed to such a horrible fate. I wanted to tell her that I was sorry, but there was no sorry for her kind of trouble, and I slid past her with my eyes lowered. I would do what I could.

Cassandra wasn't waiting for me just inside the room as I had been half afraid she would be. After I checked suspiciously behind the door I took a few more steps into the room, discovering myself to be in Cassandra's bedroom. It was the size of a ballroom: all high, ornate ceiling and chandeliers enough to light the room like a light-tower even in daylight. The effect of spaciousness was accentuated by floor-to-ceiling mirrored glass just like in the hall, but in this room the mirrors were on all of the four walls. There was no escaping myself. In them I could see that I had a dirty face and that my pinafore was crooked.

I felt that the mirrors, used to Cassandra's beauty, were mocking me. I straightened my apron self-consciously and rubbed at the dirt on my face, but only managed to smudge it worse than before. I shrugged, resigning myself to grubbiness, and continued with my search.

There wasn't much to be seen, but the little girl must have opened the door to me for a reason. I opened my forest sight on the room. There were barely any lines in all the marble, which didn't really surprise me. The only two things that showed any glimmer of change were a paperweight on the writing desk and a hair comb on the dressing table.

I picked up the paperweight first. It was perfectly round, sitting on a black base, and at first glance it seemed to be an ordinary blown glass paperweight. It had a red burst of colour inside it, but when I picked it up the scarlet burst faded for an instant, and in that instant, I thought I saw faces: imploring, desperate faces peering out at me.

I almost dropped it in revulsion, but something made me tuck it into my pinafore pocket instead, where it made a heavy bulge. It might be that this was what the little girl had wanted me to find, and I found that I couldn't bring myself to leave it. It thumped against my leg as I crossed over to inspect the comb—which, no matter how many times I turned it over and examined it with my forest sight, remained a normal, wooden hair comb.

Faint threads of forest magic ran through it, showing that it had once been a part of forest wood, but there was nothing else interesting about it. I tried putting it in my pocket with the paperweight, but the wooden tines made a loud *tap tap* against the glass that put me on edge, so I tucked it into my hair instead; deep underneath, where it wouldn't be seen.

I gazed around the room one last time but there wasn't anything else of interest and I gladly turned toward the door once again. I had a feeling that I'd been in the mansion longer than it felt, as if time ran differently here, and my skin was crawling with the desire to be out. Even the marble floor beneath my feet seemed to be growing colder, and my footsteps quickened instinctively.

I was just outside the door when a cold hand seized me around the neck. I found myself looking into Cassandra's brilliant violet eyes, and with a detached sort of calm gave myself up for dead.

"What are you doing in my house, little rabbit?" Her voice was conversational, but the fingers around my throat were as unyielding as iron bars. "Did you think I wouldn't notice a rabbit darting about my house?"

Horned hedgepigs! I thought bitterly. How stupid! I should have changed my signature to something else when I entered the house. Of course Cassandra had come to investigate a rabbit running around her marble halls.

"You'd better let me go," I said, holding her eyes with mine. "Akiva is waiting for me."

"And what does the little rabbit have in its pockets?" Cassandra said, her eyes fixed on the bulge in my pocket and utterly ignoring my threat as the pitiful thing it was. "It shouldn't try to steal from me."

She pulled the paperweight from my pocket, spinning it idly from finger to finger, and her gaze wandered coldly over each of the statues in the hall. I saw the slow seep of emotion over their marble faces, from hope to horror.

"Which of my lovelies let this girl in? And why did no one call me?"

I saw the little marble girl tremble, a slow faltering of her eyelashes, and said, "No one let me in. I found your room myself."

"If you *must* lie, try not to lie so obviously," said Cassandra contemptuously. "The doors open to me, and them. No one else."

None of the statues moved but I saw Cassandra's eyes flicker to the little girl, cold and calculating. She knew exactly who had done it.

She smiled icily at them and said, "Very well. I will destroy you all one by one until the traitor steps forward."

The little girl moved as if to slide forward, but the graceful lady opposite her had already grated forward on her marble base.

Cassandra, her head on one side as if she were listening to a soundless voice, shrugged, and said, "You'll do."

The lady disintegrated into a pile of marble dust without so much as a surge of power. Pinned against the marble wall with Cassandra's hand about my throat, a chill of hot and cold shivered through me. The desolation on the stone face of the little girl told me that the graceful woman had most likely been her mother, and the satisfied curl to Cassandra's lips as she glanced back at the little girl only confirmed my guess.

Horned hedgepigs, but I was *angry*. I hadn't known I could be this angry.

After a moment the girl's eyes dropped, and her head bowed.

Cassandra turned back to me. "Why are you in my house, little rabbit? I am becoming impatient."

"I know you're helping her," I said, choking on fury.

The fingers around my throat tightened mercilessly. I'd certainly struck a nerve. David couldn't have been the attacker, and Gwydion wouldn't be. Tancred had disappeared with the other lost wardens, so the attacker could only be another woman.

"I just don't know why. What do you get out of it?"

Cassandra smiled coldly. "I get *you*, little rabbit. You, and the wolf; with no recriminations. Tell him that for me."

She threw me before I had the wit to know what was happening. Threw me clean through the marble walls and deep forest, to land heavily and painfully in Akiva's wardship not five steps from where I had started. Grass punched the breath from my lungs, tossing me willy-nilly into a tree trunk, and as the world came to a halt, I groaned with a mouth full of dirt and grass. When I spat into the earth it came out red with blood.

Through the ringing in my ears, I heard running footsteps, then I was turned carefully onto my back to look dazedly up into Bastian's furious face.

"You stupid child!" he snarled, wiping the blood from my face with fingers that were rough and slightly shaking. "Are you determined to kill yourself?"

I tried to speak, but all that came out was another groan. When I attempted to sit up, Bastian's hand locked around my shoulder unyieldingly and pressed me back into the grass.

"*Must* you always wriggle? Stay still, little witch: you're winded."

I coughed up more blood and grass and said grittily: "I'm *fine*. Let me go."

Being called a stupid child rankled, particularly since I felt that I did deserve it. I put a hand to my head where something was painfully digging in, and found that I still had the comb. It had been shoved further into my hair, drawing blood and tearing out hair as it went. It was a messy object when it came out, but I gazed at it with all the satisfaction of a triumphant victory.

Bastian wiped the blood from his hands and eyed the comb in distaste. "What is it?"

"A comb," I said, wriggling out of his reach to sit up. My crushed lungs sent a spike of pain through my chest, and I gave a small, gulping sob which I turned into another cough. It didn't help.

Bastian shot a sharp look at me that said he wasn't fooled, but he let me climb to my feet with what dignity I could muster before remarking: "I'm not an idiot, little witch. I'm perfectly well aware that it's a comb."

"It's evidence," I said, but my voice sounded unconvincing even to myself. I didn't know what it was evidence of; or what, if anything, it had to do with the disappearing wardens. I only knew that it was something of importance to Cassandra. So I looked down my nose at Bastian, who hadn't risen from his knees, and turned on my heel before he could ask any more difficult questions.

It was only a moment before his voice said agreeably beside me, "Where are you going?"

"Home to Mother," I said, wiping the comb on my apron and tucking it away into one of my pockets. My head throbbed where the hair had been torn out, and I rubbed it thoughtlessly, bloodying my fingers. I wiped the hand on my pinafore and added, "It's my birthday."

"So you mentioned," agreed Bastian. "Little witch, you can't go home all over blood and dirt."

I opened my mouth to tell him that I could go home in whatever state I pleased, when it regretfully occurred to me that he was right. I found a stream on a nearby forest line and whisked myself there, limping. I was aching all over, and the forest jerked sickeningly around me instead of proceeding in the normal swift seamlessness of deep forest lines.

Bastian followed behind, trailing little strands of gold and black along the thread as he went, and I guessed that he was not far from his wolf-phase after waiting for me outside Cassandra's wardship. He was unusually quiet, and I felt that I hadn't been quite kind, so I said, "I'm sorry I bled all over you."

"Oh, I'm beginning to get used to it," Bastian assured me.

He lounged against a tree while I washed my face and neck. Drops of blood clouded the water briefly before being swept away, and my throbbing head lost some of its ache in the coldness of the water. I washed the comb as an afterthought and wrapped it in my pinafore, making a roll just small enough to be shoved under a convenient tree root by the stream.

My dress was old, ragged and dirty, but at least it wasn't bloody, and as the only dress I had that wasn't inches too short, it would have to do. I'd gone through another growth spurt without noticing some time during the spring, and most of my dresses were now too short. It was with a little surprise that, walking beside Bastian, I realised my head now came a little past his shoulder.

"Bastian, you've shrunk," I told him, balancing perilously on tiptoes.

Bastian grinned and picked me up so that my gaze was on a level with his. "Better, little witch?"

"Put me down!" I demanded. I did not care to be treated like one of Gwendolen's ragdolls, and the pressure of Bastian's hands around my waist was hurting my ribs more than I liked to admit.

One of Bastian's brows rose mockingly. "But I haven't given you your birthday present yet!"

"You're fibbing," I said accusingly. "You haven't got a present for me."

Bastian had that black look about him again that I didn't like. Wolf-Bastian would at this point be considering eating me: I didn't know what human-Bastian would do.

"Put me down!"

The black look vanished and Bastian laughed as he set me down. "Very well; you've caught me out. I haven't got a present for you. What would you like?"

"Pecan pie," I said, turning my steps homeward. "And baked peaches and scones."

"That wasn't quite what I had in mind," Bastian remarked. "You need a new dress."

I waved a hand dismissively. "It would only get dirty. Food is what I need. Besides, Gwendolen has probably already begged Mother to make me one."

"Gwendolen is a sensible girl."

"No, she's not," I said regretfully.

Knowing Gwendolen, any dress she badgered Mother into buying or making would be all over frills and flounces. Still, I thought more cheerfully, if she did insist on forcing a dress upon me, I could always contrive to fall into a mud hole on the way home.

We walked in silence until we reached the edge of the forest. I was thinking on my adventure, wondering what would happen now that Cassandra knew I was on to her. Bastian, very shortly after I formed my intention of falling into a mud hole should Gwendolen force a dress upon me, changed back into his wolf-form. He, too, was unusually thoughtful.

When we came into sight of my house through the trees, he stopped walking and said, "Promise me you won't go into Cassandra's wardship again, Rose."

I hedged. "I will promise to *try*. Someone needs to keep an eye on her."

"Let the wardens take care of themselves," Bastian said, on a growl. "Tell Akiva. Let her deal with it."

"Cassandra's still after you," I warned, making an attempt to nudge the conversation in a different direction. "She said that's her part of the bargain: she gets you and me, without recriminations. That's why she's helping."

"Don't try to change the subject, little witch," Bastian said grimly. "*Promise* me you won't go back there."

I looked at him speculatively, measuring the distance between us and the distance to the road. I had no illusions that Bastian wouldn't prevent me leaving the forest until I promised.

"I promise to try," I said again, and slipped sideways into a thread.

Bastian was waiting for me when I came back to fetch the comb that night, a sable shadow I noticed only when he detached himself from the darkness to lope along at my side.

"Since you seem intent on injuring yourself, we may as well collaborate," he said, without preamble. "If you go into Cassandra's wardship, then so do I."

"You can't," I said, angry at his stubbornness. "She'll kill you!"

"Very likely. But if you go, so do I."

"You're trying to guilt me into behaving," I said, with new respect. Bastian was ruthless in his bossiness.

Having achieved his point, Bastian's voice was brisk and cheerful. "Nonsense. Someone has to look after you, and since I'm assuming you're not planning on telling Akiva any of this..."

I opened my mouth to protest indignantly that of *course* I was planning on telling her, when I realised that I wasn't. Perhaps I hadn't been right from the first. There was a scared little part of me that knew wardens who got too close to the truth had a tendency to disappear, and I couldn't bear it if I lost Akiva.

"Oh, very well!" I retorted crossly. "I won't go back in there. But I have to do *something*."

"*We* have to do something," corrected Bastian, and I fancied his voice was a touch smug.

I put my hands on my hips. "Very well then, smarty-britches; what should *we* do?"

"Sarcasm does not become you, little witch," said Bastian. "We reconnoitre, of course."

"Yes, but whose wardship will we scout out?" I demanded. I was a little put out to have my investigation taken over so summarily.

Bastian grinned. "All of them."

WE BEGAN OUR COLLABORATIVE INVESTIGATIONS IN THE late afternoon of the next day. For a good part of the morning, it seemed as though I would not get any spare time at all, and I became grumpier as the day progressed. The changes affecting the forest as a whole were beginning to affect us also: too many wardens had disappeared, and Mara was struggling to maintain hold of what she had.

The result was that our garden beds, along with various unrelated bits and pieces of the forest, had shifted to entirely different locations. That morning, a piece of deep forest had appeared around the side of the cottage, trailing broken forest lines through the grass; and two of the herbal garden beds had disappeared altogether.

Akiva and I spent the morning finding the missing beds and reattaching them to our garden, but there was nothing to be done for the piece of deep forest that seemed to have been actually *torn* from the forest.

It died lingeringly as the day progressed, golden threads dulling to a dark brown and then, finally, to lifeless black. It hurt me inside to feel it dying there, and the pain of it added to my grumpiness until I was ready either to burst into tears or kick something.

To add to my woes, Akiva seemed to have woken from her preoccupation; or woken at least enough to remember that I could make myself useful. She was intent on teaching me how to deal with the smaller disturbances around the forest. Fortunately, just as I thought that I wouldn't be finished before bedtime, there was an odd, calculated knock on the door which usually heralded the arrival of Akiva's more unusual guests. I was bundled out the back way with orders not to return that night.

I ran before she could change her mind, for once not even remotely interested in spying to see who the interesting visitors were. By that time dusk was beginning to creep through the forest, and when I found Bastian, he was in his wolf-shape, as disgruntled as myself. I guessed that he was angry to have used his human time waiting for me; and, feeling an urge to defend myself, I was less than cordial in reply to his snarling, "What took you so long!"

We quarrelled heatedly and childishly until our bad humour was spent, and then sat back and scowled at each other in weary, fuming silence.

At length Bastian raised his chin from his paws and said with grudging amusement, "The thing I love about you, Rose, is that you pull no punches."

"Neither do you," I pointed out. Some of his stringent remarks still stung.

"Now, now, sweetheart," Bastian reproved. "Kiss and make up."

I almost remarked that I wouldn't kiss him even if he were *not* a shaggy and possibly flea-infested wolf, but it occurred to me in time that such a comment would hardly pour oil on the troubled waters. Instead, I nodded and stood up.

"Alright. Where shall we start?"

"If I were not a wolf I would show you," Bastian said lazily, purposely misunderstanding. The tips of his teeth just barely showed in a hunting smile. "The lips are a good place to begin—"

I scowled at him. "I meant where shall we start *looking*. Which wardship?"

"Spoilsport," murmured Bastian, but he rose to his four paws, yawning. "Very well: business it shall be. Who disappeared first?"

I thought back to Kendra's disappearance, frowning. Time seemed to have telescoped, as if it had been decades ago instead of just over a year.

I said, "Kendra. But we don't know which wardship she disappeared from; she was last seen with David."

A little arrogantly, Bastian said, "I'll know. We'll start in David's wardship, and I can follow her trail from there."

I wondered what made him think he would succeed where the most powerful wardens had failed, but he was a wolf, after all; and a magically contrived one at that. No doubt he had his ways and means. I allowed him to lead the way to David's wardship without complaint, reflecting that if he failed, I would at least have the pleasure of crowing at him.

I hadn't visited David's wardship before. It bordered on Akiva's, and was slipping into the first frost of winter when Bastian and I stepped into it. I instinctively masked my forest signature as we entered, feeling the vastness of the wardship that was now Mara's. David's wardship had been added to the others when Mara took over, and now the lines between wardships were faint and nebulous.

Soon they would disappear altogether, the only evidence of their separateness the sudden changes of season between locations.

The forest didn't like it. I could feel its confusion in its struggles to right itself. I found myself thinking that Akiva had been wrong. Wrong to support Mara, wrong to allow this horrible, piecemeal amalgamation. It surprised me, because somehow I had come to think that Akiva was never wrong.

A light evening frost was crystallizing on the grass as we walked, and we proceeded in a soft, crackling of icicles, leaving a trail of dark footprints behind us.

Once, Bastian turned to ask, "Aren't your feet cold, little witch?"

I shook my head impatiently, and he said under his breath: "Ah, yes. Dragon fever."

A little while later he stopped. "Here," he said, sitting back on his haunches. "This is where she began."

"How do you know?" I demanded. I disliked the near sightlessness that came with being in another wardship, and it was annoying of Bastian to sound so assured. All I could see were very faint shadows of the forest lines.

"It's the newest trace of her."

I looked around, frowning. "Which way does it go?"

"You're not going to like this," Bastian warned, his eyes maliciously amused. "It leads right back to Akiva's border."

"That makes sense," I said, ignoring the veiled implication. "David said he helped her over the border and that was the last he saw of her."

"I gather we're not considering Akiva in the light of a suspect?"

"Of course not!" I said indignantly. "Besides, she was with me when most of the wardens disappeared."

"How annoying," Bastian remarked. "I would have enjoyed casting her as the villainess. Still, you did say that Cassandra is helping whoever is doing this; they could each have taken a part."

I was almost unsettled for a brief moment before reason took over. Bastian was only baiting me, and even if Akiva *was* perpetually grumpy, she was not an abductor or a murderer.

I put my hands on my hips and gave Bastian look for look. "Where does it go after Akiva's wardship?"

Bastian gave a lazy wolf-grin and stood up again. "This way, little witch."

We followed the trail all the way back across Akiva's wardship and into Mara's again. This time the point at which we entered was her old border, when her wardship had once been restricted to just one sector of the forest. Now that she controlled six or seven, the entire sector curled around Akiva's like a sea. We were the small island about to be overpowered in the waves, linked only to Cassandra's wardship.

The scent stopped abruptly at a tall white birch tree not long after we passed the border.

"How can it just stop?" I gazed up at the tree, ghostly in the moonlight. "Did she climb it? Did someone catch her here and carry her?"

Bastian drew in a hissing breath of annoyance that was really very commendable coming from a wolf. "There's nothing. *Nothing*. No other trail, no other person. No blood, no struggle. It's as if she ceased to exist."

"Maybe she did," I said, frowning. "What about deeper forest?"

Bastian shot me a hard look. "What do you know about deeper forest, little witch?"

"I danced with the dryads," I said airily, neglecting to mention that Akiva had very nearly boxed my ears for doing so. By the looks of it, Bastian was feeling the same urge.

"Deeper forest is highly dangerous," he said, in exasperation. "You shouldn't know anything about it."

"It's not much use telling me that when I already do," I pointed out. "Should we look there?"

"You need an invitation for deeper forest," Bastian said brusquely. "Leave it well alone."

I heaved a cross sigh so that he would think I'd abandoned the idea, and filed the thought away for future reference.

"Very well; what, then?"

Bastian gave something close to a shrug, and I got the impres-

sion that he was offended at his lack of success. "Nothing. There is
nothing we can do. Who's next?"

"Shona." She had been a tiny, slender warden with glorious red
hair; a quiet young girl who didn't much care for human company
and rarely ventured from her own wardship. "She had lovely hair."

"Your hair is lovely," Bastian said irrelevantly. "Like thistledown
or corn-silk."

"My hair doesn't matter," I said, scowling. There was a caressing
edge to his voice that I didn't like. "Shona was the next one to disappear. Her wardship is to the south of Kendra's."

Bastian grinned lazily. "Oh, very well. Let us go on to Shona's
wardship."

Thirteen

utumn was slow in coming that year, while summer stretched out long and hot. Bastian and I went from wardship to wardship, sneaking past the few remaining wardens and startling at shadows, but we found nothing but traces. Each of them ended as Kendra's trace had done: abruptly and completely. Bastian grew annoyed—more so when I told him crossly not to sulk—and we at last gave up the venture with much less enthusiasm than we had begun.

Akiva disappeared more and more often into unnamed parts, and I found myself at home with Mother and Gwendolen more frequently, just one more young person at the dinner table or in the dance set.

On one such night, I found myself washing dishes with Mother in the kitchen, while dancers kicked up their heels in a reel outside.

"Gwen's showing off," I said, grinning as I watched Gwendolen's pert head turns.

"Thomas is here tonight," Mother said, smiling a little. "She's young yet, but he wants to marry her. She's been behaving disgracefully every time he attends a party."

I narrowed my eyes and searched for the object of Gwendolen's attentions. I fancied that her gaze chanced more often in one direction than any other, and by following the line of her eyes I caught sight of an older admirer sitting at the outskirts of the dance. He was perhaps twenty-two or three, watching Gwendolen and her bevy of admirers with an amused smile.

He didn't join in the chatter and fun, but he was somehow there to put her shawl around her shoulders when it was needed, and ready with refreshments almost before Gwen had time to open her mouth to require them. I laughed to myself, because I knew then that Gideon with his bold eyes and Archen with his quick wit didn't stand a chance against this quiet, thoughtful man. Mother was right about him. I wondered if Gwendolen knew it: she was certainly making an effort to captivate him as best she knew.

Gilbert was there too: he hadn't seen me, but I could see him, stretched out quietly by the refreshment table with his booted feet up on Mother's chopping block and his plate piled high. I could have danced, I suppose: nowadays I had as many willing dance-partners as any girl except Gwendolen. But I found the noisy chatter more annoying than usual, so when I was finished with the dishes I left Mother and David alone and went to sit down next to Gilbert instead.

His face lit up when he saw me. "Rose! You're a sight for sore eyes. I thought you weren't coming."

I shrugged. Akiva had told me to leave her alone for a couple of days, and I had turned up at home only to find the house decked with decorations, and party trestles being set up in the paddock behind the back garden. Mother had hugged me distractedly and then thankfully appropriated me for the setting out of chairs, while Gwendolen danced in excited circles around me; useless for any sort of work in her beautiful green silk dress. It hadn't been a matter of my being at the party; it had been a matter of there being nowhere else for me to go. Gwendolen had tried determinedly to dress me up in my finest clothes, but I dodged all her efforts and skipped around the house doing the wards, conveniently out of sight. The only effort I'd made was to wear the only one of my dresses that was not inches too short. Still conveniently boyish, Gilbert didn't notice.

He grinned affably at me and said, "Come for a walk, Rose; it's too noisy to think around here."

We left the brightness of the lights and chatter for the quietness of the forest. I heaved a sigh of relief that had as much to do with finding myself surrounded by the forest lines as it did the peace and coolness of the forest. The grass never felt the same anywhere else.

Besides, it was pleasant to be walking quietly with someone who didn't expect me to say anything. Bastian had been uncomfortable company lately. It had begun when he came back on the day of my birthday and had only gotten worse; all charming words and black swirling amidst gold. I felt for the first time that he really could be dangerous. It was just one of those Bastian things, a need to make every woman he knew fall in love with him: but it was irritating. It was nice to be walking alongside a man who was content to stroll along with one hand in his pocket, munching at his piece of pie.

"I'm beginning to think that I was right about you after all," he remarked as we strolled beneath the low-hanging branches. "You *are* the fairy queen. You never smile unless you're near the forest."

I smiled mechanically, but the thought left me cold inside. "Believe me, you're lucky I'm not. You have no idea what I could do to you if I *was*."

Gilbert grinned and said teasingly: "I wouldn't mind being in peril from you. You're quite small: I could pick you up and hold you back with one hand."

The next thing I knew, I had been swept off my feet and into Gilbert's arms as lightly as if I were a feather. He grinned down at me again. "See?"

"Put me down!" I protested, though I couldn't help laughing at the smugness of his face. Horned hedgepigs, did everyone consider me to be a sack of potatoes?

Gilbert must have taken the laugh as encouragement, because he only said, more smugly still, "It's too muddy; you would ruin your shoes."

I wriggled my bare toes at him meaningfully, but he chose to ignore my pointed display, and said cheerfully, "Do your worst, fairy."

I bit back another laugh so as not to encourage him and gave him my best scowl. "You'll be sorry," I warned him.

"Oh, is that supposed to scare me?"

"Yes," I said austerely. "Fairies aren't to be trifled with. Neither am I."

"Do your worst," he said again, laughing. He didn't stop walking.

I said thoughtfully: "I think I shall box your ears."

Gilbert snorted. "If that's your worst, I'll be carrying you all the way back to the party."

I put my chin up in dignified silence and tweaked a few forest lines. New grown vines curled around Gilbert's ankles and fastened in a blink, jerking him to his knees and sending me tumbling from his arms. I landed on my back and lost my breath for a few moments, giggling madly up at the stars.

Gilbert groaned and pulled himself toward me, tugging at the vines around his feet. "That was not dignified," he said reprovingly.

I laughed up at him, and a reluctant grin rose to his face.

"All right, all right, I admit defeat. Do let me go, Rose; I think I've lost feeling in my left foot."

I allowed the vines to loosen, and Gilbert sat up thankfully. He leaned forward to help me up, one arm supporting my back and another beneath my elbow, and for a moment our faces were very close. I saw something I didn't recognise in his brown eyes: felt a sudden tenseness in the arm that was around me.

A reflex, perhaps mischievous, made me twitch the forest lines again swiftly, and Gilbert gave a yelp as the vines caught him off balance and tipped him onto his rump in the mud. The moment of unsettling stillness was lost as I stood and pulled him back to his feet, laughing.

He eyed his trousers rather mournfully. "My one consolation is that you're as muddy as I," he said.

I gave a little magic-laced shake to the cotton of my dress and flicked the mud out of it. Smugly, I said, "I don't know what you're talking about."

Gilbert opened and closed his mouth, then finally said, "Your majesty, I beg leave to be your fool. I think I'll feel safer back at the party."

I grinned, but inclined my head graciously. "You may leave the royal presence."

"Only if you promise to dance the next dance with me," Gilbert said, his submission short-lived. "Come to think of it, you might as well come with me."

I took the arm that he offered. "All right. But you have to introduce me to Gwendolen's Thomas."

"Happily," he said cheerfully. "And to anyone else who is safely in love. But don't expect me to introduce you to anyone else."

We were threading our way through the dancers when something slammed into my wards. I was thrown violently to my knees and the party babble silenced in an instant to a mere whisper of sound. Through dazed, fractured sight I saw Thomas looking around sharply.

His eyes met mine with a widening of understanding. He started towards me at a lope, shouldering aside dancers as Gilbert helped me to my feet, his arm around my waist. I heard the muted sound of screams around me, and dancers leaped wildly for cover as Bastian came leaping and snarling through their midst.

Thomas was speaking but I couldn't hear his voice, and my kaleidescoping sight made it hard to read his lips. I thought he was asking if I was all right; and, dimly, it occurred to me that he was a magic user himself.

I put my hand out to grasp his arm and said urgently, "Check the paddock side!"

I felt Bastian's fur beneath my hand, and said, "Go with him, Bastian."

Thomas took off at a run, but Bastian didn't move. I didn't need my full hearing to tell me that he had snarled a 'no' at me.

"Go warn Mother and David," I told Gilbert, disengaging myself from his arms. I knew it was no use arguing with Bastian; and besides, I was glad for the support. "Something just breached my warding."

Gilbert hesitated but went, and I was left leaning on Bastian, still shaken and oddly deafened.

"Where's the breach?"

"Forest side," I said shortly, through the buzzing in my ears. "Quickly!"

Thomas was approaching from the other direction by the time we found the place. It wasn't a full breach: the wards still held, but they had been weakened severely. Whoever or whatever had done this, they were still outside.

"No breach this side," Thomas reported, and ran one hand through his hair. "Is Gwendolen safe?"

"In the house," I told him. My last sight of the party had been of Gwendolen being pushed summarily inside the house by Gilbert. She didn't look pleased.

Bastian snarled. "Someone's coming."

To my surprise, Thomas darted a swift, sharp look around and demanded: "Which direction?"

He evidently had no trouble at all understanding Bastian. I made a mental note to warn Gwendolen that her most pressing suitor was a very strong magic user and that she stood a significant chance of having little wizardling babies.

"Forest!" snapped Bastian. "Rose, stay back!"

I spared an annoyed thought for his bossiness and said coldly, "It's only Akiva and Mara."

I'd sensed their approach for some time now, swift and silent through the forest.

"They felt the attack. They've probably come to check on us."

Bastian took a deep breath through his nose and nodded. "I have their scents now."

"I'll make myself scarce," Thomas said. His arms were crossed over his massive chest as if now that the emergency was over, he didn't know quite what to do. "We have a truce with the wardens; we don't draw on forest magic and they leave us and our magic alone. It's not exactly cordial."

I nodded. "Tell Gwendolen and Mother that it's safe now."

Akiva and Mara came from different directions, rather to my

surprise. Sensing them on the energy lines, I had assumed that they were walking together: but Akiva came directly through the forest as if from the cottage, and Mara appeared along the road just edging the forest. Akiva arrived first by a few seconds, her face lined and grey. I thought she looked relieved when she saw Bastian and me.

"I see you're still alive, then," she said shortly. "Did anyone make it through?"

I barely had time to shake my head before Mara's clipped tones interrupted. "What has your apprentice done this time, Akiva?"

I bristled, but Akiva only said, "Someone tried to force their way through her wards."

"Where's the breach?" Mara cast a professional look at the wards. "I don't see it."

Akiva's voice was grimly approving. "There is no breach: what you felt was the backlash."

"What made you ward your apprentice's house with such severity?" asked Mara, her eyes narrowed. There was an edge to her voice that suggested either that she didn't appreciate being kept out of the loop, or that she had begun to suspect Akiva again.

"Rose was worried about her family," Akiva said easily. "The wards are her own doing. She thought the disturbances in the forest could spill over into the outside. It seems she was right."

Mara raised an eyebrow at me. "Strong wards for an apprentice. Why is the wolf here?"

"I'm protecting my own," Bastian told her, with a touch of insolence. "What are you doing here, Mara?"

She gave him a frosty smile. "We'll see about that, wolf. What were you thinking, Akiva?"

"Rose involved herself," Akiva said, shrugging. "She broke the first clause in the curse. May I suggest we continue this discussion another time? Young Gilbert is coming."

"And the intruder?"

"We didn't find anyone," I said.

"Not even a scent," agreed Bastian. He sounded as if he were annoyed with himself. "Whoever did it had enough power to mask themselves."

Mara seemed to be satisfied, much to my relief. At all events she nodded and swept away; followed shortly by Akiva, who stopped behind only long enough to see me mouth *'He's safe'* in answer to her inquisitive look.

Gilbert arrived breathlessly just moments later. He seemed to find it necessary to put an arm around my waist even though I was leaning on Bastian for support. I was too tired and sore to object to the annoyance as I might usually have done.

"Thomas wants you to come back to the house; he says Gwendolen is worried."

Wearily, I nodded. "All right." I gave Bastian a brief hug and asked, "Will you come in too?"

Bastian shook his shaggy head. "I've already been out of the forest longer than is wise. Take care, little witch. I'd be happier if you were in the forest under my eye."

"You know I can't leave Mother and Gwen." I patted his head absently. "Whoever it was might come back."

Bastian nodded, as if he had expected as much. "At least tell that idiot to take his arm away from your waist."

I laughed, and relayed the message to Gilbert, who had demanded to know what the joke was.

"That's easily fixed," he said cheerfully. He took his arm away only to pick me up again despite my protests. I had to wave my goodbyes over his shoulder to Bastian, who looked balefully after us until we entered the house.

Inside, I was immediately accosted by a tearful Gwendolen, who brightened visibly when she saw that I was being carried. Too happily, she demanded, "Rose! Did you faint?"

I glared at her. "Of course not! Gilbert, put me down!"

Gilbert did so, grinning. I found that my knees weren't as supportive as I would have wished, and the hand that Thomas put under my elbow for support was unexpectedly welcome. His face swam a little before my eyes as he tilted my chin to look frowningly down at me.

"How's the vision?"

I blinked, and my sight cleared enough for me to be able to say truthfully, "Fine. It's fine."

He smiled down at me as if he were amused and said to Mother, "You'd better put her to bed. The wards took a nasty knock, and so did Rose."

Mother nodded, her lips compressed in a thin, worried line.

"I have to draw the wards!" I protested, only weakly resisting being shepherded up the stairs.

"Bed, Rose," said Mother. Over her shoulder, Thomas gave me a slow, deliberate wink that said he would take care of the wards. I allowed myself to be shuffled off to bed.

When I woke the next day, the wards stretched around the house, solid and neat. There was a restful quality to the air, and I caught a sense of Thomas' quiet, single-minded determination in the house wards. I wasn't surprised to find him at the breakfast table with David and Gwendolen when I made my appearance a little later. What *did* surprise me was that fact that Gilbert was there also, and that Gwendolen was looking very smug about it. I guessed from her air of self-satisfied complacency that she had invited him.

I gave her a scowling look: if Gwendolen thought that she was matchmaking, she was fair and far off. I had no intention of becoming Gilbert's sweetheart—as little, I thought crossly, as he had of becoming mine. *Bother* Gwen with her fainting princesses and enchanted princes, and curses broken by a maiden's kiss! I felt a momentary, wistful desire to burn her books one by one.

But as the thought entered my head, a memory entered with it: a memory of Liz and Harry and Gilbert, all of us discussing the curse by firelight. Elizabeth had suggested that a kiss could break the curse, too. A certain speculation entered my thoughts.

I frowned over my porridge distractedly, too busy now to shoot darkling looks at Gwendolen, who was ignoring them in any case. I answered Gilbert's morning pleasantries very much at random, my thoughts far away. Unfortunately, Gwendolen had been ignoring him as studiously as she had been ignoring my scowls, flirting with Thomas and leaving the burden of conversation with me.

At length, Gilbert said ruefully, "Copper for your thoughts, Rose."

I gazed at him blankly, then blinked. "Oh! Sorry, Gil: I was thinking about the curse. I was wondering if Liz was right, and if it takes a kiss to break it."

"You know, I'm beginning to believe in this curse of yours."

"Maybe Thomas knows," I said thoughtfully, and interrupted the conversation between Gwen and Thomas without compunction. "Thomas! Do kisses break curses? Liz says all the stories say so."

Thomas shot me a speculative look. "It depends. What sort of curse is it?"

"It's not a *real* curse," Gilbert assured him, cheerfully helping himself to the last slice of toast before Thomas could. "It's an imaginary one that we made up to go with the legend of the forest."

"The legend of the forest, eh?" Thomas sat back, willing to be amused, but Gwendolen, her conversation with him summarily cut short, didn't look as if she cared for the state of affairs. I had to bite back a grin, because it wasn't like one of her suitors to leave a conversation with her in order to follow someone else's.

"Well, Rose? What is this legend?"

It was a direct question, one the curse wouldn't allow me to answer. I chose to be sneaky, and said, "Gilbert explains it better."

"The werewolf of the forest," Gilbert said, with relish. "Who eats the hearts of any young maidens in the forest. He was cursed centuries ago, and has been looking for someone to break the curse ever since."

Thomas' brows rose; and across the table, David's brow furrowed. I kept one eye on him as Thomas asked, "What sort of curse?"

"Something to find, something to do, and something to give," Gilbert said glibly. It had taken much verbal wrangling to get him to that point, but I felt as though my efforts had been rewarded. Since Gilbert didn't truly know about the curse, he could speak as freely as he chose, whether his words were right or wrong.

I saw David open and close his mouth once and then again, a

look of frowning concentration on his face. Eventually, he said in a puzzled voice: "It sounds...familiar. But I can't—I can't seem to *say* it."

"Liz thinks that the something to find must be a ring or amulet that belonged to the werewolf, and that it has to be given back to him," Gilbert added helpfully. "That's the 'something to give' part."

Thomas folded his arms across his chest. "An imaginary curse, eh?"

"Yes," I told him firmly. I was glad that Mother wasn't there: Thomas' gaze was uncomfortably searching, and one set of sharp eyes watching me was bad enough.

He said slowly, and with slight reluctance, "It's very likely that such a curse would involve a kiss. They're risky at best, however; notoriously complicated and inclined to suck you in if you're not very careful. A person involved in a curse of that sort," he added, his eyes not wavering from mine; "Could find themselves caught a little deeper than they expect and needing to give a little more than they're willing to give."

"Oh, don't take the fun out of it!" begged Gilbert. "Ours is a simple little thing, broken by a maiden's kiss; isn't it, Rose?"

I nodded, hoping that it *was* as simple as that, but Thomas frowned.

"Curses aren't for light talk," he said, and turned back to his conversation with Gwendolen. I could tell that I had worried him, and I was sorry. David also looked quietly perturbed, but whether that was because he was worried or because memories were resurfacing, I couldn't be sure. He must have known something of the curse as a warden, or the gag clause wouldn't have stopped him talking about it. He remained preoccupied and silent for the rest of the meal, his brow furrowed and his eyes on the table, and I decided that it might prove profitable to slip into his room later and find out what he knew.

Thomas and Gwendolen disappeared shortly after breakfast— into the village, if I wasn't mistaken. I would have tried to corner David and find out what he knew, but he had sought safety with

Mother in the garden and I found myself walking with Gilbert by the edge of the wood forest instead.

Gilbert grinned and elbowed me. "They're getting along well, aren't they?"

I followed his line of sight to see Mother looking up at David. She said something in her dry, quiet way that first surprised him, and then made him laugh. It did wonders for his usually sombre face, lightening the grey of his eyes to blue and adding much-needed laugh lines to his cheeks.

"There must be something in the air," I said, grinning sardonically. "Too long of a summer. Too many twilight dances."

"Speaking of which," Gilbert said, "there's one tonight; storytelling and dancing on the village green. Will you come with me?"

"Oh, I'll be there," I said glumly. "Gwendolen will drag me there, if nothing else. It'll be nice to have some peace and quiet when I get back to the forest."

"I meant will you go to the dance with me?" he said.

I frowned, lacking the patience to sift through levels of meaning. Fortunately, before I could answer, Gilbert added: "Rose, I think your wolf is watching us through the trees."

I cast a glance forest-ward, and there was Bastian, prowling. "Ah. He must need to speak with me."

"I'll wait," Gilbert said, in a polite-but-firm way that puzzled me.

"You should go," I told him, oddly grateful to Bastian for interrupting. "I might be all day."

"What about the dance?"

"I'll meet you there," I promised.

Gilbert opened his mouth but closed it again without speaking and nodded. "I'll save a seat for you," he said.

I waited until he had gone before I slipped into deep forest. I had already disappeared around him too many times. I wasn't keen to be hailed as the fairy queen again.

When I came upon him, Bastian's ears were flattened against his skull in a way that boded no good.

I put my hands on my hips, prepared to be scolded, and

demanded without giving quarter, "What have I done this time? Or are you just grumpy today?"

"You took your time!" he accused, thrown off balance. "What are you doing trysting with woodcutters?"

"I wasn't trysting," I said, indignant in my turn. "I was *talking*. What do you want, Bastian?"

"I have a lead on Cassandra," Bastian growled. "I thought you would be interested."

"I *am* interested. What do you mean, a lead?"

"Cassandra has been wandering from her wardship on the first day of every week, late to midnight," he said, less grumpily. "She circles, but always ends up at the centre of Mara's wardship. I didn't realise it was a pattern at first, since I mostly try to avoid the old cow. Tonight she'll go out again, and we'll be waiting. From a safe distance, of course."

I grimaced, regret flooding me. "I can't come tonight."

Bastian's voice became silky. "Why not, little witch?"

"I promised I'd go to the dance tonight."

"You *were* trysting!" Bastian was snarling. "Who is this bumpkin, anyway?"

"He's not a bumpkin!" I shot back, angry in my turn, but realising in the snap of anger that Bastian was just furious enough in earnest to really listen to me. I wanted the old Bastian back: the one that teased me instead of flirting with me. "Anyway, you've *met* him. His name is Gilbert and he came to fetch the medicine for Kelsey that time."

"Gilbert, Gilbert," Bastian muttered to himself, and then, sharply, "Ah! The moonling who said you were the queen of the fairies. What was he doing whispering in your ear and putting his arm around your waist?"

"He wasn't whispering in my ear!"

Bastian shot me an angry, exasperated look, and I put my chin up.

"I enjoy his company," I said evenly, knowing that my calm would only provoke him.

Bastian's amber eyes were molten, and his teeth showed. "As opposed to *what*? Mine?"

"Actually, yes," I said grittily; and it was almost true.

"I thought we were friends, little witch." The anger was gone from Bastian's voice. He sounded stunned.

"So did I," I said tartly, hardening myself. It was difficult to tell if Bastian's hurt was in earnest or an act. "Then you came back, and everything was a pretend."

The hurt tone vanished from Bastian's voice, and he said, quite cheerfully, "What a cynical little witch you are! You should try to be rid of that: it's not becoming."

"It used to be fun," I said wistfully; because for a moment it seemed as though the real Bastian was back.

"All right, all right," he said, lowering his head in feigned submission. "No more pretending. I must be losing my touch—or you're too perceptive for your own good. Now be a good little witch and tell your bumpkin that you're busy. I'll be good."

With real regret, I said, "I can't. I promised Gilbert that I'd be there."

Bastian's eyes darkened stormily again, and I realised in surprise that his annoyance was somewhat more real than I had thought. It struck me that he might think that if I were friends with Gilbert I would be distracted from helping him break the curse.

I said, "I'm still working on your curse, you know."

Bastian gave something like a snarl mixed with a whine and stalked away to the nearest forest thread. He was gone before I could call him back, and I was left staring after him in some perplexity. What ailed him today? I put my hands on my hips and glared after him, but I felt a little badly about everything in general; and so, with a sigh, I went after him.

When I found him, Bastian was in his human form, kneeling by a placid stream and moodily skipping rocks across the waters. He looked up when he heard me approach but didn't speak.

I put my hands on my hips again and said austerely, "You're very grumpy today."

Bastian sat back with a weary laugh. "Ah, Rose; I've lived too long. Go to your dance, enjoy yourself while you can."

"The dance doesn't start until twilight. I don't have to leave yet."

"I'm not good company today, little witch."

"You're never good company," I said cheerfully, kneeling to hug him comfortingly around the neck. I didn't care to see him unhappy. "You're rude and dictatorial and most often grumpy. But I like you just the same."

Bastian laughed again, this time with real amusement, and I sat back, satisfied with myself.

"And you are always such charming company, of course, little witch. Never mind my glooms: I believe I've been wolf too long."

My eyes lit up at the reminder. "That's what I was going to tell you about!" I said. "I think I know what the second part of the curse is!"

Bastian straightened swiftly and leaned forward, his eyes sharply on me. "And, little witch? And?"

I settled myself more comfortably on my knees, ignoring the dampness that seeped through the material at my knees. "I should have seen it before, when Liz told me. I hope you don't mind, Bastian, but I think I have to kiss you."

I eyed him a little warily to gauge his reaction. He didn't *seem* to be repulsed. His face was solemn, but I thought his eyes were dancing, and there was a slight tremor at one corner of his mouth.

"Then by all means proceed, little witch," he said.

So I kissed him. Close up, Bastian the man smelt much as Bastian the wolf did, pleasantly of grass and rich earth. When my lips touched his I tasted the sharp tang of raspberries. For an instant I felt the soft huff of his breath, quick and uneven, on my cheeks. Oddly, the one thing that entered my mind in the spilt second before I kissed him, was the memory of Gwen's voice telling me some few days ago how unpleasant wet kisses were. I was careful to make this one quick and soft and dry, since it didn't seem fair to make Bastian suffer more than he really had to.

When I sat back on my heels Bastian's eyes flickered open. I realised with slight astonishment that he had closed his eyes, and that I had also done so quite naturally, without thinking about it. The fact seemed to bear out Gwendolen's opinion, set against mine, that lovers would *not* eventually become cross-eyed.

For a moment neither of us said anything, Bastian pale and somehow startled, his eyes on my face; myself uncertain whether it had worked or not.

"Did it work?" I asked, breaking the silence.

"In what way?" he said. I had an idea that he was talking more to himself than me, and that what he had said was in some way a dry joke. His face was no longer so pale, but it still seemed startled.

"To break the enchantment, silly," I told him impatiently, ignoring the joke with himself since I knew it was one of those that he wouldn't explain to me.

"I don't think so," Bastian said, and I remembered that the first time I broke part of the spell, the effect had been immediate. I could see no change in the gold swirls around him.

"*Well!*" I said, in annoyance. "What a waste!"

Bastian's eyes leapt to mine, startled again, and he burst out laughing. "Don't look daggers at me, my love. Your kisses must be defective. It *is* the second part, but there's still something missing."

"I expect that's because I haven't had the practice. Gwendolen knows more about that sort of thing." I brightened momentarily. "Of course! Gwendolen can come and kiss you!"

"Certainly not," Bastian said, and I knew the finality of that tone. Besides, it would be no good telling Gwendolen what to do— even supposing the curse would allow it—since the curse would require that she figure it out herself, just as I had.

"Maybe I didn't do it right," I suggested miserably. "I don't really know how to do it properly."

"I'll teach you how sometime, when you've got a likely lad of your own," Bastian said, grinning a little wolfishly down into my woebegone face.

"If I *had* a likely lad, I don't think he'd care for that," I pointed out. Besides, likely lads were in Gwendolen's line, not mine.

Bastian only said, "Hmm. I don't think I'd care for it either. And we can't forget that you're sworn to a life of celibate piracy."

I frowned in thought. "I'll ask Gilbert."

"He's more likely to want to kiss you himself," Bastian warned.

"Piffle!" I told him loftily. "Gwendolen is the one boys want to kiss. I'm quite safe."

Bastian looked at me with something like exasperation. "Gwendolen has nothing whatsoever to do with the case. And as to safety, I've told you often enough that you need someone to look after you."

"All right, I'll ask David," I conceded, giving in to compromise. I had meant to have a talk with him in any case. I jumped to my feet with enthusiasm and turned back to Bastian. "I'll sneak away and meet you *after* the dance."

"Ah, an assignation!" Bastian said, grinning. "Where shall we meet, little witch?"

Fourteen

⌒⌒

I was glad to get away from the dance and even from Gilbert, who tonight was awkward and different. My life, I thought peevishly, had devolved into nothing more than a succession of village dances. Besides, Akiva was busy and secretive, hiding away most days in her library or out in deep forest, and hadn't seemed at all keen for me to be back in the little cottage with her. I wondered if I'd done something wrong. At all events, I thought mulishly; after tonight I was going back to Akiva, whether or not she wanted me. I had an idea she was up to something.

Bastian was waiting for me when I finally managed to slip away without being seen, familiar and wolfish. I had masked my forest signature immediately upon entering the forest, nervous about following Cassandra even on someone else's wardship. Cassandra was not only clever, she knew every thread and vibration in the forest. I was careful not to use the rabbit signature this time.

Bastian trotted forward to me meet me, casual and relaxed. "No movement yet, but it shouldn't be long."

I breathed a sigh of relief. "I thought I wouldn't get here in time. What is she doing, do you think? Is she trying to make Mara disappear?"

"Who knows what goes on in that pretty little head of hers? No, stay *back*, little witch. She'll sense us if we get too close."

"Won't she sense you at once? You most particularly, I mean."

"I've been hiding from Cassandra long enough to have learned a few tricks, little witch. The only place I'm not safe is in her wardship. Quiet now, here she comes."

We stayed nearly a full wardship behind Cassandra, pacing along the threads just quickly enough not to lose her, and just slowly enough to avoid putting out excessive energy that Cassandra would certainly have noticed. I walked with one hand buried in the ruff of Bastian's neck, feeling somehow safer with the warmth of his fur beneath my hand.

We trailed Cassandra until we were in the amalgamated section that had once been many wardships but was now Mara's; then deeper still until we were in the portion of the forest that had always been Mara's. The forest had changed from late summer to winter, to autumn, and back to summer by the time we reached Mara's own wardship. Bastian and I prowled at the edges of the wardship, wary about diving right in.

Faint lines still showed where the division between wardships had once been, and it felt safer to be on the other side of the faintly marked wardship from Cassandra. I gently pinched a forest line between thumb and forefinger, catching a vibration of Cassandra's footsteps, and followed it until I could see her circling Mara's house. Crouched beside Bastian as I was, with my arm around his neck, he could see all that I could see. He growled a low, soft, puzzled growl.

"What's she doing?" I whispered. Bastian's ear twitched as my breath tickled his sensitive ear hairs.

"I don't know. I can't sense any magic."

"Me neither. Perhaps she really is trying to take Mara."

"Mara would be the logical choice, before she comes into the full potential of all the wardships. Hold fast, little witch, something is about to happen."

I had sensed it, too, a gathering of power on the thread I held. There was a slight snap, and then Cassandra was no longer by the house or even on the same thread. An instant later she materialized some way behind us, sending a ripple through the forest.

"The house, now!" Bastian shot at me.

We turned tail and ran. Mara's house, neat and square and orderly in the forest, was our only hope of safety. We dashed through myriad, lightning-fast threads to get there ahead of Cassandra, shocked at the suddenness of detection. Blackness pursued us, long thin tendrils of Cassandra's magic shooting along the threads after us at high speed.

Tiny, fibrous filaments of the black stuff attached themselves to Bastian's fur. His breathing became first laboured, and then strained as the spell took hold. At length so many threads had caught in the fur at the ruff of his neck that he was unceremoniously dragged backwards, growling savagely.

I dashed back to help him, my eyes wide with apprehension, but Bastian snapped at the hand I stretched out, and snarled, "Keep going, Rose!"

"No!" My voice squeaked with indignation. When I reached out again Bastian snapped more savagely, this time catching my hand between his teeth and drawing blood.

"Get Mara!" he snapped. "She's the only one who can help now."

I cradled my hand, staring at him in wide-eyed disbelief. "You bit me!"

Bastian gave a truly vicious snarl, one I had not heard since he had tried to eat me all those years ago. "Go *now*, Rose!"

I did as I was told that time. I heard Bastian yelp once, high and sharp, before I cannoned into a sharp, wiry body which immediately seized me in an iron grip. One hand pinched the nape of my neck: the other forced my head back. I found myself staring wildly up at Mara and loosened my clutching fingers from her arm.

The grip around my neck tightened painfully. "What are you playing at?" Mara demanded.

"Bastian!" I gasped, breathlessly. "Please help him! Cassandra!"

Mara seemed to understand my incoherent urgency, because she released me and strode down the thread I had arrived on without further questions. The forest was horribly silent around us after the yelp I heard from Bastian. As we travelled, cold and swift, I wondered sickeningly if Cassandra had actually killed him. A sob caught at the back of my throat at the thought, because no matter what the forest did to Cassandra in retribution, Bastian would still be *dead*.

Cassandra was standing over Bastian's motionless body when we saw her, a high colour in her cheeks that made her, if possible, even more beautiful than usual.

Mara said calmly, "What have you done, Cassandra?"

It was then that I realised the pinkness of Cassandra's cheeks was not that of triumph, but fury; and I held my breath in sudden hope.

"Breathe, child," Mara said softly to me, and her assurance filled me with relief. "He is not dead."

I let my breath out in something very like a sob, and dropped to my knees beside Bastian, laying my head on his furry chest to hear for myself the faint but steady beat of his heart. He was not quite unconscious, because I felt the huff of his breath as he nudged his nose into my neck—heard him say my name with a kind of wonder in his voice that he was still alive.

"Why isn't he dead?" demanded Cassandra. It certainly wasn't from any lack of trying on her part. There was a blackness roiling about her slender fingers, and the same darkness clouded around Bastian. I began to wonder if the forest didn't care more for preventative than punitive measures.

"He should be dead! *Why isn't he dead?*"

There was a bitter kind of mocking to Bastian's thready voice. "Self-sacrificing altruism, you old cow," he jeered, and lost consciousness.

Cassandra gave a scream of rage, her fingers curling into fists, and kicked Bastian's prone body with her soft satin slippers as if they were metal sabatons. It would almost have been funny if I weren't so concerned for Bastian. His chest still only barely rose and fell with his breath: there was no telling what Cassandra had done to him.

"Stop that at once!" Mara said sharply, taking a swift step forward.

Cassandra kicked Bastian one last time, viciously, and said sibilantly to his unresponsive ears, "I *will* kill you, wolf."

The quiet malice in her voice sent an involuntary shiver through me, but Mara stood her ground, unmoved.

"You will harm neither the wolf nor Akiva's apprentice on any of my wardship," she said coldly. "Do you understand, Cassandra?"

They locked gazes, violet eyes to icy blue ones. Cassandra's gaze dropped first.

Her smile was brittle and enchanting as she said, "I will see you another time, little rabbit."

I watched her go with a sick feeling in the pit of my stomach, but Mara allowed me no time to meditate on my fears.

"Take his legs," she said. "I'll attend to his head."

We lifted awkwardly, out of time with each other. Bastian proved to be heavier than either of us expected, and Mara pitched forward into me, tumbling us both into the dew-wet grass. The wooden comb in her neat bun caught me painfully below one eye, leaving a throbbing indent that promised to become a splendid bruise before very many minutes passed.

Mara, her bun ridiculously on one side, did not escape her share of mud and grass stains. As a result, she was rather waspish by the time she rose to her feet, scraping back tendrils of escaping hair with an attempt at dignity.

"Clearly this is not the most sensible option," she said, with a flush of pink in each cheek.

Recovering her self-possession, she plucked several evergreen leaves from the surrounding trees and fixed them together with tiny threads of ice-blue magic that had little to do with the forest. The leaves grew brittly brown at the edges and drew away from the threads, but remained fixed together; and when she made a motion as if shaking the thing out, it grew with each snap and flick until it was some ten times its original size.

Mara let it drift gently in the air before her, and then shooed it forward to wrap around Bastian swiftly and efficiently until he was a nondescript bundle hovering a foot in the air.

"*Much* better," she said in satisfaction. "You'd better walk with me, child; Cassandra won't have gone far."

I nodded meekly, relieved that I hadn't had to ask for her escort. Neither of my attempts at spying had gone particularly well, and I was feeling nastily vulnerable. I trailed humbly along behind Mara as she strode through the moonlit forest at incredible, soundless speed, and found that we had arrived in Akiva's wardship almost before I was aware of it.

I had no time to worry about what Akiva was going to say, but fortunately enough I wasn't called upon to explain myself. Mara commandeered the explanations, and I was grateful to her for failing to mention that Bastian and I had been following Cassandra, or that we had trespassed extensively on her wardship. She said only that Cassandra had attacked us, and that she had been near enough to help. I could have hugged her for her kindness.

"The wolf will need some time to recover," Mara added briefly.

To my annoyance, they then held a murmured conversation from which I was pointedly excluded by magic that was as impenetrable as it was insulting.

At length Akiva said to me, "Rose, I am afraid that Bastian will have to go with you."

Mara nodded a goodnight to us both and took herself off, and I was left to gaze worriedly down at the tightly wrapped figure of Bastian.

"Bastian said the change will be permanent if he gets caught out of the forest when he changes."

"Yes. You'll have to take some of the forest with you," Akiva said. "I won't be able to care for him. I have business in deep forest that can't wait."

I looked swiftly up at her, alerted by a change in her usually steady cadence. "You mean *deeper* forest," I said accusingly.

Akiva's brows snapped together. "That is not something you should know about! Hold your tongue, child, and do as you are told! We will take him to your mother tomorrow morning; my business can't be detained any longer."

"I could help," I said, a little sadly. I felt oddly abandoned and useless.

"You could help, or you could be killed," Akiva said, and the stiffness in her voice caused an absurd little bubble of happiness to break at the back of my throat. She was concerned for me.

"I want to be sure that no more wardens disappear. I will call on you when I need you."

And so, discontented, I was forced to be content.

Akiva and Mother discussed the matter in the kitchen, voices low and hard to hear. Bastian was in front of the hearth on a rough mattress, with a fire lit to combat his fits of shivering, while the rest of us gazed curiously on him.

Gwendolen's expression was one of nose-wrinkled curiosity, Thomas' of understanding, and David's face was furrowed with a thoughtful frown. None of them had objected to being woken in the wee hours of the morning: in fact, Thomas and David hadn't yet gone to bed and Gwendolen had only just returned from the dance.

The boys spent the night absorbed in a game of chess with a quickly dwindling bottle of brandy to keep them company, and Gwendolen, satisfied that she was beautiful in the entrancing disorder of loose curls, was perfectly content to be a party to night-time adventures so long as no one expected her to be more than decorative.

I fell asleep crouched uncomfortably beside Bastian some time before Mother and Akiva finished their discussion, and awoke many hours later to broad daylight and the information Akiva was gone.

Mother was in a surprisingly good humour. Thomas and David were still at their chess match, but Gwendolen had flitted back off to bed. Bastian, deep into a fever, was changing constantly from wolf to man and back again, surrounded imperceptibly by the forest spell that Akiva had worked on him.

"He's been doing that for the last few hours," Thomas told me, looking up while David made his move. "Two changes every hour, like clockwork."

I stayed by Bastian's side all day, taking my meals by the uncomfortably warm fire, and anxiously noting each change as it occurred. He didn't recover consciousness, but neither did his fever grow worse. When night drew on without any change, Mother chivvied me into my own bed to spend the night, and set her rocking chair by Bastian's side. As I crawled beneath the sheet, David's shadow slipped past my open door to keep her company.

IT WASN'T UNTIL NEARLY A WEEK HAD PASSED THAT Bastian regained consciousness. I wasn't there to see it: Gilbert had called around to take me for a walk, and Mother had insisted on my going with him, if only to get us out of the house. She seemed anxious to prevent anyone from seeing Bastian, and in his present state, I was no less anxious.

So I walked with Gilbert, talking agreeably; and found myself agreeing to go to the last summer dance of the season with him. My acquiescence brought a glow to his eyes that made me slightly uneasy. I wondered for the first time if perhaps I could have mistaken the feelings that Gilbert had for me. I remembered the sensation of eager warmth I'd had when we first met and found myself worried and slightly claustrophobic.

I was frowning thoughtfully as I entered the house again, just in time to hear Bastian's voice in conversation with Mother's.

"Bastian!" I flung the door shut with a careless joy that made it slam loudly, and dashed for the hearth. "You're awake!"

He was smiling up at Mother when my eyes fell on them, and it came to me with relief that they quite liked one another, even if they seemed to do so with a touch of wariness. Bastian turned his smile on me, and I thought it grew wider, his hazel eyes softer than I was used to seeing them.

"Little witch!" he hailed me, rising on one elbow. "Your mother and I have been getting acquainted."

Mother kissed my forehead briefly as I knelt beside her chair.

"Have some lunch with us, Rosie. This young man and I have been talking about his unfortunate...situation."

I eyed her warily, but she didn't *look* cross: I hoped that Bastian had not told her I kissed him, especially since it had done no good.

"Don't look so worried, Rose," Mother said, laughing. "I was merely telling him that this sorceress seems to have tricked his body into thinking that he is ill. I can find nothing wrong with him bodily."

I let a soft breath escape carefully. Oh. *That* situation. "What do you mean?"

Interest sparked in Mother's eyes. "I talked with Akiva. There's no curse—no spell—causing this weakness."

I frowningly considered Bastian, who said with some exasperation, "I'm not prone to imagination, mother! My legs lack the strength to stand."

"Not imagination, exactly," said Mother. "It's more of a suggestion, I believe."

I flicked my eyes over him once again. Mother and Akiva were right: there was no curse attached to him. Around his mind were cobwebby somethings that could have been thoughts but were more likely to be what Mother had called them: suggestions.

They were filmy and didn't look like they would last much longer, so I said to Mother, "Don't worry. I'll take care of it."

Mother looked mildly amused but took her cue anyway. "I'll be out with the washing if you need me," she said, and left us alone.

We sat for some moments in companionable silence until Bastian, playing idly with my fingers, found the puckering scar that his own teeth had caused.

He ran his thumb along it, frowning. "I apologize for that, little witch."

I shrugged, resisting an odd, shy impulse to pull my hand away. "It's only a scratch; it will fade."

"I believe I snarled at you."

"I thought you hated me for a moment," I told him candidly. There had been such an anger to his voice that night, caught in Cassandra's magic.

Bastian's eyes flicked up at me, and I thought he looked stricken. "I did, for the barest second. I hated you for making me protect you."

"You knew I wouldn't get back in time with Mara," I said, in cold realization. "I could have freed you!"

"Not in time," Bastian said tiredly. "Let's not go over it, little witch. Forgive me."

I threw my arms around his neck. "There's nothing to forgive, silly. I thought you were dead."

"You flatter me, my love," Bastian said, sitting up in order to put one arm around me. I couldn't help grinning because Mother was right: when he wasn't thinking about it, Bastian was perfectly healthy. He asked, "Would it make you sorry?"

"Of course!" I said, pushing my luck by rising to my feet. "I wouldn't have anyone to quarrel with, and that would be a shame."

Bastian rose with me, all unthinking. It wasn't until we had walked the length of the room that he stopped, thunderstruck.

"You little minx! You've bewitched me!"

"You're just grumpy because Mother was right," I said.

"The vindictive old cow!" Bastian said in amazement. "I could have thought myself into a decline!"

"It's just as well you have me to look after you, then, isn't it?" I told him pertly; and, having deprived him of both breath and speech, I skipped out into the garden to gleefully inform Mother that she had been right.

Bastian stayed with us only a few more days after that, until Akiva summoned me back to the forest. Mother seemed quietly pleased to have him there. Gwendolen was cross, but her anger was directed more at me. She took me aside indignantly after dinner one night to inform me that Bastian was *very* good-looking, and why had I not told her? I eyed her in some amazement, and replied truthfully that I hadn't noticed. Looks were not a thing I thought about when I was with Bastian.

But Gwendolen's crossness was not directed merely at me: she and Thomas had quarrelled, I gathered, from Gwendolen's somewhat incoherent mutterings. Thomas continued to visit just as usual and seemed not to notice Gwendolen turning the cold shoulder, which infuriated her all the more.

To add to her fury, Bastian was inclined to tease her in an elder-brotherly way that she wasn't at all used to in a male.

All in all, it was a relief to step back into the cool silence of the forest, late one afternoon. Summer was cooling off to autumn, and in two days the last summer dance would be held; to which, I remembered somewhat uneasily, I was accompanying Gilbert. I found that I didn't want to think about it, so I let the thought flit out of my mind like an autumn leaf and concentrated on enjoying the forest. Bastian had melted away into the forest upon my return, leaving me to find my way to Akiva alone, and before long my heart was light and free. It felt good to be home.

When I entered the cottage a few minutes later, Akiva greeted me with sharp relief. "Ah, there you are! How goes David?"

"The same," I told her, revelling in the scent of the cottage. I could smell peaches in the air, where the waving branches of the peach-tree desk wafted their scent through the room. Mixed with it was the dry, herby aroma of Akiva's supplies.

"And the wolf?"

"Better. He's in the forest."

Akiva gave her characteristic grunt. "Hm. Cassandra is unhappy. He should stick to the wardship."

"I'll tell him. Akiva, are you leaving?"

She looked at me sharply, then nodded. "My business in deep forest brought something disturbing to light. I need you to care for the wardship while I investigate."

I bit back what I knew to be a vain plea to be included in the investigation and nodded. "Will you be gone long?"

"I don't know," she said, and I saw that she was weary. "I need to speak with Mara, and I need an invitation to deeper forest."

"What does Mara know?"

"More than she has been sharing," Akiva said. "The disturbance in the forest is running even deeper than deep forest, and she knows it. Someone has been altering deeper forest to suit their needs."

I tried and failed to think of anyone powerful enough to alter deeper forest. Even Cassandra couldn't do that, *surely*. "Is that why the forest has been all wrong?"

"Yes. It could have coped with disappearing wardens, but not with alterations to deeper forest as well."

"Can you change it back?" I asked anxiously. I was not keen to see more sections of forest blackening and dying.

Akiva gave a bitter laugh. "You flatter me, child. No, I can't change it back, I can only find out who is responsible. To reverse damages to deeper forest requires a full council of wardens, and at the last count we were six short."

She was jerking tight the strings of a little rucksack as she spoke, on the point of departure. I knew I had only a few moments before she left, so I spoke quickly. "Is there anything I can do?"

"Keep the wardship safe," she said, hoisting the sack to her shoulder. "Keep Bastian close. And stay *away* from Cassandra."

The house was quiet and still after she left. I looked around me listlessly and found to my surprise that Akiva had let the cottage go all to pieces while she was busy. None of her cooking utensils were washed, nor were any of the clothes, and dust lay thick on the windowsills.

Ingredients were put down every which where instead of neatly on the workbench, and the kettle that sat on the hob was ringed in gradually lower circles of crusted tea, showing a progression of re-boiling without cleaning. I sucked in my cheeks as I considered the probable potency of the brew before deciding that discretion was the better part of valour. I threw it out.

The salamander, in its usual haunt below the tea-kettle, looked sulky and emitted only a slight glow. It did so love attention; and Akiva, by the looks of things, had been giving attention to nothing but her own, secretive business.

I pottered about the house, tidying and straightening everything that didn't need to be washed. I would have to draw water for washing the dishes later, and the clothes would have to wait until tomorrow to be taken to the stream for washing. After a little while the salamander crawled out of the fireplace and climbed up my leg to curl about my shoulder in the familiar way it used to.

I thought it looked reproachfully at me, and I said excusingly, "I didn't go away on purpose, you know. Akiva sent me away."

The salamander clicked twice and seemed satisfied, because it tucked its head down under my chin, and went to sleep.

The next day was bright and sunny, and I went down to the stream with my basketful of washing to get an early start on the day. Instead, I found myself sitting by the stream, daydreaming in the warm sunlight with the pile of dirty clothes beside me on the hot rock. One of Akiva's petticoats dangled from my fingers, fabric rippling on the current. Beside me were my old boots, polished to take away the dust and forgotten while I ruminated.

It had occurred to me, you see, that it would be a marvellous idea to try and match Gilbert with Gwendolen. By the time I left Mother and Gwen, Gwendolen had proceeded to the stage of whipping around the house like a miniature whirlwind, tidying and angrily declaring her perfect indifference for Thomas every few moments. I thought that if she weren't to have Thomas she could have Gilbert, and make him not interested in me anymore.

I was so deeply immersed in my scheming that when Bastian strolled from the forest and said affably, "Rose, my lovely!" I started and nearly lost Akiva's petticoat.

He grinned his peculiarly wolfish grin down at me, and said: "Daydreaming, Rose? About me, I hope."

I grinned back up at him and resumed washing the petticoat. "No: Gilbert."

"Pleasant daydreams, then," jeered Bastian, his affability vanishing. "Asked you to marry him, has he?"

"No, of course not!" I said impatiently, offended at his tone and stung because his jibe hit a little closer to home than I was comfortable with. "I was thinking it would be a good thing if he and Gwen got married."

Bastian looked at me narrowly for a moment and then gave a short laugh. "It won't work," he said, settling himself down on the other side of the pile of dirty washing and beginning on another of Akiva's petticoats with surprising proficiency.

"Why not?" I demanded.

"Because no man who looks twice at you is likely to be fobbed off with Gwendolen," Bastian said lazily. "But by all means try it. In fact, tell me when you mean to, because I want to see his face."

"But Gwendolen is *much* prettier than me," I argued. I began to think that it was all one big Bastian-joke, because of course anyone would rather marry Gwen than me.

"I believe the time has come to explain to you just how delicious you are," said Bastian, with the hunting smile that showed the tips of his teeth.

It was an unsettling smile, and I found his face too close for comfort, so I put one wet hand over it and pushed him away. "No."

Bastian's voice, muffled and softly amused, said, "Little witch, take away your hand."

"No. You're being silly."

"If you don't, I'll have to do something drastic," he warned.

"Like what?" I asked speculatively, and felt the curve of a smile on the palm of my hand.

"Kiss you, of course."

I dropped my hand in surprise, looking doubtfully at him for signs of the blackness. All I could see was gold.

"That won't help break the curse," I said. "I have to kiss you, not the other way around."

It would probably be unfair to say that Bastian howled with laughter. But when, after a moment of incredulous silence, he began to laugh, it was no gentle chuckle. I eyed him sourly, unsure if I were being laughed at or if Bastian were merely being silly, and threw a wet pillowcase at his head.

"Bufflehead!"

His laughter didn't abate, and I went on with my washing in cross silence, ignoring him. When at last Bastian's hilarity did die away, the silence was pleasant enough that I didn't notice until a few moments later that he had picked up one of the shoes I had been polishing earlier. They were my only shoes, perhaps a little small for me now, and I had polished them until they shone, much to my own bemusement.

"I'm going to the last summer dance," I said, annoyed to feel a slight flush in my cheeks. I wasn't sure quite why I had put my shoes out after so many years barefoot: I thought that it had something to do with my sudden conviction that Gilbert liked me better than I had thought. It had occurred to me that I wanted not to embarrass him. I found that thought unsettling also.

Bastian looked up with a narrowed gaze, the laughter quite gone from his eyes. "With whom?"

"With Gilbert," I said defiantly, refusing to meet his eyes. There was a sharp *snap!* and when I turned my head, startled, Bastian was still holding my shoe, its lace broken.

He tossed it to me carelessly and said, "I suppose I might have known."

I turned back to my washing, annoyed to find that I was still blushing.

"Akiva has gone again," I said, hoping to change the subject. There was a bare ripple of movement beside me, and then Bastian had gone, leaving me to stare after him in perplexed indignation. I had wanted, I thought resentfully, to invite him to the dance. Now I would be left alone with Gilbert, not to mention Gwendolen and her coy glances.

I finished the washing in a decidedly worse mood than I had begun it and pegged the wet garments to the clothes-line with some asperity. We had been good friends only yesterday, Bastian and me. I felt aggrieved at his irritability, as aggrieved as I was bemused. I could talk to him as I couldn't talk to Akiva, or even Mother; and I had become used to his teasing. I didn't like the feeling that we were at outs.

I returned to the cottage moodily, striding through deep forest without delay or detour. It wasn't until I got back that I realised I had left my shoes, broken and alone, by the stream. I left them there.

Fifteen

I scowled at my reflection in the mirror. I had been pacing in my shift for some time now, trying to decide what to wear, and I was thoroughly sick of the business already.

I didn't *want* to go to the dance, I thought sulkily. All of my dresses were too short, and my hair wouldn't behave, slipping free from any confines I tried to impose upon it, light and whispy. I understood for the first time why Gwendolen would be in and out of clothes a dozen times before she was finally dressed to her satisfaction.

My bed was a mess of bedclothes and old skirts, my small closet woefully empty, before I found the package Mother had given me some years ago when Gwendolen had a new dress.

I opened it now with nervous fingers, discovering a creamy mass of off-white material beneath the crackling folds of brown paper. When I shook it out there was less to it than I had supposed at first, which made me slightly uneasy. It was a light summer dress with an odd, low waist that would sit at my hips. I tried it on, hardly daring to believe that it would fit; but fit it did, the girdle snug about my hips and the smooth bodice comfortably loose and light. None of Gwendolen's tight-corseted dresses, this!

I wondered if Mother had seen the dryads dance, for surely this was a dryad dress. Tiny flowers chased each other over the long, sheer sleeves and about the kirtle, and the skirt, almost scandalous with its gauzy petticoat, was light and cool against my bare legs. I felt a sudden stab of excitement that tickled in my stomach very like nervousness, and left the room without daring to look in the mirror.

Akiva's hood was still a convenient shade of summer green that went well with my new dress, and it seemed to me that it was more leafy than usual in the twilight, with the flowers of my dress nestling amongst the leaves. I skipped lightly through the shadowy forest with a fizzing excitement quickly building in me. I had a brief wish that Bastian could see me in my new dress, but I quashed it, determined not to think of Bastian and his moods. I would enjoy myself.

I arrived at home with sparkling eyes, and time to spare. Gwendolen opened the door to me, dressed all in green muslin, and stood with her mouth in a scandalized 'o' of surprise.

"Rose!"

"What?" I demanded, on the offensive. I was feeling new and slightly unsteady in my dryad dress. "I'm not late."

"Oh, never mind," Gwendolen said, making a face. "You're as ugly as usual. Happy?"

I grinned reluctantly. "Thanks, Gwen. Is Thomas here?"

Immediately Gwen stiffened. "Yes, the cheek of him! I told him I wouldn't go to the dance with him, and what do you think he said?"

"I have no idea."

"He said he wasn't going with *me*, if you please! He said he was going with Mother and David!"

"Why don't you make up with him, Gwen?"

"*I* didn't begin the quarrel!" she began mulishly. "*I* don't fuss when other girls flirt with him. *I* don't insist that he should never speak to anyone else."

"Thomas doesn't flirt with anyone else," I pointed out. Gwendolen would certainly take a dim view of it if any such thing happened, despite her protests. "If you're going to marry him, you can't keep flirting with everyone else."

"I can't help it if they all like me!" Gwendolen said, her face flushed. "And I am *not* going to marry Thomas! I'm *not*."

"I suppose it's a good thing that I haven't asked you yet, then," said Thomas' voice, calmly amused. "Good evening, Rose. You're beautiful."

I blushed hotly, but Gwendolen scowled at him, and put her little nose in the air.

"I shall see if Mother and David are ready to go yet," she said haughtily, and floated coldly away, ignoring Thomas' quiet interjection that they were on their way downstairs. He smiled at her retreating back, but when he looked at me again his face was serious.

"I've learned a little more of your wolf and his situation," he said softly. "Enough to make it strangely hard to speak of it, I might add."

I nodded in understanding. "It does that to me, too. The only person I can speak to freely is Bastian."

"You'll be careful won't you, Rose?" There was a crease between his brows that spoke of consideration for me as well as for Gwen, so I stood on tiptoes to kiss his cheek.

"You're very nice, and I thoroughly approve. I'll be careful, I promise."

To my surprise, a dull red flush crept up in his cheeks. "Thank you. Now all I need is Gwendolen's approval.'"

"I'd give you advice, but you seem to be doing very well on your own," I said. "I've never seen her mope over her beaux before. Or mutter. It's quite good for her, I think."

A reluctant smile stole into his eyes. "I flatter myself that I know her quite well. She's young yet, and I can afford to wait."

I looked up at him thoughtfully as he stood before me, rock-like and steady, and knew that he would do just that. Wait and wait until Gwendolen was ready, and be there to catch her when she was. It occurred to me that Gwendolen, all unknowing, had been very fortunate.

Gilbert was waiting by the front gate when we emerged, whistling at the early moon with his hands in his pockets. He grinned in greeting and offered one arm to me, remarking with a nod at the flowers of my dress and the leafiness of Akiva's hood, "You've brought the forest with you tonight."

He offered the other arm to Gwendolen, who was still refusing to acknowledge Thomas' presence and accepted the arm grandly. Mother and David strolled ahead of us, Thomas with them and seeming not to notice Gwendolen's ire. He was behaving as if he really had come to accompany them and not Gwen.

Despite Gwendolen's annoyance, there was an air of happiness and hilarity to our little group as we approached the dancing green and saw the lights twinkling. The only reminder that all was not quite right was Akiva's hood, nestling warmly about my shoulders.

Gwendolen flitted away almost immediately, and Liz Gantry, her arm linked with Harry's, immediately took her place. She darted toward Gilbert and I, dragging us irresistibly into the dance that was forming.

"It's a four-square," she explained. "We'll make up our own set. Then we can step on each other's toes and dance the wrong steps all night if we want to."

So we danced and we laughed, amusing ourselves with everyone and everything, and in particular our own bad dancing. It was pleasant not to be serious for a little while.

Later, when passing in the reel, Gilbert enquired, "Your watchdog couldn't make it?"

"He doesn't leave the forest often," I said watchfully, turning lightly on my toes at my corner to face him. "I don't think he likes people very much."

"That explains why he's always glaring at me, I suppose?" Gilbert was grinning as we performed the obligatory last doci-do. Opposite us, Harry swerved wildly to avoid jostling Liz's shoulder with his own, and collided with another couple. We were laughing then, and I wasn't obliged to answer Gilbert's question, much to my relief.

To tell the truth, I wasn't entirely sure why Bastian disliked Gilbert. Toward most humans he showed only indifference, Thomas and Mother being the only notable exceptions to whom

Bastian seemed to have taken a liking, apart from myself. Gilbert he seemed to actively dislike, and I could see no reason for it.

Thinking about it, I found to my surprise that I was missing Bastian. I was by now so used to having him around that when he wasn't there I felt his absence like a hole in the background. It occurred to me in a moment of clarity that every time I turned to laugh and share a joke with Gilbert, I was startled that the face I turned to wasn't Bastian's.

My thoughts left me unsettled, and when the others suggested a walk along the mill road after the dance, I excused myself to seek out Mother and David. I found David first: he was watching Mother dance with Thomas, a smile on his thin face. It was a warm, personal smile, so I sat beside him without speaking, my eyes also on the dancers; and after a moment David put his arm around me in an absentminded, fatherly hug.

"Well, Rose? And what is it you want from me?"

"Want?" I demanded, pretending injury. "Perhaps I like your company."

That got me a sideways look and a real smile. "Strange," he said, turning his gaze back on the dancers. "I could have sworn you only come to see me when you want to pick my brains."

I laughed, and we watched the dancers in silence for a moment longer. Then David, with a frown deepening on his face, said suddenly, "You feel it too, don't you, Rose? I keep thinking I'm imagining it; but it feels like someone has left a door open near the birches. I think something is coming through."

I looked at him curiously but felt a few of the lines nearby and found that he was right.

"How did you notice that?" I demanded, a little put out that he had sensed something I had not.

"I don't know. I didn't know that no one else could sense it until I asked Margot what it was. She didn't know what I was talking about."

Now that it had been pointed out, I could see what he saw. It wasn't quite a door, as David had thought, it was more of a tiny, deep hole in the small copse of birches that the younger children liked to dance rings around. The copse was clear of the forest but still quite close, and the lines glimmering between it and the forest told me that it was still part of the forest: and more importantly, of *deep* forest.

There was no telling what could come through with the forest in the state it was in. The children were lively tonight: not unusually so, but there was an energy in their leaping and a dexterity in their dancing feet that sent a danger signal prickling across my scalp. It was disturbingly reminiscent of deeper forest and the wildly dancing dryads.

I stood unhurriedly, but my heart was beating more quickly with a touch of fear.

"Maybe I'll dance with the children," I said. "No one's chaperoning."

"And I will join you," David said, pulling my hand through his arm. We strolled around the outskirts of the grownup dancers, David's thin, strong hand clasping mine tightly enough to keep me at an unhurried, unnoticeable pace that matched his.

"Don't frighten them," he said in a low voice. "If they're panicked it will be impossible to keep them all in sight."

I nodded, but my hand felt very cold where I grasped the light cloth of his shirt, my fingers hidden beneath his. He patted my hand once and then released it, as if he were satisfied that I wouldn't do anything foolish. I kept it tucked in the crook of his arm nevertheless, feeling safer with him there. We joined the children briefly, spinning into the circle and through it in one swift, graceful swirl, and they let us pass without acknowledging us. Their eyes were wide and starry.

Before long we were at the centre of their straggling loop, the point at which the birch trees were thinnest. The whole patch of trees was no wider than twenty feet, and we should have been able to see party lights and silhouetted figures dancing between the pale trunks. Instead, we saw only inky blackness, as if we were gazing into the deepest, thickest of forest. I gazed pensively at the darkness and knew that though the trees were merging into deeper forest, what we were looking for was no longer between the trees.

"There's nothing here," I said, my voice small in the face of the massiveness of deeper forest. "Whatever it is has already come through."

We turned back slowly to face the circle of dancing children, and found that, beyond them, the party had grown strangely unfocused.

"We should go back," I said, a deep thrill of fear leaving me breathless and strangely euphoric; because David wasn't looking at me any longer. He was gazing intently at a graceful, pale figure as it glimmered among the children, passing from hand to hand through the dance.

"I don't think we can," he said huskily. Just beyond the dancing line I could see Mother standing, her face white and her eyes intent on us, while the dancing figure came ever closer with graceful, strathspey deliberation. It turned in the dance, lights shining full on its face, and I saw, with a jolt of cold recognition, that it was Kendra. Beside me, I heard David's breath hiss between his teeth, and I shot a look up at him in the conviction that he had got his memory back at last. The look on his face was not one of remembrance, however; it was one of deep confusion.

And as Kendra threaded her way closer, I was ashamed to discover in myself a deep desire that he would *not* remember, that he would *not* recognise her. I didn't know how Kendra could be here, but I did know how Mother felt about David, and how he felt about her. For once the thought of David's memory returning was an undeniably unwelcome one.

I heard the sound of Mother's voice calling but it sounded faded and far off. She wasn't calling my name: she was calling David's. The sound of it must have penetrated David's ears, because he tore his eyes away from Kendra with a shuddering breath and fixed his gaze on Mother instead, with the desperate look a drowning sailor has for the wooden plank that will save him. I risked another glance at Kendra, and thought I saw her mouth form my name, but David didn't look back again.

Step by laborious step, he surged through the murkiness, dragging me with him until we were through the dancers. I looked back to catch another sight of Kendra, but she was gone and the dance was breaking up. The clump of birches was just a plot of trees again.

David gave something like a sob, then Mother had her arms around him, stroking his hair and murmuring in his ear as if he were a little boy, his face pressed tight into her neck and his eyes squeezed shut.

She spared me a swift look to ask, "What happened?"

"I don't know," I said shortly. "Someone came out of deeper forest and I'm not supposed to know about deeper forest."

"You both went blurry," said Thomas. He had been there beside Mother all the time, though I hadn't seen him. He put his arm around my waist in a friendly fashion and added, "I'll get you some hot chocolate."

Mother nodded approvingly at us. "I'll take David home with me," she said, gently pushing the hair away from his forehead.

David raised his head to look wonderingly down at her as if he had not quite seen her before. And then, just like that, Mother was being kissed long and hard before the whole party, David's thin hands cupped around her face. Someone raised a cheer and several more whistled, but neither of them seemed to care, or even to hear. Thomas chuckled and pulled me away.

"Close your mouth, Rose. You're not blind, you must have seen it coming."

"Well, yes; but I didn't think David had *that* in him," I said, impressed. "Let go of me, clot! I have to tell Mother to keep away from the forest as they go home." I was instinctively and perhaps unreasonably convinced that it was me and not David that Kendra had tried to talk to, but I didn't want to take any chances.

"Mother knows," Thomas said calmly, ignoring the insult. "Just as soon as I get you some hot chocolate, I will escort them home myself."

He was as good as his word. As soon as I was sitting down on a stray chair with a mug of rich chocolate, Thomas was off after Mother and David. I saw them moments later through the throng, Thomas beside and slightly behind them; and it was with gratitude that I noticed he had chosen to walk nearest the forest.

They had barely gone when Gwendolen swept up to me, simmering with indignation and mortification. "Why didn't you stop them!" she hissed, sweeping her skirts aside with an angry flourish to sit beside me.

"What on earth could I have done?" I inquired caustically. "Besides, I think it's sweet."

"*Sweet!*" Gwendolen squeaked, in a strangled whisper. "*Sweet?* She was kissing him in front of the entire village! Our *mother!*"

"I think he was kissing her," I pointed out, but without much hope that it would abate her anger. It didn't. I cut in on her tirade to say, experimentally, "You're only cross because Thomas went with them. None of your young men have ever left a dance while you're still at it, have they?"

"*Thomas is not my young man!*" almost shrieked Gwendolen. Heads turned, and she lowered her voice with flushed cheeks. "I don't care if he is here or a thousand miles away! I don't care if I never see him again!"

A last, angry swirl of muslin, and she was gone. I sat by myself thoughtfully until Gilbert returned with Liz and Harry, demanding a dance. Deep in my thoughts, I hadn't heard them approach, and Gilbert's voiced startled me enough to make me spill my hot chocolate. They laughed at me, teasing that I was daydreaming about a certain someone, and I pulled a face at them without denying it.

If I had denied it, I would have had to tell them what I *had* been thinking of, and I had no intention of telling them that I had been on the point of slipping away into the forest in an attempt to find Bastian. Kendra's reappearance had made me uneasy, and I wasn't entirely sure that Bastian would come if I called. He was still cross at me, and even if I didn't know why he was so cross, I *did* know that I didn't like being at odds with him. I hadn't sensed him in the forest since he had left me by the creek, and the lack of his familiar presence even in the distance was beginning to make me truly, ridiculously miserable. And I had found myself, surrounded by partygoers as I was, suddenly forlorn and alone, wanting nothing more than to sense his presence at the edges of my mind.

Fortunately, Harry was in too boisterous a mood to allow

anyone time to notice my quietness, and I was borne away to dance with him before Gilbert could laughingly protest that he had asked me first. Elizabeth pulled him along with the cheerful aside that at least she would not be knocked to the ground this dance, to which Harry replied by making a rude noise over his shoulder.

The dance was an energetic polka, which we romped through with hilarity, Harry's high spirits inevitably cheering me up. Around us the party grew louder and more jolly: midnight was fast approaching, but the dance showed no signs of breaking up and the refreshments flowed as freely as before. Well before the end of the dance, I had begun to think wistfully of Akiva's cottage and my comfortable little bed.

Almost before the last hop of my polka with Harry, Gilbert was by my side again.

"My turn," he said gaily; and swept me away into the ring that was forming.

I found myself in an unfamiliar setting and tried to back away, but Gilbert wasn't minded to let me pull away, and he swung me into a waltz hold with a teasing grin.

"It's easy; and you can tread on my toes as much as you please. Just stick with me when everyone else changes partners and I'll make sure you don't get lost."

I assured him sourly that I would make sure to take advantage of his kind permission to tread on his toes, but when the dance began, the tiny, foot-flicking movements were oddly familiar. It took me a few revolutions to discover that I was dancing a variation of the dryad's wedding dance: less sweeping and spectacular, but unmistakably the same dance.

I huffed a breath of relief that lasted only until I caught sight of a tall figure threading swiftly through the dance behind us. My first, startled thought, was that Kendra had broken though again; but as my eyes followed it through the dance, it became quickly evident that it was a male figure.

My breath quickened and I kept him in my sight, caught up with the sudden hope that the golden-haired stranger was Bastian. I couldn't sense him with my forest sight, and I knew my hope was ridiculous, but I still couldn't help craning my head to keep him in sight. He passed from partner to partner as Gilbert and I dallied together, but I only ever caught glimpses of the back of his head; and once, a patch of corn-golden stubble on his turned cheek.

I lost sight of him a moment later, and an almost crushing disappointment settled on me as I furled out in what was meant to be the last movement before switching partners, my hand in Gilbert's. With each change we had taken a waltz hold instead, ducking out and then back into the dance to remain together, but this time when I unfurled from the waltz hold, I didn't get a chance to spin back into Gilbert. Instead, my free hand was seized, and I was nipped breathlessly away from Gilbert, circled closely about my waist by a strong arm and held tight to a certain someone whose scent was as familiar as the forest.

Absurdly happy, I said, "You're wearing a shirt."

It was a simple, exquisitely made shirt; though he wore it unlaced and untucked, as if he weren't quite comfortable in one anymore.

Bastian looked down at it with the disinterested, cursory look of one who is used to the finest linens and said, "Your bumpkin seems to want you back."

I peeked around him to find that Gilbert and his new partner were just behind us, ready for the next change when he might reasonably hope to partner me again.

Bastian, his eyes glittering with sardonic amusement, said softly, "Hold tight, love," and whisked us from the outer to the inner dancing circle, just before the change.

I sputtered my laughter into his shirt, not willing to look up at him because I knew that if I did, I would laugh aloud. Gilbert was looking a touch aggrieved, and I didn't want him to think that I was mocking him.

We passed safely through two more partner changes before it occurred to me to say, in some surprise, "Bastian! You can dance!"

Bastian swept me exhilaratingly high into the air and back down again, and the smile he held steadily on me was warm enough to make me look away in confusion.

"There are a great many things you have yet to learn about me, little witch."

"Why are you here?" I asked quietly, keeping my eyes on level with the yoke of that beautiful shirt and no higher. Without knowing quite why, I was afraid to meet his eyes. "And how did you get here without me sensing you?"

Bastian manoeuvred us through another change with careless expertise. "The cocoon Akiva spun from the forest was stronger than she thought: it's still around me. You wouldn't have noticed it beside the forest."

"If you change outside the forest, you'll still be safe," I nodded, understanding. Bastian took advantage of my upturned gaze to bestow another of his disturbingly warm smiles down on me, and I dropped my eyes.

"As to why I came," he said softly in my ear, "I decided that I was not going to give you up to your bumpkin without a fight."

I was tired of protesting that Gilbert was not a bumpkin, so I merely said, "He's quite nice really, when you get to know him."

"But I don't want to know him," Bastian murmured, still close to my ear. "Gilbert doesn't interest me in the slightest. Once more, little witch."

He spun me once, twice, as the tempo quickened; and then we were in the centre of the two circling rings. I caught my breath in dismay, but my feet remembered what my memory didn't, and I couldn't help chuckling once in the sheer joy of the dance. For a brief moment it felt as though it really could have been deeper forest, the dancers dryads, and Bastian and I the bride and groom.

The pulse of the music picked up once again in the last tempo change for the dance that allowed me to be swung joyfully in the air one last time and brought down lightly on my toes. Around us the flying draperies of the other ladies swished one last time, then came the last unfurl and the swift curl back in. I found myself wrapped tight in Bastian's arms, my head tilted back to laugh up at him and his eyes laughing back down at me.

The dance ended with a shout and a stamp, but Bastian didn't release me.

"It's time I gave you that birthday present," he said, smiling down at me. He bent his head and for a moment I thought—I thought—I didn't know quite *what* I thought.

Before I had time to feel more than startled, Gilbert's voice said beside us, "Who's your friend, Rose?"

Bastian snarled something softly through his teeth and let me go, but kept one arm lightly around my waist.

"He's from the forest," I said truthfully, because the curse wouldn't let me say his name. I added, more helpfully and still strictly truthfully: "An acquaintance of Akiva's."

Gilbert acknowledged the information with a stiff nod at Bastian; and Bastian, as curtly, nodded back.

"My dance, I think," Gilbert said, and I thought there was a touch of challenge in his voice. His hand was held out to me, but Bastian didn't drop his arm from around my waist.

"Rose was just about to walk me home," he said, the smallest edge of a cold smile lifting his lips. There was a shimmer to his forest skin that seemed to suggest that he wouldn't long be in human form. Even if the skin did hold, it wouldn't do to have the whole party see him change from human to wolf.

I was cross with both of them for behaving so boorishly to each other for no reason, so I knocked Bastian's arm from my waist and ignored Gilbert's outstretched hand.

"I'll walk you as far as the forest," I said to Bastian, and added to Gilbert, "I'll be back shortly." It made me feel as though I was having two conversations at once, and that made me crosser.

Gilbert said, "No need; I'll walk along with you," and though Bastian looked annoyed, at least he made no demur.

I put one hand through Bastian's arm, the other through Gilbert's, and they were forced to continue to be civil.

We got Bastian back to the forest just in time. As Gilbert and I turned away, I felt the shock of his transformation, a wave of energy so bright and exuberant that I knew his protective barrier had shattered and let out all the extra energy it had been catching during his illness.

"So he's a friend of Akiva's," Gilbert remarked thoughtfully, ignorant of the deluge.

I said non-committally, "Mmmm."

"He seemed to know you very well."

I let the remark hang in the air unanswered and said without preamble, "I don't feel like dancing anymore."

"Even better," Gilbert said equably, allowing the subject to drop. "Let's go for a walk instead."

I'd been thinking of going home, but Gilbert sounded so pleased at the idea of a walk that I didn't like to disappoint him. So we walked further away from the party instead of back to it, the glowing lights fading behind us in the darkness as we strolled by the edges of the forest. I half expected Bastian to be prowling along beside us under cover of the trees, but he was unusually far away, giving Gilbert and me our privacy.

We wandered in a pleasantly aimless way, leisurely making our way around the curvature of the forest through the hills until we reached the highest point to be had, where we sat on a rock, dangling our feet and gazing down at the lights of the village. To the side of the village, the forest stretched out, dark velvet green and silent, and I was content to hear its quiet whisper beside me, threaded through with the faint strains of music that floated up to us from the dance.

"Rose, you're unlike any other girl I've met," Gilbert said at last, breaking the silence. He was sitting back with his hands propping him up while I stretched out full length beside him, gazing up at the stars, having tired of the village lights. "You don't chatter. I suppose you're still alive?"

He poked me in the ribs, and I laughed softly but didn't stir, too content to lay quietly in the peacefulness of the overhanging forest.

Gilbert stretched himself out beside me, leaning his weight onto one elbow to gaze at my profile, and asked idly, "If you could do anything, what would you do?"

"I'd like to fly," I said hungrily, my eyes on the wide expanse of starry sky. The remembrance of my dragon-fever dreams came back sometimes at night, when I remembered the freedom of flight I'd felt with useless longing.

"I don't think I would be surprised if you told me you *could* fly," Gilbert observed.

I hitched myself up on my elbows and regarded the view before us. "What would you do?"

"Do you really want to know?"

There was a question in his voice that I didn't quite understand, but I shrugged, and said, "Yes, if you like."

He didn't answer at once, and I turned my head to look enquiringly at him just as he leaned in and kissed me. It wasn't like the time I had kissed Bastian—that quick, formal kiss to try and break the spell—this one was warm and sweet and pleasant, and wholly unexpected.

I didn't react as quickly as I might have done: first, because I found that being kissed was a startlingly nice feeling, and then because the realization of what I needed to do to break the second part of Bastian's curse descended on me with blinding effect. For a moment I remained frozen, then I put my palm on Gilbert's chest and pushed him back firmly.

"No."

Gilbert looked part annoyed, part amused. He didn't look surprised.

"Rose—"

"No," I said again, shaking my head. "It was very nice, but—"

"But no," nodded Gilbert, and took in a quick, regretful breath. He ran one rueful hand through his hair. "I knew it was too soon to kiss you. I should have waited until later, but the dance scared me, and I thought—"

"It wouldn't have mattered," I said. I felt clumsy and wrongfooted, but I didn't want things to be odd between us. "I don't like you in that way, Gil. I didn't mean to make you think I did."

Gilbert smiled a little wryly. "I think I knew that when I saw you with *him*. I thought that if I could just get to you in time, I might have a chance to win you over."

I tried to protest that it wasn't like that with Bastian and I, but

Gilbert only said, "He's the wolf, isn't he? The wolf from the stories, the one you're always going on about?"

The curse wouldn't let me agree to it or deny it, but Gilbert's face told me that he knew anyway. I slid my arm through his and there was a moment of quiet as we both gazed out into the darkened forest.

"I wish I'd met you when I was younger," I said, a little sadly. Gilbert would have been an ideal companion for my many escapades, and maybe with time I would have come to feel for him the same way that he did for me.

"I wish you had, too." There was a little rough edge to his voice, but not enough to make me think that he wouldn't recover from my refusal. "Then I might have had some chance."

"We can still be friends, can't we?"

I was surprised to hear the wistful tone to my voice—more surprised to discover that I was unwilling to lose Gilbert's friend-ship, and perhaps with it the friendship of Elizabeth and Harry.

I found that I really was sorry as I said, "I'm sorry I couldn't be your sweetheart."

"So am I," Gilbert said; but he laughed a little, and kissed me on the cheek. "Goodnight, Rose."

He sauntered back downhill with his hands in his pockets, but I don't think he went back to the party. I stayed where I was for a long time until a sniff surprised me by suggesting I was near tears. I took myself fiercely to task, sniffing away the impulse, and slipped into the forest where I wandered aimlessly in search of distraction.

It wasn't until some minutes later that I found I'd made my way instinctively towards the patch of forest that was distinctly Bastian-tinted. A few steps later I came upon Bastian himself, dozing with his snout cushioned on his paws. Feeling absurdly comforted, I dropped down on the grass beside him and curled up with my head on his side like we used to sit. Bastian turned his head to sleepily snuff at my face.

"What's wrong, little love?"

I buried my face in his fur and heaved a big, huffy breath. "Don't want to talk about it."

The forest lines twanged and pulsed around me, and then I was curled up against human Bastian, one of his arms around me comfortably. He was still wearing his shirt from the party, and it was cool and soft against my cheek. He sat up, pulling me a little closer, and laughed at my surprise.

"Midnight, little witch. It's a whole new day. What have you done?"

I tucked my head into his shoulder as if he were still the furry, wolfish Bastian and said moodily, "I don't want to talk about it. I just want a hug."

"It's my pleasure, little witch," Bastian said in his laughing voice. He took my far hand and pulled it across his stomach until I had one arm around him too, and moved slightly so that his chin could rest comfortably on the top of my head. "There. Is that better?"

"Yes."

Bastian's warm, quiet presence made the churning feeling in my stomach go away, and I began to feel more comfortable. I said: "I'm glad you came to the dance."

"So am I, little witch; so am I," Bastian murmured into my hair. He sounded as if he were talking more to himself. "It's odd; I've never worked so hard for so little. And yet it has never been sweeter."

It was a Bastian-remark, no making sense of it. I said cautiously: "I don't know what you mean."

His stomach contracted with laughter under my arm, and I felt the stir in my hair from his chuckle. "That's what makes it so amusing, my love. How is it that your dance has finished so soon?"

"It hasn't," I admitted. "I just didn't feel like dancing anymore."

"Evidently you didn't have the right partner," Bastian said, a little arrogantly. "Come, little witch; I can still hear the music."

He pulled me easily to my feet, but instead of settling into a traditional dance hold we remained as we had been before, my head on his shoulder and my arm around him. His hands clasped loosely about my waist and guided me in a series of small, slow steps that mirrored his own.

"You see, little witch? I can hug you and dance at the same time."

"This is a nice way to dance," I said approvingly. For the first time since leaving the dance I felt properly cheerful. Bastian laughed.

"My thought exactly," he agreed. "Now, little witch, tell me: did you come all this way for a hug or was there something else?"

"Why does everyone think I must want something when I talk to them?" I demanded, pulling my head away from his shoulder indignantly.

Bastian firmly pushed it back down again into the snowy folds of his shirt and said soothingly, "Hush now. I acknowledge the purity of your motives, little witch."

"Besides, it was more of an idea," I added. "I wanted to try and break the second part of the curse again. I think I know how to do it now."

Bastian's steps stilled and he allowed me to take my head away this time without interfering. I thought he looked suddenly unsure, or perhaps a little uneasy; and it occurred to me to think that perhaps Bastian might want me to kiss him as little as I had wanted Gilbert to kiss me.

Uncertainly, I added, "Only if you don't mind, Bastian."

"I can't think of any better way to begin the day," Bastian said, and there was a queer little smile hovering about his mouth. "Take your best shot, little witch."

"Hold still, then," I said, but I needn't have bothered to tell him: Bastian was standing wolf-still, his eyes intent on me and somehow nervous.

It amused me a little at the back of my mind that *he* should be nervous when he had once courted three women together. I reached up to draw Bastian's head down to me and found that his hair was long enough to thread my fingers through. It was a nice feeling, and it made me forget suddenly the nervousness that had made me keep so far away from Bastian the first time I tried to break the curse.

This time when I turned up my face to kiss him, I was near enough to feel the warmth of his body. I felt the uneven brush of his breath on my face and pressed the kiss firmly into his lips, drawing from my memory of Gilbert's kiss and trying to recapture my sudden knowledge of what needed to be done. The curse didn't want the businesslike kind of kiss I had tried before: it wanted the curious, soft kind that asked a question, just like Gilbert's had done.

Somehow or other Bastian's arms had gone right around my waist again. Finding this an advantage, I pressed the kiss more firmly into his lips, asking the question. I felt Bastian's lips part slightly at the same time that mine did, and his arms tightened suddenly around me as he returned the kiss without my urging.

At that moment, as I had been certain it would, the second part of the curse broke. A shock of magic burst through us in glowing shades of brilliant gold and rich amber, fizzing where our lips met and all the way to my toes.

I broke the kiss off with a crow of delight; and Bastian's arms, which had locked suddenly and tightly around me, pinning me distractingly close to him at the moment the second part of the curse broke, loosened enough for me to disengage my fingers from his hair.

"It worked, it worked!" I was tingling with euphoria that must have been residue from the shock of magic, and pounced with delight rather than wisdom at the slight flush in Bastian's cheeks. "Bastian! Why are you blushing?"

His arms loosened around my waist and then tightened. "You've been practicing, little witch!"

I flushed bright red and tried to twitch myself away, but Bastian was too strong, and I was forced to stay where I was. "Who have you been kissing, Rose?"

"It was Gilbert, and he kissed *me*!" I defended myself, but I couldn't subdue the ruddy tinge in my cheeks. "Anyway, that's how I learned how to do it so it would break the spell, so be grateful. I didn't *want* to kiss him."

"Perhaps I should be having a word with your bumpkin, then," Bastian said in his thoughtful growling-yet-silky voice.

"I can look after myself!" I snapped, with an air of authority that was ruined by the fact that I still couldn't wriggle myself free.

"Stop wriggling, little witch." Bastian's arms constricted again, and I knew that they would continue to do so, boy-like, for every wriggle; so I stopped struggling. "It's not polite to break off a kiss after you get what you want, little witch. It's polite to finish what you start."

"I didn't want you to have to put up with it any longer than you had to," I explained, resignedly resting my arms on his shoulders since it didn't seem likely that he would let me go until he had finished teasing me. "I thought you'd rather have it over with more quickly."

Close as we were, I felt a familiar tightening of the muscles in his stomach that meant he was holding back a laugh. "Oh, did you? Well, let me tell you, little witch, I've no intention of being short-changed, and that means you still owe me half a kiss. But as I'm obliged to you for breaking the second part of the curse, I will allow you to defer payment."

I said, "Hah!" darkly, but my rudeness didn't affect Bastian at all except to make him smile faintly and offer to walk me home.

I allowed it since he didn't seem inclined to let me go whether or not I acquiesced, and we wandered leisurely through deep forest hand in hand until Akiva's cottage segued out of the darkness and halted our progress.

I must have been wearier than I thought, because when I flopped down on the bed to rest my weary feet for a moment, I fell asleep straight away, fully dressed and with Akiva's hood spread neatly in a half circle on the pillows about me.

Sixteen

I was jerked suddenly and immediately awake the next morning before sunrise, crushed into the bed by an immense weight. I sat up with difficulty and knew in a single, terrified moment that the weight was not physical: it was the weight of the wardship descending on me.

I screamed. "Bastian! *Bastian!*"

Akiva's hood was blood-red around my shoulders, and I knew without having to think about it that she was either dead or taken. I screamed for Bastian again as I tumbled out of the bedclothes and into the hall, barking my shin on the door as it swung back from my tempestuous shove. I collided with him at the front gate, and he caught me by the forearms, swinging me swiftly behind him as if he thought the danger was coming from the house.

"What is it, Rose? Are you hurt?"

"We have to find Cassandra," I said curtly, pulling away and busying myself with the strings of Akiva's hood. Now that I was warden it no longer obeyed Akiva, and I wanted to be sure it was on tight. I jerked my chin to indicate its colour to Bastian, and said in a tight voice, "The wardship fell to me this morning. Akiva's dead or taken."

"We will find her, Rose," Bastian said insistently. "Rose! Listen to me: you can't go charging into Cassandra's wardship!"

"She's the only one we're *certain* about!"

"Let me track Akiva first." Bastian caught me by the arms again, and this time I couldn't wriggle away. "It's not safe to go after Cassandra."

I put up my chin but eventually nodded because I knew he wouldn't let me go until I agreed. "All right. But if we can't find her—"

Bastian nodded at the dropped sentence. "We'll go after Cassandra. I promise. Did Akiva give you any inkling of what she was up to before she went?"

"She said there was something she needed to do. I think she had an idea who was behind it."

"Who would she have talked to before or after she left, apart from David?" At my startled look, he added: "I saw her slipping through the forest last night to see him.

"I don't know," I said, furious at the helplessness in my voice. "Mara? I haven't seen Akiva in days, and when she left, she wouldn't tell me what she was doing or where she was going."

"Then we should speak to David and Mara. They might know something we do not."

"All right," I said again. "If David told her anything he remembered it might give us an idea where she was last."

"Could he have recovered his memory?"

My heart sank. "Perhaps," I said, and told him about Kendra's brief reappearance. "I think she was trying to talk to me, but David saw her, too."

"Did he recognise her?" Bastian's eyes were sharp.

"No." I hesitated. "That is, I didn't think so, not really. He was confused."

"He may have been less confused when Akiva visited him last night," Bastian said, a little grimly. "Little witch; I hate to ask, but are you *sure* David is to be trusted?"

I nodded sharply. I didn't know what David had been like

before he lost his memory, but the David I knew, the one without a memory, I trusted absolutely.

"Then let us pay him a visit."

When we found him, David was sitting in the back garden, looking silently out into the fields. He was wan and somehow thinner than usual, and I thought with a pang that he looked like the war-scarred soldier we had claimed him to be. I knew at once that he had somehow got his memory back: he had the same tortured look I had seen once before, when Kendra disappeared and he thought it was his fault.

He continued to gaze out onto the fields without acknowledging us, but said quietly: "I suppose you want to know what I told Akiva?"

"She's gone," I said shortly. I could feel tears of frustration and fear gathering at the corners of my eyes, and I didn't want to give them a chance to escape.

David nodded, but still didn't look at me. "I know. I felt...a change, I think: only a little after she left."

"Where was she going?"

David rubbed a weary hand across his brow. "I don't know. She asked about what happened when I was taken, that's all. When she found out for certain that it was a gryphon that had taken me she left."

"I told Akiva I thought it was," I nodded. "I went to the place you disappeared, and I saw claw marks."

He nodded. "Cassandra was the one who threw the curse, but someone else was controlling the gryphon. I don't know who."

I said, "I only met a gryphon once, and it was Mara who saved me from it."

"Then we will speak with Mara," Bastian said, pulling me gently away. "She might know who has the power to control a mythic as powerful as a gryphon."

I wanted to stay and talk with David until the smile came back to his face, but his face was closed to me and I let Bastian draw me back into the forest without protest.

I didn't notice that I was edging imperceptibly closer to Cassandra's wardship until I felt Bastian's hand under my elbow, lightly guiding me away.

"Mara first," he said gently, edging us toward Akiva's cottage. "And fetch that comb of yours. I've a feeling it will prove important."

Fretting at the delay, I left Bastian at the gate and dashed into the silent cottage. The salamander, who had been lying in a patch of warm sunlight on the kitchen window sill, scuttled after me and climbed up to my shoulders, burning strands of my hair when I tried, impatiently, to remove it. Hot and bothered and cross, I fetched the comb from beneath the pillow of my bed and noticed belatedly that I seemed to be still wearing my party dress, which most inconveniently had no pockets. Crosser still, I shoved the comb into the back of my singed hair, hoping with an annoyed huff of air that made the salamander's skin glow from red to white briefly, that it would stay put.

Mara's wardship was unhealthy and darkening even though it was hot, bright noon. The scowling line of trees that greeted us made me uneasy. Things were out of place in small, creeping ways that pricked at the back of my neck, and as Bastian and I entered the wardship we even passed a gnarled old strangler fig with roots in both my wardship and Mara's. I thought briefly that it looked as though it were trying to flee to the safety and light of my wardship.

Something was going wrong with Mara's power as well, and the forest was reflecting it. I wondered if it could be more than just teething trouble the forest was going through as it adjusted to Mara's control: perhaps she simply couldn't keep so much forest in health and order. Bastian raised his brows at the disorder as we walked, but didn't speak.

The salamander, which had shown its determination to accompany us by continuing to curl about my shoulders and refusing to be dislodged, raised its head and cheeped in distress.

"Well, you *would* come," I told it crossly. The shorter strands of my hair had only just recovered from being burned off, and I didn't appreciate the faint aroma of singed hair that was at present following me about. "It serves you right."

The salamander gave me a reproachful look and tucked its head back down into my neck, sulking. To tell the truth, I could empathise with its distress: the forest's dark, brooding air gave the uncomfortable feeling that it was somehow angry with us. The lines were crooked and overlapping, sending confusingly mixed signals of the forest around, and as we continued further, I wondered how Mara could sense anything at all in her wardship.

She was planting precise rows of chives with a poker-straight back when we found her, and such was the confusion of the threads around her that she didn't sense us until she saw us. I thought she looked frowningly surprised and wondered if we were unwelcome.

To my relief, Mara's voice was light and even a little amused when she spoke. "What brings Akiva's apprentice to see me?"

"Akiva's vanished," I said baldly.

Mara's eyes sharpened on me, and she dug her trowel into the ground, giving us her full attention. "When?"

"This morning," I said shortly. It would take too long to explain that Akiva had been gone for much longer, and that I simply *knew* that she was gone for good now. "We need your help."

Mara stood up, stripping dirty gloves from her hands. "Protection? My dear child, I'm barely keeping these wardships together as it is. The lines are in disarray, and frankly, the dryads have been uncooperative at best. I doubt I could even protect you on my own wardship."

"We don't want protection," I said grittily. "We want Cassandra brought before the warden council."

Mara was visibly startled, but said with her usual calmness: "Then you had better come in. I'll make tea while we talk."

Mara's cottage was as spare and tidy as her person. The floor-boards were spotless, scrubbed to within an inch of their lives, and each tea cup and utensil hung exactly an inch from the whitewashed plaster of the wall and no further. It struck me, suddenly and uncomfortably, that I hadn't wiped my feet before coming in.

"What charges will you bring against her? I believe nothing less than the apprehension of the attacker will draw the other wardens out of the safety of their wardships."

I nodded, absently stroking the salamander. It was disturbed, its tail curling and uncurling about my neck. "I sneaked into Cassandra's wardship," I said quietly. I found myself looking back on the episode with faint wonder. What had I been thinking? It had been slightly less than a year ago, but I felt older and quieter and somehow less sure of my own expertise. "I thought she'd kill me, but she admitted it all to me: she didn't care. She also told me that someone else has been helping her: she said that her part of the bargain was that she would get Bastian and I to herself without fear of punishment from the warden council."

Mara set her kettle on the hob slowly, her cool blue gaze on me. "Do you have proof of this?"

I nodded. "Akiva found David the day he disappeared. We've been keeping him hidden ever since, waiting for him to recover his memory."

"So he recovered his memory," she said with quiet finality: a statement rather than a question. Her eyes dropped to the kettle, and it seemed to me that thoughts crossed her face swiftly, as if she were trying to decide something.

"His story agrees with Cassandra's," I pointed out, because I knew that to convince the council I would first need to convince Mara. "He told us that Cassandra cursed him, but that someone else was directing the attack; someone who was strong enough to control a gryphon."

"I see." Mara had turned to fetch three mugs from their appointed hooks, and now she gazed silently out of the window, the three teacups balanced delicately in her capable hands. "Have you spoken to anyone else about this?"

"No," said Bastian, his eyes flicking from me to Mara. "We came straight to you. You were the one Akiva trusted the most."

"Very well," Mara said calmly, not turning from the window. "I will call the council. You said you visited Cassandra's wardship:

what did you find there? The council will require more information."

I drew the comb out of my hair to show her and was puzzled to find that it was glowing softly. My stomach did a queer flip-flop as I looked up from it to see the single, matching comb in Mara's tidy bun. I'd seen it before, the day Bastian and I followed Cassandra. I simply hadn't realised it.

"I wish you hadn't found that," she said quietly, and I knew she must have sensed it from the moment we stepped in the house. She wasn't calling the council. "I would have let you go, you know."

"You swapped pieces of wardship," I said, understanding at last. I should have noticed the bright, gaudy bracelet dropping just below the cuff of Mara's sleeve. It didn't suit her, but it would have fit any of Cassandra's bright ensembles. "You had to be able to trust each other absolutely."

"It restricts my movements more than I like," Mara said, still gazing out the window. "I'll be glad to have it back. Cassandra wouldn't deal with me unless we swapped anchors, and even then, she would keep visiting me every few days to make sure I was looking after it. If I'd had my own, I would have known David still had his piece of wardship on him, and he would never have been a problem."

There was a storm of magic approaching on the forest lines. As twisted and confused as the threads were, I couldn't tell what was approaching, but I could guess. Cassandra may have cursed David, but she hadn't called on a gryphon. Horned hedgepigs, but it irked me to think that I'd believed Mara was the one who saved me from the gryphon! She had been trying to kill me, even then.

No doubt that was why she had never claimed the rescue: she must have thought the dragon-fever had driven away all memories of that day. I wondered how long I would have remained safe if she hadn't thought so, and found something for which to be thankful.

"Why did you try to kill me that time?" I asked her.

"You were meant to be the start of it," she said. "A whim on my part. But Kendra turned out to be more effective in any case. Once you're gone, I shall of course gracefully step in and claim

Akiva's wardship. I was planning on stepping in after she was gone, but this will be much easier: no claimants to the wardship, you see."

My mind began to work very quickly indeed, seizing on the single, important fact that Mara didn't know the wardship had fallen to me. I felt a little boost of hope; perhaps Bastian and I could get out of this with a whole skin after all. The storm of magic was rushing toward us at an increasing rate of speed, and it was all I could do now not to show that I had sensed it. I didn't know how well I succeeded in hiding my apprehension, but Mara didn't seem to notice anything amiss, and I thought in brief, brittle annoyance that she probably expected me to be afraid.

It was with difficulty that I swallowed my wounded pride, and tried to prepare myself for the gryphon's arrival. Would a startled look be enough, or would Mara expect me to scream?

As it turned out, I had no need to pretend. I'd forgotten that as a deep forest creature, gryphons didn't necessarily exist on the same plane of material existence as the rest of the forest, and when the splendidly plumed head with its cruel, curving beak and molten eyes thrust through the wall as if the wall weren't there, I yelped and instinctively leaped for cover.

Bastian was in front of me in a moment, swinging me behind him in a swift, tight arc, but by that time my jumping heart had come to rest again with a thump, and I was able to take my stand beside him, my fingers tight around his wrist to stop him doing anything rash.

The gryphon's voice was more cat-like, purring, than bird-like as it said, *Well met, human child.*

The golden eye roved from my face to Bastian's, and then, amusingly birdlike, it twitched its head to the other side and did the same with its left eye. *You have grown. Wolf; we meet again.*

I stole a brief look up at Bastian, who was looking with narrowed eyes at the gryphon. The gryphon eyed us both in amusement.

He never told you? He and I have met: I believe he rescued you from my, er—attentions.

261

Mara's fingers curled tightly around the gaudy bracelet that had once graced Cassandra's wrist.

"Kill them both," she said.

The gryphon turned a look of bird-like consideration on her, and said with cold amusement, *No.*

"What are you waiting for?" demanded Mara. "You are under my command: you will do as I say!"

Bastian, beside me, was breathing in quick, shallow breaths, his legs tensed and his eyes intent on the gryphon. I found that I knew what it meant: he was preparing for swift action. The gryphon turned a single eye to me, and I heard an edge of deadly amusement in its voice.

Ignorant human! it said, and the edge in its voice was sharper, more dangerous.

Regardless of the fact that it was referring to Mara, I felt distinctly uneasy. My fingers were cold where they gripped Bastian's wrist. The gryphon took one step and then another toward Mara, who stumbled backward, fear and anger fighting for dominance in her face. Huge, muscled legs followed the magnificently plumed head, razor sharp claws scraping against Mara's spotless floorboards and raising curls of wood. The scent of cedar filled the room, rising on hot, salty air.

It was hard to see quite how the gryphon was managing the wall: the plastered stones were still there, they and the gryphon equally present, equally intact. I found that I couldn't wrap my head around it and abandoned the attempt to understand as another step brought the gryphon's muscled chest and shoulders level with Bastian and me.

Mara's voice was an undignified squeak. "I order you to kill them both! Remove them from the forest and kill them!"

Ignorant human, the gryphon said again, in a caressing purr that I found distinctly more unnerving than its cold, deadly tones. *Our contract forces me to do as you order, but gryphon law, like deep forest law, prohibits me from killing one who has already escaped death at my hands. You have violated our contract by ordering me to do so. I claim my freedom forthwith, and you may be sure I will prevent any others from falling into your traps.*

There was a surge of immense heat, and Mara, with great presence of mind, threw up a wall of powerful magic. In the resulting calmness of cool air, I realised that the salamander, traitor that it was, had slipped away from my neck, and was now lovingly curled under the gryphon's neck-quills.

Amiably, the gryphon said, *I can wait. You cannot stay awake forever.*

Mara turned swiftly, pinioning me with her eyes. "Give me the comb!"

"No," I said.

Mara gripped the bracelet until the beads dug into her palm, and I saw the sweat on her brow. It was not until a stifled groan broke from Bastian and I looked up to find his face white and narrowed with pain that I realised she was using a torture spell on him.

I gave a snarl of rage and held the comb taut between two hands. "Stop or I'll break it!"

"Give me the comb or I will kill him," Mara countered, and there was neither remorse nor shrinking in her face.

She would kill him, forest law or no.

In desperation, I found the trace of magic leading from her to Bastian and tore savagely at it. Bastian gave a gasp of pain, or relief, and Mara was thrown back with a choked cry of anguish.

She pulled herself up with the help of one of the kitchen chairs, and I braced myself for a battle that I couldn't hope to win. The gryphon gave a laugh, satisfied to watch us fight it out, but Mara, one side of her perpetually neat bun hanging loosely by her left ear, was visibly beginning to lose her calm.

"What are you doing?" Her voice retained a vestige of calm, but her fingers were white around the chair back where the bracelet beads clicked against wood. "You can't see the lines here, and your little touch of magic is hardly strong enough to fight me."

I curled my hand a little more tightly around the comb. Mara still hadn't realised that I had come into the wardship instead of

Akiva. Now that I had, Akiva's cloak was no longer merely a protection: it performed for me the same function that it had for her, providing part of my wardship for me to draw on.

And I suddenly knew what to do: because I had another advantage...

I slipped my hand into Bastian's, lacing my fingers through his, and he looked down at me swiftly, enquiringly. I smiled up at him, then found a single, straight thread running through the house and leapt for it. I tore all the other threads as I leapt, and the house fell down around our ears as we ran, the only whole thread glowing ahead of us, true and strong.

Bastian was laughing, a gleeful, wolfish sound; and with my heart pounding in my ears and Bastian's fingers strongly clasping mine, I laughed too. Mara was close behind, but she was old, notwithstanding her great magic, and her wardship thoroughly hated her now. As she ran the trees reached out and caught at her, and the energy lines twisted around her until she was gasping in rage and fatigue.

Bastian and I ran and dodged, feeling the hiss of deathly magic that flew around us more and more wildly as Mara lost focus. The other threads twisted around us in a sickening vortex of power, but I ignored them all to follow the one, true thread that led us to the very thing I wanted to find.

I burst back into my wardship with Bastian by my side, gasping for breath. The strangler fig was still there, ancient and gnarled, and so Akiva-like that I wondered why I hadn't known her at once. Mara must have caught her off guard or such a thing could never have happened. Still, she'd fought impressively to get home, and she had almost made it.

Bastian, bright-eyed and hardly panting at all, caught himself up beside me. "What's in the wind, little witch?"

"Deeper forest," I said, without waiting to explain.

I plunged desperately in, leaving him far behind, and layers of forest swept past me in a moment. I experienced again the cold, falling sensation I had felt when the dryads invited me into deeper forest for their wedding dance.

My heart jumped, because I was right, it *was* Akiva. Hadn't she said one didn't get into deeper forest without an invitation? That one, straight, glowing thread had been her doing: the invitation had come from her.

The strangler fig before me didn't seem to grow more human, nor could I see the branches melding into limbs and skin; but quietly, suddenly, Akiva was there.

"You took your time," she said, but it was said with a grim smile. Pulsing threads announced Mara's imminent arrival as she began to take shape beside me, faint and nebulous, and somehow slower than I had been. My fingers shook as I untied the strings of my hood to give to Akiva, my haste making me clumsy.

"It's too late for that, child," Akiva said, forestalling me with a gnarled, twiggy hand. "It's yours now. I will not be escaping this place in a hurry. Deeper forest tends to cling to its own, and I've not the strength to break free."

"But I'll give it to you!" I said, a little desperately. "The wardship is yours, I'll give it back!"

"You can't," she said. "Once a new warden is chosen, the old is no longer recognised. The forest chose you; it will remain yours until your death."

I saw my plans crumbling in a horrifying heap around me as Mara grew more solid beside me, and desperately gulped back a sob.

Akiva saw it, and her grimness softened into something very like a grin.

"I can't escape, but I can help," she said. "I'm very well content to remain as I am—it has been peaceful and quiet."

"And no feckless apprentice to make your life a misery," I said gruffly, sniffling in an attempt to keep the tears at bay a little longer.

She really did grin then, but didn't answer. I had the idea that she was too busy to do so. Her arms (or perhaps they were branches, now; it was hard to tell) had snaked out to encircle Mara, who though nebulous and weak, was fighting back. She had tried to enter deeper forest without an invitation shortly before crossing into my wardship, but without her comb she was as helpless as she would have been in my wardship. The fig branches curled and tightened about her, and I watched as her mouth opened and closed in dead silence. I couldn't tell whether she was yelling or cursing or pleading, for her voice, along with the colours in her clothes, hadn't yet penetrated to deeper forest. She was a silent, black-and-white figure squirming against the backdrop of living green. Akiva, without mercy and without pity, tightened her branches until Mara was still and tree-like herself, and then turned toward me.

"You'd best be off now," she said, her voice strained. No matter what she said, I knew that she had a fierce desire to be human once more, to stomp out her days in the free air of the forest. "Remember me to your mother. And to the wolf, I suppose."

"I won't!" I said, with glittering eyes. "You'll see them yourself!"

There was a kaleidoscopic swirl of colour radiating toward us, whether a natural effect of deeper forest or from the tears in my eyes I couldn't tell: but I knew at once that Kendra had appeared again.

Akiva didn't turn, but a shiver of relief seemed to pass through her old body. "Kendra, child; we've missed you."

"I am here now," Kendra said obliquely. She wasn't at all like the quiet, almost painfully shy young woman I had met once. She was tall and willowy and utterly confident; at home in deeper forest as neither Akiva nor I could be. Memory mounted upon memory, and when I realised the truth, it wasn't a surprise to me.

"You've turned dryad," I said, guilty relief flowing through me. She would never leave the forest again: Mother was safe. David could—well, David could at least *choose* now. "It was me you came to see at the dance."

She nodded and smiled down at me, her eyes at once bright and distant. "Tell David it's well with me. I don't want to leave. He is free."

I nodded respectfully, but I didn't dare look her in the eyes again for fear that she would see the joy blazing in my own.

She turned from me to Akiva, and said with quiet command, "Let go now."

Akiva did so without question. I think she knew as I did that there was little of humanity left in Kendra, no pity and no hesitation. As she let go, Mara flashed into colour and sound, her hair

266

now utterly free from its comb. I gripped the other tightly in my hand, afraid that she would somehow seize it and escape after all.

"You can't do this to me!" she snapped, but there was a cold watchfulness in her eyes, and I think that not even she believed it. She had broken too many of the forest's laws, and it wouldn't help her now.

Kendra considered her quietly as if weighing options, and then said, "If I let you go it will cause mischief in the forest. That cannot be allowed."

"I'll leave the forest!" There was dawning horror in Mara's eyes, and I found I could still pity her even though it was the fate she herself had foisted upon Akiva. "I'll take a house well away from the forest and the village!"

Again Kendra gave her that considering look. It occurred to me that she was communicating with someone, somewhere, in a way that I couldn't understand.

"You have been judged and sentenced," she said. "You will remain in deeper forest confined to the form of this tree. Your wardships will be kept in trust by Akiva until such time as the other wardens are found and returned to their wardships."

Kendra's eyes turned to me, and I realised that she was waiting for me to give Mara's comb to Akiva. I did so, skirting widely around Mara, who looked as if she would try any desperate attempt to escape. At once Akiva became clearer and less treelike.

"Ah, that's better!" she said, stretching as if her bones had been cramped. Beside me, Mara was slowly and horribly being swallowed up in strangler fig boughs that wound about her far more tightly than Akiva's had. Akiva's face was flint-like, without compassion, and I wondered what exactly had passed between her and Mara.

When there was nothing left of Mara but the vague, lasting impression of a face, Akiva let out a sigh and hugged me roughly. "There's nothing else we can do here, Rose. Come along."

I turned back once to ask Kendra, "What about the others? Can we do the same for them?"

"Some are dead, some are not," she said quietly. "Find the ones that are not and free them."

Deeper forest passed by in a rush under Akiva's hand. Before I could blink, I was snatched up and hugged roughly to Bastian's chest more tightly than my already breathless body appreciated. He let me go at last and swept Akiva into a crushing hug that made her first groan in protest and then box his ears. "None of that, wolf! Save your hugs for those who want 'em!"

Bastian planted a smacking kiss on her cheek, and I chuckled through a yawn, as exhausted as if I had been running wild in the forest all day.

Akiva said briskly, "Off home with you, Rose! No, I'm not coming with you; there are far too many things to do around here. Wolf, make sure she gets home safely."

"I can look after myself," I interposed with some asperity, stifling another yawn. I was annoyed to find myself so sleepy. Horned hedgepigs, at this rate I wouldn't ever be more than a two-copper warden!

"I'll look after her," Bastian said, ignoring me.

"And be careful where you walk," added Akiva. She slid the comb that had been Mara's into her hair, and I felt a little hum buzzing on the air as the wardship took to her. "The forest is coming apart at the seams with flyaway threads: some of them are loose and dangerous. Try to keep to the paths."

She left us there and melted away into her new wardship, leaving me with the rather dazed realisation that I was no longer a temporary warden. I was full warden of a vast and magical piece of forest that needed more attention to bring it to rights than I could give it in one day, one week, or even perhaps one year.

I took a deep breath to quell a moment of panic. "At least," I said tightly, "at least Mara is gone. There might be a chance of straightening out the forest threads now, if only we can get rid of Cassandra as well. How long were we gone, Bastian?"

"A few moments," he said, slipping his arm around my waist to dance me a few steps forward.

He seemed light-headed and merry, and I thought in a flash of knowing that he had been very much worried for those few moments. So I allowed him to twirl me about, grateful in truth for his arms around me, since I felt that there was nothing I would like better than to be in my bed. Setting the wardship—*my* wardship!—to rights could wait a little longer.

"It was much longer than that," I told him, looking up from a merry promenade through two birches. Bastian spun me elegantly, and this time instead of dancing he was hugging me again, close and fierce as though he didn't want to let go.

"I know," he said. "Oh, little witch, I know!"

Seventeen

I found a hard dirt path for us, prosaic and staid, and Bastian and I strolled along it slowly, his arm comfortably around my waist. I vainly tried to stifle my yawns for a while and then allowed myself to succumb, grateful to Bastian for holding me up. The ground felt as though it were dancing beneath my feet in a slow, shallow, dizzying swing.

It wasn't until Bastian, his voice startled, demanded, "Is the ground moving, little witch?" that I was brought to the fuzzy realisation that it was not simply my tired mind playing tricks on me.

"Yes—no. Perhaps." I cast my forest sight around, but exhaustion made it hard to focus, and the threads blended together in a confused, golden tangle. I swiped a hand over my eyes and then sat down suddenly, slipping away from Bastian's arm with determined abandon. "Can't see. I'm going to sleep now."

I think I remember being carried, and dappled afternoon sunlight slipping across my face in golden warmth, then there was silence and cool shadow as I slipped into dreamless sleep.

I woke to a gentle rocking sensation that made me think for a sleep-heavy moment that I was still being carried. As I blinked my eyes open I saw the furry form of wolf-Bastian, dropped forward on his belly, head erect and watchful. I lurched up into a sitting position to try and account for the sensation, feeling a little peculiar. Pre-dawn light was stealing through the trees, chasing a wispy early morning mist, and my feeling of disorientation increased.

"Did I sleep all day?"

Bastian, who had been watching me, gave a wolfish nod and sat up. "Most of the night, too. My change will come again shortly."

"I'm sorry," I said, hugging him. "Thank you for staying."

One of Bastian's ears quirked humorously. "I would love to accept your thanks with a gratified smirk, little witch, but the plain truth of the matter is that I couldn't leave if I wanted to."

I sat back and regarded him with a narrowed look to see if I were being laughed at. Odd. He was laughing and serious at the same time. "What do you mean?"

"Look around, Rose." The laughing lilt was suddenly gone from Bastian's voice. I sensed a still, tense note to his voice that I hadn't heard before, and it struck me with a chill that Bastian was *frightened*.

"Look with your forest sight."

I opened my forest sight, and a small, stifled sound escaped me. Bastian and I were curled on a tiny piece of forest that trailed torn forest lines out into a vast, inky blackness, the path we had been travelling on now simply a fragment that ended as abruptly as it began, in a jagged line of dirt.

I rose to my knees in wide-eyed horror, understanding all at once the stiffness with which Bastian sat. "Oh! Oh, oh, *oh*. Bastian, what happened?"

"Don't move too quickly," he warned, carefully rising on all four legs. "It tilts if you unbalance it. I was carrying you home along the path, not too far from the cottage, and suddenly the path wasn't there."

His voice was tense, and I wondered just how close we had both come to tumbling into the hungry blackness. "There are other bits of forest further on; I can see them sometimes."

I stood, shaking a little, with the steadying help of a sturdy young birch. My fingers curled around it, white at the knuckles, as I gazed out into the terrifying expanse of blackness.

Bastian was right: there *were* other islands of forest adrift in the dark. Some of them were small, barely bigger than the one we were on; others were quite large. One was even large enough for a tiny stone hut. Once I knew they were there, they were easier to see, threads trailing out around them like tentacles on a creeping underwater creature. It sent a nasty shiver through me, the kind of shiver that a particularly large and hairy spider brings on.

"They're pieces of my wardship," I said, feeling sick. There was a violet kind of flickering around the edge of my forest sight, too far away to see clearly. I found I knew what it was.

"Cassandra's out there, isn't she?"

"Yes." Bastian's voice was so quiet I almost didn't hear it. "The tears in the wardship aren't Mara's doing."

"Does she know where we are?"

"No." Bastian hesitated, then swung his muzzle at the darkness around us. "I think it's all this. I don't think she can sense us through it, or she would have found us hours ago."

"You should have woken me," I said angrily. He must have stayed awake for hours, waiting each moment with nerves straining for Cassandra to pounce. I was surprised to find how furious that made me. I wasn't sure who it was I was angriest at: Cassandra, Bastian, or myself.

"No need, little witch," Bastian said lightly, nosing my hand comfortingly. "Cassandra hasn't seen us, and we remain in the same place without drifting. I left you sleeping with the purely selfish motivation that you would need all the strength you could get to bring us out of this scrape safely."

He said it to make me laugh, and I gave a mechanical smile. "I can't do it, Bastian," I said baldly. "I don't know how—I don't even know where we are."

"We're on your wardship," he said, with a quiet confidence that warmed me. "This is your home: you make the rules. Make it do what you want it to do."

I gazed out on the torn pieces of wardship, hoping for inspiration. There were thirteen of them, green shards against a black velvet backdrop. I found that if I narrowed my eyes and concentrated hard enough, my vision scoped outward until the closest chunk of green wardship seemed to hang in the air just before me, perfect in detail.

Broken forest. Thirteen pieces of broken forest. *Thirteen pieces.*

I stooped to the ground, absently feeling for pebbles between the roots of the slim birch tree. Thirteen pieces. Thirteen milestones. A grim smile grew on my face, maturing until it became a tough, humourless grin. Perhaps I could get us home after all.

I narrowed my vision on the torn piece of wardship furthest away, a fuzzy greenness far away. It wouldn't clear entirely, but I could see enough to know that it was the rest of the wardship. Thirteen milestones to mark the way.

"Rose?" Bastian's voice was strained.

I looked across at him, and saw a pale glow of gold emanating from his fur that took on a vaguely human form as I watched.

"I can't hold it off much longer," he said, hackles up in spiky discomfort. "When it happens, she'll hone onto us like a moth to flame."

I nodded, my grin so fierce now that it was almost a grimace. It was going to be chancy at best. A quick glance down showed that I had gathered exactly thirteen assorted unlovely and unpolished stones: just enough. The game allowed for fifteen, a kind of two-life bonus, but I didn't think that would work here: the forest seemed to play for keeps. I would need to make each throw count.

"This might not work," I said, my eyes on the next, closest chunk of wardship. "Be ready for the shift in balance when we jump."

The only answer Bastian vouchsafed me was a snarl, accompanied by a small but potent surge of magic that catapulted a spurt of gold into the void. Somewhere beyond us, the bright purple presence froze and turned, quivering.

I hefted one pebble in my hand. "Change now."

Bastian, still straining against the change, shuddered and snarled again.

"*Now!*" I snapped, my eyes flashing. I didn't wait for a reply: there was no time, and Cassandra had found us. The pebble was hard and cold between my fingers, the others clutched tight in my left hand, where they dug grittily into my skin. I couldn't afford to lose any of them.

I drew a line in the turf with one bare foot, streaking my big toe with rich black sod and crushed grass. Feet behind, I thought mechanically, and checked that they were well away from the line. I swung my arm gently by my side, measuring the impossible distance, and began.

> *"Into the woods to grandmother's house,*
> *Thirteen milestones mark the way;*
> *Keep to the path and never stray,*
> *There and back by light of day."*

As I finished, Bastian's change shocked through the void in a dazzle of gold.

"One for luck," I said, and tossed the pebble. Its muted green sparkle arced improbably far, hidden in the splendour of Bastian's change to human. It fell to rest on the distant bank of the next wardship piece, leaving behind a faint, tenuous forest thread. My heart gave one, thudding leap, forcing a gasp of relief from me.

Horned hedgepigs, it had worked!

Behind me, I felt Bastian rise, swiftly. A cloud of dark magic was forming around us, and when I turned my head, his eyes were glittering in the shadows.

"She's here. Quickly!"

His hand fastened around mine, and then we were leaping; leaping through cold space along a wavering thread of forest magic that should have been too insubstantial to hold us but somehow did anyway.

The hard grassy bank hit us hard, and for a moment the world tipped wildly around us as I gasped for breath. Bastian, groaning, heaved me into the middle of the tiny knoll, and the sickening swell subsided enough for me to drag myself clumsily to my feet, still gulping for breath. The pebble was there in my hand: I pinched the forest line from it and cast it away to flutter loose in the void, where it would give Cassandra no help. I dropped the pebble again and chose another; a smaller, sharper stone that had a good weight to it.

"Two for chance!" I gasped, and threw it.

We leapt again, this time to a bigger chunk of earth that didn't sway so perilously at our landing. I snatched the used thread away to float freely, feeling the dull, aching pinch of bruised ribs, and chose another pebble mechanically. I noticed dimly that there was blood on it: my clenched hand had gripped tightly, and the sharp pebbles had bitten deeply in revenge.

"Three for faith!" My voice broke, but I had breath enough for the jump to a large, saucer-like patch of wardship.

This time the thread was stronger.

The breathless leaping fell into a routine; throw, jump, snap forest line, throw. One for luck, two for chance, three for faith, four for romance; five brings trouble and six follows grief, seven takes joy and eight holds belief; nine brings learning, ten holds a place, eleven for virtue and twelve for grace...

> "Thirteen is hardest, be quick or too late;
> To grandmother's house through the white picket
> gate."

The last pebble was there in my fingers, and I felt my hand tremble. We had arrived last of all on the wardship shard with the little stone hut, and I had found to my dismay that it was not a piece of my wardship at all. If I had a guess, I would have guessed it was Cassandra's.

Be quick or too late, mocked the rhyme, but my hand still shook and I didn't dare throw the pebble.

"Rest," Bastian said quietly. He was leaning against the stone wall with one hand, head bowed, pulling in deep breaths through his nose.

I gripped my shaking right hand with my left. "We can't. She'll see us again soon."

Bastian's long fingers closed over both my hands in a warm, firm grip, pulling me through the doorless stone arch of the house. "Rest, love. Even Cassandra's magic can't penetrate stone."

The floor of the cottage was bare, brushed dirt, with no furniture or decoration. It obviously hadn't been used in some time, but though it was old and abandoned, it was also clean of cobwebs. There was a back doorway immediately before us that seemed to shimmer. I felt a touch of unease as Bastian sat me gently against a wall; unease that quickly disappeared in the harsh, present reality of two bruised ribs, freshly jarred. I involuntarily whimpered, and Bastian looked down sharply.

"Little witch?"

"It's nothing," I snapped, swallowing once to clear the ache from my throat. I felt perilously close to tears. The stone was quiet and silent around me, and I couldn't even feel forest lines beneath my feet. I wondered why, until Bastian sat beside me, scuffing dirt aside to reveal smooth stone. The dirt was barely an inch deep over great white flagstones that emanated a slight but distinct chill. The quietness seemed to creep around us, a silent and threatening stillness.

I would have leaped to my feet and dashed from the cottage then and there, but Bastian's arm closed around me, vice-like, and held me still as a violet shadow flitted past the stone archway. We remained still for many minutes: through the stone it was impossible to sense whether or not Cassandra had gone.

At last, Bastian's arm slid away from me. "Come, little witch," he said softly, lifting me gently to my feet. "Keep behind me."

He paused for a moment in the doorway for a quick scouting look. "She's gone. Quickly now, Rose."

The hair of my arms stood on end in the stone silence for a brief second before I saw the shimmer misting the front doorway. Then Bastian stepped through, and the pain hit me.

I remember screaming. I thought once that I would be the defiant Cutlass Rose, impervious to pain and torture; but when the pain seized me with savage claws, all I could do was scream. Scream over and over, while fire coursed through my body, searing my flesh and burning from the inside out.

It ended as suddenly as it had begun. I came to myself, bruised and cut, but unburned, on the stone floor of the hut while Bastian wiped the blood from my face with horror in his eyes.

As if from far away, I heard his voice. "Rose! *Rose!* What happened?"

I choked on a sob, only dimly understanding. "Ca—Cassandra! Won't be able—to get out."

"Of course you can get out," Bastian said, very white about the lips. "You saw me leave just now. If need be, I will carry you out."

"Oh, *you* can leave," said Cassandra's voice, terrifyingly close behind us.

Bastian turned swiftly, stooped over me in protection, and she laughed at him.

"That's uncharacteristically brave of you, darling. But you can leave. *She* can't."

Bastian had gone very pale. "A witch hut? This is a *witch hut?*"

A breathtaking smile swept over Cassandra's face. "Now show me that self-sacrificing altruism of yours if you can!"

I looked at Bastian. His face was white, his breathing too fast. "Bastian? What's she talking about?"

There was a glitter of triumph and malice in Cassandra's eyes, but I didn't know what it meant: nor what it meant that she hadn't killed Bastian already. Mara wouldn't stop her: Akiva couldn't. What was I missing?

"She doesn't know what it is!" Cassandra's eyes travelled scornfully over me as I struggled to rise to my feet. "Will you tell her, I wonder? I think you will."

"Bastian, what does she mean?" I was remembering the fiery pain that had taken hold of me when Bastian stepped through the stone doorway. I tried to make my voice angry but it came out small and scratched instead. "What is a witch hut?"

"It's nothing," Bastian said, coldly dismissive. "Just the old witch trying to play off her tricks."

"What are you playing at, wolf? Tell her and be done with it."

"Either kill me now or leave us alone," Bastian said coolly. "I've had enough of this foolery."

She made an air-kiss teasingly at him. "Darling, you should know by now that I'll never leave you alone. Besides, this is so much more amusing! You understand, don't you?"

"Oh, I understand," Bastian said.

He made a great show of sitting down leisurely and stretching his legs out comfortably before him. A quick flicker of his eyes bid me do the same, so I joined him on the dirt floor. Still Cassandra didn't attack.

"She's not beautiful," Cassandra said disdainfully. "She's not beautiful or powerful, or very clever. Why don't you just tell her?"

Bastian, ignoring her, pulled me closer with one arm and began gently to wipe away the mingled blood and dirt from my face. "Smile at me," he murmured. "Keep her off balance. No, not like that, little witch, you look like you're in pain."

The typically Bastian remark brought a real smile to my face. Whatever game he was playing, it looked as though Cassandra was not going to attack. I had begun to wonder if perhaps she *couldn't* attack.

"Much better," he approved softly, smiling down at me. "But I think we can do better again."

The hand that had been caressing the dirt away from my face dropped, and slid around me instead, pulling me closer.

Oh! I thought, interestingly close to Bastian and discovering with faint surprise that I was enjoying myself. *That* was how he meant to unbalance Cassandra. Bastian, for reasons best known to himself, was trying to convince Cassandra that I had broken the curse in the only way she would understand. I tilted my face up at an inviting angle and let him kiss me.

"Stop that!" Cassandra said, through her teeth. "Bastian, I warn you!"

To my satisfaction, Bastian ignored her. I was enjoying myself far too much in consideration of the fact that Bastian was only attempting to break the curse, while at the same time trying to convince Cassandra that it was already done. I looked at Cassandra through my eyelashes. She was flushed with anger, and as I watched, she took a furious step forward—a step that took her almost through the doorway.

Almost, but not quite. Bastian stiffened, his eyelashes brushing my cheek as his eyes opened a slit, and in that moment Cassandra froze.

I heard her laugh. "That was quite clever of you, darling!"

Bastian let me go and rested his forehead against mine for a brief moment. Under his breath, he said, "Sorry, little witch."

"I almost stepped in!" her voice rich with amusement. "You've made it so much more enjoyable, darling. Now, will you tell her, or shall I?"

"I don't know what you're talking about," Bastian said. His voice was very hard. "It seems to me that you've lost."

Cassandra shrugged. "I lose a little. You lose a lot."

"Get on with it, then," I said impatiently. Bastian was sitting very still despite his casual tone, and his hands were cold. "Tell me what is so important."

"He's pretending, you know," said Cassandra, her eyes flicking to me for the first time. "He's trying to make me think that he's changed, but it won't work. You'll see, before the end."

"You're boring me, Cassandra," said Bastian coolly.

"Do you want to know how much time is left?" she asked. There was less amusement in her eyes now.

"Not particularly. Go away, Cassandra."

"You have four hours," she said. "Time passes differently here; every jump steals away a little more time. Do you want to know how much time the last jump will take away?"

Bastian ignored her, but she prattled away to herself in spite of his patent disinterest, "It will take off a full hour."

My first thought was that Cassandra had badly mistaken the situation: Bastian was still in the forest, and his change wouldn't be the irreversible one he was always afraid of. My second, more cautious thought, was that Cassandra knew very well what she was about, and would have planned more carefully than that.

So it was cautiously that I said, "We're still in the forest. Even if Bastian turns, he's safe."

"Stupid rabbit! I went to some trouble to find this piece of ground. It's a piece of the village outskirts. No forest."

I stood with murder in my thoughts. "You're cheating!"

"I'm doing you a favour, rabbit," said Cassandra coldly. "Watch and wait. If it's a choice between you and him, he'll leave you for dead."

"It's nothing to do with choices," I said fiercely. "You're trying to cheat by locking us in here while time runs out for Bastian."

"You should be more worried about time running out for you," said Cassandra. "The witch hut eats away at your magic: once the wolf leaves, it will begin. It only hurts witches, you see."

"I can live without my magic," I said, with a suddenly dry throat.

The coldness grew in me until there was a chill right through my bones, so I put my chin up.

"You can't, you know," she said. "It eats away at your magic until there's no more left, and then it eats away at *you*. You'll see who he chooses when it's between you and him."

She gave us one last, enchanting smile; then, with a flick of blue-black hair, she turned on her heel and left us.

"I'll kill her," I said.

The icy coldness had taken over my body, and I found that I didn't recognise my own voice. I didn't turn to look at Bastian because I wasn't quite sure I wanted to see him. I was ashamed to find that a tiny part of me expected him to leave, and I was afraid to face that horrible pain again as the witch hut ate the small amount of magic I possessed.

"No you won't," Bastian said firmly, surprising me by slipping his arms around me from behind. He leaned his head into mine and kissed my hair lightly. "You will wait until we can get out safely, and then you will go home. I will deal with Cassandra."

"Neither of us can deal with Cassandra," I said flatly. "That's the problem. I *won't* have you getting yourself killed."

Bastian chuckled into my hair. "You seem to have the most adorable idea that you can stop me, little witch."

"If you go after Cassandra, she'll only kill you," I said stubbornly, turning around to scowl at him. Bastian made this more difficult by kissing my nose as I turned.

"It won't matter," he said; and I understood then that he wouldn't leave me. There was acceptance in his eyes: even a kind of lightness. "The forest has ways of dealing with the Cassandras of the world. She's gone just a little too far this time."

"Bastian—"

"No."

"You have to leave."

Bastian kissed me on the nose again, and said with finality: "No."

"She means for you to be wolf forever!"

"Or you to die," he said. "What do you want from me, little witch? Cassandra expects me to save myself at your expense, but I'm not that man anymore. I won't do it."

"I don't want you to be trapped," I said angrily, furious at Cassandra for cheating, furious at Bastian for sitting quietly and letting it happen. "I want you to be free again. You have to go *now*, while you still can!"

"Little witch, I would have eaten you—I almost did eat you—and I would have done more harm by you. I had been trying my hardest to do worse by you. Don't ask me again."

"I'm not asking," I said, and shoved with all my strength.

He should have gone through the door—I even remembered to inch my toe behind his heel to keep him off balance—but he caught the door frame with one quick hand and spun himself back. He was *laughing*.

"Little witch, I'll never know how I lived without you all these years! No, don't try to throw me out again; I'll only come back in. Sit down peaceably with me."

The fury vanished, and I found myself laughing. "You horrible man, you were meant to fall over!"

"You constantly surprise me, my love; but that was not at all surprising," Bastian said, his eyes alight with laugher. "Sit down and be comfortable."

It didn't feel like an ending. We sat and talked and laughed, with

Bastian's arm around my waist and my legs curled up against him in the dirt, as if we were safe in the forest on any ordinary day. This is how is should always be, I thought, in a moment of quiet clarity; just Bastian and I, talking together.

The change came quietly and almost unnoticeably, as if unaware of its own importance. I felt the hut leaching the magic away as Bastian exuded it, and wrapped my arms around him, drawing in a deep, Bastian-scented breath until I felt fur against my face instead of skin. There was a soft huff of breath as Bastian sighed once, and then his head lifted, pulling away gently from my arms.

"Ah well, that's that."

I sniffed, seeing him through a teary haze of gold, and said roughly, "I'm sorry, Bastian."

"You have nothing to be sorry for," he said quietly.

I dashed a hand over my eyes, but Bastian's face remained blurry, and a cold tingle swept up my neck, because he was still glowing gold! I sat up straight with a caught breath, hope kindling, and looked more carefully.

The golden aura usually surrounding him had formed into spirals and figures that looked distinctly like writing, airy yet immovable. Every clause and injunction of the curse was written there, curling around Bastian's body; and every condition had been met and completed.

The glow waned and waxed, brighter and then fainter by turns, but the brightness grew greater and the faintness less faint with each surge in luminosity.

There was a hum in the air, low and grating, and Bastian said, startled, "Rose? What's happening?"

"Don't know," I said tersely. The hum was not coming from Bastian, and it took me some time to realise that it was the sound of the stones grinding together in the walls.

There was a huge surge in Bastian's aura that filled the air with warm golden brightness, and the hum rose to a roar, shaking the hut.

I threaded my fingers through Bastian's ruff. "Hold on!"

"To what?" Bastian's forelegs were braced wide, claws scrabbling for grip, and around us the house drew in magic greedily as his glow faltered once more and then grew in strength.

I gave a breathless giggle. "I don't know. Here it comes!"

An explosion of molten gold magic burst stone and buckled the ceiling above us in a great crashing cacophony, showering us with shards of stone. The witch hut split around us in a shattering of stone, flooding my mind with memory upon memory while the released magic flowed into me relentlessly.

I saw them all—an old woman, dark and evil; a beautiful young girl, her brown eyes wide with fright; even a child of barely three years old, her mouth opened in a prolonged, uncomprehending scream of pain; and so, so many more—all the witches who had finished their days here.

I saw them all, felt their pain; and as their magic flowed into me I screamed, dying death after death. Dimly, I felt Bastian's arms around me, but the pain swept everything else aside, as ruthless as the unstoppable tide of magic that poured into me until I felt that I couldn't possibly hold any more.

The rush stopped eventually, and I seemed to float toward the surface of a pool of raw, uncontained magic. I found that I was no longer in pain, but my head felt as though it contained a plethora of butterflies, flitting here and flitting there. It was hard to tell which thought to follow.

One solid constant was the pressure of arms around me, and slowly it came to me that someone was holding me. Bastian, I thought; and opened my eyes with a sigh of contentment, to see him, dishevelled and wild-eyed, but very human. He cupped one shaking hand around my face and then pulled me close, shuddering. It was some time before I recognised his huge, gulping breaths for the sobs that they were, and realised blankly that Bastian was *crying*.

The world shifted, and suddenly I was the comforter, murmuring quiet nonsense into his ear and stroking his hair steadily with my free hand. A light trickle of magic flowed instinctively from my fingers, soothing; and with it I caught the sense of a young girl with caramel eyes that were very familiar. They were not wide and frightened anymore, but without a doubt she was the second witch

I had seen. This was *her* magic; something she had known. Now it was mine.

For once I felt sure of myself. My own magic had been chancy and accidental at best, but this magic was assured and certain: it knew what it had to do, and how to do it. I surrounded Bastian with comfort and peace.

At last, he disengaged himself, but it was only to gather me closer in his arms, wrapping them tightly about me as if he thought I was about to slip away.

He said, "Oh, little witch, I thought I'd lost you!"

"Oh no!" I said, hugging him back fiercely. "You're stuck with me now."

Around us, the witch hut was a blasted field of sharp, rocky edges, some of them still faintly smoking. I knew with certainty that it would never kill another witch.

When Bastian raised his head at last, he gazed on it in blank wonder. "What did you do? What happened?"

"It wasn't me, bufflehead! It was you! You broke the last part of the curse!"

There was a nasty type of magic mixed with the others in me, and it told me, with the sharpness of an old woman who had cursed many times in her life, that the last part of the curse had never been mine to break. "Something to find, something to do, and something to give—*you* know. It wasn't me that had to give!"

"I see," Bastian said quietly. I think he was still shaking. He flopped back in the scattered dirt and debris, and for a moment I thought he was sobbing again; but this time he was convulsing with laughter.

I left him to laugh himself sane and climbed to my feet to inspect the damage. One of the witches in my head was suggesting distantly that there was something I needed to find, and though their personalities had faded quickly since I woke, it was still a strong enough sensation to cause me to wander through the ruins, shifting small piles of rubble somewhat absently with one foot. In my peripheral I saw Bastian sit up again, slowly and quietly, but it wasn't until I sifted my way through the rubbish toward him again that I saw that he was frowning down at a thick, furry skin that was bunched between his hands.

"Oh, there it is," I said, in quiet recognition.

I saw a glint of gold amidst the layers of glossy pelt as Bastian turned it over. The residue of the curse had taken a solid shape.

"It's your wolf-skin," I told him. "Put it on, you might need it."

"It's not that I don't trust you, little witch," Bastian said, holding the skin at arm's length and cocking an eyebrow at me; "But I really have no desire to be a wolf again."

The nasty old crone muttered in my head, useful for once. "You'll only change if you latch the clasp, and it won't be permanent. You should be able to come and go as you please now, forest or no forest."

Bastian looked unconvinced, but he allowed me to arrange the pelt over his shoulders without demur, and the stiffness in his shoulders gradually subsided as no change took place. I wondered how long it would be before he could bring himself to fasten the catch he was fingering so uneasily.

Eighteen

❧

W e didn't talk about it because we both knew it. Sooner or later, we were going to have to make the last jump. Sooner or later, we would have to return to the forest. And when we did, Cassandra would be waiting for us. I could feel the last stone in my pocket, scraping against my leg as I walked through the debris of the witch hut, and in my mind the old witch muttered old, dangerous spells.

"Oh, hush, you!" I murmured. Her sourness clung to the back of my mind like a bad taste, and I pulled at a trace of the brown-eyed girl to block her out.

Bastian, who had been running his fingers through the wolf pelt, cocked his head at me. "Little witch?"

"Hush. I need to think."

His hand snaked out, caught my own, and twirled me irresistibly into himself. I found myself sitting on Bastian's knee while he said conversationally, "Little witch, you and I will one day have words about your practise of hushing me. For now, I would like to know why your eyes have changed colour three times in as many minutes."

"Oh, that."

"Yes, *that!*"

"Just something tricky the witch hut did when it exploded," I said evasively. "Some of the witches weren't quite gone, I think."

"What do you mean, they're not gone?"

I shrugged. "Little bits were left. Sort of misty bits of magic and personality that stayed behind when they died."

"And these bits of magic and personality—"

"Are in my head now," I nodded. I sorted curiously through the information that bobbed to the surface of my mind and added: "I don't know how long it'll last. A long time, I think. One of them knows about time and trickery like that: I think he was the one who made sure something of them stayed behind."

Bastian still looked distinctly worried, and I found myself patting his head from sheer habit, as if he were still wolf-Bastian.

"It's all right; they're not properly real anymore. It's just magic and old memories. Are you ready to jump again?"

"Is she waiting?"

"Oh yes," I said. I didn't have to check, but I did anyway: there was a purple haze to the horizon beyond the sea of black nothingness.

"Not just yet, then."

"All right," I said.

I slipped one arm around Bastian's neck and nestled into his chest. It was strange: I hadn't noticed myself falling in love with him, but I was quite sure that I *was*. When had that happened? I tilted my head up at Bastian, wondering if he knew, and he smiled down at me with a quiet warmth that made me certain he did know.

We sat so for a little while longer before I regretfully withdrew my arm from about Bastian's neck and stood.

"It's time?"

"Yes."

"The stone?"

"I have it."

I gazed out at the sparkle of green amidst the black, weighing the stone in my hand.

"Ready?"

"Yes."

Bastian's hand was around mine, cold and rough; the stone flew, fast and true. The earth was firm this time, when we landed. And there, far away but still in the wardship, was Cassandra's presence.

Her presence didn't spur up magic from the old witch or the brown-eyed one, as I had half hoped it would; instead, the infant witch blossomed in my mind, reaching out to the forest in utter trust. The child had no defensive spells and no notion of attack: she radiated a complete and unshaken conviction in the forest that hadn't diminished despite a swift and excruciating death.

It occurred to me, with a shiver, that Cassandra's time had come, one way or the other. The forest was stirring into powerful life ahead of us: the time for equivocations was over.

"Can you reach Akiva?" Bastian's voice was non-committal, but I could feel the quivering essence of fear that exuded from him in waves. No, not fear: expectancy. He was preparing himself.

I shook my head soundlessly: there hadn't been a sense or sight of Akiva since yesterday. I pressed Bastian's hand, and he smiled down at me, leaving me oddly comforted.

With a certainty I didn't quite feel, I said: "She can't hurt us anymore. The forest is waking, and she'll have to answer for what she's done."

"I hope so, little witch," Bastian said, swinging my hand gently, and we walked through the shadowy tree trunks toward Akiva's cottage.

"How. *Sweet.*"

The two words were icy and diamond-edged in all of Cassandra's fury, dropped into the silent shadows of the forest. She approached us swiftly, her feet twinkling through the grass, and her smile was sharp and brilliantly furious. "Why," she asked in a brittle voice, her violet eyes pinioning first me and then Bastian; "Are *you* not dead? And why are *you* human?"

"I told you last time," Bastian said, through his teeth. "Pure, self-sacrificing altruism. The forest loves that sort of thing."

A million threads of blackness pierced him from Cassandra's accusingly pointed finger, and I felt the first sinking of cold desperation in my stomach, because none of the witches were volunteering magic.

The infant witch said, *Quiet, and wait,* unfurling into the forest, which was now crouching around us, poised and intent. I wondered that Cassandra didn't notice. She must have stopped listening to the forest long ago.

I said, "Stop it!" and the words seemed to swim in the thick air as the forest drew closer.

Cassandra circled us with small, angry steps. "No reprisals, she said. No interference. And now she is *gone!* You've been very busy, rabbit."

Bastian's fingers tightened painfully about mine as the torture spell sharpened, but the infant witch still said *Wait.*

"The forest took Mara," I said. "She went against it, and it took her. Be very careful, Cassandra."

"The forest loves me, rabbit: it has always loved me. He might have chosen you, but *it* will choose me!"

The forest grew darker around us, and the air thickened still more until it felt as though I were breathing in the very trees and grass.

"You pushed the boundaries by trying to break Bastian," I said grimly. "Don't make the mistake of trying to kill him."

"You think he loves you, but he doesn't," said Cassandra contemptuously. "He engineered it all, right from the beginning! Your first meeting, every meeting after that. He needed to make you fall in love with him. *Tell* her, wolf!"

"It's true," Bastian said quietly; and I saw that it tortured him more than the pain of Cassandra's spell. "I thought that if I could make you fall in love with me, I would be free of the curse. I knew a heart had to be given as the last part to break the curse, and I couldn't let you go. Ah, Rose, you were so sweet, but I was desperate."

I laughed scornfully, provoking a violet flash in Cassandra's eyes. "I've known that since I was a child! Why else would he bother to flirt with me?"

Her eyes darted between Bastian and I, furious but arrested, and

Bastian laughed low and ragged as she yanked the torture threads tight.

"You attacked us in Mara's wardship," he gasped, rocking back and forth in agony but still laughing. "I was so furious with Rose. I was so furious because I knew that I'd be tortured, or die, or stay wolf forever just to save her from a moment's pain. It was my heart, you old cow! *My* heart!"

Cassandra forgot her magic and hit him; actually slapped him with all the power in her slender arm. The torture spell snapped, and as Bastian staggered into me I caught him by the waist.

"He owes you nothing!" I panted. "The curse is broken, and all debts are paid! Leave us be!"

Cassandra only laughed, low and soft. "Oh, he will pay," she promised. "Not in death but in blood and pain and disappointment."

I saw the curls of black around her wrists just a second too late. By the time the old witch tried to push through my mind with a defence it was too late: the blackness had punctured my heart. Bastian gave a hoarse yell of anger and grief, but that was too late as well.

Ah! I thought, in the quietness that fell as my heart stopped beating. *So I'm her revenge.*

There were moments or ages of nothingness, and then I was somehow alive, my head and shoulders supported by Bastian's arms and my legs stretched out in the grass. Bastian's face was frozen in grey lines, his mouth determined, or angry, or perhaps both.

I heard him say, "Rose, I will not have you die! You bested a witch hut: what's a mere enchantress?"

The air had thinned around us again and the forest was no longer a pulsing, heavy weight. It was delightfully easy to sit up.

I did so, reaching instinctively for Bastian, and was kissed three times in quick succession, hard and insistent. I wriggled against Bastian's grip, and he let me go, looking rather pale again; but since I had only wriggled free in order to fling my arms around his neck, I was soon able to return his kisses with a fervour that made him chuckle at the back of his throat.

"Oh, Rose, my little love, I thought I'd lost you!"

"I told you before," I said. "You're stuck with me now. What has happened to Cassandra? I didn't see: I think I might have been dead for a little while."

"I find I don't care, my little witch," said Bastian, who was engaged in kissing each of my fingers in turn. "Cassandra holds no interest for me at all."

"She'll hold a bit more interest for you if she turns up unexpectedly again," I pointed out, and disengaged my hand in an attempt to stand up.

Bastian promptly caught me by the waist and sat me down beside him again. I laughed but protested, and was in the process of fending off kisses when, somewhere ridiculously nearby, a baby began to cry.

I scrambled to my feet, Bastian rising swiftly beside me: and there, where Cassandra had been standing not so long ago, was a squirming pile of clothes. The infant wails, if I was not very much mistaken, were emanating from the clothes.

I approached the silken pile cautiously and pulled back the cloak to reveal a pink-and-white face, rapidly staining to blotchy red with tears, and two little fists that clenched tight and flailed in the air.

It was Cassandra, and she was a baby.

"Rose, is this—"

I nodded, quite speechless as I looked down into the violet eyes. At last, I found my voice and said, "Yes. It's Cassandra."

Bastian picked up the struggling infant with surprising proficiency and patted it briskly on the back. "How? *Why?*"

"It was the forest," I said in wonder, and took the infant Cassandra unhandily from him. A quick survey of the infant's aura of magic was sufficient to show that she hadn't lost any of her power in the transformation. "She misused it and so it turned back on her; but instead of killing her it's given her a new start. She still has all her magic."

"But what do we do with her?"

"We raise her as our own, I suppose," I said, awkwardly patting the tiny rump. "No one else will be able to handle her."

Cassandra the infant was wriggling in a way I suspected meant she had wind, but despite burping once she looked distinctly uncomfortable. I believe she was as much afraid as *I* was that I would drop her.

"Good heavens, not like that, little witch," Bastian objected. He took Cassandra and slung her over one shoulder, patting her miraculously cloth-covered backside in a natural way that I envied.

"What will we do if she remembers? When she's older? Will we tell her?"

"She's not Cassandra anymore; there aren't any memories for her *to* remember," I said. I found that I very much approved of the forest's way of dealing with people. "She's whatever Cassandra she makes of herself, now. She must have been different once, or the forest wouldn't have accepted her. Now she can be again."

"The other wardens might not see it in the same light," Bastian warned, but his smile held more resignation than mockery. He set Cassandra down gently in the grass and piled her previous clothes around her for a cot, where she burbled happily at the tree boughs above her.

"You will have to excuse me," he said solemnly to her chuckling face, "but there is a little witch over here whom I really must kiss."

WE TOLD MOTHER FIRST. SHE GAVE US ONE OF HER SLOW, amused looks, and said, "It was about time you sorted yourselves out."

Bastian grinned and kissed her promptly on the cheek, but Gwendolen said petulantly: "It's not fair, Rose. *I* was supposed to get married first; you didn't even care!" by which I understood that she and Thomas were still in their quarrel.

Bastian grinned his most wolfish grin at her and said with brutal candour, "And unless you stop being such a little princess you won't be married at all, Gwen. Tell your butcher—"

"Blacksmith!"

"Tell your blacksmith you're sorry, and kiss and make up."

Gwendolen regarded him dangerously for a moment, torn

between laughter and outrage, but eventually went off into her infectious peal of laughter. "You're horrible and I don't understand at *all* why Rose wants to marry you," she told him roundly; and then sighed. "Oh well; I suppose you're right. I'll tell him I'm sorry and then we can dance at your wedding."

"If you want to be my bridesmaid, you'll need a groomsman to walk you down the aisle," I pointed out, in a practical spirit. For good measure, I added, "You'll need a new dress, too."

Gwendolen brightened immediately, her dudgeon at having to admit she was at fault quickly put aside by the thought of a new frock. She darted away at once to see what materials she had available, returning only once to ask me what colour I wanted it to be.

Akiva took the news with as little surprise as Mother but said in her caustic way, "Very nice for you both, but not yet. It's far too busy, and the forest needs to be set to rights first."

"Bastian says we won't be married until I'm eighteen," I told her gloomily. For the next few months, I was still only in my seventeenth year, and Bastian had insisted that he wanted me to be sure of it. He had an absurd idea of fairness. It didn't please me, but Akiva gave an approving nod.

"Sensible," she said. "What will you do with the child?"

"She doesn't like being outside the forest," I shrugged. This was an understatement: every attempt to remove Cassandra from the vicinity of the forest, even to take her to Mother, had met with an outburst of screaming and red-faced limb-flailing that was at odds with baby Cassandra's usually sunny disposition.

"I'll keep her with me."

Akiva grunted. "She might prove useful in finding the wardens."

This, I felt, was a tacit approval of my adoption of Cassandra, for which I was thankful. I wanted her under my eye, and I had a feeling that the forest, insofar as it was capable of rational thought, had decided that she should stay. It had done its best by her, and I was determined to do the same. That would have to be enough for everyone else, too; for the forest knew how to protect its own.

Epilogue

The search for the missing wardens began almost immediately. Akiva organized us into parties and sent us on our way, methodically covering every blade and leaf of the forest.

Sometimes I walked with Bastian, who slipped reluctantly into his wolf-form, the better to smell; sometimes Akiva sent us out separately. Cassandra had begun to reach out chubby hands to the forest threads so I took her with me whenever I went out alone: it made me feel less solitary, and it kept Cassandra happy.

We found them slowly. Some were alive and well, but more were dead or gone beyond any help we could give. Tancred, who was luckier than most, had been turned into an eagle, and aside from an inclination to hunt for field-mice and a tendency to snap his head around with a glare whenever one of us moved too quickly, he was healthy and whole.

Akiva, in addition to arranging the systematic search of the forest, had begun the onerous task of finding wardens to replace those who were dead, and the setting of the forest to rights. She was exhausted more often than not. It was a long process, and a weary one, but by and by the forest began to settle back into its quiet rest.

A collective sigh of relief went up the day we found the last warden. Gwydion had found one too many milestones along the

Queen's Highway, and retrieved at last a grim-faced warden called Katerina. I looked at her face, stony in its silence as Akiva pulled away the last remaining threads of the spell and found myself guiltily appreciating Cassandra's choice of spell.

Katerina looked once at the baby Cassandra, and said, "You should kill her now, while you still can."

I didn't need the sideways grin that Gwydion shot at me behind Katerina's back to remind me to hold my tongue. Bastian moved between Katerina and I, his wolf-form a warning without overtly threatening, but I only tickled his ears. It was something we were all going to have to learn to live with.

Nevertheless, I left them ministering to Katerina and took myself and Cassandra into the forest where she wouldn't be an unpleasant reminder to anyone of the friends they had lost.

WE NEVER FOUND CASSANDRA'S HOUSE AGAIN. IT WAS A dark blot that blackened the past along with the few wardens who were irreparably lost. I hoped that somehow the statues had escaped, and it cheered me to think, as Akiva said, that the forest knew very well what it was about. What needed to be done would be done, in time.

I could say so much more. I could say how Bastian and I were married beneath the canopy of the forest in the cool and shadow, with David to give me away, and Gwen to prance after me with her hand in Thomas' arm. I could tell how Cassandra began to walk shortly after, and how she filled the house with living forest as her infant hands reached out to the forest lines.

But I think only one thing really needs to be said, after all, and that is this: we lived happily ever after.

www.ingramcontent.com/pod-product-compliance
Lightning Source LLC
Chambersburg PA
CBHW070114120726
47909CB00002B/592